3.00

BEVERLY
HILLS

PAT BOOTH

BEVERLY HILLS

CROWN PUBLISHERS, INC.
NEW YORK

Copyright © 1989 by Orcam Corporation

All rights reserved. No part of this book may be reproduced or transmitted in any form or by any means, electronic or mechanical, including photocopying, recording, or by any information storage and retrieval system, without permission in writing from the publisher.
Published by Crown Publishers, Inc., 201 East 50th Street, New York, New York 10022
CROWN is a trademark of Crown Publishers, Inc.
Manufactured in the United States of America
Library of Congress Cataloging-in-Publication Data
Booth, Pat.
Beverly Hills / by Pat Booth.
    p.   cm.
I. Title
PS3552.0646B49 1989
813'.54—dc19   89-1252
ISBN 0-517-57241-9   CIP
10 9 8 7 6 5 4 3 2 1
First Edition

To my husband,

G A R T H ,

with all my love

BEVERLY HILLS

ONE

Paula Hope was numb with tiredness, but she had never been more determined. On sun-washed Melrose Avenue, half a mile from the Hollywood freeway, the street people didn't know that. All they could see was an exhausted girl in dirty blue jeans and a dirtier shirt. They saw only her dramatically beautiful face, and her straggly blond hair, matted with dust and held in a ponytail bob by a plain red elastic band. Those who looked longer noticed the limp, of course. That was something to watch in the caldron of the L.A. summer evening, as the wind from the desert waved the fronds of the Paramount Studios' palm trees against the sun-bleached sky.

Paula sighed as she struggled on. She was used to the steam heat of the Everglades, but this was a different kind of hot. It was the relentless heat of the fan oven, the crisp, brittle heat of the sauna. It was clean and clear like a bright white flame, and she could smell its burning ozone in her nostrils. Blow-torch sharp, it scorched her, and beneath her feet the paving stones shimmered like a mirage. She stayed to the north of Melrose because she didn't have the strength to cross to the shady side, and anyway here she was closer to the Hollywood Hills, their famous sign visible at the street intersections, swathed in the fluffy brown haze of the heatscape. The words of the psalm came back to her. The hills, from whence cometh my help. She smiled grimly and stopped. She would have to ask directions, but on the L.A. sidewalk everyone looked as if they belonged somewhere else. "Which way is Beverly Hills?" she said to a passerby.

"Keep going," he muttered, hurrying on.

1

How long? How far? But up ahead she could see the answer. God had made a glorious crown for Beverly Hills. To the left the sun was dying, and before Paula's eyes the heavens were alive with color. The clouds, stretched out in layered ribbons against a powder-blue sky, were tinged with pink. Now, as she watched, they deepened to a burnished orange, silhouetting a thousand finger-thin palm trees against the pastel painting of the early sunset. On a whim she turned to look back, and over her shoulder, ghostly pale against the distant San Gabriel Mountains, was the moon. At once Paula recognized it as a symbol of the hell that had been her past, while up ahead was the paradise of Beverly Hills, the place where she would find her future.

Paula knew with crystal clarity what she wanted from it. She wanted to be loved. She wanted to be adored. She wanted someone to take care of her forever and wrap her in a cocoon of happiness in which there would be no more tragedy, no more loss, no more wickedness. In her brave new world there would be security, safety, and excitement, in the arms of someone who would hold and never let go, who would love but never leave, who would be brimful of life and would never die. In her magic future she would *be* someone, respected and admired, and she would have friends like ordinary people and she would have the luxury of leisure and the time simply to *exist*. She wanted to surround herself with beauty, and at least to see if not to own some of the wonderful things her teacher Emily Carstairs had told her about. Most of all she wanted never again to be poor and hungry, and at the mercy of a cruel world in which evil had stolen away the precious people she had loved more than her own life.

And then she wanted the revenge she had promised Seth Baker. Only in the music of his screams could the squatting toad of hatred be banished from her mind. Only in the river of his blood could her loathing be washed away. Only as the foul breath rattled in death from his lungs could she be reborn.

But Paula was a realist. Before she could have any of the things she desired so desperately, she would have to create a future for herself. God knew how, but she had to escape from the bottomland of life where she had always lived. Right now, however, the problem was to find a place to sleep, somewhere safe and free if that wasn't a contradiction. Luckily on her long walk from the freeway the neighborhood had steadily improved, and Paula hoped that it was a metaphor for her life. The boarded liquor stores, ninety-nine-cent movie rentals, and poverty-stricken Hispanics of early Melrose had been replaced by delicious-smelling restaurants and frivolous boutiques, as low-end retro-punk merged imperceptibly into credit-card-crunching chic. Now, as she hauled one bejeaned leg in front of the other, past the fruits and the nuts and the flakes of the muësli that was Southern California, the storefronts were getting grander by the minute. One in particular caught her eye, and she walked over and gazed through its broad windows.

It was an antiques store, but that description was ridiculously inadequate. It was an Aladdin's cave of beauty that sent Paula's tired heart leaping in her chest. Ornate mirrors, gold leaf, ancient smoky glass, hung complacently over delicate half tables of faded, highly polished wood. On the walls rich tapestries danced with color, their needlework executed with the intricacy of the painter, depicting heroic scenes of glory and triumph. Multicolored rugs, dusty and dark with messages from distant lands, were scattered like giant postage stamps over the floors and on them languished furniture the likes of which she had never seen. Great bow-fronted chests covered with ornate giltwork merged happily with severe geometrical ones, and the infinite varieties of the wood shaded into each other beneath the glow of a discrete lighting system. On and on the "store" went. Over the years it had consumed its neighbors and now the marginally different, yet at the same time homogenous, storefronts stretched the entire length of the block.

Paula stopped. The wall of beauty had brought her up short. She stood close to the gray glass, smoked to keep out the harmful rays of the sun, and she pressed her face against it as her eyes roamed over the trove of treasures. Apart from the artwork there seemed to be nobody inside. No human marred the splendor of the ancient Roman busts as they stared grandly from their columns in their terra-cotta marble tunics. Their unseeing alabaster eyes seemed to peer back at Paula, mocking her from their positions of eternal security. On an impulse she stuck out her tongue at them and their haughtiness, leaving a little wet mark on the immaculate window of the storefront.

Winthrop Tower wondered why the street girl was bothering to stick out her tongue at him. He arched an eyebrow as he watched her, and his practiced eyes slid over her visuals. The fact that women were not his bag did not diminish his interest. Neither was Sheraton, but he could still spot a fake secretaire at forty feet across a coal cellar in the dead of night. She was certainly beautiful, if in need of a little cleaning, perhaps a tad of judicious restoration. She would need polish and wax in terms of makeup and all the funny things that women wore, and if he allowed himself to be perfectionistic with a capital P, then some cunning sculptor might improve the line of the nose. But if in profile, and to the connoisseur, her features were marginally less than classic—face on, she was stunning.

The eyes and the mouth, both partially hidden from the side, were the jewels in the crown. Her eyes were great marbles of blue light glistening with irreverence and interest, and Winthrop's gaze was swept down the bridge of an upturned nose, to the slash of the voluptuous mouth.

And the cheekbones! Oh dear, they were very good. A touch of the Eurasian? Well not *really*, but the hint of that sort of thing, all high and proud and in marvelously happy triangular relationship to that pouting mouth from which the pink tongue had so surprisingly protruded. Her hair was a mess of course, but it was obviously American hair, which meant it was the best stuff in the world. Which left the teeth—tombstone correct; and the jaw—no-nonsense, jutting geometry; and things like the neck—swans, pedestals (Carrara marble ones)—and the skin, smooth, honey-brown basted; and those pretty, neat little ears. In his orderly mind Winthrop Tower ticked off the inventory, and with a frisson of surprise he added up her score. My oh my, she *was* good. Take away the tiredness and sharpen her up a bit and she would sparkle and shine in mint showroom condition. Park Avenue Winter Antiques Show quality. No question. Had she been a Longton Hall owl at a Sotheby's sale he'd have bought her. He chortled to himself and looked down again at the catalogue on his knee. The girl was forgotten.

Paula wondered at first what the store was called. The Tower Design plaque was discreet—simple black roman letters on a highly polished brass plate, the legend partially worn away by daily polishing over more years than a town like L.A. was supposed to have existed. The feeling inside her was overwhelming. She wanted to go in, and so she did.

Inside it was quiet and cool and apparently she was alone in what might easily have been a Pharaoh's tomb. Up close, the things were far more lovely; the textures, the subtlety, the workmanship; the shades, the architecture, the amazingly sensitive juxtaposition of the art. The cavernous rooms were crammed with priceless objects and yet there was no sensation of overcrowding. Her eyes picked out a group—a painting, a chair, a table, a rug, which made up a whole far more interesting than the sum of the individual parts. Each set seemed to bear a relationship to a neighboring grouping until she could not escape the feeling that everything was related by progressive degree to everything else. The room made sense to her eye. If you moved anything the fairy castle of visual pleasure would fall.

The chair next to her spoke directly to her soul. It was a great throne of a chair standing majestically on sturdy, bowed feet. It was upholstered in a pink silk damask, but the intricacy of its wood carving scoffed at the necessity for that. "I'm for looking at," it seemed to say. "I am a statement. The fact that I am a chair is merely incidental. Rest on me and you will *become* someone."

Paula couldn't resist its siren call. She was sucked toward it, and to reach it she squeezed her taut bottom past a table on which sat a large, complacent Chinese vase.

For a second or two she paused, her denim-encrusted butt poised over the pink silk. Should she be doing this in someone else's store? The hell with it. The worst they could do was throw her out, and it would be so wonderful to sit, and to be a queen . . . for just a minute.

Winthrop Tower stood up and dropped the Christie's catalogue onto the green leather top of the Chippendale desk. The important furniture sale in New York looked vaguely interesting. It was difficult to know whether to bother to go or not. He might get one of the girls to ask the Algonquin if they had his usual suite. That would decide it. Right now it was about time to close.

He walked to the front door of the store, which was when he saw her. The rude street beauty with the irreverent tongue had her grubby blue jeans in the only piece of furniture that wasn't for sale. She was sitting in Queen Marie Antoinette's and Tower's favorite chair. It was lèse-majesté.

The girl saw him and the fright passed across her beautiful face like a cloud scudding across the fullest of full moons. It didn't last. The moment it arrived it was gone, to be replaced by a devil-may-care insolence all wrapped up in the spicy aroma of irreverent charm.

"I wanted to know what it felt like to be a queen," she said simply.

"Oh, it has its moments," said the most famous and successful designer in the Western world. Tower stood back, hand on hip, and struck a pose. Inside, he was already beginning to laugh.

Paula cocked her head to one side as she tried to sum up the situation. She had followed her natural instincts and showed no weakness when the stranger had confronted her. Now she smiled back at him, because she felt somehow that he was kind, and because she needed kindness.

He was tall but lopsided in a seemingly intentional way, as if he wanted to catch you off balance and felt he was more likely to do so by setting a good example. He was around sixty, but Paula was picking up much younger vibes, and his face had the well-worn look that could have come from either speedy living or anno domini. His eyes sparkled but the bags beneath them said "booze" while the reading glasses perched on the end of his Roman nose looked like they might be merely a prop. Small tufts of hair grew from commodious nostrils and although he was shaved he was hardly "clean shaven." The male process had obviously been hurried, perhaps always was, and there was a clump of untouched hairs beneath a receding chin. His mouth, thin but not mean, was maybe a little merciless.

Now he smiled as he spoke. "First you put out your tongue at me. Next you sit in my favorite chair. You're not, I hope . . ." and he wrinkled up his nose in pseudodisgust, "a kissing telegram?"

Paula smiled. "Gee, no. Of course not." The thought suddenly dawned on her. "Oh God, no I wasn't sticking out my tongue at *you*. I didn't know you were in here. I was doing it at all those Romans. They looked so pleased with themselves."

She stood up. Somehow that seemed the proper thing to do. The stranger's whole manner was casual but his clothes indicated clearly that he wasn't the hired help. His shirt was button-down gray linen, and the tie looked like that of a college that would mean something to people who knew, but the rest of him was far more impressive. He wore a suit of the palest brown corduroy, and, although he looked completely at home in it, it didn't really fit him. The shoulders of the jacket were round and it ballooned out at the waist to accommodate a healthy paunch. The pants of the suit were voluminous. Baggy and a little threadbare at the knee, they were turned up where they met ancient, highly polished brown brogue lace-up walking shoes.

"Are you Mr. Tower?" she asked. "Is this your store? I think it's the most wonderful place I've ever seen in my life."

Once again his eyes appraised her, as the honest compliment hung in the air. The girl was liquid glory. She flowed into his mind like Rodin, the curves of Moore, Michelangelo, and da Vinci on a good chiseling day. Her breasts weren't large, but they were far from small, and in terms of perspective they sang in harmony with the belted waist he might enclose in the palms of two hands if he squeezed tightly enough. For a butt man, like Winthrop, it was a good day, too. Inside the filthy Levi's the proud bottom was snare-drum tight. And then there were the legs. Away they went, zipping like good news down to the dirt-streaked Adidas sneakers, but why was the thigh of the left noticeably thinner than the one on the right? An injury? A leg in plaster recently? After some accident?

Winthrop Tower stroked at a droopy earlobe. "You're right about the Romans. Ancient yuppies, really. Dreadfully nouveau, and no

sense of humor. I'm glad it wasn't me. And thanks for the compliment
. . . about all this, I mean." He waved a lazy hand to encapsulate
several million dollars' worth of museum pieces, and the pleasure
swooped from his face. He didn't know why he was pleased. Compliments about his "taste" from the art arbiters of the globe were usually
about as interesting as small earthquakes in Chile in which nobody had
been hurt.

"Oh, and yes, I *am* Winthrop Tower. And you're *not* a kissing
telegram or anything like that?"

Paula thrust out a grubby hand. "I wish I was," she said with a
laugh. "That would mean I had some money. I'm down to my last ten
bucks." It was a billion miles from a pitch.

"What made you sit in *that* chair?"

Paula looked at it carefully. "Oh, I don't know, it's sort of unique,
I mean, it looks as if it's *used* to being a seat, but only for special
people. It sort of rises above being a chair, but isn't ashamed to do the
job if it approves of the sitter. Sounds silly doesn't it, but that's what I
felt when I saw it." She laughed self-consciously as if she were almost
ashamed to say such pompous things, but not quite.

Winthrop Tower's wise eyes widened. He didn't often experience
the spark of intense artistic interest. Once a year, less, when at the back
of some crumbling Scottish castle a grubby unidentified Rembrandt
peeped shyly from some damp wall. Occasionally, very rarely, when
he met some "new" artist whose work transcended Madison Avenue
bullshit and dealer hype. Now, it had happened. The girl from
nowhere, with the tongue, the tits, and the dirty jeans, had told the
"truth" about his chair. She had plumbed his secret fantasy as if it had
been written above his head in blood-red neon.

"How did you know?" he asked simply. Was this some joke? Would
the girl now reveal herself as the great-niece of the immortal designer
Sister Parish, sent on a whim to plague him?

Paula laughed, pleased by his agreement, a bit puzzled by his
question. "Well, I didn't *know*. I mean, that's just what the chair made
me feel."

"So you're not a furniture expert." The gray-painted Louis XVI
fauteuil, *à la Reine*, was museum quality. It bore the stamp of Dubois,
and the carving of its channeled seat rails, and the fluid lines of its
down-curved arm-supports transcended mere beauty.

"I'm not an anything expert."

"I wonder," said Tower slowly. It was just possible. Only just. There
was a way to find out.

All along the back of his neck the flesh was crawling with the premonition. Was it about to happen? At long last. "Come with me," he said, and he took her arm as he steered her safely past the green T'ang dynasty urn that a little old lady from Pasadena had been using as a table lamp before he had liberated it.

Paula went with him. If she handled this well, she might get some food. At least a drink of water. Perhaps even some sort of help.

He hurried into the bowels of the showroom toward a set of dining-room chairs arranged in a semicircle about a round table. They were made of a peculiar milky wood, with black horsehair seats, and on their backs mythological figures were carved on a darker and more traditional-colored wood.

"What do you think of those?" he asked.

"I think they are magnificent. Very simple. Very secure. They're beautiful."

"They're German Biedermeier. Eighteen ten. We call that wood 'blonde.' The ones with the arms are sometimes called 'carvers.' I've never seen a finer set." He watched her like a lynx. She would need a hint. The curator of the Smithsonian would. "I should say . . ."

But she cut into his speech. "Except for that one, over there on the left. It seems out of place. Sort of sad, by comparison, but it looks like all the others . . ."

Winthrop Tower felt the thrill of excitement. Of course it *looked* like the others. It was meant to. The skills of the greatest restoration firm in the world—Oxford Restorers of Long Island—had *made* it look like all the others. But it didn't *feel* like all the others. To the eye that could feel, it was wrong. It was a fake, a great big bogus lie in the middle of the purest beauty. But only half a dozen people in the world had that aesthetic vision, and they were all titans in the field of fine furniture. Now, this girl, apparently a kid from nowhere, had picked an imposter at the Biedermeier feast, only seconds after she had divined the truth about the two queens' chair.

He took a step back and opened his mouth to speak, but still he could not believe it. He wanted confirmation. "Which rug is your favorite?"

The glorious pistachio-green Tabriz from the late Shah's collection— it was not perhaps the most expensive carpet in the world but he had never walked on one more beautiful.

"This drawing by Fragonard . . ."

Yes, of course, it was Angelica's hands that weren't quite right as they reached for Orlando—great frankfurter fingers from the supposed brush of the master of feminine delicacy.

"Let's rearrange this corner of the showroom. I'll do it. You direct me. Now let's put a picture in place of this Chinese Chippendale looking-glass. You pick it. From anywhere in the room. And let's find some different objects for this little table. No. Let's find another table altogether. You choose it. You just say."

He couldn't keep the enthusiasm from his voice. All his life, since the flowering of his artistic brilliance at Yale, he had believed that beauty existed despite the opinion of the observer. All that was required to recognize it was a person born with eyes that could "see." This was a talent, he had always maintained, that could not be learned or taught. It could be refined by experience and by endless exposure to great art, but it predated education. It was more fundamental. It had to be there first. Now, of course, it was too late to demonstrate that *his* monumental taste had been innate. At the height of his fame that could hardly be proved, and in the early days when his raw genius had been plain for anyone to see, nobody had known him and no one had wanted to. His fellow countrymen, obsessed by the value of "learning" and with an instinctive belief in the value of "expertise," had always scoffed at his theory, and he had been unable to provide evidence for its truth.

At last here before him was the living proof, a blue-jeaned Venus hot from heaven, the ultimate untrained "eye" who would show the world that he had been right all along. Paula didn't hesitate. "Well, I think perhaps that horse picture would be good there, with that gilt wood table and perhaps that clock. Of course we'd need to change the rug to that one with the tree design with all the things in the branches . . ."

"Oh God. Oh God," Winthrop murmured to himself as he struggled with the Sartorius equine painting that had cost him a quarter of a million dollars at the Bridport sale. Could he manage to move the fabulous Venetian marble-topped baroque side table he had found in the Brandolini Venice palazzo, and swapped with the Fiat heiress for a tired Guardi? Probably not, but his mind's eye could already see the Thomas Eardley tortoiseshell table clock sitting beneath the head of the Derby winner. And of course the girl was right. The whole needed nothing more than the Persian Isfahan depicting the traditional tree of life. The exquisite grouping would bring tears to the eyes of a half-switched-on beholder. The corner of some Beverly Hills drawing room would remain forever a shrine of beauty and the photographers from *World of Interiors* and *Architectural Digest* would home in on it like Navy missiles on a Libyan jet.

He stood back. There was no point in carrying on. It had been proved. Beyond reasonable doubt. She had it. She knew nothing, but she could do it all. Goddamn it, he had been *right*.

"What's your name?"

"Paula Hope."

He laughed and held out his hands in a gesture that said for once in his life he didn't know what to say. "Do you know what you have just done, Paula? Have you any *idea* what you can do?"

But as he spoke, he saw she didn't know. He looked quickly at his watch. It was getting late. He had agreed to meet a client for cocktails. It would have been a big commission. A million, maybe one point two. But he didn't hesitate. "Paula, if you're not doing anything else, would you let me take you somewhere to eat?"

Paula's eyes widened. God, food! She'd almost forgotten. Now she remembered and her stomach screamed at her to accept. "I'd love to," she said.

T W O

'd like you all to give me a minute or two before I make
up my mind.

Robert Hartford picked up the horn-rimmed glasses from the
Barcelona cut-glass coffee table, and he breathed in deeply. All around
him was the pungent smell of fear. It wasn't physical fear. The six men
who sat on the edges of the comfortable Osborne and Little chintz-
covered sofas and chairs were not afraid of bodily injury. It was a more
comprehensive fear than that. All of them stood very, very close to a
deal that would reinvent their careers. A yes from Hartford and they
were home free, movie heroes in La-la Land, up-to-the-millisecond
Oscar creamers with the best tables at Morton's and Spago to prove it.

A no and they were yesterday's men, the crowd for whom the
bigtime had been just too hot to handle. Their personal reputations
would be shot in the town where image was money, where money was
power, and where power was sex. Six careers, six mighty mortgages,
three and a half mistresses, fleets of high-end cars, love, respect, and
marriages were suspended in the Havana cigar smoke of the Sunset
Hotel bungalow, and fingers of panic plucked at the studio executives
as they waited for the star's decision.

Robert Hartford gave them the little-boy smile—the one that turned
on the moviegoers coast to coast—and he watched the Galaxy top
management sweat.

He didn't look like a fifty-six-million-dollar man, but he did look far
too good to eat. His face was simply perfect. No more, no less. Women
thought so. Men thought so. Children thought so. Animals given the

gift of speech would have said that they thought so, too. There was just no possible argument about it. To say that he was not beautiful was to brand the judge insane, blind, mendacious, or a blend of all three. The emotions in his eyes depended on the perspective of the person watching him. They were sad eyes, shy eyes, laughing eyes, strong eyes. They were all of those things at once . . . and none of them, their infinite variety confusing as it excited, shocking as it soothed. Although he was thirty-six, the crow had not landed. In fact the crow hadn't even flown overhead, and the skin at the corners of his remarkable eyes was a smooth honey color, totally devoid of wrinkles. The Hartford hair, dark brown and unfashionably short at the top and sides, was nonetheless long at the back, reaching down the nape of a graceful neck. Its cut was geometric, offsetting the square, dimpled jaw, the high cheekbones, the glint of the cobalt-blue eyes. It was these last that saved the face from a bland perfection. He didn't look like a model, nor did he resemble some Marlboro man, a swaggering macho pseudocowboy with two left feet and ten-minute reflexes. It wasn't even, in the end analysis, an "interesting" face—the sort of good looks that depended on shock value to deliver, a crooked nose, hooded eyes, an overly ripe mouth. But although it was none of them, it was all of them, merged in a secret harmony. It was the face of a man that women, all women, would love. His clothes didn't detract from his visual splendor. Their simplicity emphasized it. His plain white T-shirt was squeaky clean and free of mindless chatter, and it covered a lean torso from which brown, wiry arms protruded, the muscles rangy and businesslike—far from the designer triceps and biceps of the bodybuilder crowd. He wore pressed blue jeans, colorless Nike sneakers, and simple white socks that drew attention to the length of his legs and the tautness of his bottom. In short, Robert Hartford's beauty had an edge that could cut, and all around the immaculately decorated Sunset Hotel bungalow, his captive audience knew it.

"If there's anything we can say to influence you in any way . . ."

Bos Liebowitz's voice was shaking. He couldn't bear the silence. You were supposed to have learned how to deal with those in the sixties when it was a measure of your "cool." Well, he hadn't. Right now he cared more desperately than he had ever cared before and it was pointless to hide it. What could he do to make the superstar say what he wanted to hear? What could he give him? How could he flatter him? Hartford had more girls than he could ever use, and Bos had told him a hundred times that he loved him more than God. Galaxy had broken its piggybank to offer the record-breaking guarantee that the

studio was floating at the movie hero, but perhaps he could have lined
up a little more bank finance, hocked a few more old movies from the
studio library, begged for it, stolen it.

Robert lifted up a bronzed hand and waved it in the air in a gesture
that said "shut up."

"Just a few minutes. Bear with me, Bos. And I'll let you have my
answer."

Again he smiled the shy, unassuming smile, and inside he laughed
at the enormity of his assumption. He knew what he was going to say.
He had known for two weeks, but the beauty of life at the top of the
heap was that you could shower it down on the ants who lived at the
bottom. That was what he was doing right now. It was better than sex.
Almost.

Bos Liebowitz, too, held up his hand in the universal gesture of
surrender.

"Forgive me, Robert. Forgive me. It's just I can't help thinking of all
those wonderful movies we could make . . . all those wonderful
movies . . ." And those rentals, and tie-ins, and video rights, those
sequels and the lists in *Variety* and the *Reporter* and the angst at the
other studios. Robert Hartford movies didn't just "open." They never
closed. They had legs that went on forever, and first-weekend theater
returns so large they looked like misprints. Why couldn't the bastard
just say yes? Seven pictures, ten percent of the producers' gross, eight
big ones guaranteed per movie. It was unheard of. It might never
happen again in the history of the industry. It certainly hadn't come
anywhere near to happening yet. But whatever it cost it was worth it,
because Hartford was more bankable than the banks, the nearest thing
to certainty in the Hollywood dice game, with a profit graph on his last
four pictures that aimed straight at heaven.

Robert Hartford's baby-blue eyes had gone dreamy. He seemed to
have left them. Oblivious to the mutterings of the mere mortals, he
peered imperiously around his Mark Hampton–designed drawing
room. How clever of Mark to decide on the tetrad color scheme, rather
than the boring monotone, monochrome, or analogous schemes that
the West Coast designers slavishly employed. The four hues melded in
a perfect mix—the delicate pink and russet reds of the sofas; the creamy
yellow of the lampshades against the tan walls; the rich browns of the
Sheraton furniture; and the turquoise blue of the garden-of-paradise
silk rug from the Persian holy city of Qum. The style was aristocratic,
but it was not a cold room, and the important early cubist Picassos,
daughters of the Demoiselles d'Avignon, were at home amidst the

ambience of understated tradition. Yes, it was a beautiful room, dripping with good taste—and crowded with some of the ugliest men Robert had ever seen.

Robert tugged at an ear, placed his glasses on his perfect nose, and cleared his throat. "I'd have artistic control, script, casting approval and final cut, and veto over choice of product."

It was a statement posing as a question. Bos nodded quickly.

"Which shall not be unreasonably withheld," added Cal Brewer, who headed up the Galaxy contracts department.

Robert Hartford's eyes narrowed, his sensuous mouth thinned, his jaw jutted.

Liebowitz's heart stopped. He whirled on the attorney. "Shut up, Cal!" he hissed.

The explosion of his command roared around the room, vibrating the Limoges coffee cups on the three-quarter-inch-thick coffee table and bouncing off the beige of the Thai silk walls. "Sorry," he added almost immediately. It had been an overreaction, a potentially disastrous loss of control, very un-Hollywood. But, God, he was nervous. Later, if Hartford didn't accept their offer, Cal Brewer could and would be let go. For now, it was more important that they all appear one big happy family, riding to glory on the back of the legend's name.

"What I meant to say was that what Robert finds reasonable, *we* will find reasonable. We always have in the past, and we always will in the future. You have my personal word on that." Bos actually rubbed his hands together as he made oil for the suddenly troubled waters.

When the contract was signed they could fight with Robert Hartford until he was boxed, but until the ink was dry on the contract there would *be* no deal. And no deal might mean no studio, or worse, a studio with a boss whose name was no longer Liebowitz.

He leaned forward, acutely aware that sweat was staining the front of his Sea Island cotton Bijan shirt. He watched Hartford like he would the Maker on Judgment Day.

Robert Hartford didn't even bother to look pacified. He flicked his head away from all of them and began to study the ceiling, his long, sensitive fingers reaching up to massage the back of his neck.

"Do you know this place is for sale?" he said at last into the anguished silence.

Six minds whirred to a stop. What place? For sale? What the hell was he talking about?

Robert Hartford beamed around the room. He seemed to want an answer to his totally out-of-context question at the very moment when the only thing anybody else wanted was an answer to theirs.

The vice president of production, insulated to some extent from the general angst by his relatively lowly position, got his mind together first. "You mean the bungalow?" he tried.

"No. No. The whole thing. The whole hotel." Robert waved a languid arm in the air to encapsulate it all—the late afternoon Beverly Hills sun knifing through the open window, the hiss of the lawn sprinkler on the emerald grass outside, the muted rumble of a room-service trolley from beyond the ivy-covered wall that bordered the Hartford compound.

Bos Liebowitz alone knew what was happening. Robert Hartford was playing with them. They were mice to his cat. He knew exactly what he was going to do, but was enjoying the fact that they didn't. It was a Hollywood power trip pure and simple, and all they could do was tag along.

"Must be a bit of a worry . . . I mean, you living here and not knowing who the new owner's gonna be," he said as casually as he could. He had never been able to understand why Robert Hartford chose to live in a hotel, however splendid, when he could have afforded any estate in Bel-Air or Beverly Hills.

"Weeeell," Robert drawled. "I mean, I imagine the new management wouldn't throw me out!"

An explosion of anxious laughter rocked the room.

Amused, Robert Hartford watched the awesome manifestation of his power. It was moments like this when it was all worthwhile—the careful legend building, the loneliness that erected the myths, the sacrifices and the hard work as brick by brick he had constructed his mighty career. He'd never wavered from his objective; he had never varied his methods. In fashion and out of it he had plowed his furrow, and now, at last the whole world wanted him.

The Galaxy contract on the shining glass coffee table said so. Robert Hartford. A seven-picture deal. Fifty-six million bucks, big points on the gross, and no artistic indulgence "unreasonably withheld." Money had long since ceased to mean much to him. He already had far more than he could spend. But it was a method of keeping score, and in Hollywood it was the language of love, the dialect he would always understand.

He smiled carefully around the tuberose-scented room, his beguiling eyes snakecharming the studio players one by one. His smile dried their counterfeit mirth and soothed their jangled nerves. It was the smile that made the housewives feel all right, and the teenagers feel themselves. It was the smile that posed the mystery, and the sphinxlike smile that promised the conclusion would satisfy. It was the smile that

pried into the magic of motivation, and the smile that gave no clue to
its own.

"It's make-your-mind-up time," he said softly in the voice of a lover.
"With this contract I thee wed . . ." and he picked up the Bic pen with
its chewed end, and the ink running down the inside of the plastic.

He talked as he wrote, destroying the importance of the moment
with the willfulness of a child. His voice now was matter-of-fact,
devoid of the charming playfulness that had taken the edge off his
earlier banter.

"You know the best thing about this place? The staff. I don't know
where the hell Francisco gets them. They look like the usual wetbacks,
but they all speak immaculate English, and they have this instinctive
way of anticipating what you want."

He paused. He'd gotten as far as *Hart*. . . . He looked up.

Not a whisker moved; not a muscle; not a joint creaked. Their
expressions were frozen in horrendous half smiles of anticipation. But
he had the antidote in his hand: . . . *ford*. With the stroke of a Bic he
could make the studio top brass come alive. Of course it wouldn't be
as much fun then. It was the same with women. Climax and
anticlimax; the chase; the games, and the fury of the coupling; and
then the little death and the relative dullness of the life thereafter.

So, like lovemaking, he was eking it out. But, like lovemaking, too,
there was a limit beyond which things could not decently be
prolonged. Robert Hartford let out a sigh and leaned forward once
again. With no more ado, he scrawled . . . *ford*.

Cal Brewer remained rooted to the spot. The contract had five
copies. All needed the Hartford signature. Bos, however, came off the
sofa like a brain-damaged boxer at the sound of a doorbell. He was a
bottom-line man. Hartford had just signed on it. It was a done deal. A
man like him wouldn't bother to sign again. There were photocopying
machines to relieve one of drudgery like that. If the photocopying had
to be witnessed at great expense by the equivalent of a panel of bishops
to validate the signature and the facsimile, *that* was mere detail.

Right now, the trick was to glorify the moment. The blissful second
when he, Bos Liebowitz had, at the stroke of a broken ballpoint,
become the second most important man in the most important town
in the world.

The tears were thick in his eyes as he waddled across the four-
hundred-knots-to-the-inch pure silk rug toward the man who had
made him so happy. It was time for celebration, time for the laying on
of hands. His money had been accepted. There was a sense in which

it was only right and proper that he should be allowed to finger the merchandise.

Robert Hartford, however, was way ahead of him. The man who loved women could not stand the touch of men.

He was on his feet, his movements fluid, as he distanced himself from Bos. In a flash the sofa was between him and those who jostled to congratulate him. He picked up the telephone from the sun-faded sofa table and dialed once.

"Ah, Conchita," he sighed his relief. A female. "You have a cold!" His tone was intimate. He scolded. He was alarmed. The whole focus of his attention was on the disembodied Mexican voice that took the orders for food and drink. "Vitamin C. Honey. And a tequila before bed tonight," he prescribed, his words creamy with solicitation.

The senior management of what had just become the most successful studio in Hollywood were forced to put their joy on hold, as Robert Hartford sweet-talked the anonymous woman. A few of them bothered to wonder who she was.

Bos Liebowitz, however, didn't find it odd at all. He had seen this happen before, and it was part of the reason he had just promised Robert Hartford fifty-six million dollars. The movie star had the knack. It was by far the most important thing he had. Perhaps it was the only one. From dusk to dawn, and from dawn to dusk he thought of women. He thought of pleasing them, and of their softness, and he daydreamed of their divine smells, and the way they held their heads, and the funny things they worried about. He planned his conquest of them, and he worshiped their beauty, and loved their plainness also, their specialty and their ordinariness. Robert Hartford adored the stars in their heavens but he adored, too, the clerks at the Ralph's check-out counters, and the tender-age night kids outside The Roxy or Gazzarri's on the Strip and the fifty-year-old agents, and the sixty-year-old casting directors, and all the crazy girls on the Santa Monica freeway with the wild wind in their hair. He was mesmerized by them all, and they were beguiled by the bizarre intensity of his interest. In turn he vibrated to their reaction in an endless dance of positive reinforcement, until the whole world he inhabited had become a spinning vortex around his body and his bed and the secret places of wonderful strangers.

"Conchita," he murmured the name like a response in church. "Can you send me along some of that 'seventy-nine Pol Roger Rosé. Oh, two or three. And some bits and pieces, those dates rolled in bacon, smoked salmon with brown bread, the usual things. Oh, and I'll have some peach juice. Yeah, a celebration you could say . . . ." He laughed a tinkling laugh, full of conspiracy and comradeship, as he let her know that she was more important than all of them put together, all the hairy, horrible things with their smelly socks and their sexual inadequacies, with their halitosis and their hernias, their dandruff and their disgusting toes. He cradled the telephone against his cheek and clavicle, freeing his other hand, and he peered at his new partners over the edge of the horn rims.

"Now, you watch that cold. Early to bed. Promise?"

He eased the telephone back onto its holder.

"I thought some champagne," he said. "Congratulations! You boys have done a good deal."

Nobody quite knew what to say. They were all caught up in Robert Hartford's letdown. They, the rubbish, would be drinking his champagne. He, the sophisticate, would be doing the peach juice. They wanted hugs, and declarations of undying affection, and proud promises for the future. He wanted to make someone called Conchita burn up with desire at the Sunset Hotel's switchboard.

It was too soon to talk of the projects ahead. It was too late to rehash old ones. In short, there was not much to say at a time when something badly needed to be said. It was Bos Liebowitz who said it. "Well, Robert. How are you going to spend the money?" he asked.

Robert Hartford looked him straight in the eye. "I'm going to buy this hotel," he said.

Robert Hartford hurried across the faded Mexican tile of the pink-and-white impatiens-lined walkway to the adjacent bungalow of his compound, and already he was feeling better. He could tolerate a roomful of men for only so long, and he had been dangerously close to running out of emotional breath.

He knocked on the door, but he opened it as he did so, and the delicious scent of her wafted out onto the evening air. She was sitting on the edge of the bed, and she smiled up at him as he stood in the doorway. She had been waiting for him. Her expression said that. And so did her body, and the clothes that underdressed it. The girl's forehead was propped against her hand, and long black hair burrowed through her fingers before cascading down to frame the sculpted arm. Her elbow rested provocatively on the milky paleness of her thigh, indenting the creamy skin. Her lips were moist, her head leaned seductively to one side, and her eyes were ablaze.

"Hi, Robert," she murmured.

He didn't answer. He was in church. He wanted to kneel. This was the communion that gave meaning to his life. She was so white—

white as light in the town of brown women—and that made the black
so much better. Her midnight stockings were turned down at midthigh,
and the straps of her garter belt lay loose against her skin. Her silk
night-dress was short, circling her in a black band that was in contrast
to the snowy slope of her back and the flesh strips of her upper legs. But
it was her breasts that took Robert Hartford's breath away. The flimsiest
brocade fought to contain them, the material forming a sensual
latticework over the firm flesh as the girl's crouched, catlike position
magnified their fullness.

He smiled at her.

"You're so beautiful," he whispered. He breathed the words, as he
willed her to believe him, and his smile, and hers, deepened as she
did.

"Thank you." It was a murmur, brimful of pleasure, but it was also
the "thank you" of a little girl. The hint of formal politeness in the pre-
lude to the storm of bodies, delighted Robert. He moved toward her.

She sat up and turned to face him full on. Her tongue crept out to
moisten her parted lips, and she swallowed hard as she prepared to be
the lover of the man who loved women.

He stood before her and reached for her hands as his eyes reassured
her, and her fingers played lazily with his. He drew her up toward him,
and she flowed into his arms, silky smooth and sweet smelling, soft as
the black material that clothed her, her body supple and willing. His
hands caressed the velvet skin of her back, and she shuddered against
his chest as the sensation flowed through her, and he drew himself in
closer to lose himself in the tense flesh of her breasts.

She turned up her face toward his, and she closed her eyes as she
willed him to love her. "Kiss me, Robert," she murmured.

In answer, he ran his hands through her hair, twining its strands
through his fingers. Then he bent toward the long whiteness of her
neck, and his breath fanned her. He paused, deliciously unhurried,
and his hands traced the contours of her head, holding her hostage to
him, she who only wanted to be his prisoner. Then his lips descended,
warm and humid on the dry desert of her skin, and their landing was
butterfly soft, hovering between presence and absence in the delicious
mixture of threat and promise.

A sigh of longing slipped from her, and she reached up to take what
he was so tantalizingly slow to give. Her hands cupped his cheeks and
she opened her eyes wide in the stricken gaze of the frightened fawn as
she moved his lips to hers.

He sensed she could wait no more and, excited by her desire, he
matched it with his own, allowing the wonderful girl to draw him into

the sweet trap of her lips, parted hungrily to receive him. He closed his eyes, the better to feel her, and his mouth melted gratefully against hers. There was a time for control, and there was a time for letting go. Robert Hartford was no longer a conscious being. He had become an instinct, the most subtle and sophisticated sensual animal in the world, and now his every motion was designed only to capture the elusive prey of pleasure—pleasure for himself, pleasure for the goddess he was worshiping.

She fought him in the kiss, and he rode her desperate mouth, swaying, retreating, advancing, in the abundant wetness and the heat of lips. For long seconds he allowed her savage onslaught, and then as the wild passion gripped her, and the low whimper murmured in her throat, as her hands reached out to draw his buttocks in against her thrusting hips, he slowed the pace once more. Languid, liquid, his mouth captured her quivering tongue, and his hands played her hair, her neck, as if both were the reins of a crazed mustang that must learn to be ridden. His touch was gentle as he guided her to the easy calm she would learn from him. Gradually she relinquished her greedy, headstrong assault, as she allowed him to guide her to the sensuous shyness of a more delicate love. Their tongues swayed together in a velvet embrace, and she experienced at last the taste of him as she sucked the nectar from his lips with the patience and calm of a honeybee at the heart of a wide-open flower.

Now his mouth lingered on the high pallor of her cheeks, caressed the dark line of her eyebrows, slipped down to taste the fluttering lids of her nut-brown eyes. But always he returned to her lips and, like a parched traveler in the desert of her face, he drank from the fountain of her. Then, strong enough to explore once more, he set out again in the search for satisfaction: out to the lobe of her perfect ear; up to the broad brilliance of her forehead, where the glory of her face met the mane of lustrous, scented, jet-black hair.

He breathed in the perfumed essence of her and he laughed in his heart as he smelled the secrets of all the soft, seductive beauties with their beguiling ways, their brilliance, and their superhuman strengths. It was always different, so endlessly the same, as the doe-skinned wonders lent him their bodies to thrill and be thrilled. It was the way to handle women. To love them was simply not enough. They had to be adored. Only then could they give the gift of joy that was always theirs to bestow.

Her face was wet with the tracks of his tongue, and her cheeks were moist with tears of passion.

Her long legs were weak with excitement. He could feel it, as she shuddered in his embrace, as her hands picked pleadingly at his body.

She sank down against the creamy ivory of the Pratesi bed cover, until her head rested on the outsize pillow, and he smiled tenderly at her, as the love light blazed in her big round eyes, and the musky, majestic aroma of her need seeped into the scented air. She lay back, and her hands wandered to her breasts, to the fevered skin framed by the black brocade, to the pink pulses that were her nipples.

He reached out and he slipped one black strap over her shoulder, then the other, unveiling the twin monuments to terminal beauty for the eyes of the man who understood.

She lay back, and she smiled at him as she watched her reflection mirrored in his delighted eyes. The consummate sculpture had at last met the supreme aesthete. She was more beautiful than all the beautiful girls she knew, but he was more beautiful than she. And he knew how to love. He was showing her, and in the dawn of lovers' wisdom she realized that she knew nothing at all. For an age of anticipation he simply watched her. His eyes feasted from her, speaking to her, roaming lovingly over her, until her hot flesh crawled with sensation, and tingled with longing. His look was liquid intimacy. His eyes said the words that his tongue would never speak—that he loved her more completely than any perfect woman had ever been perfectly loved—and the lies of his eyes didn't matter. There was only the present, only the agonizing nearness of him.

She swallowed hard and her eyes, round with disbelief, gazed into the mystery of his. His hand moved toward her, and his touch was so feathery in its lightness, that she could hardly comprehend the crashing vibrations it sent coursing through her. "Oh God, Robert . . ." she moaned.

His finger hovered on the borders of her nipple, and his eyes asked the tender permission, as they watched for the telltale signs from her body that each stage of arousal had been filled up to its potential, and that no tiny area of sensual possibility remained unexplored.

She could feel it pulsating at the edge of his finger. All the blood in her body was there, forcing the skin into the geometrical point of the triangle.

"Touch me, touch me . . ." she pleaded.

And he did. But it was not his finger that touched her.

He leaned in toward her, and he bent down as if to the sacrament, and the tip of his tongue, wet and warm, merged with the sharp point of the center of her world.

THREE

The Georgian crystal chandelier ruled the room. On either side, flanking it like a Praetorian guard, were its lesser fellows, showering down pearls of brilliant light on the up-market swine below. The crowd was tense, and packed together on gold-painted chairs in the ballroom of the Sunset Hotel. The hum of their excited conversation waxed and waned like the Santa Monica surf, merging in uneasy harmony with the metallic Ravi Shankar sitar music that burbled from the concealed speaker system.

"Christ, Kristina, I've just signed the movie deal of the century and now you've dragged me off to some psychedelic sixties time-warp rally. What *is* this? Who on *earth* persuaded Francisco to let these fruitcakes use his hotel?"

The indulgent smile on Robert Hartford's face gave the lie to the sentiments he was expressing. He leaned toward his daughter, into the sweet aura of Dior's Poison, close to the swanlike neck with its clusters of Tina Chow astral-trip aquamarine stones, up against the shoulder-pads of her black Giorgio Armani jacket. His velvet-soft whisper was intimate, and totally unrelated to the words he spoke. Kristina Hartford was to some extent insulated from the industrial strength of his charm, but she was also a woman.

"Oh, Dad, relax. Let it all *go*. Caroline Kirkegaard could change your life if you let her."

Robert laughed dismissively. Then his nostrils began to twitch. "What's that funny smell," he asked, suspiciously.

"They've smudged the room," said Kristina, as if talking to a small child.

22

"They've done *what?*"

"They burn leaves from a cedar, and bits from sage bushes to 'clear' the room. It removes all the stored vibrations and leaves everyone receptive for the message from the crystals."

"Good God," said Robert cheerfully in a seen-it-all-now tone.

She reached for his hand and twined her fingers in among his, squeezing affectionately to show that she could live with his skepticism and appreciate his good humor. Robert squeezed back, pleased by the contact and the unconditional affection it symbolized.

He ran his practiced eye over the woman he had created. It was difficult to be objective about her, but he tried. The body was superb, and she was well dressed, even if the couture was a little unadventurous. That was a function of the ludicrously large allowance he paid her. Cash was the enemy of cachet, and cheap so often the friend of chic. There was too much of her mother in the face, a certain bland flatness that looked passable as a whole but lost points on a feature-by-feature analysis—the ripe mouth and sparky eyes scoring high; the too-large nose, the high forehead, and the fleshy cheekbones failing to deliver absolute beauty. But Robert adored her. For him Kristina represented the difference between love and sex. If it hadn't been for her, he wouldn't have had a clue that they were not the same thing.

"Listen, sweetheart, there can't be two people called Caroline Kirkegaard in this town. If it's the one I threw off my movie five years ago then I'm telling you she's really bad vibes. Believe me, *really* bad."

"Vibes, Dad. *Vibes!!!* God, it's getting to you already. Like no way was Caroline Kirkegaard ever an *actress.*" The putdown was as unintentional as it was unmistakable. In Kristina's scheme of things, psychics ranked higher than movie people.

The laughter was bubbling through Kristina's words. She'd only heard about the Kirkegaard channeling meeting an hour or so before, and she'd rushed over from the UCLA campus in Westwood and had only just made it in time. If she'd known earlier she'd have made a point of dropping in on her father, but the way things had turned out she'd bumped into him anyway saying good-bye to a tearful, dark-haired beauty in the lobby. Kristina had immediately captured him and dragged him along to the meeting, as he pretended to complain. It was fun teasing him, and basking in the glory that always accompanied public appearances with her famous father, and she was also enjoying introducing him to the New Age movement that was becoming such a large part of her life. Of course, she *expected* skepticism. If you couldn't count on a dad for that, what *could* you count on him for?

"Well, I'll recognize her when I see her. Once seen never forgotten."

It was true. He'd never totally forgotten Caroline Kirkegaard, and now, as he thought of her, he couldn't suppress the shudder of revulsion. Big, butch, ballsy as hell, she had stood out from the faceless crowd of bit players in the movie that had been constructed as his own personal vehicle. She had towered above all the rest, both literally and figuratively, and in the scenes they had done together she had all but stolen them. That in itself had been unforgivable, but it had been much more than that. Robert Hartford had found her deeply unsettling. There had been an impossible-to-ignore quality about her, and in watching her he understood about moths and flames, and the compulsion of male spiders for fatal union with black widows. She had the hypnotic immediacy of a particularly violent traffic accident, of a plane falling in flames from an angry sky.

He had acted with surgical speed and precision. The director and the producer had been summoned to his office at the studio, and he had told them—just like that—that she was history. He hadn't asked that she be given the soft soap in terms of some let-you-down-gently-excuse, and she hadn't been given any. She had been told, quite simply, that she was off the movie, because Robert Hartford had ordered it and he had never been told—although he could imagine—what her reaction had been.

He shifted in his seat, suddenly uncomfortable on the little red cushion, and he looked around the room. For all his talk of freaks and weirdos the crowd in the ballroom was actually platinum-card-carrying Beverly Hills: exuberant suntans, silver hair, buckets of gold for the predominantly middle-aged males; brave, brittle lifted faces, bright colors, and pendulous semiprecious Kenneth J. Lane necklaces and bracelets for the marginally older women. Scattered among the agents and lower-level studio-production people were a couple of screen "writers" that Robert recognized, a trio of actors that he almost did, and a swathe of support people like the doctors who made the tits and the faces stay up, the lawyers who handled the divorces, and the dentists who were responsible for the unearthly whiteness of the wall-to-wall teeth. Then there were the starlets with their expressions of desperate expectancy and their wide-open bleached, bonded smiles that belied their ugly interiors, their gold-bullion souls, their computerized hearts.

"Look, it's beginning!" said Kristina.

As if on cue the lights dimmed, stilling the roar of conversation in the Sunset ballroom. At the same time somebody turned up the tuneless music, and twin spotlights lit the stage.

Robert couldn't help being caught up in the almost palpable excitement of the crowd. "These people ought to know better," he muttered to himself as a mantra to ward off the electric enthusiasm that surrounded him on every side.

Two porters walked briskly onto the stage, carrying three black Doric columns, made of papier-mâché, each about five feet long. They searched around on the floor, looking for chalk marks, and took great care to position them with total accuracy at the points of an equilateral triangle. A third man entered from the left carrying a simple straight-backed metal chair, which he placed at a point equidistant from the columns. Then all three withdrew. The mystical music stopped. There was no sound at all in the audience. The Testarossa and Countach keys were quiet in their pockets. The thick, creamy scent of Giorgio still in their nostrils, they forced all thought of box-office returns to the back of their minds. Any minute now the channel herself would walk onto the stage, and soon they would be in touch, across vast stretches of eternal time, with the people that once they had been.

The girl who hurried onto the stage now was clearly *not* the main feature, but to Robert Hartford she was a more than acceptable trailer. She was extremely pretty. Her red hair was cut in a flashy, slightly old-fashioned Farrah Fawcett, and it framed an enthusiastic, pert face whose main features were a surgically perfect nose and pouting heart-shaped lips. She wore standard-issue 501's and a checked shirt that looked like it was from an L. L. Bean catalogue. In L.A., where they knew about such things, it was obvious that she was heavily into exercise, and from her superconfident walk, and the way her rock-hard ass stuck straight up, it was also clear that Narcissus was a close relative.

She carried a large tray strapped around her neck, holding three outside clear quartz crystals. Each was about nine inches high, brilliant and translucent, rising from an irregular base to a uniform point. Making light of what was obviously formidable weight, she placed one carefully on the top of each column. Immediately the spotlights sought them out, and there was a murmur in the crowd as three beams illuminated their beauty. The light seemed to blaze from the surface of the stones, haunting, mysterious, and totally alive. For a second the girl stood back and allowed the crystals to speak silently to the crowd. Then she walked to the center of the stage. In a soft, silky voice she said, "My name is Kanga. I am Caroline Kirkegaard's disciple. The mistress of Destiny is ready for you. May the truth of the crystal live in your hearts, and the love of the Great One illuminate your minds."

Then she turned quickly and left the stage.

"She's muddled that up," whispered Robert. "Surely she meant truth in the mind and love in the heart."

"Sssssssh," hissed Kristina, irritated. Parental skepticism was one thing, literary criticism was another, especially from her father, whose I.Q. equaled his systolic blood pressure.

"Is the Great One God?" he persevered, beginning to enjoy himself.

"We're *all* gods," whispered Kristina.

"Ah," said Robert. "That one."

"Don't think, feel," exhorted Kristina in her role as metaphysical navigator, blissfully unaware that she was mouthing a line from a sixties musical.

"If I don't think, I won't know what it is I'm feeling," said Robert.

"Be *quiet!*" ordered someone loudly from the row behind.

Robert twisted in his seat, ready, willing, and fantastically able to do battle with the shadowy bastard who had *dared* to give him an order. But Caroline Kirkegaard forestalled him. She was striding across the stage, and she was as impossible to ignore as nuclear war.

Robert felt his eyes sucked toward her by some power beyond his control. Oh yes, it was "his" Caroline Kirkegaard, all right. He recognized her instantly, and a packet of dread exploded inside him. This woman had reason to hate him, and one thing was certain. She wasn't the sort of enemy that anybody should have.

Caroline Kirkegaard sat down on the chair in the dead center of the crystal triangle. She sat quite still, her spine straight, head held high, eyes wide open, and her long pale neck stretched upward, as if longing for the kiss of some Druid's knife. The black Saint Laurent cocktail frock she wore—cut low in front, and slashed surgically up the side of the pencil skirt—had the effect and purpose of an exclamation mark. It wasn't there to hide. It was there to reveal. Her milk-white body exploded from it like toothpaste from a punctured tube, oozing out in a tight stream of flesh, and as it did so it was sculpted into muscle perfection and bone brilliance by some Valkyrian artist who had never heard of bourgeois self-control. Her yellow-blond Brylcreemed hair was slicked back from her high forehead in a fifties Tony Curtis cut and chopped off mercilessly at the back where the skyscraper neck met the Nordic head.

Her face was disturbingly beautiful. Below dangerous brows her eyes were an unnatural metallic blue, quite unlike the blue of the sky or sea, as if the color had been invented by a chance clash of the elements in a freak electrical storm. They held her eager audience with the irresistible power of cosmic blue-black holes—beckoning, demanding, insisting that they watch her if they dared. Down, down into the eyes they went—all the movie men and the groovy women, the medical mavens and Rodeo matrons—spinning gratefully into their depths. It didn't matter that they were unable to breathe. The important thing was to *be* there, safe in the sanctuary of her mysterious purpose, womb-warm in the glow of her vision, rammed up tight against the luminous knowledge of her stellar brain. Caroline Kirkegaard's wet lips dripped promises. They were vermilion, but, unlike her eyes, color was not their point. It was their lushness. They were mangoes, and papaya and kiwi and loquat, exotic in their tropical come-on, twin pads of glistening membrane parted in the unmistakable statement that they were ready to eat . . . and be eaten.

Her torso alone would have had the muscle-pumping bodybuilders of Venice Beach weeping in their steroid soup. Her shoulders, broad and strong as a rigid steel joist, supported arms that could have won wrestling matches on bars. Her breasts headed straight for the audience, shameless in the enormity of their statement, and were separated from each other by a cleavage that, in more ways than one, conjured up visions of Silicon Valley. Across the crack-of-doom divide stretched the milky way of the Caroline Kirkegaard mammary land. Most of it was visible above the low-cut black dress, and the acreage that wasn't was merely shrouded in thin cloud by the sheer silk material. Two tight nipples, icepick sharp, fought mano-a-mano with the Saint Laurent dress, and for a good reason. The half-cone tips of her bra had been removed, and the brown pigment of her areolae was a mere wisp of silk away from total visibility.

As if carved in stone, she received the homage of the audience, her hands clasped around two crystals that rested in her lap.

"She's like a goddess!" Kristina's breathless whisper was saturated with awe, and beside her in the semidarkness Robert Hartford was uncharacteristically lost for words. He swallowed hard in the somehow noisy silence. Caroline Kirkegaard had always been difficult to ignore, but this was ridiculous. Heavens, she was big! Not so much a goddess as a praying mantis, hovering over the stage, burying the chair in which she sat, and dwarfing life itself with the sheer size of her personality. She wasn't really a woman at all. She was an *event*. She transcended gender, a great statue of androgyny that spoke alike to men, women, and children in the Esperanto of universal sexuality.

Robert could feel it. It was a fine mist enveloping his delicate sensual antennae, and all around him he knew that the Hollywood power people were giving up the struggle to retain their jaded indifference as they plopped, one by one, gasping and gulping, into the sexual stew that was now the room's atmosphere. It wasn't just the men. It was the women, too, sinking gracefully into the seductive sea of the Kirkegaard charisma.

"Look, the crystals," said Kristina.

Perfectly still on their pedestals several feet from Caroline Kirke-gaard's Viking head, the crystals seemed to have come alive. The spotlights played over them as they had before, but it was the way the light reemerged that now fascinated the audience. Before it had been reflected in uniform diffusion from the facets of the stones, but now it was on the move. It began to choose direction, and it gained in strength, cascading out, as if it had been born again in the heart of the cold geometry. As the crowd watched, their bodies humming like tuning forks to the subterranean vibrations, the light that streamed from the crystals began to aim itself at Caroline Kirkegaard. Gradually the beams became more focused, until at last they were lasers darting like spears at the bone sculpture that was her head, giving off a ghostly, incandescent glow at her forehead, high up on her cheekbones, deep in her bottomless eyes.

Kristina heard her own sharp intake of breath. Her whole body was full of the absolute certainty that something wonderful was happening. She wanted to *be* that light. There, inside the vision, lost in the crystal moonbeams, she could find herself. There, bathing at the knowledge fountain, she could get drunk on meaning. There, in the warm heart of Caroline's loving mind, she could find all the truths at last.

But the light had changed direction. Funneling in from the crystal-topped columns it flowed down both sides of her, indenting at the wasp-ish waist, caressing her thighs, lapping lovingly at her stiltlike legs. It hugged Caroline closely like an aura, and Kristina, her willing ears tuned to hear such things, fancied she could hear the humming of the light, high pitched and resonant, that signaled the end of the beginning.

Caroline Kirkegaard closed her eyes. Then she breathed in deeply through her nose, inflating her majestic torso. Next the breath rushed out of her and the sound filled the room, until everyone could sense the currents of air that she was creating. Slowly, a crystal in the palm of each hand, her arms rose up from her sides until they pointed straight at the audience.

"She's directing her kundalini energy through the crystals, and using the force of the other crystals to energize her," whispered Kristina, leaning in toward her father, but keeping her eyes fixed on the stage. "Can't you feel the power in the room?"

Robert shifted in his chair. He could feel something, but it was impossible to say what it was. Irritation? The contagious enthusiasm of the gullible crowd? The appalling discomfort of not being the center of attraction? There was a sensation of strangeness, of being on a voyage, the weird exhilaration of finding yourself in a foreign country that you weren't sure you liked.

He jumped suddenly as the music struck up again. It was a hideous aural experience, loud and dissonant, tuneless and disjointed. There were synthesizers, gongs, bells and droning, chanting, Eastern voices repeating meaningless sounds amid the chaos.

"God, what a dreadful noise," said Robert.

"You're just not in *tune* with it," hissed Kristina. "*We* are."

"It's not in tune with itself," protested Robert.

"You can't '*hear*' it."

"I can. That's the problem."

"It's shamanic music. They play it all the time on that radio station, the Wave. It opens your consciousness to higher planes and it potentiates the power of the crystals. This one is called Wakan-tanka."

"Now, *that* I can believe."

She looked at him sharply, as she sensed the ridicule.

But the dialogue was over.

"Link hands," commanded Caroline Kirkegaard.

Her voice, pure Southern California, silky smooth, was a million miles from the fjords where she came from, but despite its softness it cut through the silence like the crack of a whip. No one in the audience considered disobeying her, not even Robert Hartford, who thanked the Lord in heaven that he had chosen an aisle seat as he reached for his daughter's hand.

Caroline watched them obey her, and the thrill of excitement coursed through her. This was what it was all about. Power over people. She worshiped it. The audience, however, recoiled from it. They wanted release from their responsibilities and the awesome decisions that they endlessly had to make. They wanted to retreat from self-determination to a simpler world where they danced to the tune of a piper who was no longer themselves. It was a straightforward transaction, as old as time, as old as ruler and the ruled, as ancient as leaders and the led. All their problems would melt away if they would give Caroline the control that she longed for with every fiber of her mighty will.

Holding hands made it easier. Feeling was believing but touching was
the truth, and other people's flesh was the most powerful medi-
cine. If they were linked together, then they were *connected*. To some
extent they were no longer discrete individuals. They had become a
crowd, an entity with a personality that was dramatically different
from those of the individual human beings who combined to form it.

Caroline stood up, well aware of the psychological impact of her
unusual height. She raised a hand to focus the eyes.

"I am who I was," she intoned.

"I am who I was," they dutifully responded.

"I am who I was," said Kristina.

"Bullshit," said Robert Hartford. "Reincarnation bullshit," he
repeated, quite loudly.

But Kristina wasn't listening to him. She smiled to herself. They had
all existed before, and somehow those past lives lived on in them right
now. It was reassuring to feel that life stretched back endlessly into the
distant past. It made her feel bigger, more important, *part* of something.

"I will be who I am," said Caroline Kirkegaard.

Robert Hartford was beginning to get irritated. The Kirkegaard bitch
had just said that everyone would experience an infinite number of
future lives, and the life they were leading now would be incorporated
into that endless future. Dear old reincarnation. Original as sin. No,
the maddening thing was the smiles of wonder on the faces of the
audience. On *Kristina's* face. It was unbelievable. They were looking
at age-old soft soap, and seeing the Holy Grail. It was totally ridiculous
even in bone-from-the-neck-up Beverly Hills where the nearest things
to intellectuals were screenwriters and shrinks.

"The future and the past," said Caroline Kirkegaard mysteriously,
"are one through me."

Robert Hartford stood up. It was garbage. He didn't bother to say
good-bye to Kristina. She was too busy mouthing her responses to the
High Priestess to notice that he was leaving. He would make as much
noise as possible on the way out, as he voted on the whole incredible
charade with his feet, and he vowed to recommend to Francisco
Livingstone that in future all Destiny meetings be banned from the
Sunset Hotel.

Caroline saw someone making a high-profile exit, but she wasn't
fazed. There was always somebody in the audience who couldn't stand
the competition, who resented the power she exercised. It was good he
was leaving. There was room for only one force source at a Destiny
meeting. She peered out over the flushed faces, and the glorious

feeling exploded within her. God, it was magnificent—asserting the control. They would say anything now, believe anything. They were committed, not to truth, not to knowledge, not to wisdom—but to her.

"Raise your hands above your head," she ordered, as maybe a thousand hands reached for the sky. "We are the brothers and sisters of eternity," said Caroline Kirkegaard.

Robert Hartford tried to shut his ears to the meta-claptrap that was unfolding in his wake as he made for the exit, and he avoided the eyes of the crowd on the way out. His instinct told him that the audience was too enraptured by the Kirkegaard charisma to spare a thought for a mere superstar, even one of his stature. That added insult to the intellectual injuries he had just sustained. But as he approached the exit, he noticed a man he had seen somewhere before, who seemed to be trying to communicate with him, although it was not certain what his expression meant. Despite himself Robert couldn't help returning his gaze and the corners of his mouth turned down in irritation as he realized that some sort of acknowledgment might have to be made. The familiar stranger's look seemed to be saying that he understood why Hartford was leaving while at the same time insinuating that his departure was the result of all sorts of ego problems that weren't totally admirable, were even slightly humorous. The Hartford jaw set in concrete as he sailed past the maybe acquaintance. Screw him, whoever he was. Fifty-six-million-dollar movie stars could afford to ignore people they didn't know they knew.

At the back of the room, beside the exit, and beneath a brooding, romantic landscape of the Hudson River School, the man was quite unmoved by Robert Hartford's failure to either recognize or acknowledge him. He leaned nonchalantly against the oak-paneled wall of the Sunset ballroom, wearing an expensive single-breasted dark blue worsted suit, a nondescript blue-striped tie, and an unfashionable but far from cheap white silk shirt. The jacket was tightly buttoned, and that seemed a symbol for his entire appearance—from the tips of his patent-leather hair to the soles of his highly polished thick-soled tasseled loafers. His face, like the rest of him, was giving nothing away. It was relaxed in an expression that was not quite a smile, hovering on the borders of both disdain and patronization. Broad, bushy eyebrows, black as night, bristled over wide-set eyes, and a determined, snub nose tapered off into a mean mouth, which in turn was lost in a square, aggressive jaw. His features warred with each other, suggesting he was a creature of deep contradictions, and his fastidious appearance bore that out, existing as it did in contrast to the lack of style that characterized his choice of

clothes. Right now, behind the enigmatic face, David Plutarch was
fighting back the all-but-uncontrollable desire to laugh.

He had arrived late to find that it was standing room only and for a
second or two he had wondered whether to leave immediately. Now,
however, crazed Arab stallions couldn't drive him away. It wasn't what
she said, it was the way she said it, and of course it wasn't even that
. . . it was who she *was*. He had never seen anything like her.
Anywhere. She was a dream come true, a wild fantasy figure from his
unconscious mind, and the desire bubbled up from the cess and the
muck to drown his reason with its decaying, infinitely alluring aroma.
But although he was aware that all sorts of slumbering giants were
shifting and grunting in the early dawn of arousal, his cutlass-sharp
mind was still analyzing the extraordinary spectacle he was watching.

The woman called Caroline Kirkegaard was clearly a control freak.
It took one to recognize one. But whereas he had built the fourth larg-
est fortune in America to satisfy his craving for power, this girl clearly
preferred something a little more immediate. She liked to *see* the effect
of her charisma. She liked to touch it, to taste it, to smell it, to hear
it, and the frisson of excitement rushed down his powerful back as he
admired the supreme virtuosity of her performance. It was incredible.
The grownups all around him were holding hands like soppy teenagers
on a first date as they mouthed the meaningless metaphysics, filling the
room with the sound of their chanting.

"You are the flowers, the birds, the corn in the fields . . ." Caroline
Kirkegaard paused for the sting . . . "You are the *worms!*"

There was absolutely no hesitation when the crowd reached the
"worms" bit. In this context there was clearly no shame in being a
worm at all.

"We are joined together in the protoplasm of infinity," said Caroline
Kirkegaard definitely.

Plutarch's mouth dropped open. It was far better than brilliant. She
was playing the childhood game of Simon says, and the crowd would
do anything for her. But where would it end? "Give me your money
and become my slave?" "Renounce your family and deny your
friend?" "Torture this one, kill that one in the name of the brotherhood
of transcendental rubbish?"

Plutarch loved every bit of it. If only the charisma could be distilled,
bottled, *sold*. That was how business worked. Create a need in people
for something that isn't basically good for them—drink, cigarettes,
candy, game shows—and then peddle it with high-octane energy and
adventurous advertising until they were hooked and you were rich.
This load of losers dressed as winners were all the same. They were lost

souls longing to be found. They were searching for elusive happiness, or trying to escape intolerable loneliness, and they were reaching blindly into every bizarre avenue to fill the void in their hearts. All of them, in one sense or another, had failed. Some had successful careers but were universally loathed. Others were loved but no longer had money for the rent. Some would be depressed, some anxious, others still would be deep in long-term relationships with booze or drugs. All were at a low ebb, all vulnerable, all clutching at straws, desperate for quick fixes, cheap promises, and instant transports to delight from the terminal angst that plagued them. The Kirkegaard woman would know all that. She was merely giving them what they wanted. It was the great American way.

Plutarch's lips curled in a smile of the deepest satisfaction, as he tried to climb inside her intriguing mind.

He nodded to himself. Oh yes, he could see it all. The poor lambs were lining up for the slaughter, little lost sheep who had gone astray. Not for a moment did he identify with them. After all, he was only there because he had been passing by on his way from a business meeting in one of the Sunset bungalows. He had seen the crowd, and he had popped in to take a look. Boy, was he glad he had. What a *star* she was! Clearly she adored what she was doing. Her lips were parted in a kind of sensual anguish, and her hips were thrusting out at the losers who loved her. She was throbbing with pleasure as she massaged the audience. He could see the excitement at the points of those mind-numbing tits, and he could dream about it tingling in the hot bed between those divine legs as she stretched her arms upward to impale the flock she led on the sharp shaft of her enormous will.

David Plutarch swallowed, noticing that his mouth was suddenly dry, and that he was warm in the cool of the air-conditioned ballroom. He could sense the thin film of sweat that had sprung from nowhere to coat his upper lip and he felt his heart speed up in his chest, the moths start their frivolous dance in the pit of his stomach. God in *heaven*, she was attractive. . . .

In front of Plutarch, in the body of the room, Kristina was a flower, and a worm, and was now publicly admitting that she was a part of the protoplasm of infinity. She was not sure why, but it just felt so *good* to be all those beautiful things. She didn't ask for proof. It was true because it *felt* true. It was true because Caroline Kirkegaard said so.

But Caroline Kirkegaard was flailing her arms from side to side and her mighty breasts were heaving around like twin storms at sea. "Silence!" she screamed.

Kristina's mouth, still muttering about protoplasm, shut tight.

The silence that the mistress of Destiny had ordered now filled the room. On and on it went, longer and longer, as its creator stood motionless on the stage. Kristina felt the collective anxiety. They had been on an emotional roll, strange in its intensity. Now they were all strung out in the alien territory of the unaccustomed quiet. Kristina could actually hear her heart beating as she waited.

"You . . . . are . . . . NOTHING!"

The last word erupted from the stage like a missile, and the contempt, and the accusation exploded in an air burst over the crowd.

Kristina's head shot back and her eyes widened. She was stunned, her mind shocked into blankness by the completeness of her surprise at finding herself suddenly a nothing. If *she* was nothing then perhaps all those other intriguing things were really nothing, too. Yes, that must be it. God, how clever! She'd nearly fooled herself, but at the very last moment faith had rescued her. It was true. She was nothing. Sad, but true, and it sort of gelled with the feelings she already had about herself deep inside.

"What are you?"

"Nothing," said Kristina and everyone else.

"LOUDER!"

"NOTHING."

"Again."

"NOTHING."

Kristina screamed into the growing chorus, and the louder she shouted the better she felt. She squeezed tight on the sweaty palm of the nothing beside her and she howled her nothingness at the gleaming wooden panels of the ballroom, at the high ceiling with its intricate plaster molding, at the extravagant arrangements of white phalaenopsis butterfly orchids, at the Chinese Chippendale mirrors. In her eyes there was a glistening, luminous zeal as she went for the peak experience, and the fervor and wild excitement cascaded from her bared lips, because now she knew who she was.

Relief flooded through her, shaking her with the intensity of an orgasm. She belonged at last. She was joined to everyone else in the room. They were a great and glorious team of nothings. Nobody had been picked out for special treatment. The hands they held said so. It wasn't like life where people were big failures, little failures, and all sorts of grades in between. Instead here was an equality of nobodies, a humming, throbbing conglomeration of nothingness. From this point anything would be possible. From the bedrock of nonexistence that Kristina and all the others now so cheerfully embraced there would be only one way to go: up. Then, who knew, with Caroline Kirkegaard as the spirit guide they might, one fine day, actually become something.

"NOTHING! NOTHING! NOTHING!"

Kristina's voice filled up her own ears as the sensation of listening and shouting merged into one, and she traveled on the sound surf to the grotto where she could lose the identity that plagued her. It was a wonderful place, full of light and wisdom and absolutely devoid of responsibility. In it she could swim free, unencumbered by the paraphernalia of herself, her credit cards, her matte black BMW convertible, her Cartier Panther watch, her pride, her presumption, her prejudice. As she howled the desperate hymn to her own inadequacy, she sensed that she was about to be reborn.

"NOTHING. NOTHING. NOTHING."

Once again the Kirkegaard arms were in the air, signaling for quiet, and slowly, like some ponderous oil tanker ordered to stop in the Gulf, the cacophony of sound began to fade. The nothings who would be somethings were shutting up on cue. A few couldn't stop their hysterical chanting, and their brand-new brothers cradled them in brotherly arms, and their brand-new sisters slapped them hard with sisterly palms until they obeyed the instruction.

"You have gained great insights here today," breathed Caroline into the expectant silence. "Together we can go on to learn larger truths. But first you must make a commitment—to Fate, to each other, to yourselves. Join with me in Destiny. Merge with the Cosmic Force. Please come forward if you are ready to inherit the earth."

Kristina jumped onto feet that didn't seem to belong to her any-more. All around everyone else did the same thing. Then they rushed toward the stage, jostling, pushing, pulling at the other members of their instant family as they fought to sign on. They *were* ready to inherit the earth. It sounded like the best possible deal for a gang of wall-to-wall nothings. And yes, they *wanted* the Cosmic Force on their side—in script conferences, on the tennis court, and in the bedroom, where any force at all would be enormously welcome. They thronged the edge of the dais and they tried to reach up and touch her and to speak to her, but somehow, without doing anything at all, she held them at bay. It was as if a magnetic force field surrounded her, a barrier that the uninitiated couldn't cross. There was no keep-your-distance body lan-guage, and nothing was said, nothing gestured. Somehow they recoiled from her at the very moment they wanted so badly to make contact with her, and so they stood before her in their foolish ranks, smiling stupidly as the love beamed out of their eyes toward her.

In all her life Kristina had never felt so vitally important, and yet so completely impotent.

Towering above them, Caroline Kirkegaard moistened her silky lips as a half smile of pleasure played across her face. Then, decisively, she turned to one side and stalked imperiously from the room, leaving Kristina and the others spaced out on the plateau of their own enthusiasm, the place where they so desperately wanted to be.

The corridor stretched out in front of Caroline Kirkegaard and the thick pile of the carpet sucked at her like quicksand as she strode along. She smiled as she walked, at the thought of the Destiny converts she had left behind. By now, they would be desperate to put their names down on some list, to write the checks, to "belong." But that was another trick she'd learned. She made them work for it. That way you separated the real cannon fodder from the bogus kind. Leaving them all stretched out on their adrenaline jag was another vital ingredient in the mix of their conditioning process. In half an hour's time the real enthusiasts would be besieging the Destiny offices in Century City, while others would be burning up the telephone lines with their commitments and their cash.

The girl called Kanga half-ran, half-walked beside her. It was the only way she could keep up.

Caroline Kirkegaard looked straight ahead, but she inclined her head toward her assistant as she spoke. "Good, no?"

"It was awesome, Caro. Totally awesome." The redhead's voice was full of respect.

"Who was there? Anybody worthwhile?"

"Only Robert Hartford, no less. The bad news is that he walked."

"Robert Hartford at one of *my* meetings? Which cat dragged *him* in?"

"His daughter, Kristina. Great body."

For a second or two Caroline Kirkegaard stalked on in ominous silence as she digested the information. "Fuck Hartford," she said at last. "Anyone else?"

"Oh, Silvers, the hot agent at CAA. And that actress that got eaten by the extraterrestrial in the Lucas film. Or did *she* eat the extraterrestrial? No above-the-title people. No 'go' execs. No real heavy hitters." Kanga paused, wondering if she dared to live dangerously, then decided to go for it. "Except Robert Hartford," she added.

"You missed the most important one of all."

The Kirkegaard words were heavy with accusation.

"Who?" Kanga's voice was nervous.

"Plutarch."

Caroline shot the name out like the ace of trumps.

"Plutarch?"

"He's two-point-five billion and change. He was standing at the back, and *he* didn't walk." The last bit she said reflectively, almost to herself. "Good-looking guy . . . if you like them brash and common. You should be able to recognize people like that, Kanga. You're my assistant, remember. The others are shit. Plutarch's the real thing. He just sold Stellar Communications to United Electric. Read the *Journal*, *Fortune*, *Forbes*. Forget all that mystical crap from the Bodhi Tree."

"Yes, Caroline."

" 'Yes, Caroline.' 'Yes, Caroline,' " mimicked Caroline cruelly, stealing a quick look at her crestfallen assistant as she hurried along beside her, trying valiantly to keep up. The famous wallpaper of the famous hotel—pink palm trees set in three-dimensional relief against a setting sun, gave way to a section of mirrored wall around an alcove, and Caroline Kirkegaard slowed down to catch it. The sight of herself was one of the few things on earth that had the power to stop her in her tracks. She allowed it to do that now.

She angled herself for the sideways reflection, throwing back her head and peering at herself out of the corners of her eyes. She had changed backstage into a sleek black full-length Bill Blass dress and she stood six foot three inches in her Karl Lagerfeld at Charles Jourdan black satin high-heeled pumps.

"Do you think they realized I wasn't wearing any panties?"

"I for sure did."

In the looking glass, Kanga Gillespie was watching the Kirkegaard reflection with the same concentration as Caroline.

"Ah, but then you're paid to notice such things. That's what you get presents for, isn't it, Kanga?"

The redhead blushed, all over her neck, up onto her cheeks, at the tips of her ears. She made no attempt at all to do anything about the Kirkegaard hand that had reached out to squeeze her heavily muscled thigh.

"I don't notice you because of the presents, or because you pay me, Caro."

"Tell me why you notice me."

"Because you're beautiful."

Kanga Gillespie chewed on a suddenly nervous lip. She knew what was coming. It often started like this. Out of nothing, in public, in totally impossible situations. Any second now and a waiter with his trolley would come bustling around the corner, or a bevy of hotel guests would erupt into the corridor from one of the rooms.

"No, the *real* reason, Kanga."

She towered over the younger girl and the cruelty merged with something else in the weird blue eyes. Her powerful arm snaked out and caught Kanga by the neck, her fingers intertwining roughly in the backcombed hair. A ripple passed along her biceps, drawing her assistant's face upward, backward, nearer to hers.

"Because I love you." Kanga's voice was little-girl quiet, as if the words had been forced from her at gunpoint. Her lips trembled as she spoke.

Caroline Kirkegaard moved closer, without relaxing her viselike grip, and her breath fanned out over the pert, pretty face. "You love me because I gave you your tits and your cute little nose, and because you want me to fix up your eyes so they're big and round like mine."

Kanga Gillespie took a deep breath as she felt the delicious wave of passivity flow through her. There was no resisting Caroline. From the very beginning it had been like this, from the very first day when she had been summoned to Caroline's house for the one-on-one aerobics session, and the whole of her life had been turned into wonderful, spine-tingling chaos. She had been the instructor on that occasion, but she had been learning lessons ever since. How to obey, how to serve, and yes, how to worship.

The luscious lips hovered above her, wet and wide and ripe and ready.

"I loved you from the beginning," murmured Kanga. "Please kiss me. Please, Caro, please."

Caroline Kirkegaard had seen her desire, but she would not fulfill it. She stood back and released her grip, and she laughed.

Kanga tried to stop herself from shaking, as the hot and cold sensations danced over her suddenly clammy skin. She attempted a smile. God, she had never been a lesbian. She hadn't even had crushes on other girls at school. But within three weeks of meeting Caroline Kirkegaard she had left her husband, given up her job at the gym, and moved into Caroline's house in the canyons. From that day to this, over two nerve-jangling years, she had been obsessed by her—sexually, intellectually, spiritually, and there wasn't a thing on earth she could do about it.

Caroline Kirkegaard set off again. At the elevator station she found another mirror, and she devoured her image as she waited for the doors to open. Her body *was* amazing. God and surgery hand in hand had created the scaffolding, and two or three hours a day of blood, toil, sweat, and tears had done the rest. She went through instructresses like Kleenex on a cold mountainside in Aspen. They could last maybe an hour with her, maybe more on the aerobics, but on the weights she blew them away. All except Kanga. She had been special. Not on the Nautilus. Not on the circuit training, but on the floor. Oh yes, on the floor she had been the best, which was why she had taken her on, and trained her to do all the things she did so very well.

"I love this place," said Caroline suddenly. "I always have, you know. It *is* Hollywood. It *is* Beverly Hills. If you owned this, you'd own them all, all the players, all the studios, all the dreams . . ."

Her voice trailed off, and she stroked at herself like a sleepy cat, as the Sunset elevator rose to meet her.

"There's some old guy who's had it forever. They're always doing pieces on him in magazines. He looks like father time," said a distracted Kanga.

She had to look away from Caroline as she spoke.

"Yeah, Francisco Livingstone," said Caroline. She stuck both hands on her head and smoothed down the golden hair so it looked like it had been sprayed onto her skull, high gloss, heavy lacquer, sleek and lovely. "There's a rumor he wants to sell it," she added reflectively.

The doors whirred open. The elevator had arrived, and already the eyes of the operator were bulging. Caroline ignored him. She strode into the elevator, hitched up her skirt, and adjusted her garter as if the man weren't there. "Lobby," said Caroline. She didn't say "please." Vast expanses of her milky muscled thigh merged with the black stockings below. The younger girl tried not to watch it. The elevator swooped downward from the fifth floor where their dressing room had been. "You thinking of buying it?" Kanga tried to lighten up. Caroline couldn't stand it when she moped.

But Caroline Kirkegaard didn't laugh. She leaned backward against the ancient oak paneling that Otis had imported from a Scottish castle to wall the Sunset elevator. "Destiny could buy it . . . someday," she said.

"Destiny? In the hotel business? What next? Fast food?"

"Shut up, Kanga."

Kanga Gillespie bit her lip and cursed her stupidity. She had made the cardinal error. Making fun of Destiny in public. Okay, only the elevator man had overheard her, but the George Christys of this world paid good bucks for gossip. If the word got out that Destiny didn't take itself seriously then it would be the end of everything.

In the lobby, Caroline heaped salt into the wound. "Never, ever do that again, Kanga, or you're history, understand?" she hissed. "I'll wipe you out, sweetheart, you'd better believe it."

But the mood was gone like mercury on a marble floor as Caroline Kirkegaard marched across the Carrara stone of the Sunset reception area.

When she spoke again her voice was alive with enthusiasm, almost before Kanga Gillespie's eyes had a chance to fill with tears.

"Don't you see, Kanga? It would be a perfect move. Think of it. Destiny owning the Sunset Hotel. The prestige. The PR. The instant worldwide recognition. We'd keep the hotel side going, but we could use part of the building for residential training seminars, and rallies, and channeling sessions. I mean it would be *brilliant*—the guests would be intrigued by the whole thing, and we could have good-looking chicks like you out by the pool to get people interested. And they wouldn't be just any people. They'd be the sort of people who stay at the Sunset. I mean, look at them. You can *smell* the money."

She waved a hand at the crowded lobby. It looked like Louis Vuitton had married Gucci and Mark Cross had been best man. The luggage alone was worth a few hundred thousand dollars. Only God's accountant knew what the people were worth.

Kanga objected to being one of the poolside chicks, but she was thrilled to be called good-looking by Caroline, and even more pleased that her anger was gone. "It's a cool idea, Caro. I mean it's *really* great, and it would be *so* fun. But this place would go for megabucks—and we're doing terrific, but not that well . . ."

"Okay, we're not there yet, but we will be, baby. You trust me. Just believe in me. We're closer than you think. Much, much closer."

She swept through the doors of the Sunset Hotel, scattering porters and valet parkers like a fox in a chicken coop. The metallic gray convertible 560 SL Mercedes was already there, parked by the curb as she had ordered it to be, but Caroline Kirkegaard wasn't thinking about such mundane things. A name sang in her brain. Plutarch. David Plutarch.

He had been there at the meeting where they had all but worshiped her. Had he, like Hartford, been immune to her power? One thing was certain. He hadn't walked out. And at the thought of that, the adrenaline sizzled through her arteries, and the joy reached out to every distant corner of her immaculate body as she contemplated her glittering future.

FOUR

ood Lord, what on earth have you done to your leg?" said Winthrop Tower as he shepherded Paula through the traffic toward Morton's.

Paula laughed unselfconsciously. "I had an accident when I was very young. I've had it all my life. The leg, too, I guess," she joked.

Winthrop wasn't the sort of man to be embarrassed by the things he said. Nine times out of ten his remarks were supposed to be embarrassing. If she could laugh about something as awesome as a limp, then so could he.

"They shoot horses," he chuckled.

"Where I come from they *eat* horses."

"Where *do* you come from?"

Pain flashed across her face, wiping away the smile. "Grand Cypress—a place called Placid," she managed at last. "It's in Florida. In the Everglades. It's taken me a year to get from there to here."

They had reached the other side of the street, and Tower could see the change in her. It was as if she were a rag doll crumpling before him. There were tears in her deep blue eyes and her lips were trembling as she spat out the spare description of her home. The lump would be growing in her throat. Her sudden sorrow was so real he could almost touch it.

He reached out to her, and he took her small hand in his big creased one and he squeezed the support that he couldn't put into words. He felt the tenderness well up inside him, and the unaccustomed emotion both surprised and excited him. Here at last was someone he could relate to. Not right now, perhaps. Not quite yet. But one day he could and would talk to this girl, and she to him. Then he would learn of the source of her sadness, and he would help her, and they would become friends, good friends, close friends in Temporary Town where relationships were career moves, and shifting sand was considered a firm foundation. What was she running from? What horrors had she left behind, this girl who understood the things *he* understood, this stranger who walked with beauty and knew its secret ways?

The Morton's parking lot was filling already with high-end cars, and the Mexican valet parkers were unashamedly arranging them so that the most exotic and expensive achieved the most prominence, Rollers and Beamers and Mercs to the fore, rented Chevys and Fords consigned to the anonymity of the side alley. It was cooler now but the legacy of the heat remained, sucking the scent from the night flowering jasmine, while the dry desert wind rustled the palm fronds against the discreet green neon MORTON'S sign on the stucco building. The whole restaurant was diffused in a warm, welcoming pink glow from uplighters carefully positioned among the lush green foliage of the palm and banana trees.

It was undeniably pretty and totally unthreatening, but at the same time Paula picked up the vibration that all was not as it seemed. The people erupting from the cars were good-looking and better dressed but somehow they were not completely at ease. The men laughed too loud as they smoothed down the material of their cashmere jackets over spare asses, and they looked nervous as the Hispanics clambered behind the wheels of their proudest possessions. "Ding it, and I'll sue your ass," snarled one hard charger. The women smiled brittle smiles and shook their hair in the night breeze as they looked around expectantly, checking their fellow diners, checking who was checking *them*. Tower eased Paula through the tightening knot of people that thronged around the French doors to the restaurant.

Inside the war between tension and relaxation continued. To the left of them, a large square opening showed chefs hard at work in the spotless kitchen, hinting that this was an unpretentious place where food was the major concern. Directly in front of them, however, like an interrogation team at Moscow's Lubianka prison, stood the welcoming committee. A darkly good-looking girl, tall and thin in a stylish red dress, was flanked by an unbelievably handsome man in a well-cut but casual navy-blue suit. It was Saint Peter and his assistant at the gate. Goats and sheep were about to part company. For those unfortunates unprotected by the Grace of success, it was the moment of reckoning. But not, apparently, for Winthrop Tower and Paula.

Twin smiles showed twin sets of perfect Southern California teeth.

"Good evening, Mr. Tower," they both chimed, their enthusiastic deference tinged with a hint of anxiety. "We weren't expecting you. Are you joining someone else tonight?" added the square-jawed Adonis.

That was the point. Morton's tables, even more than Spago's, were the Holy Grail in trendy L.A. One booked them via Peter's sister, Pam, at least two or three days in advance. Tonight, as always, the restaurant was full. Unless Tower was joining somebody, there was technically no room for him. But here, of course, the irresistible force and the immovable object collided, because it was completely unthinkable that a man of Tower's prestige and importance be turned away. What's more he could hardly be kept waiting. Anything more than five minutes and he would be gone. The practiced eyes of the receptionist scanned the table list, and the maître d' hovered at her side lending moral support, as she rated the tables in order of the industry status of the bookers. Tower must have one of the top ten tables. That meant someone who had scored a "good" table before would now be shifted to an intermediate one, and some hapless intermediate would get the bums' rush to the outer Siberia that was the back of the room, where an extra table would now have to be created out of thin air. Anywhere else on earth this would not have been a disaster, but here on the edge of Beverly Hills, where appearance and illusion were the only reality, it might mean the difference between career life and career oblivion.

"Any problem?" said Tower with anaconda innocence.

The implied threat concentrated the minds of the gatekeepers. The receptionist's eye fastened on to a pseudocelebrity who lurked at the bottom of the "good" table list. Her eyes flicked the question to her boss as her pencil hovered over the unfortunate's name like a hawk above a canyon mouse. He nodded, and the pencil swooped.

She turned toward Tower, her smile bright. "Yes, we have a table for you right away, sir. Please follow me." She set off down the wooden walkway into the restaurant.

"It matters where you sit," whispered Winthrop loudly, in a tone of voice insinuating that it mattered only to people who were not him. "The rule is stick to the areca palms, and avoid the bananas like the plague. Anywhere near the Francis Bacon or the Ed Ruscha is a tragedy. The serious art is the consolation prize for the losers!"

Paula took it in. She could see what Winthrop meant. The back of the room was already full, mostly men eating together, with the occasional older woman. On either side of this grouping were two pots containing miniature banana trees. A huge and very beautiful Francis Bacon hovered over them, bordered by a painting that read THINGS TO EAT. That must be the Ruscha. These people had obviously come early, and they were noticeably less attractive than those who were scattered among the front tables between the areca palms. Paula had time to notice champion dieters Dolly Parton and Oprah Winfrey sitting together as she was swept through toward the tables for two arranged along the windowed right wall of the restaurant.

Winthrop pulled back the rattan chair and she sank gratefully down, taking in the pristine pink tablecloths, the small earthenware pots of flowers, and the little candles burning in glass jars that gave a warm, romantic glow to the room.

A great-looking waiter, white jeans, white apron, white shirt, black tie, asked them if they wanted anything to drink.

"A Coke'd be fine," said Paula. She was too tired to be made nervous by the swank of the place, too hungry to be intimidated by the clean, crisp napkins, the bewildering array of knives and forks, and the heady aroma of hard cash and harder fame that bounced off the Mexican-tile and wood-inlaid floor, the rattan ceiling, the long, glittering bar. She knew she looked a mess, but somehow the exalted status of her brand new friend made that unimportant.

"I'll have a scotch and soda. Famous Grouse. No ice. A very large one," said Winthrop Tower. "You're not supposed to drink in this town," he said to Paula. "Only Perrier, or Chardonnay if you must. Anything else is considered 'unhealthful,' and by palm-tree sushi logic that makes you less lovable, and ultimately less rich. In Beverly Hills it's as close as you get to serious crime. Personally, I side with the English on the whole business. Never trust a man who doesn't trust himself to drink."

"You're not English, are you? You sound English sometimes."

"No, just pretentious." Tower giggled. "Although I did have an English period. In the sixties, I think. Can't remember much about it, but I worked in London for about seven years with a guy called John Fowler. The only people who can remember the sixties are the ones who missed the party. I'm told I had a *great* time."

The scotch arrived, and Winthrop attacked it as Paula sipped at her Coke.

"It sounds silly, but I don't quite know what it is you do, Mr. Tower. I mean, I know you sell all those beautiful things and . . ."

"I'm Winthrop, darling, actually Winty to friends like you, and I'm in the protection business. I protect the rich from their appalling taste."

Paula's laugh was incredulous. "Why would the rich have bad taste?"

"Why wouldn't they? It shows bad taste to spend all one's time making money."

"Aren't *you* rich? You *look* rich. You'd better *be* rich, 'cause no way can I chip in on this check."

"Well, there *is* a certain amount of money, but the serious stuff I made the old-fashioned way. I inherited it." Again he giggled, and he signaled for another scotch. He sat back and watched her as the whiskey wandered into his bloodstream through the lining of his mercifully empty stomach. It was the best shot of the day. None of the other drinks would be as good, but he wouldn't be discouraged by that.

The piercing voice cut into his pleasant mood like a knife through skin. "Winthrop, darling. How *are* you? Why don't you ever return my calls? Well, I've got you now, haven't I? Listen, you've just *got* to do my house. I've had a disaster with a Chilean. A decorator dear, not a husband. Anyway, it all has to be redone, top to bottom. *You've* got to do it."

Winthrop Tower winced visibly. The Cruella de Ville figure hovered over the table, in a shimmering Galanos gown and a cloud of cloying Joy. The clinging dress emphasized the spare tire around her slack stomach, and as she gushed at Winthrop a fine spray of saliva wafted over the table.

"Before you decorate your house, Miranda, don't you think you should have yourself done first?" he said.

Paula gasped.

"What do you mean?" said the dreadful interloper, her eyes wide with horror as the Tower meaning sank in.

"I was thinking of liposuction," said Winthrop Tower with a wicked smile. "Do you know that over five thousand liters of human fat are removed each year in America? I'm sure most of it comes from here, dear. It's no coincidence that 'shrivel belly' is the anagram of 'Beverly Hills.' "

She was gone, as she was intended to be. Her head held high, her jaw set, no stranger to abuse, she rejoined her ancient husband of the nanosecond at a poor table too near the bar but beneath a superb Chuck Arnoldi collage of multicolored twigs.

"What!" said Paula.

"Oh, don't worry about her, darling. She's the void beneath the Beverly Hills veneer. She's been through hundreds of husbands. Her children can't stand her. She tried to adopt a baby once. Sent it back because it wasn't a boy. Lives in an Alberto Lensi house on a hundred geologically suspect acres in the Santa Monica mountains. Very fitting. Did you know that the anagram of Santa Monica is 'satanic moan'?"

Winthrop took the second scotch fast. "Listen, Paula. While I'm still sober, can I offer you a job?"

Paula's eyes widened as she crammed a huge piece of bread into her mouth. God, a job! What kind of a job? Cleaning probably. Polishing all that beautiful furniture, in a cool store, safe, and well fed, and with a base to build on.

"What job?"

"Oh, I don't know. You'd troll around with me, and we'd talk about what I was doing, and we'd just do the sorts of things we were doing earlier across the road. What would you want? Five hundred? Five fifty?"

"A month?"

"A week, sweetheart. A week."

"Omigod!"

Winthrop could see her enthusiasm. He swept up the menu, and his heart was singing inside. It was all going to be all right.

He'd never worried about dying, not even after the coronary, but the idea of the ultimate full stop saddened him. There was a lot to be said for death, and nothing at all to recommend eternal life, but somehow it was the waste that was so irritating. All that time and effort, all that accumulated wisdom stuffed down the gullets of the worms, or blown up into the ubiquitous L.A. smog that played such havoc with his sinuses. Had it all been for nothing, the "life sucks and then you're dead" of the T-shirt legend? If so, then it was a monumental confidence trick played on humanity by a God with a warped sense of humor, to say the very least. Tower Design would be dismembered to pay the bureaucrats of whatever dreadful charity eventually starred in his will. Certainly he had no competent relatives to take the business over. But worse than that, far worse, was the loss of all the brilliant knowledge that was stuffed inside his head. If only there was someone to pass *that* on to. He looked into Paula's innocent, eager face.

"Have we dealt? Is it a deal? I'm your boss?"

"Mr. Tower, Winty, I'd love to work for you, but I mean . . . I haven't got anywhere to stay, and believe it or not, these are the only clothes I have. The rest got ripped off in New Mexico. I don't know how to do anything pretty much, and I might have given you the wrong impression in there. I was kinda winging it, you know . . ."

Winthrop Tower held up his hand to silence her. "Darling, for goodness sake don't *ever* tell the truth. It's too obvious. Anyone can do *that*. Creative lying is the name of the game in Beverly Hills.

"Seriously, though, the beauty of you is that you don't *know* that you have the thing you have. Trust me. Humor me. Patronize a silly old man. It's my money, and these jaundiced eyes are wide open, believe it or not. Clothes"—he flicked a dismissive wrist—"are a credit card away. As for somewhere to stay, that's no problem at all. You must stay with me."

"Well, with my wages I could find a room somewhere pretty nice. I wouldn't want to be a nuisance."

"Nonsense, my dear. Of *course* you must be a nuisance. All the very best people are, and I feel sure you have the makings of a superbly creative nuisance. Later on, darling, you will discover that the greatest enemy of fame and fortune is boredom, and the greatest foe of success is ease. What I need is stimulation, irritation"—he paused, his fingers together, his eyes laughing at her, as he thought out loud—"and yes, competition. I think you might be my own size, Paula Hope, and believe me when I say that not many people are."

"Well, if you pay me and feed me and house me I'll do my best to cause you some problems, and the first one is I don't understand this menu so you'll have to choose my food. What's mozzarella?"

"It's a tasteless cheese that Beverly Hills people use for dieting when they can't afford cocaine."

Paula cocked her head to one side. "You're joking."

"I'm not. Just try using a bathroom in this town. They're permanently occupied. This is *not* a place for those with weak bladders."

"Well, I'm not on a diet, and I'm starving. Maybe you should order for me. What should I have?"

"Protein, dear. What you need is some grease on the inside of your arteries," whispered Winthrop conspiratorially, peering suspiciously around the restaurant. "It's heresy to say such things in a place like this of course, but I'm a great cholesterol man. Red meat and plenty of salt to thicken the blood. That's what these people need. If they all worked a bit harder on their souls and not quite so much on their bodies there'd be a little less angst among the palm trees. Now, prawn cocktail, some of Peter's fabulous beef, potato skins with sour cream and chives, a selection of vegetables. Maybe some ice cream later. How does that sound?"

"Sweet music. Listen, Winty. You're going to have to teach me one helluva a lot. I mean, I really want to learn about everything."

48   P A T   B O O T H

"Winty!" The large pussycat of a man loomed over the table in an immaculate tuxedo.

"Merv! Hello! Do you know my new assistant, Paula Hope? Paula, this is Merv Griffin. Gave up TV to become a Master of the Universe. How are you, Merv? Love the way the Hilton's turned out."

Paula held out a hand and basked in the famous smile. She *supposed* this wasn't a dream, but she was no longer completely certain.

"Winty, I wanted to ask your advice about my place out in Palm Desert. Can I get my people to fix up a meeting sometime?"

"Sure. And what's this I hear about your place here being twenty thousand square feet bigger than the Spellings'?"

"Yeah, and it's got a view, too." Griffin displayed the stylish chuckle.

"All poor Candy gets to see is the old folk putting on Armand Hammer's miniature golf course."

Again he laughed, and he patted Winthrop's shoulder affectionately.

"Nice to meet you, Paula. See you soon, Winty." He wandered off to join a bevy of Japanese at the best table in the room, beneath the right-hand areca.

"How do you *know* all these people?" Paula laughed.

"Oh, you know, it's a small town. Like Mamet says, 'It's lonely at the top, but at least it ain't crowded.' " He laughed to show he was laughing at himself.

"Who's Mamet?"

"A brilliant playwright who among other things described all these people as 'secure whores.' " He waved his arm around to encapsulate the movie industry. The room was full of its heaviest hitters.

"And are they whores?"

"Well, as he says, 'The movie industry is like an affair—full of surprises and you're always getting fucked.' "

"Is that really true?"

"Listen, the only things that are really true about Hollywood are the things one makes up. You take Tinsel Town people as they are. Live with them, lie with them, cry with them, die with them. God, I need another scotch."

The drink came and went. Another accompanied the prawns, while number five preceded the côte de boeuf. Before the meat was finished Winthrop Tower was zoned. It didn't seem to affect the substance of his speech as much as its form. His words slurred and came more slowly, and he slumped down at the table, his eyes glassy. The sumptuous meal was punctuated by the periodic implosion of the L.A.

table-hopping elite, some like Griffin, sexy Michelle Pfeiffer, and handsome, laid-back Peter Morton, the restaurant's owner, welcomed and cherished, others unmistakably encouraged to "walk on." Stuffed shirts, the insensitive welcome outstayers, the pompous and the presumptives all got their marching orders, and Paula, marginally embarrassed at first, soon got the picture. The cruel wit was far from blanket bombing. It was surgically accurate. The good guys were insulated from it. The others were taken out one by one.

But still the scotch came, and Paula's eyes widened. She hadn't seen drinking on this scale. It wasn't the redneck Bud swilling of an Everglades Saturday night as the diner shook to the roar of the football replays and the whine of the country music on the jukebox. This was a headier, steadier, altogether more serious business. Now, before her eyes, her new boss was slipping into the next stage of drunkenness. The glass in his hand was no longer straight, and the whiskey threatened to spill out onto the tablecloth. He sank deeper into his chair, and his eyes were hooded, his movements suddenly slow and clumsy.

Paula realized that she would have to take charge. "Mr. Tower. If I can really stay overnight at your place, would you mind if we left now? I'm real tired." She said it quite firmly.

"What?" His eyes narrowed belligerently.

"Home," she said simply. Then, "Now."

"Don't piss on my party. I decide when . . ." But there was something in her eyes. Something so sad, so strong, so deeply appealing. It cut straight through the swirling mists of aggression and grandiosity that were welling up inside him.

He stood up, swaying slightly. "Quite right, Paula. Home. Yes, quite right, my dear. You must be tired. *I'm* tired. We're all tired. Let's go home."

"Where's home?" asked Paula. She didn't even know where he lived, but she prayed it was close.

"Sunset Hotel," he mumbled.

The stretch limo erupted into the Morton's parking lot from the alley that ran along the south side of the restaurant. It squealed to a stop, and a man jumped out from the driver's seat. He was in a hurry and he strode toward the brick walkway where Paula struggled to support Winthrop Tower and the monstrous glass of kümmel-on-the-rocks that he had ordered as his last semiconscious act, and insisted on taking with him as he left.

The man was dressed in a nondescript black suit, cut tight and nipped in at the waist, and he wore black socks, black shoes, and a black tie against a snow-white shirt. He was neat, seemingly obsessively so, but it was not the suit of a boss or even of a businessman. It was the suit of a servant. The clothes emphasized the body. He was thin, but strong looking, as if every ounce of fat had been burned away, and the muscle had been kept to a level that would permit maximum movement, while retaining maximum strength.

"Mr. Tower! Cor blimey, strike a light you've 'ad me pissing roun' the cafs like a bleedin' lunatic," he said cheerfully as he approached.

He looked like a fallen angel. It was a powerful, cruel face, perfectly proportioned, with wide spaces between the eyes, a short bobbed nose, and a square jaw. His hair was blond and cut short so that his features were emphasized. His narrow lips revealed straight white teeth, but it was his eyes that rang alarm bells. They weren't a cherub's eyes. They were Damien's eyes, blue but vacant, pretty but effortlessly unkind. They glinted and gleamed in his baby face, and they lied about the innocent smile he smiled.

Tower waved a limp hand that fell back almost immediately. "Graham," he said, "dear boy . . . where's my Mercedes Bass . . ." The stranger smiled at Winthrop. Then he turned toward Paula, and the smile disappeared.

" 'oo are you when you're at 'ome?" he asked rudely.

It sounded like an English accent. "I was going to ask you the same thing, but more politely," said Paula coldly.

"Paula's with me . . . coming home with me to stay . . . new assistant . . ." That was all Winthrop Tower could manage. With a grunt and a groan he lolled sideways onto Paula's shoulder, the glass of kümmel still balanced in his hand.

"I'm sorry, miss. Very sorry. I didn't know you was with Mr. Winthrop. He's a bit Brahms, ain' he? Lucky I found you. I bin all roun' the 'ouses."

" 'Brahms'?" said Paula.

He laughed an easy laugh. "Oh yeah, there I goes again. Brahms and Liszt. Pissed. That's what we say at 'ome. It's rhymin' slang. 'ere, let's get him in the Merc."

Paula went through the motions while the man called Graham did the heavy lifting. "I was supposed to meet Mr. Winthrop at the shop, but he took off like, an' I 'adn't a clue where he pissed off to," he said, effortlessly shouldering his boss's limp body. "Tried the Dôme, an' the Ivy an' that chinky Chinese on North Camden an' blimey O'Riley I didn't think of Morton's till ten minutes ago."

He cocked his head to one side and looked at Paula, smiling saucily.

Then the smile was replaced by a look of concern. "Your leg all right, darlin'?" he said.

"Oh yeah. One leg's a bit shorter than the other. It's always been like that. I'm used to it."

"Oh." His voice was flat, like his face. But it wasn't a dull flatness, nor a boring face. Both were disturbingly attractive. This man might take orders but he belonged to nobody but himself.

"I'm his wheels, dear, and I sort of smooth 'is path through life, you know. Like tonight I'm 'is bleedin' legs."

"Does he often get this drunk?"

"Does 'e ever? Never 'appier than down the boozer, cruisin' for a bruisin'. An yet durin' the day he's got nobs eatin' out of 'is 'and. Bloody fantastic, ain' it? That's what I calls it, any rate. You ever think of 'avin somefink done wiv that leg? Seems a shame to be left with that limp, an' this *is* America—the medical promised land."

Paula blushed. Most people were embarrassed by her limp and clammed up about it. Today the only two people she'd met had waded right into it. In the Everglades they took things like that for granted, like the skeeters and the hurricanes, the floods and the TB. If those were the cards you'd been dealt you played them. It took money to change them, and there wasn't any of that. Obviously in Los Angeles they saw things differently. Bodies were like cars. They could be rebuilt and redesigned, and the really strange thing was not to bother.

"It would cost thousands of dollars," she said. "It's no big deal. I'm not an athlete!"

"No, but you're very beautiful." Again he looked at her, but it was a peculiar look this time. Intense. Deep. As if he didn't say things like that to everyone.

She turned away, but her blush deepened. Her limp was the most personal thing about her. It was as if he had seen her naked and was talking about the shape of her body.

He propped Winthrop Tower among the pillows on the vast rear seat of the Mercedes. "There you are, Mr. Winthrop. Now you keep it buttoned till we get 'ome. All right, sir? That's the ticket." He winked at Paula, and she felt a little shock of surprise at how fast his mood could change. They had hardly met and yet he had revealed an emotional range that would have shamed an experienced repertory actor. Did he really feel all those things, or just some of them? Or none of them at all? Only the eyes said the last was true.

" 'op in darlin', and we'll beetle over to the Sunset. It's quite a joint. Impressive, that's what it is." In the driver's seat, he slipped on dark glasses despite the blackness of the night. Did he know about the out-to-lunch eyes? Did he want to shut the trapdoor to his soul? Why on earth did Paula want to know the answer to that?

"I didn't know Mr. Tower was takin' on no assistant," Graham said as he gunned the engine.

"Neither did I. I sort of wandered in off the street, and we got talking and I admired his store, and he offered me a job. Then he took me to that restaurant, and drank all the scotch they had, and then you showed up."

"Seventh cavalry. Well, anyway, I'm glad. Your face around'll be nice. More than nice. Bloody fantastic."

"Thanks."

"You don't look like you're from L.A."

"I'm from Florida. The Everglades."

"An' you wanted to get out?"

"I *had* to get out."

He heard the bitterness, the sadness, the anger, and the hatred. "Bad things?"

She bit at her lip.

He looked at her quickly. "We're not bad people here," he said. "We'll look after you. You see if we don't."

He put out his hand to touch her arm, a gloved hand, black leather, soft and slinky and at war with the sentiment he had just expressed.

From the back, through the glass partition that divided the car, came the faint strains of a song.

The Tower voice was fine, although the drink had taken the edge off the intonation. "Gentlemen songsters off on a spree, doomed from here to eterniteeeeeee . . ."

Graham nodded over his shoulder. " 'e always sings that when 'e's pissed. 'e used to be something called a Whiffenpoof at somewhere called Yale. More pouf than whiff, 'e always says. It goes on about black sheep and gentlemen. Just about sums Mr. Tower up, that does."

"He said he'd inherited some money."

" 'e wasn't lying, darling. 'is family's from Boston. One of the richest in America. 'e always said he became a designer to irritate them, and moved to L.A. to drive them mad. Anyway, the ones with the loot died off an' they left it to Mr. Tower 'cos 'e was the only family left. There that's the Sunset up ahead."

The Sunset Hotel loomed out of the night, like a good deed in a naughty world, and instantly Paula was mesmerized by it. She actually heard herself gasp as the reality of the "hotel" collided with her meager expectations of it. There was a wrench at her heart, and fingers clutched at the depths of her stomach as its beauty exploded all over her, taking away her breath. This was not a hotel. It was the pastel fantasy of some manic cakemaker on an icing jag; it was a latter-day Xanadu, light blazing from the windows of its pleasure dome, searching the velvet darkness for defectors from its delights; it was big and proud and wild and wonderful and it beckoned the lovers of all things bright and beautiful to experience the marvelous mysteries of its womb. Its tall central tower hovered, maybe ten stories high, above the dark section of the Strip, and a sign in green script said simply THE SUNSET HOTEL.

All around it, like an honor guard in the glow of its aura, stood tall, thin palms. Their trunks, painted ghostly white by uplighters from below, were in dramatic contrast to the vivid green of the treetops, and their height and old age emphasized the quiet statement of the ancient Spanish mission architecture. It was a dream of delicate balconies and intricate wrought iron—at once deliciously public and tantalizingly discreet—and it glowed its excitement into the night sky, and throbbed its exotic energy into the foothills of the canyons that were its backdrop. This was no parvenu. There was nothing nouveau about the Sunset's riche. It had endured, and it would endure, and its grandeur would mock the failure of those who entered its portals to do the same.

Nestling down at the base of the tower, a rambling series of buildings sprawled off into the night. Through the open window of the car came the creamy scent of gardenias. The rich aroma was thick in the balmy air, and Paula could see the dense bushes on either side of the driveway, bearing thousands of the milk-white blossoms that had turned the warm darkness into the most potent perfume. She could hear the Sunset, too. It hummed with impossible-to-identify vibrations that spoke to her heart, not her ears. It was talking to her, and Paula wanted to shake her head and get rid of the cobwebs that were inside, so that she could hear the thing it was trying to say. Even as she listened with her soul, her mind said this was ridiculous, but the message was there. "I am your future," said the stucco walls. "Within me, all things will happen to you. You will love me and you will loathe me, but you will never ignore me. I promise you that. I promise you that."

"Not a bad little pub," said Graham.

They had arrived beneath a covered portico, which allowed three lanes of cars to park side by side. From the one nearest the hotel, a blood-red carpet led toward banks of revolving, highly polished brass-and-mirrored doors. Half a dozen young men, apparently hot from the centerfold of *Surf* magazine, loitered around the entrance waiting to park the cars. The doorman, resplendent in full gold braid commissionaire's uniform, marched forward crisply to open the back door of the Mercedes.

" 'arf a mo', Fritz ol' son . . ."

But Graham wasn't quite quick enough. During the ride Winthrop Tower had shifted position. Now he was leaning against the inside of the door. As Fritz opened it, he fell, very gently, very slowly, onto the deep pile carpet. The glass of kümmel was still miraculously attached to his hand. It didn't break but its contents, largely melted ice cubes now, spilled out to form a little puddle on the immaculate carpet.

From what appeared to be the corpse the sentiment was firm. "Fuck," said Winthrop Tower, quite loudly, lying where he lay, and making no effort whatsoever to get up.

"Christ!" said Graham.

"Oh no," said Paula.

"Good evening, Mr. Tower," said the doorman. Not one syllable of his greeting contained an ounce of reproach. Nor did it go one inch toward admitting the undoubted fact that Mr. Tower was lying, apparently unconscious, on the floor of the hotel's main entrance.

By now Graham was out of the car, and he was already hauling Winthrop into the air like a drooping flag up a pole. Paula, too, hurried out to help, and at that precise moment she saw him.

He had been standing there, where the car had stopped, and as Paula jumped from it, he moved quickly to help Graham as the doorman stood back. He looked old for a busboy, and he wasn't dressed like the others. In fact, clothes-wise he looked like a drycleaned version of Paula—crisp Levi's, brown tasseled Bass Weejuns, a soft, faded brown leather bomber jacket over a plain white T-shirt. His eyes caught hers and lingered for a second, registering a spark of interest before he bent down for the Tower rescue operation.

"I'll give you a hand," he said simply to Graham.

"Thanks, mate," Graham replied.

With Tower hanging unsteadily between his two human crutches, the unlikely group set off toward the lobby. The doorman, dripping gravitas, the finally empty glass of kümmel held like a chalice in both hands, marched ahead of them.

"Home at last," slurred Winthrop Tower before letting out a burp of around seven on the Richter scale. He filled his lungs. "Lord have mercy on such as we . . . Ba! Ba! Ba!" he sang.

The stranger chuckled as the revivified Whiffenpoof song rent the
scented night air, and Paula, bringing up the rear, laughed, too, at
what she now recognized as high farce. The guy must be hotel
security. He seemed really cool. Together Graham and he looked like
they were out of a Calvin Klein Obsession advertisement. If all the
guys in L.A. looked like this, Help!

Paula was hardly ready for the beauty of the marble-columned
lobby. It had the feel and look of a vast private living room. There were
inviting sofas, and chairs and more flowers than she had ever seen in
one room in her entire life. It was almost empty, apart from two crisp,
gray-suited ice maidens manning the reception desk, and two or three
uniformed bellboys placed at strategic points across the vast space.

As the odd convoy made its way through, no one batted an eyelid.
It was clear what the party line was going to be. Doorman, busboys,
security, bellboys, receptionists, all would play this straight as a die.
Whatever Winthrop Tower sang, said, or did, he and his entourage
were going to be treated as if their behavior was totally and completely
normal. Perhaps it was. With the exception of the security guy's smile
there was no hint of mockery in anyone's demeanor, no patronage, no
supercilious condescension at all. It was quite brilliant, the more so for
being so utterly unexpected. No computerized Hilton or Westin could
have carried it off. No funky inn, or trendy watering hole, no fancy
hostelry or fashionable crash pad could have possibly known how to do
it. It was effortlessly upper class in its unflappability, and its easy
transcendence of rules and regulations. One thing was completely
clear. In this place Winthrop Tower was not a lush, a loser, or a joke.
He was a gentleman, and the gentlemen's gentlemen, and woman,
who were ministering to him in his hour of need were not forgetting
it for a second.

Paula wondered if there were any arrival formalities to be completed.
If she was going to be staying, shouldn't she check in? Apparently not.
The caravan didn't stop. It swept through the palatial lobby, clippety-
clop across the white Carrara marble to the halting melody of the
Whiffenpoof song, past the Henry Moore sculptures, the Modigliani
paintings, past the carved columns and the graceful Ming vases toward
the bank of elevators.

The elevator boy, too, appeared not to notice the state of the guest.
He nodded politely and pressed P.

"Watch out! Be careful."

The security guy had relaxed his grip and the Tower head,
suspended only by its India-rubber neck, rolled sideways and collided

sharply with the oak paneling of the elevator's interior. Paula's voice was full of reproach, and the security man's head snapped around toward her as she spoke.

It was the first time she had seen him head on, and once again she was caught short by the visual. Forget the Calvin Klein ad. He was achingly good looking, despite the irritation that had flashed into the extraordinary eyes at her outburst. But just as soon as it had appeared it was gone. His face softened, and he smiled again as if puzzled by something.

He caught the lolling Tower head, still watching Paula. "Sorry," he said. There was something strange about the way he said it. He seemed surprised, almost amused by himself, as if he weren't used to apologizing to anyone, let alone scruffy girls of uncertain origin and unspecific identity.

"It's okay. I just don't want him to hurt himself," said Paula.

" 'e's feelin' no pain, luv," said Graham.

"She's right," said the guy.

It was a rebuke. No question. He was putting Graham down for his frivolity, commending Paula for her concerned attitude. Again she tried to make sense of it. He seemed very sure of himself for an employee. Certainly rubbing a guy like Graham the wrong way was not for the faint-hearted. She'd worked *that* out.

"Yeah, 'course."

Graham had swallowed it. Not with the very best grace in the world, but he'd taken it. Paula felt the metaphorical temperature drop. There was a coldness between the two men, and it had followed some sort of subterranean clash in which the stranger had come out on top.

Again the fascinating eyes sought hers. "See," they said. "Did you catch that? You got me to apologize, and now I've made him back down. You're doing well, but you haven't a clue just how well."

They had arrived. The doors drew back, and they were in the anteroom of the Tower apartment.

"Here, I'll let you take over from here, Graham," said the stranger. But he walked out of the elevator, into the foyer of the apartment, and stood there as if he wanted something.

"Thank you very much for helping like that," said Paula. "It was very kind of you."

He didn't want to go. Again he was smiling at her, as if he was enjoying a marvelous private joke.

Paula felt the flash of irritation. "I think we all ought to be going to bed," she said, as Graham struggled past with the stuporous Winthrop.

"I think that's an excellent idea," said the security man, but still he didn't move. At his back the elevator door remained open. The boy in charge was pressing no buttons until he got his instructions.

The idea came to Paula quite suddenly. God, how crass of her. The guy wanted a tip. It must be that. There were ten bucks in her pocket. The last money she had in all the world. It was way too much, but she could hardly tear it in half, and anyway the Sunset Hotel was not small time. The battle raged in her mind only briefly. The hell with it. Mr. Smarty Pants with his outrageous face probably deserved it. She fished in her pocket, hoping that it wouldn't be too impossibly crumpled. It was. She pulled it out and thrust it at him quickly to cover her embarrassment.

He looked down at her outstretched hand, and the filthy ten lying in the middle of her palm. In all her life she had never ever seen anyone look so surprised. He was dumbfounded. He was absolutely and completely astonished. If she had pulled a samurai sword from her jeans and started to cut off his toes he couldn't have been more comprehensively flabbergasted. There was shock all over his face, and disbelief, and his wonderful mouth dropped wide open to reveal even better teeth.

From behind her came the cockney accent, too late, far too late. "Oh no, luv. Oh dear me no," said Graham.

Without knowing exactly what had happened, Paula realized she had done the wrong thing. Perhaps security guys weren't allowed to be tipped. Was the tip too big? Too *small?* Maybe tipping was a male business. Whatever. Her face registered her confusion.

But the receiver of her bucks was already undergoing a transformation. The phenomenal surprise he had clearly just experienced was apparently not an unpleasant one. There was wonder on his face now, and the humor was coming back, and there was that other thing, that intense interest, as if the rest of the world had frozen into a backdrop that existed only to frame her.

"What's your name?" he said, clutching the bill in his hand.

"Paula Hope," said Paula, thoroughly bemused, and at the same time weirdly excited by the unpredictable chain of events.

He transferred the money into his left hand, and he extended his right one.

"I'm Robert Hartford," he said, "and I want to thank you for your extremely generous tip."

FIVE

Paula was too tired to sleep—tired, confused, depressed, elated. She had expected a hard sidewalk as a mattress, and yet here she was suspended like a lily on a pond on the softest bed in the world. The gentle whir of the air conditioning merged with the muted hum of the Sunset Boulevard traffic and in her nostrils was the delicious smell of the bedside freesias. She was safe, but for how long? She had been given a future—an exciting, infinitely possible future, but would it still be there in the morning?

Along the corridor, the man called Winthrop Tower would be lying comatose. In his jingle-jangle morning would the job he had so capriciously offered her be available? Maybe he was one of those enthusiastic artists who promised the world, but who found it more difficult to deliver. She had liked him so much, and trusted him instantly, but she had never expected him to dissolve so comprehensively into unconsciousness. Then there was Graham, with his wiry body and his chirpy cockney-speak, and his unpredictable changes of mood. She felt ambivalent about him, drawn to him but unsettled by the aura of menace that hovered around him like a shroud. He had seemed to like her, but was he what he seemed?

Round and round it all went in a whirligig of doubt and hope, as the good faded into the bad and optimism merged with pessimism, murdering sleep, and sending her naked body tossing and turning beneath the cool cream linen sheets. It was creeping in, the memory that she was trying to banish. God! How could she have done it? Robert Hartford. Trying to tip him. In the darkness the sweat rushed to her skin as she allowed herself to remember the ultimate embarrassing moment. Talk about a hick from Hicksville. She had defined the term. Like the rest of America she knew what he looked like. Why the *hell* hadn't she recognized him? Okay, so she wasn't expecting him, and he wasn't supposed to be hanging around any place *she* was staying at, in blue jeans and a bomber jacket at eleven at night, but to push a ten at him like he was some servant when he'd been kind enough to help out! She buried her head in the pillow and groaned out loud in the blackness as she tried in vain to forget what she'd done. Why hadn't Graham *told* her? It must have been done on purpose. It was almost as if he'd wanted her to insult the movie star for mysterious reasons of his own. Certainly there had been a coolness between them, right from the beginning, and Paula couldn't get out of her mind the totally mad idea that in some weird way the bad vibes had been partially to do with her.

Apparently he lived there, in the hotel. For sure they would meet again if all the offers of the day before held good. But even as she shied away from the horror of that, she was drawn toward it. He had been so utterly charming, and even before her faux pas, he had been impossible to ignore. All the time she had been aware of him, of his movements, his gestures, of his otherworldly beauty. She had noticed him notice her and the lazy searchlights of his eyes had played across her, taking their time, not ashamed of their interest, pleased that she knew he was watching her. He had taken her money. He had folded it, lengthwise, as he had introduced himself, and the memory of his laugh and his exaggerated thank you were vivid in her mind. As the meaning of his name sank in, she had tried to say something, but the words just hadn't come. She had turned and fled, muttering goodnight despite the fact that she had absolutely no idea where she was, and where she was going. She had closed some door behind her and died in the darkness until Graham's gentle knock had signaled that Robert Hartford had gone.

"Sorry, luv," he'd said. "Shoulda told ya. Sort of imagined most people knew 'artford."

"Graham, I *tipped* him."

"Yeah, doll, you did. Did you see his boat?"

"His boat?"

"Boat race. Face."

"Oh God!"

"Listen, luv. Serves him right. Thinks 'e's God's bleedin' gift to women. Blimey, I bet no one's ever done *that* before."

"Mr. Tower will be furious."

"No way. Them two's good mates. They'd think it's bloody funny. But you watch out for 'artford. I saw him looking at you the way he does. Most girls in this town go at him like kamikazis, 'cos of who he is, like. The way you treated him'll really get 'im goin'."

Graham had looked discouraged at the thought. He had showed her her bedroom, and the glorious wall-to-wall marble bath with more potions and lotions than Paula had ever seen before, and he had said goodnight.

As she had lain back in the bubbles and the boiling water, Robert Hartford had not gone away. He had hovered there in the steamy scented air, exciting, embarrassing, listening, looking, and later, as she'd climbed into bed, she had felt his lingering presence. But now, in the dead of night it was difficult to make sense of anything.

She lay back on the soft pillow and squeezed her eyes shut as she struggled to still her racing mind. Damn! It was no good. She might as well get up, walk around, read, maybe watch some TV with the sound turned way down low. But paradoxically, as she decided to stop trying to sleep, she felt the first gentle waves washing over her. The thing she wanted most was being given to her only as she stopped trying to achieve it. How like life, she thought, but the tide had turned, and now she was being swept out to sea, away from the nerve-racked shore, out, onward, backward to the wide oceans of memory and the lost continent of dreams.

꒐

Paula put up her hand.

"Please, Miss Carstairs, what is 'art'?"

"Whatever I say it is," said Emily Carstairs, firmly.

The giggles erupted around the schoolroom and Paula realized that she had somehow been worsted in the exchange. Not that she had been trying to score a point off Miss Carstairs. She worshiped her.

"But what if you're wrong?" persisted Paula.

"Then it will be your duty to expose me, Paula Hope." There was a smile on the crinkly, kindly Carstairs face.

"How will I know when you're wrong?" Paula could feel the initiative running away from her.

"By trusting your heart, dear."

"Oh."

Paula's twelve-year-old mind tried to sort through her teacher's words. There were rules in art, and Emily Carstairs, her beloved teacher, knew them. But at the same time teachers could apparently be wrong, which seemed to imply that the "rules" were not really "rules" at all. Bad art, or bad artistic judgment should be exposed—even when the person producing it was a teacher, or a so-called expert. Then there was the amazing implication that a small child could do the exposing, simply by trusting her heart. Apparently you judged art with your feelings, not with your intellect. You should not be afraid to learn from the learned, but you should always reserve your right to disagree with them.

Paula peered around the schoolroom to see if her friends were picking up the same message. The blank faces stared back at her, the dirty, bored, inbred faces of the swamp. If Emily Carstairs had been talking in Mandarin Chinese they might have understood her better. It was at that very moment that Paula came to realize she was different.

It was a turning point, and the recognition of it zipped through her body to explode in a hot flush of excitement all over her cheeks. Emily Carstairs had been talking to an "art" class of thirty children, and Paula was the only one who had the remotest idea of what she was saying.

The two vases stood side by side on the table in front of Miss Carstairs.

"Now, children," she said in a weary voice. "What do you see here on the table?"

They didn't answer. It was the last class before the bell. They were thinking of food, and catfish in the shallows, and all the Mark Twain things that deep-country, waterlogged kids thought about, and they prayed collectively for merciful release from Miss Carstairs's peculiar games.

"Two vases," said Paula. She already knew what was coming. She could "see" it. For three blissful years she had been soaking up the Carstairs message.

"Yes, dear, two vases. One of them, I'm glad to say, is mine. The other, I am far more glad to say, is the proud possession of the Pahokee County school board."

They twisted their heads that way and this, as their little bottoms shifted on the hard wood seats, and they picked at their noses and willed the bell to ring. There were two more or less identical vases on the table. Big deal. Who cared?

"Now, it is the task of you budding . . . aesthetes . . . to decide which vase is 'art' and which is most decidedly not." She sniffed, and she flung her head back in a gesture that seemed an attempt to ward off terminal despair. She stood foresquare behind the table, scrawny, frail, but to Paula absolutely magnificent as her scorn flew over the heads of the children she addressed. Her face was wrinkled but her eyes were bright, flashing with life above the bags of flesh that underlined them. Her dress had clearly once been fine, but was now a little faded and not quite clean, but it was not the main event. Miss Carstairs was. Proud and valiant, she transcended her lowly position as art teacher in the Placid school. Like a colossus she hovered above the swamp. Like a soaring eagle she flew high above the bars of poverty, ignorance, and mundanity that formed the walls of their prison.

"Think of it," she added as she took in the vacant gazes, "as a quiz show on TV."

The children immediately perked up. "Ah, the flame of learning burning bright at last," mocked Emily Carstairs. "The God of the tube has not forsaken us in our hour of need. Blessed be 'Jeopardy,' and the son of the 'Wheel of Fortune.' "

Boy, did she have them now.

"Here," she said, "is the red vase, on my right. There is its fellow. Now, what color should we call that? Tan? Beige? Nasty words, I know, but I think they will do. Now the name of the game is to choose the vase that we think is beautiful. That should be roughly the same as choosing the vase that we think is 'good art,' 'has artistic value,' etcetera, etcetera." She paused patiently. "Now, children, hands up those in favor of the red vase."

A set of hands reached for the sky. Red was the color of Dad's boat, of the dress Mom wore on a Saturday night to the bingo in Ochopee, and anyway it was the color of blood.

Paula pushed her hand down toward the floor, and she thought she caught the sharp, flinty edge of a Carstairs smile as she seemed to notice her adamant decision. Paula did a lightning inventory of the room. Three other children had not put up their hands.

"It may be," said Emily Carstairs, her lopsided face slipping into a look of intense cunning, "that some among you consider both vases to be beautiful. Let us see the hands of those particular 'connoisseurs.' "

"Con a what?" said one child, as the hands of the three dissenters shot upward, their wise-ass eyes sure that they had identified the "catch."

Still Paula's hand remained solidly by her side.

"You are the only vote for the sand-colored vase, Paula Hope," said Emily Carstairs, her voice giving nothing away. "Maybe you could tell us why you choose to be in a minority of one."

They giggled again now, thoroughly enjoying what they imagined to be Paula's acute discomfort. Silly old Paula with her airs and graces *and always top of the class in everything had it wrong at last. Twenty-nine to one. Ha Ha Ha.*

But Paula didn't hear them. She was looking at the vase, at the beautiful stoneware vase.

"Its color is so unusual. It's delicate, and it's not uniform. I mean, the color has different shades as if someone mixed it by hand and then painted it on themselves. The red vase is just red, a dull, ordinary red." Her button nose wrinkled in distaste. "But that one has a wonderful, flowing shape that's elegant, and the red one is short and squat and its lines are just . . . well . . . boring. It's as if the red one just wants to hold some water and some flowers and be done with it. The sand-colored one wants to be looked at for itself. It wouldn't mind holding things, in fact it would be brilliant at that, but people would always look at it first." She stopped. The words had flowed from her, but at the same time her mind had filtered them. All those picture books, the slides that Emily had shown them of Chinese porcelain, of Florentine vases, of Japanese ones, had left their surreptitious mark on her memory.

"It's the red one, ain't it," said a loud-mouthed boy from the back.

"Ah, the red one. What shall we do with the red one?" said Emily dreamily. She picked it up, between thumb and forefinger like one might a very dirty, very nasty rag that just cleaned a squashed cockroach off the kitchen counter. Then she extended her arm to the side of the table, and then a little bit past it.

"I think we should put it out of its misery, don't you," she said, and she dropped it on the linoleum floor. The sound of the explosion as it shattered sent twenty-nine heads flicking back, and Miss Carstairs's and Paula's peals of laughter merged happily with the death rattle of the Pahokee County school board's hideous red vase.

In the thunderous silence that followed the crash, the school bell rang insistently. Art class was over. School was finished. Bemused and vaguely resentful that some trick they didn't quite understand had been played on them, the children began to file from the room.

"Paula Hope, can you stay behind for a word, please?"

"Yes, Miss Carstairs."

Paula walked up to the front.

"You were the only one who saw my vase."

"It's beautiful, Miss Carstairs."

"You're beautiful, Paula, and you can recognize beauty. That's a very rare combination in this world."

Paula blushed. "Where did it come from?"

"China. It's a Kuan-yao vase. Southern Sung dynasty. Nine-sixty to twelve seventy-nine."

"I remember you telling me about Sung, and how they invented a new glazing process."

"Yes, the monochrome feldspathic glaze. You remember everything, don't you?"

She seemed to make a decision. Her voice was suddenly excited. "Paula, I want you to come home with me now for an hour or two. I want to show you some things like this vase. Lots of wonderful things. You have a rare talent. I'm going to teach you how to use it. You're not a child anymore. You're not like all the others. You deserve more, and I'm going to make sure that you get it."

Paula looked at her and listened, and as she did so she believed. There and then, as the belief in herself flooded through her, her childhood ended. When she walked from the classroom, her teacher's arm around her shoulders, she was a woman.

The warm afterglow of Emily's memory lit up the darkness as Paula slipped out of the dream. She lay quite still, as if by doing so she could prolong the vision that was already beginning to fade, but it was impossible. It was going, and Paula sighed in the blackness as she thought of the nightmare that so often took its place. She tried to force the awful thoughts from her mind, to hang on to the happiness, but she knew as she did so it was pointless.

There was no escape from what was to come. Once again she was going to relive the past. She took a deep breath—the diver above the murky, icy pond—and then she plunged down into the depths of sleep to confront the demons that she could never slay.

$$\backsim$$

Lazily, their wings set, the mosquitoes zeroed in on Paula. She lay across the crumpled sheets, and surrendered her naked body to them, as her tears dripped onto the grubby pillow. The damp heat wrapped her up, sucking the sweat from her glistening body, and the sound of her sobbing filled the miserable room. Outside the cabin of the houseboat, the Everglades swamp provided the background music: bullfrogs croaking their raucous melody; warm wet sounds as the forest oozed and dripped; the drone of a distant pickup truck carrying a nobody to nowhere.

A moonbeam found her through the open porthole, and played over her soft skin, painting the loveliness of her body. Like some peeping voyeur the finger of light darted across her breasts, and roamed gratefully over her strong, proud shoulders, her muscular arms, her flat stomach. Then, suddenly, it was gone, obscured by some prudish cloud. Once again the blackness blanketed her.

"Damn! Damn! Damn!" she whispered with a terrible intensity as the memory of the horror howled like a hounddog in her soul.

She shuddered in the steamy heat. She could still feel the arms of the men tight around her neck and shoulders, hear their hideous laughter, smell the smoky beer hell of their breath. But mostly she could see. Holding her captive, they had forced her to watch the rape and the murder of her friend.

She had read about things like that before—some people up north in a bar somewhere, an enthusiastic audience as their friends had committed the heinous crime, but things like that didn't happen around you. Until last night, when they had happened to Laura. Laura had been the regular waitress in Seth Baker's diner, and Paula had been helping out to earn some extra money, as she often did. Seth Baker, mean and ugly, owned the liquor store, the gas station and the only "restaurant" in town, which meant he controlled the only things that anybody wanted in the place called Placid. It gave him the power of God over the drunken drifters and losers who passed for his friends. Last night, as the blue smoke had hung heavy in the fetid air, curling between the checkered tablecloths and the sawdust-covered floor, he had used it. He had raped Laura, while some drunken hero had held her by a belt coiled tight around her neck, and Paula had seen it all. And at the end poor Laura's eyes had been frosted glass and she had lain so still—so very still—on the filthy floor.

Paula had been the first to understand what had happened.

"She's dead. You've killed her. You pigs have killed her," she had screamed at the top of her voice.

They had let her go then and she had rushed to Laura and bathed her poor defiled body with tears of helplessness as they had stood back, spectators now, no longer big, no longer strong, just men at the bottom of life with nowhere further to fall.

"She was a drifter. We'll put her in the swamp. Weren't no one's fault. She did it to herself," the man who had made it happen had said at last.

Paula had turned to Seth Baker and called him a murderer, and she had promised him personally that she would watch them all burn for the hideous thing they had done. They had all recoiled from her fury, and they had drifted away. But Paula had seen the beginnings of fear creep into Baker's eyes as he had watched Paula carefully, as if weighing the possibility of her keeping her promise. She had run from the diner, as she had sensed her own danger, and, slaked on violence, they had let her go.

Now she clutched the sweat-soaked sheet around her as she shivered with fear and rage. Even as she had run through the outskirts of the *town, down the old dirt track to the edge of the lake where the houseboat was moored, she had realized that she herself had become a target. There was no point going to the sheriff—Baker owned him, and Paula knew that if he had been in that dreadful room, he would have joined in. Emily would have helped her, but Emily had died six months ago. No, in Placid she was powerless and at risk. She had to escape.*

Paula took another deep breath, as she tried to concentrate. She had no money. She had no job. And in the next room, piled on top of each other on the tiered bunks like brand-new tools in an old woodshed, were the twin brothers to whom she had been a mother for the last five years. They were six years old—"Cool Hand" Luke, and reckless Jake—and when she had put them to bed earlier, their happy, love-filled faces had shown no inkling of the shadow that was about to fall upon their little world. They had been asleep before the bed-time story had been finished as they always were, exhausted by the cheerful war against poverty that they all fought by day, and Paula had hurried to the diner for the evening shift, the boring evening with the cardboard-cutout alcoholics, hopeless, hapless, harmless. . . .

She fought against the tears, biting at her lower lip, as once again Laura's pleading face flashed from her memory. Again the rage consumed her, wiping away the sorrow from her mind.

In Placid there would be no justice for the fiends. Nobody would miss Laura. She had been a runaway, a nobody floating on the slippery surface of America, a nonperson to everyone but to Paula, who had loved her. In Baker's town they would pretend that they vaguely remembered her if anyone bothered to ask after her. Was that the waitress that moved on a few weeks back—Lana? Lori? Laura? One thing was for sure. They would stick together rehearsing their booze-wrapped lies until everyone believed them, or was too bored to care.

Quietly, Paula slipped both feet to the scuffed linoleum of the cabin floor, and she moved toward the door. On the deck it was hotter than it had been inside, as once again the silver-white of the moonlight bathed her nakedness. There was no one there to watch her. The rotting wood of the jetty had long since led to its abandonment, and the hulk that was her home was the only "boat" tied to it.

She tossed her head in the super-still air, stretching her long neck, and sending her tousled blond hair dancing in the moonbeams. She looked back toward the aft cabin where the twins were, and then she tiptoed gently to the porthole and peeped in. They lay like dead soldiers slain in battle across the bunks, their small limbs abandoned in the deep commitment of children's sleep. Their little chests rose and fell and their parted lips smiled the contentment they had no right to feel. In the dreamland they would be frolicking like spring lambs unaware of the tragedy that had already engulfed them. Tomorrow they would all have to leave Placid forever. The killers knew where she lived, and she had seen in Baker's eyes that he wanted her dead.

Paula sighed as she stared at their beauty, and she felt their tiny fingers clutching at her heart. God, how she loved them. Luke, quiet, brave, honest, and shy—the one she called Cool Hand after the old movie because he kept it all inside. Jake—the extrovert who kept despair at bay with the powerful weapon of his smile. The Mr. Bear he slept with didn't really look like an animal at all—it was a sad, shapeless thing that Paula had thrown together from a bundle of rags—but it was Jake's most prized possession.

She walked back to the guardrail and peered out over the lake. Beneath the shimmering light of the full moon it stretched out before her like the glassy sea of the hymn. At once, as they always did, the fond memories came winging back. The lake was Daddy, and Daddy was fun, and happiness and safety in those far-off days before the laughter had died. A huge tear trickled down Paula's cheek, and she knelt down, squatting near the splintered, bleached-out wood of the deck, touching it so that she could remember better those far-off days.

"Oh, Daddy, darling Daddy," she whispered. "Help me. Tell me what I should do."

Her voice broke on the hopeless words and she began to sob once more as the loneliness crowded in on her. But only the forest was listening— areca and sable palms bending solicitously to catch her words; tall royal palms reaching straight to the sky impervious to human grief; the buttonwoods and tangled mangroves at the water's edge with sad, dark tales of their own to tell.

There below her, tethered to the gangplank, was the boat he'd built, its wood rotting, its green paint faded and peeled. Six years ago next month her mother had died giving birth to the twins, and five short months later a hit-and-run driver had killed her father as he had returned from fishing a creek off the Miccosukee Strand. At fifteen she had become both a mother and a father instead of the sister she had been intended to be. The rented house had gone, and the meager savings of a carpenter had left nothing after Paula had bought the run-down houseboat. From that moment to this she had battled to keep it all together. And all the time, pushed down deep in the undergrowth of her mind—the loss of her beloved father lived on to plague her.

She wanted so much to be near him, and she moved to the

gangplank, and looked down into the small boat he had built. She could see the heavy rock, and the coil of rope attached to it, sitting in the bow. It was the anchor they used to hold the boat still in the shallows off the mangroves. She could see him now as he heaved the rock into the lake—and she could hear her own squeals of mock irritation as the water from the splash soaked her.

She stepped carefully down the rusty ladder, into the boat, and sat down on the seat that had always been hers. It seemed to comfort her, this link with the past, and suddenly she moved forward, picked up the paddle, and untied the bowline from the ladder. Reaching out over the side she pushed hard with the paddle against the sandy bottom, propelling the boat out into the darkness, as green parrots shrieked overhead and bonefish plopped in the shadows that danced at the water's edge.

For a minute or two she was lost in the rhythm of the movement as she paddled the boat toward deeper water until the houseboat was small behind her, and was soon cut off from sight behind a low ridge of mangroves that jutted fingerlike into the lake. She knew this place so well. How many times had they come here for long lazy afternoons of fishing and philosophy in the golden age of her childhood? Paula stopped paddling. She picked up the stone—so light now, so heavy then—and heaved it into the water. Then she sat back in the stern and peered up at the stars. In the morning she'd be gone. Now she would say good-bye to the sacred places to which she would never return. So she cuddled up tight, wrapped in the night and the old days, naked as the baby she wished she still was. She squashed her full breasts against the skin of her forearms and pushed her knees to her elbows like a child in a womb and the comfort coursed through her at long last. Then she pulled the ancient tarpaulin around her and, gloriously, the horror and fear began to fade into the woolly haze of sleep.

Paula sat bolt upright as she crashed into terrified wakefulness.

She knew with absolute certainty that something horrible was happening. But what? Where? Then she saw it. In the sky. Above the place where the houseboat would be. The sky was glowing. The sky was red. The sky was alight.

She tore up the anchor and grabbed at the paddle, thrusting it like a dagger into the gleaming water. A cry gathered at the back of her throat.

"Fire," she whispered.

"Fire!" she shouted.

"Fire!" she screamed across the empty lake, at the teeming, careless forest.

She tore at the smooth surface of the water, and the old boat groaned *with the power of her strokes as it began to obey. She was separated from the houseboat by a small mangrove island, and in minutes she would be around it. Long, endless minutes as the fire burned. God, let it be the jetty, or some camper's fire igniting the undergrowth farther inland.*

She broke around the edge of the island, and the flames lit up her eyes. It was a torch. The old boat was on fire from its bow to its stern, from its water line to the roof of the two cabins on its deck. The still, hot air was full of the crackling roar of the flames, and the smell of the smoke, campfire clean, wandered with the innocence of Satan amidst the streaks of silver moonlight.

"Luke! Jake!"

Her body trembled with the effort of the scream as she tried to alert them to the danger. Her wild eyes combed the banks of the lake for the twins. Surely they had escaped. But the dread filled her, strangling hope. There was only the sound of the flames. Only the shadowy, deserted shoreline. Only the searing heat plucking at her eyes and melting her heart. Her home was an inferno. Bright, infinitely bright it burned, the old wood glowing and sparkling as it had never done before. Exploding, falling, crunching in upon themselves the timbers surrendered to the fire, and bits broke away, burned to a crispy lightness, as they spiraled upward toward the sky.

Paula paddled furiously, but the wall of heat was rock solid against her face as she approached the blaze. It singed her, angry against her exposed nipples, cross against her sweat-soaked stomach, enraged against her bare thighs, but still there was no room for pain in her racing mind.

"Noooooooo," she howled at the moon to forbid the disaster.

"Jake! Luke! Oh, dear God, noooooo!"

The flames roared back. She looked around desperately. What should she do? No way to stop the burning. No possibility of getting closer. Then, on the edge of vision, she saw the movement. Out near the old towpath, where the jetty met the bank, something was moving. Her heart leaped for joy. It was all right. They were there, safe on land. Her little brothers had been delivered from the fire. She peered desperately into the shadows and tried to focus through the crazy patterns of light. There was something, someone in the bushes, half hidden, half revealed. Then, as she watched, the figure began to move. It was the figure of a man and he was hurrying away from the fire.

"Help! Help!" she screamed.

But he ran on, turning only once to look over his shoulder as he heard her shout. It was the precise moment that a shaft of moonlight caught him, illuminating him plainly in the phosphorus glow.

Seth Baker was running away from her burning home.

Seth Baker! In the midst of her panic she knew instantly what had happened. He had done this. He had started the fire. He had tried to murder her, thinking that she would be asleep inside. To protect himself he had tried to kill her.

Helpless, she turned once again to face the agonizing vision, as her life burned before her. The twins' cabin was a red ball of flame. Nothing could live in there. Nothing. Paula clenched her fists and she beat on her knees as the nausea gripped her, the bile rose in her throat, and the horrible world danced before her eyes.

Then it happened.

The door of the cabin where the twins slept disintegrated. There was a muffled explosion, and a tongue of flame speared out through the space where the door had been. Flame . . . and something else.

Two small marionettes, their puppetlike arms outstretched, stumbled through the door. They walked in slow motion, their movements jerky, and sometimes it looked as if they would fall, as they swayed from side to side. From top to toe they burned. They were tiny beacons of flame, small torches of flickering light as they struggled away from the fire they had become. One led the other, his blazing arm held high, and on the end of it was a blob of flame that burned brighter than all the rest. Rooted to the spot by the glue of horror, Paula knew instantly what it was. It was Mr. Bear. It was Jake's Mr. Bear, and he was carrying it with him to Paradise.

Despite the heat Paula paddled closer, and, as she did so the twins gave up their doomed march to freedom. Jake staggered and toppled and the animal he loved flew away from him as he fell, his hands still reaching for the grown-up arms that would never comfort him. Luke fell at the same time, crashing into Jake, merging with him in a burning fiery embrace and together the twins who had been born together died together in a crumpled heap of flames at the edge of the deck.

Like a stricken animal, moaning softly, Paula crouched down in the bottom of the boat, her hand raised above her head as if to protect herself from the evil she had seen, as a part of her died forever with the little brothers she loved.

For an age she was still, locked in anguish, her soul tossed on the sea of her torment. Then, at last, quite quietly, her voice shaking with a transcendent conviction, she made her promise.

"I swear on the blood of my family that you will die, Seth Baker, for what you have done. You will die in horror and terror as they have died, and you will scream for the mercy that you never gave."

S I X

t was one of those days when you could see forever. L.A. was clear and crisp and across the valley the mountains were sharply focused—massive, brooding, complacent as they watched the San Fernando matchstick men and women doing the bizarre things that humans did. David Plutarch peered out at them from his poolside gazebo before turning slowly to savor the other half of his panorama. On one side lay the humble valley with its magnificent mountains, on the other the proud palaces of Beverly Hills and Bel-Air, the boxlike towers of Century City, and out there in the distance across the Malibu hills, Catalina Island and the sparkling ocean, the water already polka-dotted by the white sails of yachts.

He smiled to himself as a strange happiness wafted through him. Days like this made it all worthwhile.

Here he was, high above the City of Angels, safe in his twenty-million-dollar estate above the old Sinatra house, with Caroline Kirkegaard by his side.

He walked toward her and flopped down on the terrycloth sun bed next to her, his lean, oil-slicked body the color of a newly minted penny against the pure white background. He looked down at himself. Not bad for the mid-forties. Tight, but not stringy; creased but very far from wrinkled; the tan exuberant but not the mahogany dark of the obsessive sunbather.

Now he looked over at Caroline, and at once the music began to play inside him. She was magnificent in a jet-black Norma Kamali nylon-and-spandex one-piece, a slingshot thong steamy from the sands of Ipanema that bisected her buttocks with geometrical precision. All

71

the ends of her seemed to be blood red, her toes; her fingernails; her glistening, half-parted lips. She lay flat, on her side, her eyes open, but although they were pointed in Plutarch's direction they didn't appear to be watching him.

"Pretty special, huh?" he tried, half meaning the day, half meaning her.

Caroline Kirkegaard ignored him, but the beginnings of a smile flirted with the edges of her lips. She knew what she was doing. She wasn't answering when spoken to; she was injecting a bolus of angst into a serene situation; she was being predictably unpredictable.

Plutarch was acutely aware that she hadn't responded to his innocent remark, and although this should be no big deal, somehow, maddeningly, it was.

"What made you want to make so much money?" asked Caroline dreamily, noticing how eagerly his eyes darted toward her, how hurt they'd been when she had blocked him out before. Her question was conciliatory. At the same time there was a leitmotif of mockery in its background, the veiled insinuation that making money was a pretty tawdry ambition.

"I never wanted to be rich. I just wanted to create things, and to have my own way." He smiled a childlike smile when he said that. It was true. He'd never wanted to stare complacently from the covers of *Fortune* and *Business Week*. He'd never longed for the trains and boats and planes and all the other toys of the Forbes 500 boys.

"You were wise. Only losers try to make *money*. It's like working at being happy. Do what you have to do and everything falls into place—the loot, the contentedness, everything."

"And if you don't *have* a goal, or a talent?" Plutarch asked.

"Then get one, quick, or it's all over."

He laughed. People who lived by the will had a way of taking it for granted that the rare commodity was available to everyone.

She sat up, her stupendous torso emasculating gravity. Then she leaned forward, resting her breasts on her knees. "Have you got your own way now, Mr. David Plutarch?" she asked, staring deep into his hungry eyes.

The question was laden with innuendo. She leaned forward farther, squashing her breasts into her knees, then rocked back, then forward again, squeezing, pushing, relaxing, and all the time watching him, watching . . .

He swallowed hard. Did he have his own way? It was impossible to say. Yes. She was there beside him, inside his life, filling it up with anxious excitement. No. Because he didn't own her. He had not broken her, defeated her, dominated her. And he had never touched her. That was the worst bit of all . . . the waiting, the planning, the hoping.

"Partly," he answered, turning his face from hers. "Do you want a drink?" he added as camouflage.

"No."

Again Plutarch recognized the power play. How often had he played the same game himself, hovering on the verge of rudeness to assert his superiority, and to show that he didn't feel he had to be polite? The evening he had first set eyes on Caroline he had recognized a virtuoso performer in the exercise of power. She was as good as he was, as strong as he, possibly even more single-minded, and all his life he had never met anyone who was those things. From that moment he had longed to control *her* and in doing so to win a contest of will with perhaps the only person on earth who was a match for him.

"So, how did you do it, David? How did you put it all together?"

"Oh, I don't know," he mumbled casually. "I just built a little company and sold it to United Electric for two point five. U.E. paid too much. It was maybe worth two." David Plutarch couldn't help the evasion. It was second nature to him, coded into his genes. Winners hoarded information like fine jewels.

Caroline smiled as she watched him shortchange her. He was almost good looking, the brooding brow, the deep-set green eyes, the aggressive jaw. But there was something undeniably crude about him. It wasn't just the bikini-style, Club Méditerranée swimming briefs, or even the heavy gold ring with its vulgar diamond; it was more fundamental than that. There was something mean about his soul, something crass about it, some fundamental absence of class that all the millions would never ever quite dispel. She had wanted something from him—to pick the brains of the billionaire, and unlock some of the secrets of his success, but he had seen what she wanted and he had automatically backed away from giving it to her. Not that it mattered. In a little while she would pluck him like ripe fruit from the tree. And afterward, he would beg to be allowed to make all her dreams come true.

"So, now your only problem is to know what to do with the money." Again her voice had that mocking lilt, because she knew she was on target. The Plutarchs of this world did not thrive on spare time. It might have been a shrewd financial move to peddle Stellar to U.E. It almost certainly hadn't been good for his peace of mind.

"It's the kind of problem I like," lied Plutarch.

"Sometimes when your life changes it's not so easy. Despite money. Despite all this." She threw out a statuesque arm to take in the world spread out like a magic carpet around them. "Then you have to have a spirituality to fall back on."

"New Age?"

"Destiny."

"Yes, of course, Destiny."

In his former life as the hard-nosed entrepreneur, Plutarch had had no time for such things. Now he was definitely interested. All around him the material world seemed to be in retreat. It was the first thing he'd noticed when he'd cast off his business blinders. Everywhere there was a new interest in the metaphysical, and he had set out to explore that alien world as an antidote to the vast stretches of spare time that threatened to engulf him. It had been an eye-opening journey. Unbeknown to him there existed a parallel New Age culture.

It was a sensual world of massage and messages, of Maharishis, mediums, and mind-trips, a world of passive passion and steely gentleness as gurus filled up the vacuums of empty lives and dreamers dared to experience their elusive dreams. Hypnotists, telepathists, clairvoyants, and astrologers were guides on the supposed journeys to the center of self. Channelers, numerologists, psychics, and metaphysicians led the group gropers to peak experiences that gave new meaning to the bittersweet sigh between two mysteries that went by the name of life.

He had not embraced the counterculture entirely, but he had been at least partially seduced by it.

Then he had on a whim decided to go to the Kirkegaard meeting, and at once he had realized that all the disparate elements of his life could come together in her persona. The woman had it all, and something more. He had never seen anyone so beautiful, and he was drawn toward the flame of her unapproachable sexuality. In her, mysticism and Mammon merged deliciously as Plutarch hoped that they would in *his* life. He wanted more of her. In his dreams that night they had been joined together into a cohesive force that would transcend this world and reach out into uncharted, unconquered realms of cosmic time and space.

Caroline watched him carefully as she reached for the Mario Badescu number thirty sun-block. She squeezed a huge blob onto her hand and massaged it languorously onto her legs, her inner thighs, up high where they vanished into the minimal swimsuit, as his eyes roamed over her. She had recognized him early on at the Destiny meeting and although he didn't know it she had been doing it all for him, analyzing his every reaction. She had noted the bits that seemed to excite him, the parts that didn't, and slowly but surely the jigsaw had fitted into place. He loved her when she was dominant. He became alive when she insulted the crowd of which he was a part, as a demonstration of her power over them. The ultimate voyeur, he couldn't take his eyes off her when she strutted, macho and masculine, across the stage.

At last the picture was perfect. Plutarch was obsessed not with Destiny but with her, and it was a sexual obsession. The man who had so recently dealt in power had discovered the alien delights of subservience.

Over the past couple of days she had noticed that he loved nothing more than to watch her lithe body cutting like an otter through the waters of his pool; her muscles ballooning deliciously on the Nautilus machines, the oiled leather belt biting into her straining waist; and most of all he loved to watch the sweat-soaked aerobics lessons with little Kanga, as their bodies melted and the smell of them merged deliciously in his twitching nostrils. It wasn't so very strange that a powerful man had at last discovered the awesome world of sexual desire, but Caroline's knowledge was the key to owning him, and soon she would be turning the key in a padlock around his heart.

Plutarch seemed to sense her thought process. He wanted to get back to more tangible things, but he couldn't take his eyes off the legs. "The computerized astrological-chart thing . . . It's a good idea. The guy came up with a neat program and the advertising people think it'll play . . ."

Caroline laughed inside. It had been merely a ruse to get to him, and boy, had it paid off. The moment she had seen him at the Sunset Hotel she had decided to meet him. She hadn't bothered to make an appointment. First thing the next morning, she had simply banged at his door, or rather at his security-guarded, TV-monitored, Door King-communication-rigged, electronically operated gate. He had rushed to see her, and her calling card had been a business scheme— computerized astrological charts. You feed in the birthdate, time, and place at one end, and your future pops out at the other. Ground-breaking idea. Neat. Sure fire. And neither Plutarch nor Caroline had mentioned it again until now, because it had served its purpose—by allowing them to meet. They had circled each other like gladiators in the Roman arena, but it had been no contest. Caroline had already discovered the Achilles' heel of his sexuality, and she had held her glorious body over him like the unanswerable weapon it was. By the end of the meeting, Plutarch had trotted in front of her like a broken mustang, and it had been merely a question of slipping into the saddle.

"Good," she said dismissively, banishing astrology, computers, charts, and all such mundane things from their relationship. "David?" Her voice was husky. It was almost time.

"Yes."

"Come here."

He stood up, wanting to ask why, ashamed to be doing her bidding, not daring, not wanting to refuse.

"I want you to rub some of this into my feet," she said.

He moved toward her. "Your feet . . . ?" His voice was strangled. It was the first invitation to touch her. But her feet! He knew what it meant, yet he couldn't fight against it.

She didn't explain. She handed him the Chanel Hydrafilm Protective Moisturizer, and her whirlpool eyes were hooded, as she lay back and sent her legs snaking out toward him. He couldn't sit beside her. There was no room. There wasn't meant to be. He took the cream, and he knelt down before the feet that he was to serve.

With shaking hands he reached out to do her bidding.

Plutarch's whole body was tingling. It was like superreality—those moments when fear or excitement made everything crystal clear. The smells amplified in his bared nostrils—the heady scent of the Chanel, the crisp ozone of the midmorning canyon air—the soothing aroma of the pines. Beneath his trembling hands was the body of his dreams, the feet of the woman who obsessed him. He worked reverently at them, rubbing them gently, neither too hard nor too soft, as he struggled to prolong the moment.

Her voice melted into the maelstrom of his mind. "David," she said, "I have a fantasy and I'd like you to indulge me."

He couldn't answer. There was no room in his crammed brain for fantasies other than his own. His hands lay still on her, unable to move in the thunderstorm of sensation that had engulfed him.

"I want you to give me dinner. In one of the bungalows at the Sunset Hotel. Pink champagne, flowers, beautiful music . . . everything."

He fought to concentrate.

"We could do it here," he managed at last.

"No, it has to be the Sunset," she insisted dreamily. "Tonight." Her feet moved lazily, encouragingly, against his hands.

"Of course," he mumbled. "Of course I can arrange that."

"Oh, and David," she purred, "I almost forgot. The dinner should be for three."

Caroline Kirkegaard stepped into the gardens of the Sunset Hotel and was immediately enveloped by the lush foliage—pink and white double hibiscus, oleander, banana trees, schefflera, Benjamina, ficus, cypress, acacia, and Washingtonia palms.

Here, near the lobby, the restaurant, and the Star Room, waiter and guest noise was loudest. It was where the cheaper bungalows started, where the relatively impoverished stayed, able to afford only a miserly thousand dollars a night, there but not really *there* in the shadowy world of Beverly Hills scorekeeping. As she headed along the azalea-lined walkways, down worn stone steps, past bowls of bougainvillea and tinkling fountains, beneath Spanish-tiled arches, the houses got grander. The one to the right of her was more a compound than a bungalow, and Caroline knew that behind its faded terra-cotta wall was a pool that would have done credit to estates in Brentwood, Bel-Air, or Holmby Hills.

She jerked an accusing finger at the wall. "Robert Hartford lives there," she hissed, the pilot light of her permanent loathing bursting briefly into flame.

"Asshole," Kanga murmured in a conciliatory tone of voice, imagining that Caroline was irritated that Hartford had walked out of the Destiny meeting. "Does this guy we are going to meet have anything to do with Destiny?" she tried, knowing as she did so that it was hopeless. If Caroline had intended to tell her more, then she wouldn't have had to ask the question.

"He will have . . . after tonight."

Kanga sighed, but she said nothing.

The door said BUNGALOW 9, and to reach it you passed beneath an archway of ficus, and another of wrought iron on which white roses twined. There was a heady scent of jasmine, and the faint sound of what might have been Wagner filtered through the carved oak door. Caroline Kirkegaard pressed the bell.

He opened the door himself and the stirring music surged past his stocky body. He looked nervous, and yet elated. He didn't speak.

Neither did Caroline. Nor did Kanga.

The room was full of flowers, all of them white—lilies, orchids, gladiolus, gardenias.

The TV, set in a mahogany mock Chippendale cabinet, was

switched to CNN, and stock prices ran along the bottom of the picture, but the sound was switched off. The Wagner, *Tannhauser*, exploded from twin speakers on either side of one end of the room.

On the coffee table stood three bottles of what looked like pink champagne nestling in the traditional plastic Sunset Hotel ice buckets bearing the setting-sun logo of the most famous hotel in the world. There were three Baccarat flute glasses, and somebody had bothered to frost them in the fridge. A huge silver ice bucket contained a bowl packed to the brim with beluga caviar, and three spoons protruded from the top of it.

Caroline walked quickly across the room and flicked the switch of the Carver amplifier. Wagner died.

Plutarch broke the noisy silence. He licked nervously at dry lips and said, "You don't like Wagner?"

"I like champagne," said Caroline as she smiled at him.

His eyes never left Caroline as he picked up a bottle, eased the wire and gold foil from the neck, and pressed the pads of both thumbs beneath either side of the cork.

The tiny *pop* seemed to surprise him, but not nearly so much as Caroline Kirkegaard's next remark.

"Get undressed, Kanga," she snapped.

"What . . ."

"DO IT!"

Caroline smiled sweetly as she issued the extraordinary command, and her serene facial expression was totally at odds with the explosive force of her words. She held out her hand and watched David Plutarch swallow nervously as the drama she was directing began to unfold. Next he would fill a glass with champagne and hand it to her, and his mind would boil as he anticipated the enormity of what was to come. She threw back her head and laughed as she saw that she had him. His eyes were wide, and his hands shook as he tried to control the bottle. The crushed pink petals of the champagne spilled onto the walnut table and it took him long seconds to fill the flute to the correct two-thirds level. Was that sweat breaking out around the careful lips? Was that the thumping of his heart beneath the navy-blue Polo shirt? Yes, yes it was, and she laughed some more as the liquid power flowed in her veins, and the drums began to pound in the pit of her stomach.

She took the glass he offered and her eyes watched his as he stared first at her . . . and then at Kanga. Now, as she sipped delicately on the champagne, she turned to see if she had been obeyed.

Kanga's mouth was half open as she tried to make sense of what was going on. The surprise was all over her beautiful features, the upturned nose, the trembling lips, the firm set of her brave chin.

The Kirkegaard eyebrows arched upward, questioning why she had not been instantly obeyed. Then her features softened in a smile of encouragement as she added the carrot to the stick.

Once, just once, she nodded imperceptibly. Go ahead, Kanga. Trust me. Do it for me. Because you love me. Because you must.

Kanga's arms moved slowly, serpents to the flute of the charmer, toward the buttons of her shirt. All the time she stared straight at Caroline, as if to say, "I don't know what's going on, but I'll do this for you. Only for you." One by one the bone buttons surrendered until they were all undone. Now, draped by the soft linen of the pure white Calvin Klein shirt, the divide of her breasts was visible, her freckled, suntanned skin painted by the faint glow of embarrassment, anxiety, and, despite herself, the warm flush of early desire. It was quite obvious that she wore no bra.

She paused. Then with a sudden movement she took the plunge, throwing back the shirt, and at the same time thrusting her chest forward at the hungry eyes in a gesture of hopeless defiance.

Caroline had never seen her quite like this, so shy, so afraid, and so very appealing. Kanga stood foresquare, her legs apart, one hand hiding coyly behind her back, the thumb of the other hooked with make-believe bravado behind the tight leather of the belt, and her breasts, two unutterably lovely documents of surrender, seemed to fill the room. The curve of their upper slope ran from the tense turned-up tips of the pink triangular nipples to tighter pectorals, and below the contours formed a smooth, flattened U from the apex of the breast to the vertical, high-tone muscles of her chest wall. There was a voluptuous fullness about them, a sort of pendulous tension, that underlined their defiance of gravity.

Caroline walked toward her, as Kanga stood her ground, her head held back, and angled very slightly away from the woman who was her obsession. She reached out with her left hand and she ran a lazy finger along Kanga's upper lip, catching the moisture that had gathered there. Then, languorously, she transferred the finger to her own mouth, all the time staring deep into the young girl's eyes. Now, she reached down to the cold champagne and she dipped her thumb and forefinger into the pink bubbles and her hand moved toward Kanga's breast. Pink on pink, cold on warm, first one side and then the other, she anointed them with wine as the breath shuddered from Kanga's lungs and the sigh of want rustled between her desert-dry lips at the intimacy of the gesture. Then Caroline bent down slowly, cupping one breast with her hand as her tongue slid out to taste the warm tightness of the champagne-and-sweat-drenched nipple. For delicious seconds it lingered there, soft and slippery against the murmuring flesh, and Kanga's moan of ecstasy filled the room as she reached in desperation, first for her own free nipple and then for the buckle of her belt.

Caroline drew back, and her voice was hoarse with desire as she breathed the words. "Yes, darling. You're so beautiful. Yes, my darling. Take off your jeans." Kanga's fumbling fingers tore at the belt, and ripped at the buttons of the Levi's. She squirmed from side to side as the skin-tight denim thwarted her and she pushed down to release the hot heart of her to the eyes of her must-be lover. Caroline smiled. Like some lovely ice creation, the girl was melting in the sizzling heat of her lust.

"Come here," she ordered. Kanga did as she was told. Stumbling across the carpet, her movement hampered by the pants she hadn't time to remove, she struggled toward Caroline.

A reigning monarch now, Caroline placed one hand upon the hot skin of the girl's naked shoulder, and gently, but firmly, she forced Kanga to kneel before her.

For a second Caroline paused, then she, too, bent at the knees and, reaching down with both hands, she took hold of the hem of her skirt. Slowly, she began to lift. It seemed that her legs themselves were moving inexorably upward. The thighs elongated, slinking toward the ceiling, long and luscious and full of wicked promises. The tops of her stockings gripped them firmly, black on cream, and in turn the pure white of the garter straps clutched at the dark silk and all the time the knowledge of what was to come scrambled the minds of her two eager victims. At the uppermost edge of her thigh she paused and Kanga's heart stopped with the dress that had become a veil. She couldn't hold herself back. The groan of abandonment floated free of her.

"Please," she murmured.

"Do you want it?"

"Yes." Kanga's voice was soft, defeated.

"How much do you want me?"

But Caroline didn't wait for an answer to her question. She raised the dress to her waist.

"Oooooh," murmured Kanga, leaning forward eagerly.

"Wait for my permission."

At the moment of truth Caroline Kirkegaard had not forgotten her ultimate objective, and now she turned toward him, and a smile of triumph broke across her face. David Plutarch lay slumped across the sofa. His breath was coming fast, and, lost in wonder at what he was seeing, it was clear he could think only of what was to come. Caroline was turning his ultimate fantasy into reality. She was in control of the man she had set out to dominate, and the expression on his face was the eloquent confirmation of her victory. It was time.

Her hand came up slowly, undoing the still life she had created, and her forefinger beckoned to him. It pulled him up from the sofa, and across the carpet, and he hurried toward his fate.

"Look at her, David Plutarch. She's mine, isn't she?"

Standing awkwardly beside the two women, he nodded his assent.

"She'd do anything I asked. She'd steal, she'd kill for me."

It was strange. Caroline had won but she still wanted to prove her power. Plutarch was beneath her, but in some way he was still an equal to be impressed as he was being humiliated, to be pleased while he was being punished.

"Kanga!" Caroline's voice was taut. "Undo his fly."

The redhead came out of her dream, her face suddenly stricken. "Now, Kanga!"

Plutarch held Caroline's eyes as the fumbling, obedient fingers sought him. He understood at last. Caroline would not be touched by him, nor would she touch. And it didn't matter that the one he wanted wanted nothing to do with him. It was right. It was fitting. She was a superior being. It was enough that he would be allowed to stare into her eyes as the business was concluded. Kanga's fingers had obeyed their mistress. He was exposed.

"Go ahead, Kanga!" ordered Caroline Kirkegaard.

There was a pause. So short. So unthreatening. Because of course she would be obeyed. And she was.

Plutarch's eyes, glassy with ecstasy, locked onto Caroline's as the sublime sensations flowed through his body. "Is it good? Do you like it?" asked Caroline, her tone triumphant.

His voice was hoarse as he spoke.

"How do you do it, Caroline Kirkegaard?"

"Better than you, David Plutarch."

He stared at her helplessly, already rushing toward the conclusion that could not be delayed. She saw it in his eyes.

"I'll tell you when. Not before." Caroline's voice was sharp.

Yes, she wanted to control that too.

But she couldn't. Surely she couldn't. Not that. His whole being was hovering on the edge of the chasm. He only wanted to float free on the wild wind of release. In this one thing he would assert independence. No mere spectator could control the mystery of his orgasm. In the very last round of all he would save face with a minor victory.

But he couldn't do it. He remained there, poised on the brink of the cliff, unable to step forward, unwilling to step back. Time and again he steeled himself for the leap into the pleasure space, but each time the invisible wall forced him to retreat.

He heard her laughter. He saw her smiling face. She knew. She could sense his struggle, she could predict its outcome. The moment would be hers, not his.

"Please," he murmured as he admitted it.

Again she laughed, and she threw back her head, reveling in her absolute authority. The pause seemed like an eternity.

"Okay, David Plutarch. Do it," she said at last.

Her words unlocked the gate and David Plutarch flowed through it. His knees buckled and he staggered sideways as the mighty river of pent-up lust rushed from him. Kanga reached for the carpet to steady herself as she recoiled from the incredible force of his orgasm, and the triumphant smile shone from her face, as she looked up at her mistress for the reward that surely now would be hers.

Caroline's lips broke into a soft smile as she glanced down at Kanga, and her voice, caressing yet still commanding, was urgent. "Kanga. Go! Now! Right this minute! I'll call you later, but only if you do what I say *immediately*."

There was no time to dress properly. There was time only to grab her shirt and pull up her blue jeans before the door crashed shut behind her and she was outside the bungalow, half naked and alone in the jasmine-scented garden.

David Plutarch staggered toward the sofa and fell onto it, burying his face in the pillows. He half turned toward Caroline. "What do you want?" he murmured.

"I want you to buy me the Sunset Hotel," she said.

SEVEN

Robert Hartford loped across the Star Room of the Sunset Hotel like a wolf who had just fed. He looked neither to right nor to left, because he knew what he would see if he did. The clientele were the most sophisticated in the world when it came to celebrities—and small-town gawkers and gapers were conspicuous by their absence—but there were limits, and Robert Hartford transcended them. It had to do with rationing, with mystery, with the careful attention to career building that had always been his trademark. Robert didn't do the coast-to-coast chats. He wasn't rent-a-mouth for the glossy magazines. The details of his private life were shrouded in the mystery that only great care, and a carnivorous Century City law firm on a monstrous retainer, could guarantee.

So now the eyes of the women devoured him. They sniffed at the air to savor the smell of his charisma. They willed him to look at them, to shine the light of his countenance upon them, and give them, not peace, but wild hope. What they wanted from him was fuel for the fires of their daydreams, gasoline for the furnace of their night ones. That they wouldn't get it simply added to the potency of the Hartford myth.

The men watched him, too, the Hollywood men, short on short and long on longing. They watched him carefully, like small children a conjuror. They wanted to know how he did it. What was the trick? Could it be learned? Could it be performed? It was his sexuality. That was what they wanted. They wanted to bottle it, to distill it, to concentrate it. They wanted to pour the delicious charm juice all over their hairy chests and their short little dicks and to smoothe it liberally all over the shiny skin of their bald, glistening heads. Then, then, one fine day, they, too, would achieve superstud status in Star Town, and the wall-to-wall women who ignored them now would howl at the moon while they came.

Everyone knew exactly who he was. His recognition factor was at least one hundred percent, possibly more. If he'd had a buck for each murmured "Robert Hartford" his meal would have been free.

Francisco Livingstone half rose to greet him. He smiled, crinkling up his leathery, heavily suntanned face as his fingers pulled at a neatly cut, snow-white mustache.

"Morning, Robert," he said.

The tones were mellifluous, the accent upper class. That went with the clothes. Francisco looked like a walking fashion plate transported from an era when even to *think* about male "fashion" demonstrated a lack of good taste. He didn't, therefore, buy his clothes from the obvious places, expatriate stores like Dunhill and Kent and Curwen that specialized in the Beverly Hills idea of the "English" look. He didn't get his shoes from Church's or his sweaters from Carroll and Co., and he avoided Ralph Lauren's Polo store on Rodeo like the plague. Instead he fitted himself out in London, where the genuine articles were, thus establishing himself as the ultimate in Beverly Hills aristocracy, that rare creature who was totally at home outside its city limits. His silver hair, slicked down with Royal Yacht hair oil from Thomas's in London's Duke Street, was parted at one side in a line that was the shortest possible distance between two points. The herringbone-tweed hacking jacket from Savile Row's Kilgour, French and Stanbury was patched at the elbows with worn, dark green leather, and it enclosed a pale blue cotton Harvie and Hudson shirt, knotted at the deep collar by a blue-and-white polka-dotted silk tie. One and a half inches of cuff peeped from the sleeves of his coat, showing plain, oval gold cuff links engraved with the faded remains of some indecipherable family crest. His trousers were dark gray worsted, belted around his thin waist by a navy-blue belt that sported a single brick-red line along its middle, and they broke over the laces of forty-year-old Lobb's shoes, cracked and weathered by years of diligent polishing. A red-and-white handkerchief cascaded in careful confusion from his breast pocket.

Robert Hartford took the parchment hand, noting the firmness of the old man's grip. "You're looking well, Francisco," said Robert. "Sometimes I think you've found the fountain of eternal youth." It was a fantasy of Robert's that such a thing existed. The aging process was one of the few things he had not been able to control.

"Hah, it's called Lafite, dear boy. And do you know I'm doing a *very* wicked thing." He chuckled charmingly at his naughtiness. "I'm drinking up the 'sixty-ones. I'm told it's a capital offense as they won't peak for years yet. But when you reach my age time is of the essence, isn't it? Yes, it is, my word, it is." He nodded sagely to himself, his gimlet eyes twinkling, as his old head wagged up and down.

Robert Hartford was seldom on this side of a conversation, and there were few people that he would allow to put him there. Livingstone knew exactly what the lunch was all about, but he would take his time before he got to the bottom line. Men like him hated bluntness. Instead they dealt in manners, and courtesy, in rituals and in delicacy.

"Are you a claret man, Robert?"

Robert Hartford laughed. The question assumed so much—that the world was divided into "claret men" and "Burgundy men"; that any civilized person would be a drinker of fine French wine; that "both" was no possible answer.

"Actually, I'm a great lover of the better white Burgundies. Corton Charlemagne. Le Montrachet. I've been meaning to ask you to beef up the Century Room's list in that area. Otherwise, and I know you'll disapprove, I'm rather fond of champagne."

Francisco Livingstone threw up his hands in mock horror. Few old people could drink much of that. "Dear me, no! I can't be doing with it. Girl's drink."

Robert laughed. "In that case, Francisco, I suspect you have quite a store of it tucked away in your bedroom cooler."

It was no secret. Francisco had never let the weakness of his flesh stand in the way of the willingness of his spirit. In the fifty years since he had bought and built up the fabled Sunset Hotel he had ground his way through most of distaff Hollywood. Few women were safe from his gallant conversational sallies, and those who signaled their interest were, there and then, investigated by his courtly fingers. Robert Hartford had never quite understood how the old boy managed it. Admirers of women such as he could seldom see the charms of another man. But although Francisco Livingstone had been a widower for thirty years, he seldom slept alone, and hardly ever with the same person. If anything had changed, it was the age of his bedmates. This seemed to vary in inverse proportion to his own. As Livingstone got older the chicks got younger. Now he slept with women less than half his age. And that made him, in Robert Hartford's eyes at least, a very impressive figure indeed.

"Aha, you know my secret. Dear me, have the chambermaids been

talking? Is that the gossip?" He appeared delighted, leaning forward in
his chair for corroboration of his virility. He wanted chapter and verse.

Robert Hartford froze a little inside. Women were for loving, they
were not for leering over. They were too wonderful for that, too gentle,
too delicate, too strong, too resilient.

He reached for a piece of bread, broke it, and scooped on a dollop
of saltless butter. He said nothing, but his talkative eyes registered their
disapproval. A man's man would have given the old boy his moment
of male pride, but Robert Hartford was not a man's man, and he didn't
care who knew it.

Francisco Livingstone picked up the rebuke, and the sunshine left
his face. He did not hold it against Hartford. He held it against
himself. That was how he had gotten to be the most admired and
respected hotelier in America. Hotels required sensitivity. You had to
vibrate in tune with them, as you anticipated every whim of your
guests. You had to charm your staff, and retain the demeanor of the
aesthete as you moved with fashion, and yet never forsook good taste.
A second or two ago he had allowed his creaky hormones to dictate a
remark that lacked delicacy. Most men in Hollywood wouldn't have
recognized that.

Robert had, and he hadn't liked it.

The old man swept up the menu, the gesture symbolically closing
the subject.

"Now, dear boy. A little luncheon, I think, don't you? The smoked
salmon is always fresh from the Dee, but then you know that. Can't
think why I'm selling the stuff to you. You *live* here!" He waved for the
waiter, and the hovering servant shot forward to the most important
table in the room.

"A bottle of Krug—yes, I think Mr. Hartford would approve of the
1969. Now, not too cold. Don't murder it." He turned to Robert. "I'm
told Krug needs bottle time, isn't that right?"

Robert smiled back, letting the silence linger a bit. In business, as
perhaps in life, the trick was to be a watcher, a listener, a collector of
the facts. It wasn't necessarily a way to be liked, but it was the way to
win.

"Sounds good to me," he drawled, well aware that Francisco had
deferred to him in the choice of the wine. He leaned back against the
comfortable upholstery of the banquette and looked around the
familiar restaurant.

It was an endlessly fascinating place, the hub of Beverly Hills deal
talk since Francisco had opened it maybe forty years earlier. It existed
on all sorts of secret levels that were not apparent to the majority of its

customers. The nub of the Star Room was the four or five tables at one of which they now sat. These power tables controlled the entrances to the glass-enclosed loggia, which was the *only* place for breakfast, and the charming al fresco courtyard that was *the* only place to have lunch.

From this pole position, anyone who was anybody could be checked out, and as they left they had to run the gauntlet of the Livingstone/Hartford table, from which they could either be graciously acknowledged or cruelly snubbed. Robert ticked off the "faces." Sleek Whitney Houston lunching with bright Jodie Foster. Ex-skier Ivana Trump eating à deux with tennis star Martina Navratilova. Superproducer Jerry Weintraub and Sylvester Stallone doubtless discussing their new movie *Polo* that Stallone would direct. Robert peered over to his left, toward the Outer Mongolia that was the entrance of the room where nobody but the cameramen, the Japanese, the Eurotrash, and the single ladies sat. The hungry eyes stared back, as the outsiders looked in, as far from the real Star Room as the Devil from Grace. He smiled to himself and to the cooled-out pianist, who was running through a selection from *Phantom* for the inattentive restaurant.

Vibing in on Hartford's detachment, Livingstone decided to start flirting with the point. "I shan't really miss it, you know," he said wistfully.

"It was about a year ago I first heard you were thinking of selling. Now it's definite. Is that right?" Robert had known immediately what Francisco was talking about.

Livingstone gazed dreamily around the room, filling up now with the lunchtime powerbrokers. As much as anyone he had created this industry. Not the studios, of course, but the *style* of it all. The Sunset was a symbol of Hollywood. It was the center of Los Angeles, the city that wasn't supposed to have a center, and its majestic aura of unflappable calm defined Mellow Yellow Land.

"Yes. I'm going to sell it. I've had enough. I want some peace. I want to travel. I need a rest from Beverly Hills. The whole place has changed. The traffic's a disaster. All the old houses are being pulled down. Nobody talks about anything but crime, cholesterol, and couture. The bookshops have gone. So have the toy stores, and there's nothing *cheap* anymore. It's just car phones with call waiting, the boredom of the endless real-estate boom and all those perfect bloody palm trees and steam-ironed lawns. And the Sunset's such a responsibility. It's like a banana republic—I feel I can't leave without either getting deposed or the whole place falling to bits. The *real* cost of living here's about half a million brain cells a day. More if you drink."

He laughed to show he wasn't serious. Beverly Hills was still paradise and the Sunset was no Panama. It was a superbly functioning machine. Every rule in the hotel was made to be broken, but you had to know who to allow to break the rules. No dogs for the salesman from Ohio. A pack of beagles if Robert Redford or Warren Beatty expressed the wish for them. And the hotel was never, ever "full," even when all the bedrooms had people sleeping in them, never "full," that is, to the "right" person. On one memorable occasion Francisco Livingstone had moved out of his own apartment to accommodate Princess Grace of Monaco, and on another even more auspicious one he had personally supervised the erection of a tent in the hotel gardens when Onassis and Callas had asked for a room. So luxurious had been its appointments, so lavish its decoration that ever since guests had been asking if they, too, could be afforded the privilege of sleeping in one. Little things like that made the difference, and decisions of that sort could only be made by an entrepreneur, a man who knew the powerful people he entertained because he was one himself.

"Do you have a buyer?"

"Not yet." An enigmatic smile.

"Are you advertising it?"

"Well, *you've* heard it's for sale."

The champagne arrived then. Two waiters. A bucket of ice. The cork made no vulgar *pop*. There was no nonsense about tasting it.

Robert raised the glass to his lips, and he watched Livingstone carefully as he drank. "I might be interested in buying it."

"Ah!" It was Livingstone's turn to drink. He paused. "If I have to drink champagne it must be Krug. I know everyone swears by Moët's Dom Pérignon and Louis Roederer's Cristal, but I think it's because the bottles are pretty more than anything else. I've blind-tasted all of them—here and in France—and Krug wins. In my book, anyway. Of course, most Americans are drawn to wines like Taittinger that are made predominantly with the sweeter Chardonnay grape. I prefer champagnes like Krug that rely on the dryer Pinot noir."

"It's very strong, very rich, Francisco."

Again there was a silence. Who would break it? Who was more interested? Buyer or seller? Interest would cost money.

"Forgive my asking, Robert, but why on earth would you be interested in buying the Sunset Hotel?"

Robert Hartford knew there was no way to tell him, and he knew also that it would be unwise to try.

How could he describe an obsession? How could he talk about a childhood fantasy that had bubbled and fizzed within him since he had been old enough to walk? He had come to the Sunset for children's parties and even now he could remember the sticky pink cakes and the wonderful ice creams piled high on the groaning buffet tables, festooned with streamers and balloons and all the things that made life worth living. Magicians and party favors, rabbits popping nervously from silk top hats, the jugglers and the clowns, and the wonderful sprints along the endless corridors as the old retainers turned a blind eye to the screaming antics of the children of the Hollywood elite. Later, as he had grown, it had come to mean other things.

When his father and his mother had fought, which they did with the regularity of a metronome, his father would move out of the Rexford Drive house to take up residence in the Sunset Hotel. Then he would do what all bad parents did. First he bribed his only child in an attempt to turn him against his mother. Second, he cheated on his wife. Third, he spent money with a wild extravagance, both to assert his individuality and to hammer his partner's share of the often precarious family finances. Thus, through his formative years Robert had come to associate the Sunset with excitement and with scenes of spectacularly conspicuous license and consumption.

Breaking glass and drunken oaths in the middle of the night would signal the parental row. Next morning he would tiptoe down to find his enraged mother packing up his father's things for the Sunset. "This is the last time," she would scream. "That pig is never coming home again." All of which meant that his father was already ensconced in a bungalow at the hotel. The telephone calls would come later in the day, after school, and sooner or later one of them would sneak past his mother's defensive screen. "Darling, it's Daddy. I'm at the Sunset. Why don't you walk over for tea. The icebox is full of good things, oh, and I've bought you some things I know you'll like."

The bungalow would be stuffed to bursting with extravagant presents, and room service would be a never-ending source of good things to eat. He would pretend to listen to the antimother propaganda, but mostly he would just have the time of his life until his father slunk back home. And during the blissful ten days or so, the girls would come and the girls would go. He'd find them, long-legged beauties barely twice his age, douching themselves in the marble bathrooms, or turning sleepily in darkened bedrooms, the half-empty bottles of Dom Pérignon guarding them on the mahogany bedside tables. Some ignored him as if he didn't exist as they made their cryptic phone calls in the living room, their white panties poking out from beneath outsize T-shirts. Others would try to befriend him, muttering flattering things about his father in little-girl voices, in a transparent attempt to do themselves a bit of good in the industry in which his father's influence waxed and waned.

And a few, very few, had noticed how beautiful he was and had not held back from showing it. They had stroked his hair, and breathed their sweet breath over his face, and they had allowed their silken, half-clothed bodies to rub gently against him as they had talked about the color of his eyes and the straightness of his teeth, and about how big and strong he was, how more like a man than a boy . . .

Had it started there? He had loved them all. The indifferent hookers, so hard and strong and single-minded in their pursuit of cash; the soft-brained doe-skinned starlets, so tenacious, so exotically ambitious in their search for fame; the lust-driven sensualists, on fire with the unscratchable itch, so determined to please themselves in the act of pleasing others. Each one he could remember. The haunting scent of them, their sleepy gestures, their sex-soaked eyes. And he had wanted them. He had wanted to own them all and have them do for him the dreamy things they would do for his father, and above all he wanted to worship them, and they to return his adoration until they sank deep into the vortex of the physical and the wild world went spinning round.

Later the Sunset had marked the milestones on his path to fame. He had married at the hotel, the terrible, fruitful marriage that had been the first step on the road to stardom, and when he had divorced the legend who had briefly been his wife, he had moved into a small room at the Sunset as his father had before him. He had never left. When his own movie career had hit, he had attended the Oscar night parties there, and the banquets for the visiting celebrities, the fund-raisers and the charity balls. As his career had headed into the stratosphere, he had taken over a suite, then adjoining suites, a bungalow, then adjacent bungalows, until he had achieved the compound he had now—four thousand square feet of Spanish hacienda in the grounds of the most expensive hotel in the world.

He loved the Sunset because it was his life, and he wanted it because he wanted to own himself. That was the truth, and, as always, the truth could not be told.

So Robert Hartford looked Francisco Livingstone directly in the eye, and told him the story he had prepared.

"You see, Francisco, running a hotel and making movies are really the same business. You have the set, and endless plots and subplots, and you have the cast—the guests and the all-important staff. I want to direct *The Sunset Hotel*. I want to tell the beautiful visual story, and I want to write the script and I want the crew to harmonize and to improvise and to reach new heights of technical excellence. I want it to be a bigger hit than it has ever been and to make more money, and to be critically acclaimed until the world agrees that it is a work of art so complete, so brilliant that it is the standard against which all others are judged."

Francisco laughed out loud and his laugh managed to be both respectful and disparaging at the same time. It had been the sort of thing he'd wanted to hear. Almost. The Sunset turned into a hundred miserable condominiums had not been his plan for the extraordinary hotel he had created. Yet, Robert Hartford *daring* to imagine he knew how to do something as impossibly difficult as running the greatest and most exclusive hotel on earth just had to be a joke. God, people were amazing. Their gall. Their effrontery. Their sheer bloody chutzpa. He had never suffered from the sin of pride. Gluttony, maybe; lust, definitely, and lots of other ones. But he would never, for instance, in his wildest dreams, imagine that he could carry off a few supporting roles in Robert Hartford's pictures. Here, however, before his eyes, the best-looking man in the world was cheerfully boasting that he could pull off the part of best hotelier, too. He filed it away in the voluminous drawer that was his life's experience. Never underestimate the power of the famous to overestimate themselves. Was it their strength or their weakness? Perhaps both.

"Well, why not?" said Francisco. "God knows the place could do with a few new characters and plot twists." He peered around the clockwork-smooth restaurant, the perfectly operating bar, the waiters drilled to Prussian parade-ground standard. To his practiced eye it looked like the top. The only place to go from here would be down. Still, flattery was what the Hartfords of this world understood. They could never get enough. That was what drove them on. To excuse any disrespect in his earlier laugh he added, "I couldn't imagine anyone I'd rather sell to."

Nobody had mentioned money, but then nobody had picked his nose.

Robert watched him with hawklike eyes. Was this the moment to mention it?

His gut said yes.

"How much are you looking for, Francisco?" said Robert casually. He paused. "From a friendly buyer, like myself."

Livingstone sipped at the champagne, rolling it around his mouth as if he were at a professional tasting. He swallowed, and he smiled as he watched the movie star bobbing like a cork on the sea of nervous anticipation. "Oh, I don't know, Robert. I'm not much good at things like that. Jack Douglas and Fred Sands say one thing, Drexel, Burnham says another. You know how it is. Who do you believe? The realtors or the banks? You pay everyone for advice, and the advice cancels itself out. What do you think it's worth?"

Robert laughed. It was the oldest trick in the book. It didn't matter what the sums were. You got the *other* person to come out with a price. "I don't know, what, a hundred million?" he said, after a short pause.

Livingstone knew all about the Hartford contract with Galaxy. Fifty-six guaranteed over seven pictures. Seven years? A bank would lend him around thirty on that sort of security. His net worth before the deal was probably ten, give or take a few. He could put up around forty million cash for his equity interest and raise a mortgage of an additional seventy-five. He wouldn't be able to afford any more than a hundred and fifteen million, and that would be stretching him.

"To be honest, Robert, I'm looking for around a hundred and seventy. It's a lot I know, but the Sunset's unique, isn't it? You couldn't build it, and the goodwill must be worth a third of that."

Robert Hartford's face was expressionless, but inside the sinking feeling had taken the bottom out of his stomach. Okay, so Francisco would drop from the asker, but probably not much more than fifteen percent. It seemed there would be a gap that financially he couldn't bridge.

"That's too much for me." Robert's voice was quick, matter of fact.

Livingstone shrugged.

Robert Hartford stuck out his dimpled jaw. The blue eyes flashed and the famed nostrils flared. He leaned forward across the table and his suntanned fingers gripped the powder-pink cloth. "I'm not messing around, Francisco," he said. "I don't do that."

"Good heavens, dear boy, I didn't think you were for a minute. Lord no, never entered my mind. It's just that I owe it to my old age to get the market price, don't I? I know you understand that. You better than anyone."

Robert was not placated. "I don't blame your trying for a fancy price, but asking isn't getting. Frankly, the hotel needs a facelift. It's looking a little tired, Francisco. When you live in a place you see these things. A buyer would want to spend big bucks doing it up. I certainly would."

Francisco snorted his derision. "Oh, you would, would you? And are you quite sure your 'improvements' would *be* an improvement? You make marvelous movies, but I didn't know that interior design was a 'hobby' of yours."

"I'd have Winty do it." Robert floated the trump card onto the table with the innocence of an asp.

"Ah, yes. Tower. Yes."

Winthrop Tower, the taste arbiter of America. Winthrop Tower, the West Coast designer who had single-handedly shifted the style center away from New York, if not quite to Los Angeles then at least to some indefinable place in the middle. Tower was beyond reproach. If you didn't like his work, then you were wrong. It was as simple as that.

"You could get Tower to do it?" Livingstone had to ask the question. After all, he'd tried and failed on occasions far too numerous to remember, despite the fact that Tower had been living in the hotel for the past five years. "Sorry, darling, hotels aren't my thing. They're for living in, not designing," the designer had always replied to Livingstone's increasingly desperate entreaties.

"For sure he'd do it." Robert paused. "For *me*. We've been friends for a very long time," he added enigmatically.

Livingstone knew that. Tower was drawn naturally to a man as beautiful as Robert. Whether it was animate or inanimate, Tower loved beauty wherever it existed.

Inside the old man's head the glorious vision was falling into place. The Sunset, remodeled by the best designer in the world. The Sunset, a style Mecca, transformed by the hands of the guru into a work of extraordinary art. He might not own it then, but at least he would live to see it, and everybody in the world would always think of the Sunset as Livingstone's monument. Yes, that would indeed be something. He could even continue living there, powerless maybe, but rich beyond dreams and with the respect for the founding father shining in everyone's eyes. That would be better than an extra million or two in the bank and the horror of watching them tack up a cheap neon sign on the hotel tower.

Robert Hartford had just discovered Francisco Livingstone's weakness, but with the instinct of the born dealer he immediately backed away. He waved a dismissive hand in the air. "Anyway, Francisco. Enough of all this business. Let's enjoy our lunch. Keep me in mind, and if you can't face the other potential buyers then you know where to find me."

He picked up the menu that he knew by heart, and he studied it as he might the early box-office returns. But he couldn't resist the last word. "My God," he muttered, almost to himself, "old Winty would do an amazing job on this hotel."

"Omigod, mirrors," said Winthrop Tower, holding on to his forehead as if trying to keep his brains inside. "Why on earth do people want to keep looking at themselves? I mean, I could understand it if *Robert* walled his bungalow in mirrors. But the *Coriarchis*. It makes one wonder how on earth they keep their food down."

Paula fought back the blush, but it was hopeless. She shifted her weight onto the other foot, trying not to sink completely into the quicksand of the vomit-colored carpet. The very mention of Robert's name was more than enough to paint her red all over. Winthrop cocked an all-seeing eye in her direction. Colors were his thing. He never missed a change in one. "What*ever* you do, dear, don't tip Antoine Coriarchi's butler if he brings you a drink. He's British. He'd be appalled. On the other hand you have my permission to tip Mr. Coriarchi. He's so obsessed by money he'd be thrilled."

"That's enough of that, Mr. Tower, sir. Any more of that an' I'll remind you what you said to that nice Mr. Stallone in the St. James's Club last night," said Graham cheerfully.

"*Thank* you, Graham," said Paula, as Tower groaned theatrically, and her embarrassment at the memory of her first meeting with Robert Hartford subsided. She had only known them all for a few weeks but already she was part of a team that shared private jokes, a boisterous camaraderie, and an easy acceptance of each other's strengths and limitations. But although Tower and Graham were now her friends, she couldn't help feeling somehow that the whole thing would soon be revealed as a gigantic mistake. She had landed on her feet so rapidly, and the memories of tragedy and despair were still fresh in her mind. She had no right to be there, standing beneath the monstrous oil painting of Corelli Coriarchi in the huge drawing room as part of a design team whose commission on this job alone would top three-quarters of a million dollars. She might have lucked out, but she still had so much to learn. The mirrors were a case in point. What was wrong with them? They made the vast room even bigger, and it was true that they were a rather yucky shade of gray and sported some nasty engraved twiddly bits, but she couldn't quite understand the global objection to mirrored walls. That was no problem. She would ask.

"Why are mirrors a no-no, Winty?"

"Last year, dear, and one tries to forget last year as hard as one tries to forget last night. Then of course they're faux, and we're off 'faux.' And they're pretentious, trying to give the impression that the space is bigger than it is. We don't allow pretension unless it's *us* pretending, dear. What else? They're too easy. Much more fun to get light into rooms using lovely lacquers and glosses, and windows, and skylights, and Florida ceilings. I'm *definitely* going to bring those back. You probably had one in the Everglades, didn't you, sweetheart?"

"We didn't have electricity, let alone electrically operated ceilings."

"Good Lord, how did you keep the booze cold?"

"Mr. and Mrs. Coriarchi will be joining you shortly," boomed the butler from the huge double doorway. "May I get you something to drink?" He sounded enormously pleased with himself. His lip curled over the "Mr. and Mrs. Coriarchi" as if it was a subtle, but enormously funny joke. At the same time he managed to raise an eyebrow in muted disdain at the appearance of the trio in "his" drawing room. A footman had shown them in and he, as head servant, was viewing them for the first time. Mr. Tower he knew, and approved of. The girl, however, didn't look at all at home. Very pretty, but definitely an outsider, in those odd beige trousers and funny brown jacket, and those hilarious old shoes. The other one was definitely a servant. It took one to recognize one. It took one to despise one.

"I'll have a glass of champagne," said Winthrop Tower, adding no nonsense about "if you have any," "if you have a bottle open," etc.

"Miss?" Again the surreptitiously witty delivery.

"I'll have a root beer, please," said Paula.

"A root *beer?*" said the butler. His mouth was open. He was incredulous. Had Paula asked for a glass of piss he couldn't possibly have been more appalled. "I'm very sorry, 'miss', but we don't have any . . . such drink . . . in the house."

Paula's face registered the direct hit. She deflated visibly before the supercilious servant's eyes. "Why on earth not?" said Tower, peering ostentatiously around the room. "You seem to have stocked up on most of the other disgusting things."

"Miss Paula'll have a Coke," said Graham quickly. "I'll 'ave one, too." He was acutely aware that the butler had rumbled his lowly status and had no intention of even *offering* him a drink.

"Very well," said the now thoroughly disgruntled servant, as he withdrew from the room.

"Imagine having to live in the same house as a butler with a personality that could ice champagne," said Winthrop loudly at the Englishman's disappearing back. "Apart from wanting to look at themselves in mirrors we must now add masochism to the list of the Coriarchis' perversions."

Paula could have sworn that she saw the Englishman's back wince.

"What's that about our perversions?" said Corelli Coriarchi.

She stood there in the doorway, where the butler had been, and more than anything else she looked like the cracked crab salad they served at the Bistro Garden. Her skin was faintly pink from an unjudicious and half-hearted exposure to the vicious August sun, and she had chosen to clothe herself in variations of that color. A pastel pink chiffon scarf hid the scrawny neck and clashed exuberantly with the darker shade of the unfortunate suit. She wore stockings that themselves glowed pinkly, and her large feet were crammed into frankly orange shoes. Blood-red talons, layer upon layer of some plastic material almost certainly developed in the space program, were the claws, and her hyperthyroid eyes bulged menacingly from a small, pinched face. Her upper lip said "electrolysis time" quite clearly, and her hair, tortured, maimed beyond retrieval by years of wicked chemical warfare, would have settled gratefully for being straw. Pendulous bracelets, solid gold, platinum, and silver, drooped from her undernourished forearms, a potent testament to her strength and determination rather than to her irrelevant wealth.

If she was cracked crab, the man who stood by her side was crème brulée. He'd gone the whole hog on the sun. His skin was baked mahogany brown, George Hamilton–style, as if he had been attempting suicide and had chosen skin cancer as his method of self-destruction. He wore a seriously unpleasant cream suit, a red shirt, and in the hairs that sprouted from its open neck a hilarious medallion nestled complacently on a thick gold chain. He looked Levantine, and indeed he was, his mighty fortune founded on the sale of very cheap movies to cheaper people. Despite his burnished exterior, his whole persona reeked of an almost unnatural softness, a sort of sybaritic hedonism, and it was quite certain that inside the caramel-coated brulée the texture of his crème would be just right. When he farted, thought Winthrop Tower, there would be absolutely no noise at all.

But it was the frightful wife who wore the pants, and right now the expression on her face said that she was going to give them an outing. She had caught the "decorator" in an unguarded aside. Now she would make him pay for it.

Her expression was quizzical, almost haughty. She wanted some kind of explanation.

Winthrop Tower looked her right in the eye. "I was just saying," said Winthrop evenly, "that living in this house, and employing that butler, indicated that you must derive a certain pleasure from pain."

Paula's hand rushed to her face to cram the laugh back inside. Graham tried to keep his mouth straight. Tower stared pugnaciously at the Coriarchis.

It was simple. Either they could take offense, and Tower and his employees would walk there and then—or they could pocket their pride, and be allowed the privilege of paying the best interior designer in America three-quarters of a million dollars. The debate raged in

Corelli Coriarchi's eyes, as the neutral smile flitted backward and forward across the face of her husband. It didn't rage for long. She had tried to score a point, and she had been outgunned by a far higher-caliber social confidence. And she had been left an "out." It would be possible—*just* possible—to write the Tower remark off as a joke.

"Ha. Ha," she said rather than laughed.

"Ha. Ha," agreed her husband.

"Good," said Winthrop Tower. "May I introduce my assistant, Paula Hope. She'll be working closely with me on the design."

Mrs. Coriarchi edged forward in a curious sideways approach that gelled perfectly with her crab persona. She extended a claw toward Paula as if probing a possible piece of food. Paula shook her hand, but the fish eyes evaded hers, circling instead to fasten on Winthrop in an expression that said she was going to make one last attempt to even things up. "So young," she said to Winthrop. "Has Ms. Hope had a lot of experience?" Her eyes swiveled back to take in the absence of Hope heirlooms, the dubious appearance of the Hope wardrobe, the slightly scuffed leather of the Hope loafers.

"Good God, I hope not," said Winthrop. "Experience is the name we give to our mistakes."

"Ha. Ha," said Antoine Coriarchi mirthlessly. "Oscar Wilde."

"He got it from me," said Tower without missing a beat. "So you've decided to do away with the 'work' of poor Hugh Gates," he continued, flourishing an expansive hand to take in the safe-but-sorry California oatmeal/ficus/abstract painting school of interior design.

"How clever of you to recognize Mr. Gates's work," said Antoine Coriarchi in an attempt at reconciliation.

"Oh, we designers are like dogs," said Winthrop. "We recognize each other from the smell of the messes we leave behind."

"You don't think you can work around the existing design," tried the male Coriarchi.

"Work around it? Work around it? Good God, don't you realize this stuff is *dead*. It's crying out for a decent burial." He stalked over to one of the two Greek-style mock columns that flanked the doorway in a pretense at holding it up. He pointed an appalled finger at it. "Do you know what we call that? We call it a Gates post. And do you know its only use? To piss against when you're too drunk to make it to the john."

Mrs. Coriarchi took one step backward. She couldn't take much more. But with the steely determination of her breed she was not going to let go of her objective.

She had dragged her husband halfway across the world to America, and she had chosen Beverly Hills because it was the only place in the whole country that remained vaguely grand while at the same time quite definitely preferring money to class. Now she was here, but a few million dollars later she had still not arrived. Winthrop Tower would change all that. If he could be persuaded to "do" her house, to take her money, then she stood a good chance of graduating to be insulted by a superior brand of person. It was that glittering prize into which she had sunk her bonded teeth, and she was not about to let go. "I'm not feeling very well, Mr. Tower. If you'll excuse me, I think I'll go and lie down. Antoine can deal with everything. He knows what I like."

"Fine," said Tower, removing a glass of champagne from the silver salver that a footman, not the butler, had offered him. He made no reference at all to the supposed Coriarchi indisposition.

"I hope you feel better," said Paula.

"*Thank* you, dear," said Corelli Coriarchi. With a flick, sniff, and a pout she was gone.

Antoine Coriarchi poured himself across the carpet. "Where do we start?" he said.

"With the cash," said Winthrop easily. "Just like the movie business."

"We don't get to explore your ideas for the house to see if they're compatible with ours?"

"That," said Winthrop Tower, taking a deep gulp of the champagne, "would be an exercise in futility. I can tell you here and now," and he peered, horrified, around the room, "that our tastes will *not* be compatible. It is because you have zero expertise in this area that you are buying mine."

Paula could hardly believe her ears. In the Everglades Coriarchi would be either a murderer or the coward of the county by now.

"I suppose I wouldn't expect you to know how to make my movies," he managed at last in a desperate attempt to excuse his abject lack of pride.

"Good," said Winthrop. "I'm glad we've got that settled. Now, what happens is this. You pay me a design fee of two hundred and fifty thousand dollars, half now before I give away all my secrets and half on submission of the detailed design scheme. In addition I pocket thirty percent of the wholesale cost of the entire job. You get a house designed from top to bottom by me." The "with all the social benefits that such a deal implies" was unspoken.

Tower chuckled inside. It was far from the way he usually did business, but this was different. The Coriarchis were beyond the pale, and he had decided to take the job for the money, not because he needed it but because he *felt* like it. In this life it was vital to practice one's whims. They were an antidote to old age.

Normally Tower's relationship with a client was not nearly so autocratic. It didn't have to be. His godlike status in the design world meant that he could pick and choose who he worked for, or rather with, and he insisted that all his customers have at least the rudiments of taste. Conflict over his suggested schemes was rare, because a filtering process had occurred before he was actually hired. People came to him because they had seen his work, liked it and admired it—either in the shelter books (*Architectural Digest, HG, World of Interiors*) or in the homes of friends. Already, therefore, there was invariably some form of meeting of the minds before the design schemes were submitted and discussed. At this point Tower would meet several times with the clients and form an impression of the sort of people they were, of their artistic psychology, of the type of life they led. Did they own a billion cats? Then, detachable slipcovers for the sofas and chairs. Did they spend all their lives watching TV in bed? The concealed video systems and bedroom cabinetry could set them back a quarter of a million dollars. Were they grand entertainers with a wide circle of friends/enemies? If so they would be given imposing vistas, expensive art, drawing rooms like aircraft hangars. Did they like to hide from the world surrounded by clutter and the wife of the moment in dark wombs? In which case he would provide them with textured fabrics, rich colors, deeply subtle lighting. The Tower Design schemes were works of art all by themselves, and some had already changed hands for money at Sotheby's in New York. There would be hand-painted room interiors, intricate cards showing swatches of materials for the curtains, the carpets, the sofas, the chairs, glossy color photographs of pieces of furniture and paintings, intricate line drawings of the innards of closets, the fine details of cornices and moldings, diagrams of hydraulically operated hidden TVs, mobile walls, sliding panels. There would be examples of the vitally important details, the door furniture, the light-switch panels, the covers of the electrical boxes, things that lesser designers ignored.

The client would be allowed to pass judgment on the design scheme, and within reason, and more important "within taste," modifications would be made. Rigidity was not a Tower problem. If there was more than one way to skin a cat there were an almost infinite number of ways to design a room. The limit was the border of his artistic vision, and he hadn't reached it yet.

The Coriarchis, however, were a different kettle of oily fish. It was quite possible that they had never set eyes on a single example of his work. They had hired him for his social cachet, for his vaulting reputation, the way people sometimes gravitated toward infinitely grand designers like Henri Samuel (Rothschilds, Wrightsmans, and, oh dear, Gutfreunds), Mrs. Henry Parish II, a.k.a. Sister Parish (the Kennedy White House, the Duke and Duchess of York), or Mark Hampton (everyone else). What the Coriarchis wanted was not a beautiful environment but a rocket up their drooping social life. In exchange for giving them that, Tower would exert upon them maximum artistic discipline. Like unruly, rude, and ill-educated schoolchildren they would be taken severely in hand. They would be given what was good for them, and by God they would like it.

He smiled to himself because there was one more reason he had agreed to take the Coriarchi commission. He was going to leave it to Paula. He'd supervise her closely of course, but basically the job would be hers.

"You'd like the check now? Right here?" asked Coriarchi in a gloomy voice.

"That's right. Then we can get cracking."

The moviemaker mooned over to a large, almost certainly fake, Queen Anne walnut bureau, peddled, definitely, by the dreadful Gates as the real thing. He wrote out a check for $125,000 and, walking back, his shoulders sagging, he handed it to Winthrop, who peered at it suspiciously.

"Now I'll tell you what, old luv, why don't you potter off and administer to poor Mrs. Coriarchi while I take my rescue team on a lightning tour of the disaster area. We can leave the bedroom until another time. Don't worry, we'll find our way around. Shouldn't take more than half an hour." He waved his champagne glass in the air like a flag ordering the troops into line. "Come on, gang. We come to bury Gates not to praise him," he chortled. "Death to the California style. Onward to designing glory."

He set off at a brisk trot, Paula and Graham hurrying behind, as Coriarchi slunk from the room.

"Always start in the hallway," he said. "Back to the front door. Actually it's better to stand *outside* the front door and look into the house through it, but we'll stand here rather than on ceremony."

The trio stood crammed together, their backs plastered against the fussy carving of the massive mahogany front door.

Tower winced theatrically. "Well I'm glad I did *that*. Graham, make a note to scrap this terrible, fussy door. I'll have scenes from the rites of spring imprinted on my back for weeks.

"Okay, Paula. Away you go. What are we going to do with all this, short of bulldozing it?"

The white marble hallway stretched away toward the "Gates post" columns that flanked the double doors leading into the drawing room. To their left a wide corridor ran for about a hundred feet before joining at a T junction with another corridor, which crossed at right angles to it. The top of the T, they all knew, contained the bedrooms, which looked out over a sumptuous pool to a splendid city view of Los Angeles. The wall on either side of the passage was dotted with an untidy arrangement of assorted ultramodern prints, predominantly home-grown California artists—Ed Moses, Billy Al Bengston, Bob Graham, Richard Diebenkorn.

Paula swallowed. How had Emily Carstairs told her to do it? "First you have to look, dear. But much more important you have to see. Clear all the rubbish away. Block it out. Look at the space. Feel the architecture."

"Well," she started hesitantly. "I think it would be wonderful to open up the ceiling, and let some sunlight in. Then I think the marble floor is too severe, and too white against the white walls. I'd . . . maybe . . . leave the marble at the edges but perhaps scoop out the middle and inlay some oak boards, quite dark, if we had the skylight. I'd carry that floor design through to the cross bar of the T where the other passageway meets this one. Then, where they meet there could be an alcove . . . square I think, and rather classical with a fine piece of Renaissance sculpture, big, male probably, and carefully lit from below, with the natural light coming in on it from above."

Winthrop Tower's smile was that of the proud father for the winning child.

"Wonderful. Perfect. And your metaphor?"

"What do you mean?" said Paula, pleased but bemused.

"Dear God. You do it, but you don't know it. It's scary. It frightens me. The cross," he said.

"I still don't get it."

"Dear girl . . . Christ on the cross is your metaphor. Crucifixion actually took place on a T bar. You've put in the dark wooden bars of the cross. You've hung a godlike figure at the intersection. You've made it open air. It's out-of-this-world brilliant. And you didn't know. I really don't think you knew what you were doing."

Paula saw it at once. He was right. There was a unifying theme to her design suggestion, and it was religious.

The wise old eyes were on her now, boring deep into her, proud but also vaguely suspicious. "Okay, Ms. Superdesigner. Own up. Where did it come from? Where did you learn all about inlays, and Renaissance statues, and mixing textures like wood and stone? You didn't learn that in the Everglades. They don't know about things like that . . . in . . . 'Florida.' "

"Oh, but they do," said Paula. "My best friend in the whole world knew all about those things, and we both lived in the swamp."

"What friend?"

"Her name was Emily Carstairs. And she was a drunk. A lovely, wonderful, kind old drunk, who taught me everything she knew about design. She worked in New York once, and then she sort of dropped out, and she ended up living in Grand Cypress."

"Emily Carstairs . . . ? Emily Carstairs . . . ? *I* remember Emily Carstairs. She had a store in the nineties on Madison. Wonderful fabrics, and a few bits of odd furniture. Must have been fifteen years ago. God, we all used to go in there and steal her stuff from her. No idea at all about what to charge. She used to drink more than I did. She'd fall asleep on an ottoman in the store window and forget to lock the door at night. You could see her in there sleeping as you motored past. And although that shop was on the edge of the civilized world, she was never robbed. Can you believe it? It used to shake my faith in the evil of the human race."

Paula laughed, thrilled to find that her new friend had known her old one.

"That's my Emily. She could fall asleep in the middle of a sentence. Well, she lived in the Everglades. She taught the art class in the school at Placid, and I used to just about live at her house, going through all her books, and her drawings, and listening to her stories. I guess that was where I learned whatever it is I've learned. She used to fascinate me. You know what she used to say about gin. 'Gin doesn't destroy your art, it just destroys your ability to profit from it.' "

Tower laughed.

"It may be true about gin but I haven't done so badly at turning a buck on scotch."

"*And* the rest of it, Mr. Tower."

"That's enough from you, Graham. We're talking about *art* here." He turned back to Paula. "What happened to dear old Emily? Is she still in the Everglades getting the mosquitoes plastered?"

"No. She died nearly two years ago."

"Oh, I'm sorry."

"So was I. Devastated. But she was longing for it. 'So exciting, dear, don't you think, to find out the answer to *that* one,' she used to say to me." Paula mimicked the patrician Bostonian nasal twang.

"Know what she meant. Know what she meant. Hell sounds like great fun. Not so sure about heaven. Not at *all* sure about that. Oh, and talking of hell, are you organized for Livingstone's ball tonight? You know he's calling it a black ball and everyone has to dress in black. Can't think where he got the idea from unless he's just had mumps. You can get that in the balls you know, and they go black and drop off." He paused deep in reflection on the serious subject of Livingstone's potential testicular problems.

"Oh, Winty, you are dreadful. Livingstone's a lovely old man. People give white balls. Why shouldn't he give a black one? Anyway, yes, I am ready for it. I picked up a great dress at that store you told me about on Rodeo."

"Wonderful, darling. Wait till you see mine!" laughed Winthrop. Then his expression went wicked. "Can't wait for the rematch," he added.

"What rematch?" But Paula knew. The color high up on her cheeks said so.

"You and the bellboy, dear. The one on seven million a year. Whatsisname. The actor. Tip of my tongue. Made a movie or two." He smiled wickedly.

"Oh God," said Paula, her heart thumping suddenly in her chest. "He won't be there, will he?"

"Oh yes, he will. I promise you that. And I'll tell you something else. He'll be all over you like a hot rash, or I don't know Robert Hartford."

"He won't remember me." How could you dread a thing you hoped for?

"Yes, he will. Bellboys *never* forget good tippers."

"Winty, *stop* it! God, how awful! That was the very worst moment of my life. I mean . . . should I go and try to apologize? He must have thought I was such a hick."

" 'e thought you was beautiful, Paula." There was a trace of bitterness in Graham's voice. At Tower's ribbing of Paula? At the memory of Robert Hartford's eyes?

"Yes, Graham, I'm sure you're right. I do believe he would have thought that, darling, and I'd advise a chastity belt beneath your pretty black dress, although the last time I looked for one of those in Giorgio they'd been out of them for some time."

She gestured as if to hit him, but he ducked away from her.

"Listen, you two, I'm off to track down the rest of that champagne. You don't need me. You and Graham wander around the house. He'll take notes for you, dear. See you later."

He was gone. Paula and Graham were alone.

"Blimey," said Graham. The boss was on form today. " 'e's a brutal little bugger isn't he?"

"You'd better believe it."

A different mood had descended. It was as if Winthrop had been the sun and had darted suddenly behind a cloud, plunging the world into shadow. Or was it Graham's undiluted presence that had cast the subtle gloom? There was an intensity about him when they were alone that was not apparent when he was locked in his role as the Tower foil, the straight man to his master's voice. It was difficult to pinpoint, a brooding, know-what-you're-thinking camaraderie that Paula found unsettling, yet very real. When she was alone with Graham, Tower's irreverent jokiness faded into illusion. Possibly he was a brutal little bugger, but he was a pastry-cake pussycat compared with the brutality of the world, the brutishness that *she* knew about, that Graham knew about, too. She was ashamed now of her flustered little-girl act when she had confronted the thought of meeting Robert Hartford again. Did she honestly care what some movie star thought of her? How could she stoop so low, she, Paula who had seen her brothers burn before her eyes? How could she play the pathetic film fan at the idea of being confronted by Robert Hartford at Francisco Livingstone's silly, frothy "black" ball? The frivolity she had allowed herself mocked the solemnity of the sacred memories.

She tried to say it, but it wouldn't be said. There was no way. She waved an impotent hand. "Sometimes I wonder how I got here . . . I mean . . . after everything . . ."

"Yeah. I know, doll."

They both knew that. It was the thing they had in common. They couldn't talk about it, but they were joined in the conspiracy of those who had experienced genuine poverty. Not the cosmetic kind—one TV, an ancient car, and no holidays—but the real, dreaded thing. The cold for Graham, painful in his damp bones; the East End flat with its leaking roof and the outside khazi down at the end of the back yard through the dripping, stinking eel boxes, its walls lined with frozen corrugated iron. The mosquito-laden heat for Paula, sucking at her sweaty skin, as it turned her mind to fire and her soul to cinders, unrelieved by air conditioning or the electric fans that the merely poor enjoyed. Dirty clothes, shoes that couldn't keep the outside out,

Christmas and birthdays carefully and cruelly spaced-out reminders of the nothing that they had, of the nothings that therefore they were. And the hunger, worst of all by far, the rumbling anxiety in the pits of stomachs that didn't know the feeling of enough and only knew the desire for more. There was no nobility in such suffering. It didn't make you fine and admirable as you learned to survive. It made you mean, and vicious, and callous, and insensitive. It made you angry, and tense and nervous, and fearful. You could think only of escape, and of the blood of those who stood in your way, and you longed and wanted with a terrible intensity that the haves of this world would never, ever understand. And worst of all, the poverty and the suffering lived on to plague you in the land of plenty. There they were standing in the middle of one of the richest houses in the richest town in the richest country in the world, and yet the poison of terminal deprivation still coursed like venom through their veins. So poor Mrs. Coriarchi's feelings had been hurt, and Tower had insulted the porno-movie millionaire, and Paula had thought of an imaginative way to blow some of his ill-gotten gains. So what? At the end of the day, so what? Because the only thing that really mattered was that neither Paula nor Graham would ever, ever have to go back to the places they had been. No word had passed between them, but in the fellowship of the damned it hadn't had to. It was the kind of thing that eyes spoke about far more eloquently than tongues.

For a second they watched each other, daring to think back, their memories horrified yet fascinated by what once they had been.

Paula broke the moment. She smiled wryly. "Come on, Graham. Let's get to work." And then, her smile lightening, brightening—"And Graham . . . let's pretend it's ours."

EIGHT

Why is Livingstone giving a ball, Dad?"

Robert Hartford winced despite himself. The word *Dad* could do that to him, because although he was one technically, he had never *thought* of himself as one. That had always been his problem with Kristina. He loved her deeply but in his own special way—a way that was light years from normal paternal affection.

"Francisco's been giving balls all his life in this town . . . They help decide whether you are dead or alive socially. Some people find it useful to know."

Robert Hartford peered at himself in the mirror. The famed annual Livingstone ball at the Sunset Hotel had black as its theme this year, but he hadn't really bothered about that. He never did. A dinner jacket was black, so was a bow tie and a pair of velvet slippers. About the only concession he had made to the "black" party spirit was a double-breasted waistcoat his father had always worn. Even now he could visualize it, slung across the back of a chair in the sitting room of another dim distant bungalow in the same hotel. The rest of his father's clothes would be in a heap around it, and in the bedroom the gentle moans of some soft-skinned dream would be the evidence that his father was "entertaining." Robert smiled as he remembered him. He, too, had never been a "dad."

"Did you know this is your grandfather's waistcoat? Whenever I saw it hanging over a chair, I knew he was on the job in the bedroom."

"That's gross, Daddy." Kristina Hartford didn't mean the rebuke, and there was laughter in her words. Just to make sure he didn't get it wrong, she shook her short blond hair and let him see her smile in the mirror.

Robert smiled back.

"You look good, Kristina. Very beautiful. That dress is perfect. Is it Chanel?"

"Thank you, Daddy," she said. "You look pretty good yourself. And how do you know about things like Chanel?"

"It's my business to know such things." Then he laughed. "No, really. I may not be much of a father, but I still pay the bills."

It was true he never had been much of a father. Most of her life Kristina had been brought up by the mother that Robert himself could hardly remember. His marriage to the famous actress hadn't survived the fact that he had become better box office than she—that potent reason for Hollywood marriage breakdown—and she had slunk off to the East Coast, taking the baby Kristina with her.

Now, he walked over to his daughter and he put his arms around her waist, and he felt her melt in them, with all the love she had never had, with all the love he didn't know how to give her.

"Oh, Daddy, it's so great to be with you, sort of *properly*. Not just visiting. Thank God, UCLA accepted me."

He squeezed her to him, but even as he did so he was uncomfortable. He could feel her breasts against his chest, firm and hard, and her tiny waist, and the heat of her and the glorious smell. Christ! Why couldn't he be like other people? They experienced normal emotions like warmth and tenderness and sympathy. They empathized and they comforted, and they used tough love, all the myriad of decent human feelings that made parenthood possible, and allowed children to be childlike. But he had only one means of communication. He could speak only the language of sex. It was the sole emotional dialect that he could understand. Already, he had felt her respond to the siren call of his sexuality. Everybody did. The animals did. The flowers did. The servants were always remarking on the fact that flowers lived twice as long in his rooms as in anyone else's. The guilt coursed through him and merged with satisfaction in the soup of his ambivalence. He could do it. Always. He had it. But it meant he was a failure while he was winning, a freak at the pinnacle of his success, a loser at life in the middle of the endless victories of lust.

There was a gentle knock on the door. "Who is it?" he called out.

"It's Joe, sir, with the drinks you ordered." The disembodied voice of the servant wafted into the bedroom.

"Okay, Joe, I'll be right out. Wonderful." He patted his daughter lightly on the bottom. "Go and say hello to Joe, darling. He'd love to see you."

Kristina smiled wryly at him. "Don't be long," she said.

In the bedroom Robert Hartford stood back to admire himself in the mirror, and the vanity began to smooth the worries away. He practiced a smile, and then another, and then one that merged with a little frown, before springing back again. Yes, it was all there. The tricks were packed away in the box ready for use. He would conjure his way to what he wanted. He would use his magic to win the Sunset Hotel.

Since the Star Room lunch with Livingstone he had thought of little else but the hotel and the buying of it. That was why he was going to the party. In the ordinary way he wouldn't have bothered. Parties were politics, and he floated above that in the Milky Way where the serious stars lived. Tonight, however, it was different.

Without naming names Francisco had intimated that there was another bidder in the wings. That might be a negotiating ploy, but if it wasn't then it was more than likely that the rival would be at the ball, and Robert would be on the lookout for someone who appeared to be dealing in ulterior motives. The sultan of Brunei, maybe, always a great buyer of up-market hotels. Or it could be anyone of half a dozen megarich wheeler-dealers like Perelman, Merv Griffin, or Donald Trump, who were into buying quality, uniqueness, and prestige wherever they could find it.

He straightened his tie. What he needed was one of Joe's cocktails to get him into the party spirit. Kristina's enthusiasm already had him heading in that direction.

Robert strolled casually back into the drawing room.

"Joe, how are you? You're looking well. Who is Livingstone allowing you to make drinks for this evening?"

It was an in-joke. Joe had been the barman at the Savoy in London under the immortal Harry Craddock of *Savoy Cocktail Book* fame, until Francisco Livingstone had spirited him over to Beverly Hills. Now he occupied an illustrious position as adviser to the barmen at the Sunset Hotel, and as cocktail maker to Mr. Livingstone himself. On special occasions such as this Joe was allowed to wait on carefully selected guests. The whole hotel had been taken over for the party, and the rooms allocated to out-of-towners or to L.A. residents who preferred to stay the night rather than drive home in the small hours. It was a potent symbol of importance to be allowed the services of Joe.

"Good evening, sir. Thank you, sir. Well, sir, I've been to Mr.

Tower sir, of course. I always do him, as well as yourself. And a Mr. Trump, sir. He's from the East Coast, I think, sir. Some sort of businessman there, I'm told. Then, Mr. David Plutarch over in bungalow nine. Apart from Ms. Streisand, that's about it, I think, sir. Isn't Miss Kristina looking beautiful? It's been ages since I last saw her."

Kristina blushed as Joe held the silver salver out toward Robert.

"What have you got here, Joe?" Robert put the drink to his nose. "Peach juice. Gin. Cointreau. Angostura?"

"Nearly sir, nearly."

He tasted it, and as always the elixir lifted his spirits. It was an extraordinarily delicate cocktail, the balance perfect, colder than ice, its top still frothy. The fresh fruit harmonized perfectly with the alcohol, bittersweet, strong, and satisfying.

"How did Harry Craddock say you should drink a cocktail?"

"Quickly, sir, while it's still laughing at you."

"Well, it's certainly a pleasure to obey him," said Robert, downing the delicious drink. "Who is in Mr. Tower's party?"

Normally Joe would be the soul of discretion, but Robert Hartford was Sunset Hotel family. So was Winthrop Tower.

"Just that man who does for him, Gordon is it." The old servant wrinkled his eyes up in distaste. "Oh, and a *very* pretty young girl, sir. Absolutely gorgeous, in a very stylish dress. She was ever so nice, sir. Miss Hope I think she was called." Joe knew where Robert Hartford's interests lay.

"I've met her. You're right, she *is* beautiful. The last time I saw her she tipped me ten bucks."

"She did what?" Kristina exploded her disbelief.

"Surely not, sir," said a scandalized Joe.

"Yes, she did. She put it right in my hand, after I'd helped Winty upstairs one evening."

"She's very young, sir," said Joe. He'd really liked the girl.

"I think she sounds absolutely divine." Kristina laughed.

"She thought I was a security man, or something," said Robert thoughtfully. "Anyway, she's going to the party?"

"Oh yes, sir, she is. Looks like a film star, sir. More than the real thing."

"If you're nice to her, perhaps she'll slip you a twenty next time. I don't know how you struggle by on your income," teased Kristina.

"Mmmmmmm," said Robert absentmindedly. "Joe, be an angel and do me another one of these in about ten minutes, could you. Oh, and while you're here could you bring out some canapés. The room-service people put them in the refrigerator a little earlier."

They were alone, sitting opposite each other across the glass table with its neat piles of blue bound scripts, its Waterford bowl full of floating gardenias, its exquisite Rodin bronze.

"Is Galaxy really paying you seven million a picture, Dad? That's what they say on campus."

Robert tried to put on his weary "it's only money" expression, but it didn't quite come off.

"Yes, as a matter of fact they are."

She leaned forward, and clasped both hands around her face. "That's *amazing.*" Her enthusiasm didn't quite ring true. Kristina wasn't very interested in cash. Too tangible.

Robert Hartford felt the sudden surge of adrenaline. "Actually, it *is* rather amazing. Shall I tell you why? Do you know what I'm going to buy?"

"A fantastic estate."

"Well, yes and no. I'm going to buy the Sunset Hotel."

"You're not! I mean, I heard a rumor it was for sale, but . . ."

"I can't afford it? Apparently I can. My accountants have been over the figures, and my business people say it will be a disaster, but they all agree I can do it. The bank's falling over itself to lend the money. No credit-worthy people left in America apparently. The Galaxy contract I've just signed is better security than any of their Third World loans and most of their farm ones. In the worst scenario, if I default, they'll end up owning a totally prestigious asset that's worth more than money in the bank. They say I can afford to bid a hundred and fifteen million, if I gear myself up to the hilt."

"Are you going to *do* it?"

Robert sipped deep on the drink, as Joe reentered. He took a carefully rolled brown-bread-and-smoked-salmon canapé from the tray and popped it into his mouth.

"Yeah," he drawled, "why the hell not?"

"When do you bid?"

"When the moment's right. The credit lines are open now. The offer document is drawn up. It's just a question of dealing with the psychology. I think there's going to be some sort of announcement tonight."

He put a surreptitious finger to his lips. Joe wouldn't know what they were talking about. He'd been out of the room when he'd mentioned the hotel. It was best to keep it that way.

"My *God*, it's the most exciting thing I've ever *heard*, Dad. Can I come and work for you? I'd do anything. PR. Accounts. The linen."

"What, and drop out of UCLA?"

Immediately he relented. Responsible father was not a favored Robert Hartford role. "Yes, of course you could come and work for me. *With* me. You're my only child. Part of it would be yours."

Kristina clapped her hands together in glee. "I just knew this whole weekend was going to be exciting karma," she said. "The sun and the moon are in a tight relationship with Jupiter any minute now. That means it's make-your-mind-up-time for Pisceans."

"You don't believe all that crap."

"Of course I do. Everyone does. It's a new age dawning, Dad. Ultimate knowledge didn't end with the sixties."

Robert groaned out loud. He'd forgotten that side of Kristina. The problem was that the sixties hadn't ended with the sixties.

"Don't knock it, Dad. It's commitment time for Virgos, too. Maybe you'll meet a woman who isn't just a tooth on a circular saw."

Usually Robert couldn't stand jokes like that, but now he laughed. He was in a good mood that wasn't just a sexy mood. It was going to be fun. He was taking his only daughter to a ball, like the best father in the world, and there was a hotel to buy, and an old boy to sell it. Maybe Kristina was right, and Virgo was rising or falling or whatever. And, at the back of his mind, there was something else. The girl with the proud, sad face who'd paid him ten bucks to go away because she was tired, and she hadn't known what else to do.

He stood up. "Come on, you," he said cheerfully. "Stop making fun of your father, and let's go to the party."

The swimming pool at the Sunset Hotel had been transformed into a steaming caldron of Hades. Smoke rose from it, and the surface bubbled with tantalizing menace, as if it longed only to claim the black-and-midnight people who clustered around it. Occasionally, through the mist, loomed one of many huge black swans, its back alight with candles. For a moment or two each would hover, partially visible in the constantly moving vapor clouds, before disappearing once more into the darkness.

The orchestra, too, was consumed by smoke, but the music transcended it. It reached out into every corner of the ghostly gathering, trembling, rising, falling, swooping onto the ears of the guests, filling them up with delicious dread, and touching their quivering spines with fingers of ice. It was Wagnerian in its grandiosity,

rococo on Gothic on baroque, and as they sipped nervously on their
'79 Perrier-Jouët Rosé champagne everyone agreed that Francisco
Livingstone's black ball was exceeding expectations.

The sweet scents of the night-flowering jasmine and the gardenias
argued that this was in reality paradise, not hell, but the flaming, fiery
torches that hung from the darkened fan palm trees allowed the exotic
myth to live, as they painted anxious shadows on the faces of the
partygoers. And there was something else out there on the lake.

A figure of unearthly gloom was ferrying his boat across the sulfurous
surface of the water. He was stooped, cloaked in black, and his face was
hidden beneath the wide brim of his hat. About his movements there
was an otherworldly weariness, as if he were doomed forever to ferry
souls in torment to the burning gates of external damnation. Now,
suddenly, he burst into song, and his words filled the music of the
orchestra as they sank into the psyches of all who listened. It was a
magnificent voice, powerful, compelling, a cry from the heart, the
message of the collective unconscious demanding that it be obeyed.

> "Come to me now, now that life here is ending,
> Come to me now, now the death knell is sounding . . ."

"It's so *spooky*. I mean, that guy is just wonderful. How do they get
all that smoke?"

"Dry ice, luv. Packed on wooden platforms on the swans' backs.
They've each got little clockwork motors underneath." Graham
answered Paula quickly, as if he had been waiting for her to speak.

"God, Francisco's really gone for it tonight, hasn't he? Looks like
he's practicing for the Grim Reaper. Hellfire, damnation, and purgatory. Deals with the devil. It's just like Spago on a Thursday night,"
said Winthrop Tower.

They stood on the edge of the crowd, a party within the party,
thoroughly enjoying themselves.

Especially Paula. Unbelievably, she felt she had a new home.
Certainly she had a dear new friend. By day he was kind, charming,
and infinitely wise, and he moved through the world of interior design
on a cloud of brilliance that everyone recognized and all respected. At
night the alcohol would unleash the poet in him and for a while his wit
would sparkle and he would declare unconditional war on hypocrisy
and the tawdry values of the society in which he had chosen to live.
Then, usually quite suddenly, he would go over the top, and at
lightning speed it would all be over. Next morning, however, he would

be back on line, a little rueful maybe, mildly apologetic, but hard at work in the business he had elevated to a fine art form.

He had kept his promise, and Paula knew that she had more than fulfilled hers. He was teaching her everything, and she was storing the information away and merging it with her uncanny natural eye to excel in every area of the trade. Together they trolled what "antique" shops L.A. possessed and they talked to the cabinetmakers and the fabric manufacturers, and they went through swatches and sat down with architects, and they endured endless sessions with bemused clients.

But if Winty was a joy, Graham was an enigma. Only one thing was for sure. He had become very interested in her. His eyes never left her, and when she caught them she couldn't help but recognize their burning intensity. She liked him, but his quicksilver moods unnerved her, and often his gaiety seemed merely a cover for darker feelings that blackened the water around the tip of his emotional iceberg.

"So death takes all, and life bows down to serve her,
In black we die, and in despair we surrender . . ."

The hellish gondolier's voice sailed above the crowd.

"Dear, oh dear," said Winthrop. "All this talk of death is giving me the most *marvelous* appetite. *Such* an underexposed topic. How very *clever* of Francisco."

"Hello, Winty, gloomy enough for you?"

"Hi, Kelly, sweetheart. Yes, darling, I'm feeling incredibly optimistic about it all. Death's so reassuring, isn't it? Imagine the *horror* of endless life. It'd be like that torture, you know, when they won't allow you to sleep. Have you ever done a transatlantic economy class?"

Kelly McGillis had done several. In the days when she'd been a waitress. Not anymore. "Do you think there's anything *wrong* with Livingstone?" she asked.

"Nothing that death can't fix, dear."

"Winty!" they all chorused.

"Well, all I can say is that I hope this isn't the last party he ever gives," said Winthrop. "This is the fourteenth I've been to, and I can't remember any of them, which is the ultimate test of an excellent host."

Francisco Livingstone's parties at the Sunset Hotel were legendary and when they happened, Hollywood talked of nothing else for weeks before and didn't change the subject for weeks afterward. It wasn't just the inventiveness of the food and drink, of the bands, of the exotic themes and the superb timing with which they were stage managed.

The real action was in the guest list. It wasn't a total disaster not to be invited. But then earthquakes weren't total disasters, and there were those who maintained there could be life after nuclear war. Leprosy, the Greenhouse Effect, Black Monday were all examples of things that *could* be survived, and so life went on after the Livingstone invitations had failed to arrive. Shrinks, however, saw their income spike upward, and post-office workers encountered a whole gamut of the strangest emotions in the month or two that preceded a Sunset Hotel ball.

The European invitations would go out first, followed ten days later by the East Coast ones. Finally, four days later, out would go the invitations to the ones who cared the most. To minimize nervous breakdowns they would be posted simultaneously at the baroque Beverly Hills post office on Santa Monica Boulevard. Then the trouble would start. As anxiety rose, fueled by unkind calls from "friends" in Europe and New York, the tougher and more desperate wives would contact Livingstone's office, to wonder if their invitation had "gone astray" because of their "change of address," or whether it had been among the batch of mail destroyed that very morning by the dog. This was L.A., so the guest list was an infinitely mobile one. Old friends were safe, but meritocrats were judged on merit, or rather box office, it being Hollywood's idiosyncratic tendency to confuse the two. This was why everyone cared so much. To be a new invitee meant you were on the way up. To be culled from the list meant you were dying if not dead. Thus the absence or presence of the black engraved card on the hall table had potent messages for the future. It told you what you would or wouldn't be able to afford, who might or might not cut you dead at the hairdresser. There was one rule, and it had only been broken twice. The list would be neither added to, nor subtracted from. Princess Margaret, passing through New York from her house on Mustique, had once been added at the request of Drue Heinz, a mutual friend of hers and Francisco's. She had been one exception. On another occasion there had been a call from a Beverly Hills psychiatrist ringing from the house of one of his patients. He had been trying to talk her down from the roof. The only thing that would prevent her suicide would be a Livingstone invitation. Francisco had thought about it long and hard before capitulating. No way, however, would she get away with the ploy again. Next time she could jump. From Elsa Maxwell, Livingstone had learned that in planning a guest list there was no place at all for pity, sentiment, or a sense of obligation.

The superb baritone was finishing his aria. His voice breaking with transcendental doom, he slipped away into the mists, to the thunderous applause of the partygoers.

"Paula! You're not going to have a glass of champagne? It's a 'seventy-nine. You ought to *try* it."

"Okay, Winty, if you think there'll be enough for you."

A waiter rushed past and Paula spun around to get his attention. "Would you bring me a glass of champagne?"

"With the tips you give, it would be a positive pleasure," said Robert Hartford.

He was standing beside her, so close they were almost touching. He leaned in closer, and his eyes were dancing with her. She could smell his warmth, she could sense his heart, she could hear the things his body was saying to her.

I've thought about you. I've remembered you. In bed at night I have dreamed of you, he was saying. You've been to my secret places, and walked in my forbidden cities, and I know you and you know me, and we will know each other.

His seductive power lasered in on Paula. In his sultry gaze there was the ultimate intimacy—quiet, intense, targeted solely at her. Despite the crowd, they were alone, communing together in the first sweet moments of the thing that could be love. She did not know what to say, but it didn't matter. Now she realized that he had been with her every moment since their first meeting, as his sex-ray eyes told her she had been with him. Somewhere just beneath the surface, they had been joined together.

He put out his hand and he touched her arm, and she fought back the desire to hold on to him, and to pull him toward her, and admit to the world what was going on.

But the world already knew. As they recognized the moment, nobody spoke. Winthrop Tower saw it through the prism of ambivalence. Kristina saw it, warped by the spectacles of daughterly possession. Graham felt it, like a knife in his heart.

"We haven't been properly introduced," said Robert.

"Paula Hope," said Paula.

"God, I thought you two had met. Now, where on earth did I get that idea from? Paula, this is Robert Hartford, the man the Lord created with women in mind."

Winthrop Tower's introduction was way too late. "You know the good Graham, our friend from across the water," he added.

Graham's nod was curt. Robert's was curter.

"Omigod, now I know who you are. You're the girl who tipped my dad," said Kristina suddenly.

Color rushed into Paula's cheeks. At the memory of her faux pas, at the far more unsettling reference to Robert Hartford as a "dad." The blonde could have been her sister.

"I didn't recognize him!" Paula's response was *not* an apology.

"Where have you been *living?*" Kristina's incredulity was cunning. She said it with a laugh that hid most, but not all, of the scorn. "You're a hick," she was saying. Now, Paula's only real escape would be to say something about how there was no law about people having to recognize Robert Hartford. To her dad, who'd made it his life's work to be totally recognizable by everyone in America, that would be bad vibes. She would have succeeded in driving a wedge between them. Such a move was out of character for her, but she only had one father, and this girl was *startlingly* beautiful.

"There's no law that says I have to be recognized," said Robert with an incredibly lazy smile. "Maybe Paula's had more important things to do with her life than paint her nails, watch movies, and generally carry on like an empty-headed mall Val with an inexhaustible supply of plastic."

"No, Kristina's quite right. It was incredibly naïve of me, and anyway I *have* seen most of your movies. I just never expected to meet you. Not then, not ever."

She held out the olive branch to the defeated daughter without thinking, without any ulterior motive, just at the sight of her crestfallen face.

Her reward was Kristina's look of surprised gratitude. "What sign are you?" asked Kristina.

"Taurus," said Paula warily, not entirely convinced that the attack was over.

"It's a good time for you. There's only the moon in your sign this month. And there's a brilliant aspect between the Sun and Neptune."

"Oh," said Paula, wanting to say "thank you" but feeling somehow it would be inappropriate.

The Hartford eyes were probing her deeply. "Now that we more or less live under the same roof we can go *on* meeting each other," he murmured.

"Yeah, on 'an on 'an on . . ." said Graham. He made it sound cheerful, but his cockney cockiness was heavy with sarcasm.

Robert half turned toward him, his eyes blazing with anger, but there was nothing that could be said. Graham stared evenly back. They knew they were rivals now.

"I'd like that very much." Paula ignored the bad feelings that had swirled up like the mists over Francisco Livingstone's swimming pool. She was still in psychic touch with him, and, in the delicious metaphysical clinch, she didn't want to let go. They were getting to know each other at lightning speed. She was tuned into him and already she felt like a lover, quivering at the brink of him.

Winthrop Tower understood it all. Graham had fallen hard for Paula. That Tower could live with. Robert Hartford, however, was something else. He specialized in making women unhappy, *after* the most blissful happiness of all. Nor could Tower control him. Nobody could. If Paula was sucked into the whirling Hartford girl pool, which looked far more than likely, she might easily drown. As her protector, he wasn't about to allow that.

"Robert, what's all this I hear about the hotel being for sale, and you being a potential buyer?" he said quickly.

It was the only thing that could have broken Robert and Paula's communion. Robert had wanted badly to have this conversation with Winthrop, and now the best thing of all had happened. Tower himself had brought the subject up. "If I bought it, would you redesign it?" Robert went straight for it. His gut told him it was the thing to do.

"If I had a choirboy for each time Francisco asked me to do that, dear, I could have the Hallelujah chorus whenever I snapped my fingers."

"But what if *I* asked you, Winty?"

Winthrop laughed, as the spray of fine charm wafted over him. It *would* be different if Robert asked him. He had known and liked him for years. Francisco, however, was from an older generation. One of the things he had learned in the design business was to pick out the clients who would be potential trouble and those who would not. Livingstone would have been trouble. At every stage of the design process he would have resisted change. He would have given up the old with the greatest difficulty and he would have resisted the new with every fiber of his being. Despite the fact that intellectually Francisco Livingstone knew that Tower would transform the Sunset into a design masterpiece, emotionally he would not be able to deal with it. Robert, in contrast, would let him get on with it. That was the only way he, Tower, would ever agree to take the job.

"I'd say a definite 'maybe.' "

"How would I get you firmer than that?"

"One of your famous candlelit dinners for two, sweetheart."

He struck the famous Tower hand-on-hip pose as he laughed

outrageously at the double entendre. So did everyone else. Laughed, that is.

"No, come on, Winty."

"I'm coming, sweetheart, I'm coming. Don't rush me. Not at my age!"

More laughter.

"You'd have carte blanche."

"Loo seats to lampshades?"

"Finger bowls to toothpicks."

"And Paula is my design assistant on the entire job, working as liaison between us?" said Winthrop, quite unable to resist the temptation.

Then an amazing thing happened. Robert Hartford began to blush. The twin spots appeared like headlights on the sunburned cheeks, but then they became bloodstains spreading out to cover his entire face. He put a finger in the neck of his shirt, and he looked down in confusion, as if completely dumbfounded by the alien feeling that had suddenly overcome him.

To those who saw it, it was remarkably charming, so much so that Winthrop actually wondered whether it was a secret weapon, a newly unveiled armament in Robert's constantly expanding romantic arsenal. If so, then he should learn how to duplicate it on the screen. He would have been showered with Oscars.

Still staring at his shoes, Robert mumbled, "Well, that's settled then," and he looked up again at Paula.

A crashing, booming noise reverberated over the loudspeaker system. "Dinner is served," intoned an extravagant English accent.

"Saved by the gong," said Winthrop Tower.

He hurried off, encircling Graham's elbow in the classical older man's steering grip, bearing his servant away with him. Somehow Kristina was sucked into their wake.

Robert didn't move. Neither did Paula.

"I'll enjoy working with you," said Paula. Her cheeks were rosy red as she spoke, and the smile she wore lit up the words. It was as far from the traditional remark at the end of a successful job interview as the moon from Mars.

He didn't answer at first. He simply turned the light of his countenance upon her. The blue of his eyes, surreal, hypnotic, shone bright beneath the hooded, lazy lids, and his mouth softened at the corners in a smile that was a million miles from humor. He leaned his head to one side, in a gesture that said his whole mighty concentration was focused exclusively on her. He appeared to be about to speak, and the smile that wasn't a smile seemed to broaden as his whole face shone with an otherworldly warmth.

Their silence was an island in the middle of a sea of noise, and although no words were spoken they were speaking at the most fundamental level of their being.

Paula swallowed hard as the magic moment wrapped her up.

She knew what she was doing. She was falling in love. With the most famous movie star in the whole wide world. It was crazy. It was mad. It was deeply wonderful.

When Robert Hartford spoke his voice was low, husky, frighteningly intense.

"We're going to be lovers," he said.

The great banqueting hall at the Sunset Hotel had never looked so evil. It was like a black hole sucking you into its ghostly intrigue and delicious spookiness. The Georgian central chandelier was still there, the one that had adorned the ballroom of the duchess of Richmond at her dance before the battle of Waterloo. From all around it, huge areas of black damask swooped out in folds to tent the entire ceiling. It formed the walls, too, and at strategic points flaming torches burned, sending tongues of flickering light dancing across the smooth oak of the floor. Thirty tables, each seating ten, were clustered at one end of the room, their tablecloths black, their Wedgwood Colonnade bone-china dinner services milk-white and black, their centerpieces Waterford crystal bowls of floating gardenias in which Rigaud candles drifted on rafts of midnight blue. The scent from the flowers was heavy in the ethereal air, and from hidden loudspeakers the soft strains of the poolside death aria reminded everyone of the theme for Francisco Livingstone's extraordinary ball.

The atmosphere of another world, however, had not entirely succeeded in diverting the Hollywood elite from the priorities of this one. They wanted to know who else was there and what this meant about *their* status.

Everyone knew that these days the A-list/B-list grading system for L.A. parties no longer applied. The old guard—the Gregory Pecks, the Charlton Hestons, the Lew Wassermans, the Ray Starks, the Robert Stacks, the Irving Lazars—were slowing down and staying home while the new party people—the Marvin Davises, the Leonard Goldbergs, the Deutsches, the mighty Quinns, the proud peacock Tartikoffs, foxy Barry Diller, artful Doug Cramer, Mr. and Mrs. Barbara Walters, the revivified Sue Mengers, Princess Zsa Zsa von Anhalt, and the increasingly more beautiful and vivacious Cristina Ferrare and her husband, Tony Thomopoulos—couldn't replace them. New blood was required, and the name of the up-to-date game was to fill one's parties with a judicious balance of up-to-date people who were strangers to Beverly Hills. So, apart from the new and the old party people, Livingstone had invited top rock band Guns N' Roses; George Bush's brother, Prescott Bush, who had been a fellow Whiffenpoof of Winthrop Tower's at Yale; Michael Crawford, soon to open *Phantom* in L.A.; top black Jesse Jackson; top gun Tom Cruise, and top party bikers Justine Bateman and boyfriend Leif Garrett, who'd pitched up on their Heritage Harley. Culture was catered for by beautiful Baryshnikov, the other coast by Tom Wolfe, and couture by the dashing Kleins. It being Beverly Hills rather than New York, everyone who'd been invited had turned up, and now they were all marveling at the "mix."

But if being invited to the Livingstone party meant that you had jumped the first hurdle into the inner sanctum, there was still a final fence to be negotiated. Those who had at last relaxed on the invitation obstacle were now experiencing varying degrees of adrenaline surge as they confronted the placement one. At which table were you sitting? And with whom?

Believing, with the divine Elsa, that a good host should treat his guests like children, no matter what their age, Livingstone had erected a huge blackboard at the entrance to the room with a diagram showing the position and seating arrangement at each table. Around this oracle of triumph or doom, three hundred of the most important people in the entertainment business were crammed like Japanese commuters waiting for a train. Livingstone had expected that. That was why the blackboard was so big. It had taken him two glorious weeks to plan the seating of his guests, fourteen spite-filled days in which old scores were settled and new alliances cemented. He had not shrunk from the incendiary task. He was too old and powerful for that. Instead, he had reveled in it. Former partners in feuds, sour business deals, marriages and dissolutions (Beverly Hills's new word for divorce) were stuck mercilessly together, on the principle that high tension provided party energy. To add insult to injury, the tables were named shamelessly from one to thirty, and it didn't take a professor of mathematics to work out which one was the most important . . . and which the least.

Robert Hartford stood back from the milling crowd. The hand on his elbow confirmed that he had been right to do so. It was Martin, an assistant manager at the hotel. "You and Miss Kristina are at Mr. Livingstone's table, Mr. Hartford, sir. If you'll follow me, I'll lead the way."

All around the room this little scenario was being repeated. The real movers and shakers were holding back. Barbra Streisand didn't look at blackboards. Nor did the Armand Hammers, the Mike Ovitzes, or the David Plutarchs of this world. Sunset Hotel employees had been surreptitiously detailed to look after the people who weren't used to anything else.

The first table, Livingstone's, was in the middle nearest to the dance floor, and apart from the fact that it wasn't actually raised on a separate dais and lit by multiple spotlights, it was quite apparent that it was the place to be. Livingstone was already there, standing proudly behind a chair. He made little waving gestures of greeting to Robert Hartford.

"Robert, my dear chap, glad you could make the arduous journey. And this must be Kristina, who I haven't seen for *far* too long. You used to sit on my knee, m'dear. Oh, yes, a long time ago. Robert you're over there, one away from me, and Kristina, you're three away from me on the other side. Yes, that should do it. A billionaire on each side and you the filling for the sandwich. Dear me, *isn't* this fun?"

Robert peered over the table. There were no name cards. Both his dinner companions remained a mystery. In the normal way that would have been irritating, but potluck at a Livingstone party was like a lucky dip in which all the tickets scored Rolls-Royces. Who would it be? Whoever was immediately to Francisco's left would be good business, good fun, possibly both. He was enjoying himself. It was a wonderful party, and the face of the girl called Paula still lingered hauntingly in his memory.

"Ah, there's Barbra. Darling, don't you look divine? How did a poor old wreck like me end up sitting next to a goddess at his own party. My, my, isn't this just fantastic."

Barbra Streisand did look divine. Wearing a Scaasi dress, yellow diamonds, her hair piled high by Victor Vidal, she sat down in the pole position on Livingstone's right like the genuine superstar she was.

"And there's David. You found us. Good. Next to Barbra, old boy. You two know each other of course, and I'm sure you both know Robert, and his daughter, Kristina. David Plutarch made his fortune by keeping us in touch with the heavens, or was it the other way around? Stellar communications of one sort or another anyway, which means he should get on well with Robert and Barbra. Ha, Ha! Yes! Ah, there you are, my dear. Another of our great communicators. In between myself and Robert, please. Do you all know Caroline Kirkegaard?"

She hovered above the table like a genie released from Aladdin's lamp. She, too, wore a tuxedo, but there all similarities to the men's dinner jackets disappeared. The Donna Karan creation flowed over shoulders rendered even more than usually massive by rounded pads. The silk facings were curved as well, but it was all but impossible to notice their cunning shape because of the vision they framed. From her long bare neck to the slash of her belly button, Caroline Kirkegaard was exposed; from the edge of one melonious breast to its rock hard companion she was visible. The great expanse of delicious whiteness was in dramatic contrast to the jet black sheath of the "dress" that stuck to her body, defining a gigantic double hourglass—the top of which nipped in at the waist, the bottom one at the knees. Her Hemingway-esque lashes and brows were emphasized with mascara, and her drowning-pool eyes, under- and overlined in vivid amethyst, sang in tense harmony with the powerful red coromandel of her lips. Despite the stylish sophistication of the Chanel makeup and the fashionable inventiveness of the couture evening dress, the nervous fallout from her presence settled over the table like radioactive dust.

Robert Hartford took an involuntary step back, recoiling from her. Livingstone was motioning her down beside him. She was an honored guest at the top table in the room. Caroline Kirkegaard, whose fledgling movie career he had personally ruined. Caroline Kirkegaard, who had apparently risen phoenixlike from the flames of the defeat he had engineered, to a position of undoubted power once again. Since the Destiny meeting he had walked out of, her squalid little cult had gone from strength to strength, but what the hell was she doing *here?* With him. With Barbra Streisand. With Livingstone. With Plutarch. The thoughts stopped there as the man who majored in passion read the neon eyes. Plutarch! He was watching Caroline the way the bewitched watched their mistresses. There was hunger in his look, and a slavelike devotion mixed in with the pride of the possessed for the possessor. It was plain for all to see. David Plutarch and Caroline Kirkegaard had, through the workings of the devil, come together, which meant that now she stood close to his billions, to his power, to his possibility.

Robert took a deep breath. He was caged with her for a couple of hours. There was no way he could walk out. Not on Livingstone, at this time. It would not be forgiven, and the thing he so desperately wanted would be denied him. Livingstone's table placements were notorious for their cruelty, but why Kirkegaard next to him? Did Livingstone, who knew everything, know the story? And if so, what wayward perversity had encouraged him to thrust them together?

"Now, Caroline, I'm not sure that you have met Barbra and perhaps you don't know Robert Hartford, because I think this is the first time you have been to one of our little get-togethers. We have David to thank for that."

"Hello, Robert," said Caroline Kirkegaard.

There was amusement in her voice, the amusement of the surpriser for the predicament of the surprised. She flicked her head down, looked hard at her chair, and Robert reached out toward it and pulled it back for her. Immediately he was aware of what he had done. He had behaved with reflex gallantry toward a woman who must be his enemy. Somehow she had "made" him do it. The first point was hers. The second wouldn't be.

"Not since *Angels in Heaven*," he said.

"Yes, you destroyed my acting career, didn't you, Robert? All by yourself. But perhaps you did me a favor."

She turned on her smile at him—unfazed, seemingly unfazable.

With the curiosity of the connoisseur he tried to work out what he felt about her. Physically, she still repulsed him. She was too hard, too tough, too menacing. He didn't bear her much personal animosity. He had dumped her from the movie because he found her vibrations deeply unsettling, because her charisma made her a rival, and because he had wanted to exercise his power and his hypocrisy at the same time. Exercising those were as much a part of making it in Hollywood as the money and the fame.

"I was surprised to see you at one of my meetings. In this very room, wasn't it?" said Caroline. Again she smiled serenely, and the message was clear. The past was ancient history, "forgotten" not forgiven, by a person who had moved on to bigger and better things. She had audiences of her own now, and people like Robert Hartford sat in them.

"Yes, my daughter dragged me along to it." He paused for the putdown: "She's going through an impossible stage. I was able to resist the message." The last sentence dripped sarcasm.

"I'm glad there aren't many like you." She smiled an enigmatic smile. Their eyes locked in combat.

She leaned forward to reach for a glass of water, and her cleavage opened wide. Robert's eyes crawled right in. He couldn't help it. Neither, on Caroline's other side, could Livingstone.

"What's all this I hear about you selling the hotel, Francisco?" said Barbra Streisand.

"Ah, Barbra, you've preempted me. I was going to make a little speech about it after dinner. You know how I love to 'say a few words,' and it would quite spoil it if I let my secret out of the bag too soon."

"Well, all I can say is that if it *is* for sale then someone very sympathetic must buy it. I couldn't *bear* it if it went to some faceless hotel chain." She beamed around the half-empty table for potential buyers with taste.

"Now, why doesn't nice Mr. Plutarch buy it? I'm sure he wouldn't change a thing and we could all keep coming back as if nothing had happened. We could even embalm you, Francisco, and put you in the lobby, and then, each night when we went out to dinner we could stroke your foot for good luck like they do the statue of the horse in the Hôtel de Paris in Monte Carlo."

An icy silence descended on the table. Plutarch studied his linen napkin. The half smile of the Sphinx played around the lips of Caroline Kirkegaard. Robert Hartford's sensuous mouth was pencil thin across his face.

"Or, Robert, what about you? You live here. You must love the place as much as anyone, and now that you're so rich, couldn't *you* buy it? I think that would make *so* much sense, don't you, Francisco? I mean, Robert's a part of your décor around here. It would be like selling the hotel to itself."

The silence got even colder.

Francisco Livingstone's laugh was gentle, but not entirely kind. "Just in time, Donald," he said, as he stood up. "Barbra is auctioning my hotel here at the table, and you're just in time for the bidding. Ivana, how lovely you look, as always. Now, I know everyone knows the Trumps, because the Trumps know *everyone*."

Caroline Kirkegaard did the math. The table was approaching the four-billion-dollar mark. It made her feel warm inside, the more so because nearly three billion was hers. Plutarch was hers. He'd caved in more comprehensively than she had dreamed possible, and after the fun and games with Kanga in bungalow 9 he wanted more and more. He was fascinated by her, dangling on her sexual hook, like a recently hanged man. She had asked for the hotel, and he had promised it to her, but even in his obsession his business sense had not totally deserted him. He would retain a controlling interest and nearly all the money would be borrowed against the asset of the hotel itself so that his own downside risk was strictly limited. How much would it cost? So far

Livingstone hadn't named a price, but at the meeting the three of them had had the night before he had intimated that there was another serious bidder. Caroline didn't necessarily believe him, but she was worried, and the warmth in her gut at the proximity of so much money was tempered by anxiety that Donald Trump could be just the sort of person to be interested in the hotel. He owned hotels already, casinos in Atlantic City and the Bahamas; his recent acquisition of the Plaza in New York, the mention in his book *The Art of the Deal* that Ivan Boesky had once offered him the Beverly Hills Hotel. The Sunset might fit well into his empire. It was prestigious enough, and more than anything else the high-profile developer dealt in prestige.

Behind the Trumps were the last two guests, and in many ways they were the most surprising of all, because they were totally faceless. Nobody had the remotest clue who they were.

"Now, last but not least," said Livingstone, with the barest and most subtle indication that here *were* the least among the gathering, "are Henry and Freda Cox of Cox, Cox and Playfair, the very best attorneys on the West Coast, in my humble opinion."

Everyone arrived at the same conclusion at once. Livingstone was going to sell the hotel. The buyers were at the table. So was his lawyer. Could it be conceivably possible that the deal was going to be done here, now, in the middle of dinner in the Sunset ballroom?

Francisco's next remark did little to dispel the speculation.

"I have an idea," he said as ten silver tureens packed tight with beluga caviar hit the table simultaneously, and as ten waiters leaned forward to pour Stolichnaya vodka from bottles frozen into foot-square cubes of ice.

"Why don't we play a little game? We go around the table, and we all say what we would do if we owned the Sunset Hotel. How we would change it. How we would do things differently. Oh, I forget. I don't get a turn. I *do* own the hotel, and of course I'd change nothing!" He laughed pleasantly. "Barbra?"

"I'd throw out all the guests and have the whole place running exclusively for me. A staff-to-guest ratio of about four hundred to one would suit me fine."

They all laughed at that. Some with relief. At least *she* wasn't a serious buyer.

"Caroline?"

"I'd bring the Sunset triumphantly into the New Age. I'd hold Destiny seminars here, and spread the word to the other guests until everyone was caught up in the excitement of the future, the glory of the past, and the infinite possibility of the present. It would grow and grow until it was the center of the universe, the paradise for the brave new world that I know will come to banish all sorrow and to bring new hope to humanity."

"David?"

"Caroline has just said what I would have said had I the power and the knowledge . . . and the brilliance." Plutarch's face gleamed with wild enthusiasm as he spoke.

"Ivana?"

"I'd keep it just as it is, as you would, Francisco. If it ain't broke, don't fix it."

"Thank you, my dear. I can't believe you really mean it, because I know you have wonderful ideas about interior design, but thank you anyway."

"Donald?"

"Gambling in California? I don't think the economy needs it, do you? Now, Florida . . . that's another question entirely. No, I think that the California game is real estate. I'd buy it, hold it, get someone good to run it, trade it. The money'd be safer than in the Bank of America, if I didn't have to pay too much."

"Henry?"

"I have to be very careful what I say . . ." Lawyers often started out like that. "Because I'm the only one at the table here who couldn't afford it." He got a bit of a laugh, but heavy hitters didn't laugh hard and long at lightweights' jokes. "I guess I'd just soldier on, and hope that Livingstone didn't open up down the street. In fact I'd have a clause in the purchase contract about that."

His wife wasn't asked. "Kristina?"

"I'd give it to my father," she said at last, but her eyes were fixed on Caroline Kirkegaard as she spoke. All around the table there was a little ripple of applause at her generosity.

It was Robert's turn. He tried to separate the fact from the fiction. Was this just games, or was Francisco in earnest? It was difficult to say. Would his speech be important, or just meaningless chitchat at the whim of a cunning, courtly old man? He paused, sipped pensively at his vodka, and his voice was quiet when at last he spoke.

"I'd have Winthrop Tower draw up plans for a total rebuilding and redecoration of the Sunset Hotel," he said, "and I'd build a house for Francisco on the grounds and make it part of the agreement that he remained in a consultant's capacity until the day he died."

"And boy, would you be praying for *that*," whispered Caroline sotto voce.

"I didn't think you believed in death," he shot back out loud.

"It's a transition."

"Can it," said Robert rudely.

If Francisco Livingstone had heard the interchange he chose to ignore it. He sat there like a bird on a perch, a wise old owl, and the spoon of caviar hovered at his blue-tinged lips. He was deep in thought.

"Moonies, loonies, bucks, and bores," he said at last to no one in particular.

There was ragged laughter. Everyone, with the egos of the super-successful, imagined he was being rude about someone else.

Caroline felt the excitement build within her. Francisco was going to sell for sure, and the other serious buyer was almost certainly Trump. She knew as much about the New Yorker as anyone else, but no more. One fact stuck in her mind. He liked to buy assets cheap, from sellers who were hurting. He was a patient man who would wait for years before striking. Plutarch, however, was a different sort of businessman. He saw a deal and went for it, happy to pay over the top now for something that he truly believed would be worth much more later. Trump would come in low, and wouldn't chase it because there were hundreds of other irons in his fire. Plutarch, awash with cash, and besotted by her, would pay Livingstone his asking price or damn near it. And as for Robert Hartford, well, she had never thought of him as a joke before. He might be a power in Hollywood, but he wasn't serious money. He was out of his league at last, a dilettante movie star with delusions of grandeur and sexual complexes that made Don Juan seem as psychically wholesome as an astronaut. It would be more fun than she had had in years to dump on his Mickey Mouse dreams, if indeed he dared to entertain them.

She took the caviar fast, rolling it around her cavernous mouth, and her eyes sparkled their encouragement at the bankroll across the table.

She turned toward Robert, eager to patronize the man who had so capriciously destroyed what she had once wanted more than anything. Intuitively she knew where he would be weakest. "Is that your daughter across the table?" she asked.

"Yeah."

"She's a lovely girl, isn't she? We had a little talk earlier, out by the pool."

Robert turned to watch her, the way he would a serpent.

"Yes, she is." His voice was flat, noncommittal. "Who introduced you?"

"She did. She's been to more than one of my meetings, you know."

"Yes, I gather they're very profitable. You should be proud. Cash from weakness. Money from losers." Immediately he regretted his last words.

"And is Kristina a loser, Robert? Surely not."

"My daughter has no money of her own, Caroline."

"Just a rich, doting father."

"Do you see much of *your* family, Caroline?"

Twin specks began to glow high on the alabaster cheeks. She laughed, but there was no humor in the sound. "Touché, Robert. Yes, families are difficult, aren't they, when one wants things so badly."

In the silence they both called the truce. Happy families was a game that neither of them had played. Somewhere back in Scandinavia, there would be a Kirkegaard family—proud daddy, sad mummy, a Kirkegaard boyfriend, husband, child? There, in some safe suburb she would have existed for a while and then, when lofty ambition soared above the dreary status quo, it would have been make-your-mind-up time. To stay or not to stay? Was it nobler in the mind to batten down and heave to on the sea of promises and responsibility, or braver and better to take up arms against dull decency and fly away? She had chosen flight. So had he. That made them allies against mediocrity at least, and it made them both sinners against themselves and against those who had trusted and depended on them. Robert had often wrestled with the dilemma. There was only one life to lead, and for so many the question had become not how did you live, but how would you die. For such people the future was the place, and the present merely the valley of the shadow, where you made your dispositions, and did the right thing, and hoped that in some far-off one-day world you would be repaid for your sacrifice.

Or there was his way, Caroline's way. Their goal had never been safety, security, the absence of pain. Those things frightened them, because they clipped their wings and caged them. Robert's power was sexual. Hers was the force of her extraordinary will. They were oil and water, but together they dressed the salad of life. They gave it taste. They made people want it. They gave surrogate hope to the dreary survivors. They were the soapiate of the people.

She was thinking that, too. Her wry smile said it, and then, mysteriously, it changed until it was saying something else entirely. His antennae trembled in the path of her smile, and he couldn't help returning it to say he knew.

She was so big, so beautiful, so hard. She was a diamond, an icicle, a mountain peak in a cold, bleak range, and she would be incredible, this half woman, this half man, with her muscles and her madness, her cunning and her inventive cruelty. Could he have her? Just once—screaming for him, in the way some did. Could he throw her out, and hurt her badly for the crime of being like him? Could he exorcise the ghosts within himself by conjuring up her orgasm, and killing her with the weapon of his attraction?

"No," said her eyes. "But try, do try. We deserve that contest, and I will win and you will lose."

The caviar had gone, and so had the Dover sole bonne femme, flown in that day from the North Sea. And now, inexplicably, before the beef Wellington and the soufflé Grand Marnier, Francisco Livingstone was on his feet, and the major domo's booming voice was praying for silence.

"My lords, ladies and gentlemen, pray silence for your host, Mr. Francisco Livingstone."

Slowly the hum of conversation faded.

He stood there like some immaculate scarecrow, the kind some nouvelle society billionaire would buy for his King Edward potato patch.

His dinner jacket hung like a sentence of death from his scrawny shoulders, but it was as perfect a fit as Huntsman of Savile Row could arrange within the confines of good taste. His bow tie was droopy enough to reassure everyone that it was tied not clipped, and his perfectly plain cream silk shirt was what you would expect from New and Lingwood, the Eton tailor's shop, understated, devoid of horrible frills, and with a soft, deep collar. There were plain bone buttons down its front and pretentious studs were mercifully absent. The simple, worn links, eighteen-carat gold but wafer thin, were just visible at the cuffs that protruded from the sleeves of the dinner jacket he never, *ever*, referred to as a tuxedo. A cream silk handkerchief tumbled untidily from his breast pocket, and his ancient, patrician voice creaked as he spoke.

"Dear friends," he lied. "Dear, dear friends, thank you for coming to my party." He paused like a hound sniffing the track of a fox. "We have had so many of these balls, over the years, haven't we? Wonderful evenings. So much fun. Some of you have been to all of them. Others of you are marvelous *new* friends. But tonight, I am so very sad to say, is the last one of all."

The murmur rustled around the room like wind in the willows.

Caroline leaned forward in her seat, her lips parted in anticipation. Plutarch fought for, and found, her eye. Robert, too, was alert, a runner at the starting gate, waiting for the gun.

"What I am going to say now may surprise some of you. You may think I am being unnecessarily dramatic, and the last thing I want to do is spoil the delicious dinner that I planned for you, but here it is. I live alone. I am an old man. Funny as it may seem to many of you, I have no one to talk to and yet I have something very important to say. So I thought I would tell you all—all at once—all my friends who have made my life so very happy and the Sunset Hotel such a joy on this earth . . ."

Spit it out, thought Caroline.

"I went a while back to see my doctor, as I do from time to time, when the man at the bank says I can afford to go . . ."

They all laughed uneasily.

"And do you know what he told me?"

In the silence nobody knew, but a few had guessed.

"He told me I was dying."

"Ooooooooh!"

"Nooooooooh!"

Mumble.

Rumble. The murmuring earthquake of shock and disbelief shook the room. Livingstone waited until the sound had subsided. When he spoke again his tone was cheerfully conversational. "In fact, he was quite specific. He said I had only a couple of years to go. Maybe three at the most."

Caroline Kirkegaard's eyes were alive with excitement. Across the table Plutarch's calculator mind was humming. Both had reached the same conclusion. He would sell fast to the man who could put the money on the table first. Plutarch fought back the compulsion to grab the old boy's arm and put in his bid then and there.

Robert Hartford was thinking what the others were thinking as his heart sank, and the prize slipped away from his outstretched hand.

"So I thought, as my little joke, that I would give a black ball, so that I could enjoy an evening of my own mourning. Not, perhaps, in the very best of taste, but it tickled my fancy, and when you haven't long to go one wants that tickled as much as possible . . ."

There was the odd nervous laugh. Francisco Livingstone's reputation as an eccentric was certainly being lived up to tonight.

"So, reluctantly I have decided to sell my life's work. I have decided to sell the Sunset Hotel. So wish me well, and bon voyage, and I love you all." Quite suddenly he sat down.

The tears rolled down Barbra Streisand's cheeks. "Oh, Francisco . . . I'm so sorry. I had no idea . . ." The others, too, struggled to find the appropriate words.

But Livingstone's hand was up. He was still in control and he wanted action. "Now, which one of you buggers is going to buy my hotel?" he said.

Robert Hartford's right hand was tingling, and his feet weren't touching the floor. He could remember the parchment touch, the arthritic fingers, the little squeeze that had said, "I'm pleased. I trust you. Don't let me down." And he chuckled to himself as he weaved among the black-draped tables toward his destination. All around him rose the flak of would-be friends, business acquaintances, former lovers, all united in their aim of deflecting his purpose. They bounced off him. He nodded and smiled and made little warding-off gestures with his hands, but he didn't stop, he didn't even slow down. It was too important. Things were far too wonderful. He had to find Winthrop Tower. He had to tell him he had just bought the Sunset Hotel.

The crowd around the tables was breaking up now, with the coffee and liqueurs, and people were beginning to dance to the Lester Lanin orchestra that Livingstone had flown in specially from the East Coast. Some of the tables were half empty, a few deserted. Where the hell was Winty? He was hardly a dancing man. He would be sticking tight somewhere to a glass of the genuine 1812 Grande Fine Champagne Napoleon Cognac that Livingstone was offering among the liqueurs.

There he was. Sitting all alone. Doing what came naturally.

"Winty!"

"Robert! Hello, old dear. Good God, what a bombshell! The old boy sure has balls even if they are black. Poor old Livingstone. The Big C, I imagine. Awful thing is, it didn't spoil my appetite. Amazing dinner. Didn't you think?"

Robert grabbed Tower by the shoulders. "Who is the owner of the Sunset Hotel?" he asked.

"Heavens, Robert, I didn't think you drank. I mean, not seriously. Mind you, I can understand the lapse from grace. The Haut Brion was out of this world."

"I am!"

"You are what, dear? Pissed? Yes, I can see that. Good for you. I've got about half an hour to go, if I can get them to bring me another cognac."

"Listen to me, Winty! Listen to me! I've just bought the hotel. I shook hands with Livingstone, in a verbal agreement witnessed by his lawyer. It's legal. I've done it. I'm the new owner."

In his mind the glorious vision danced. Plutarch had been the first to respond to Francisco Livingstone's bombshell when most of the others at the table had thought that the old boy was joking. "I would be interested in making an offer," he had said. "Do we know the price?" He had sat back, calm and confident in the certain knowledge that whatever the price was he could easily afford it, and he had smiled across the table at Caroline, his face reassuring, smug, totally at ease.

"I would like to hear your offer first, if you don't mind indulging me," Livingstone had replied.

"A hundred and sixty million cash."

Robert's heart had headed south as he had realized he could never match Plutarch's bid.

The Plutarch eyes had gleamed their triumph, as Livingstone had turned to Trump, but Trump had simply shaken his head from side to side.

"Robert?"

Robert had been aware of Caroline Kirkegaard's eyes upon him at his moment of defeat. "I can't match it," he had said, his head low, his spirits far, far lower. Across the table, he had felt Kristina's sympathy. There had been tears in her eyes.

"What would be your very best offer, Robert? I'd like to know."

A hundred and fifteen, he had said.

The old fox had smiled then, a slow, lazy, self-confident smile. "Subject to certain conditions, I accept."

"WHAT?"

The Plutarch/Kirkegaard question had not been a harmonious duet. It had exploded into the previously genteel dinner-table atmosphere, hers high pitched, piercing; his strangled, disbelieving. And it had been the wonderful beginning of Robert Hartford's first major nonsexual high.

Tower's expression said the message was beginning to sink in. "Robert, that's incredible. Were there other bidders? You mean he did the deal there and then, at the table?"

"You'd better believe he did. He was all ready for it. He had some lawyer sitting there. Plutarch bid a hundred and sixty million."

"Christ, Robert, you didn't top that?"

"I didn't have to. Livingstone told Plutarch that he wouldn't sell to him for a billion dollars. Didn't want the Sunset to fall into the 'wrong' hands. I thought Plutarch was going to have a fit."

"So, what'd you pay for it—if you don't mind my asking?"

"A hundred and fifteen million, with strings."

"Strings?"

"I, or my family, hold it for ten years minimum. Within a year you submit plans to redecorate and redesign it."

"I *do?*"

"You do. You shook my hand on it earlier, in front of that beautiful girl. . . ."

He looked around quickly. Where was she? He'd wanted her to be there to hear of his triumph.

"Robert, you're on. I said I'd do it. I'd love to do it."

"Where's your assistant?"

"Around somewhere. There, there she is. Over there with Graham. God, she's going to be thrilled."

"What on earth's the matter with her leg?" asked Robert.

She was limping. She'd hurt herself. He felt the concern well up inside him, and he was surprised that there was room for any such emotion at this the moment of his triumph. He walked quickly toward her, his worried look conflicting with her open smile of welcome.

"Are you all right? Have you hurt yourself? What's the matter with your leg?"

"Oh, that. It's nothing. I've had it since I was two. I had an accident. One leg's shorter than the other. It's no big deal. I'm used to it." She laughed to prove it.

"No, it's not," he said. "It can't be."

Paula looked puzzled. She didn't reply, but her expression was asking for elaboration.

"I mean, you can't have one leg shorter than the other. You can't have a limp."

"What do you mean, Robert?"

In the face of the question he wasn't sure. The women he liked were perfect in their way. If not perfectly beautiful, then perfectly powerful, or perfectly amusing, or even perfectly rich. He liked Paula very much—more than he'd realized—and she was supremely beautiful, so she couldn't possibly be . . . crippled. The word burst in his mind like a bomb, and he was completely aware of the wave of irrationality that had so suddenly submerged him. But the awareness didn't change anything. His intellect had been completely blocked by his emotion, and outside it was beginning to show.

"I mean . . . I mean . . . that you should have something done about it," he blurted out at last.

It seemed a wildly callous thing to say, but it was the way he said it that did the damage. There was disgust in his voice. The disgust of the aesthete for the ugly, of the clean for the dirty, of the virtuous for the sinner. His words meant that he was repulsed by her deformity, that he couldn't ignore it, that it actually made a difference in what he thought of her.

It happened so fast that everyone was astonished, but the pain and the hurt hadn't made it to Paula's eyes by the time Graham's lightning reactions allowed him to speak.

"Limps upset you, do they, Mr. Hartford? You look like you seen a bleedin' ghost. 'ad a friend once who felt like that about 'ospitals."

"No. I didn't mean that . . . I meant . . ." But he *did* mean it. The horror in his eyes said so. It was done. He had revealed the flaw within him, as he had beheld the flaw in her.

"I was going to ask you to dance," he said, and his hands splayed out to show their helplessness at the ridiculous inadequacy of his response, at its inevitability.

There was no way for him to make any sense of it. There *was* no sense. Only feeling. Only emotion. Only his naked self. So he backed away from her and then turned his back, and he hurried away through the tables, toward the big double doors, and in seconds he was lost in the bowels of the hotel he had so recently bought.

The muted roar of the party wafted out into the scented gardens of the Sunset Hotel. It waxed and waned on the idiosyncratic night breeze, now loud and insistent with aggressive merriment, then muted, a soft, surrogate happiness blowing on the wind. Around Paula, however, the sounds of Francisco Livingstone's black ball were crashing against a massive breakwater of solid misery.

She sat, still as a dancer in repose, on the weathered seat beneath the jasmine-entwined arbor, and the white, moonlit flowers seemed to weep in sympathy with her. All around her the black chiffon of the Mary McFadden skirt billowed out. Its folds, plucked by the warm air, danced up around the thick black suede belt and rustled about her ankles and the plain black Chanel satin pumps that until this evening had been her pride and her joy. She shivered with sadness, and despite the heat of the far from silent night, her skin was chilled beneath the skimpy material of the black camisole.

Next to her, formal, uncomfortable, like a suitor in a stilted play, sat Graham. As a concession to the "black" theme of the party he wore a frockcoat, pin-stripe trousers, a wing collar, and a black silk stock in an attempt at period style that succeeded only in making him look like a cockney music-hall villain.

"I can't believe what he just did," said Paula.

There were tears in her eyes and her voice broke, as she fought to hold it all together. All through dinner she had been thinking only of Robert. He had haunted her, and she had hovered on the delicious brink where intense physical attraction merges with something else. Now, distracted in the moon-softened darkness, she tried to tell Graham what she felt.

"It was weird," agreed Graham. He sat close to her, and his face was turned toward hers, his eyes wide with wonder at her beauty, with alarm at her agony.

"I mean, nobody's ever reacted like that before. Ever. It was as if I were a leper. He couldn't even look at me. You saw it, didn't you? It wasn't just me."

"It weren't just you, Paula." He spoke softly, as if he didn't want the words to hurt, and as if lowering his voice would take away some of the pain. But his sympathy for her was tinged with satisfaction. Hartford had behaved like a pig. It was quite extraordinary. His legendary sophistication and charm had vanished into thin air. He had hurt Paula badly, and she wasn't the sort of girl who would put up with that. It was an ill wind, and it had brought Graham luck.

"Listen, luv, forget it. They're all nuts here. They're not real people."

"I never think about it anymore—the way I walk. I've never thought about it. It's just there." She picked at the delicate material of the skirt, rolling it between her thumb and forefinger in a forlorn attempt to comfort herself. She had done that as a child, to the red satin dress her mother wore.

"I know, luv. I know. I don't notice it. There's too much else to look at."

"Sometimes my little brothers would joke about it, but they were just tiny kids."

Graham was instantly alert. All he knew of Paula's past was that there had been some terrible disaster, and both he and Winthrop had somehow known not to probe too deep. He moved closer to her.

"I never told you about my family," she continued. Her voice had a dreamy, disembodied feel to it. It was painted in sadness, but it was a sorrow somehow too fundamental for the obvious symptoms of grief.

Again Graham was silent. It seemed the most likely way to unlock the secret gates.

Paula gazed up at the stars twinkling in the satin sky, at the clouds hurrying across the complacent moon, as she looked for answers she would never receive. Was it time now, to let it out, to unleash all the horror? He liked her, this blue-eyed boy who sat beside her, and he wanted to know all the things she hadn't been able to bring herself to tell. She didn't make the decision. Somehow, like all the important ones in life, it made itself.

"I'll tell you about it, if you like. If you can believe it . . . if you can stand it . . . if I can . . ." said Paula, but she wasn't really talking to Graham anymore, she was talking to herself.

Graham's face was close to hers, close to the tears, and the soft regret, and the hatred that flowed from her as she told her story—told of the poverty and the happiness; of her dear, dead father and the struggle to bring up the twins; of Laura's terrible death and the holocaust that Seth Baker had wreaked on her little brothers; of the night her world had died.

She was dimly aware of his face, and now, as her cup of sorrow emptied, she noticed for the first time the extraordinary change that had come over it.

He seemed frozen, his attention absolute, but somehow he was separated from her by a wall of feeling that she couldn't cross. His eyes were without bottoms as they stared into hers, and his mouth, so often cheerful, was now a slit trench across his chiseled jaw. His brow was furrowed, and he leaned forward, his hand clasped tight against his thigh, his knuckles white.

"What did you do, Paula?" His voice was arctic cold; soft and deadly as he asked the question.

"It rained in the early morning, and they never sent the fire engine. But they sent a truck with two little coffins, and they pretended to find something to put inside them. It was funny, nobody seemed to mind very much."

"You didn't go to the sheriff?"

"Seth Baker owned Sheriff Mardon. Oh, I thought about it, as far as I could think about anything. But I didn't see him light the fire and it was dark, and he's important there, and I never was. . . . Maybe they'd even have blamed me. You know, what was I doing on the lake in the middle of the night. . . . And even if they'd believed me, and arrested him and found him guilty, what would have happened to him? Nothing, most likely. The lawyers would have gotten him off with a few years in jail."

"Yeah," said Graham softly, and he reached out to touch her, to comfort the girl he loved. "I'm sorry, darlin'," he said. "I'm very sorry."

He *was* sorry, but far more he was angry, and he was good at that.

There were villains in the East End of London who could swear to it, and had. But he was also puzzled, and the surprise was up there with the icy fury all over his beautiful, cruel face. Inside him the strange emotion felt all wrong. He had never felt like this about anyone before. Not about his mother who had brought him up and who he thought he "loved"; not about the tough, talkative cockney girls with their brittle glitz and their sparky humor who'd catered to the lusts of his formative years; not even for the mates who'd drunk with him pint for pint from the Elephant and Castle to Green Gate—the villains he'd called "friends" in the old days. Now, however, he felt strangely protective. He wanted to touch this girl, but softly. He wanted to stroke her, feel her skin, and conjure up a smile in the so-sad eyes. Above all he wanted to be with her. Just sitting side by side was almost enough, so that they could be together against the world that had mistreated them. It was called "love," and Graham smiled to himself like a foreigner in a strange country as he saw it for the very first time.

"You really understand it all, don't you?" said Paula.

"Yeah, doll, in a way I do." He squeezed her hand and he looked away, embarrassed that she had felt him care.

"Did terrible things happen to you?" she asked.

"Yeah, a few. But it's different, ain't it?"

He knew what he meant. It *was* different. She was a bird, wasn't she, and a wounded one. In the East End, men who attempted rape were outcasts, and those who harmed children were doubly so. A fella was fair game in the life contest, but a bird wasn't. Baker was roach slime, and he, Graham, longed to hurt him for what he had done to the innocents. Yeah, it would be good to see him hurting, and screaming and doing the things they did when they could see in your eyes that you didn't know what mercy meant.

"Why is it different? Because you're strong and I'm weak?" said Paula.

"Something like that."

"Well, I'm not weak. Nobody will ever understand what's going on inside my mind. One day I'll kill him. It's all I think about."

Her eyes flashed her determination, and her brow furrowed with the intensity of her desire for vengeance.

"Don't think about it, Paula. Try not to think about it."

She bit on her lip and tried to stop the tears, but they rolled on down her cheeks anyway, great big round tears of accusation and despair.

He put his arm around her and squeezed her tight, as if his strength could stop the memories, and she leaned in against his shoulder in the gratitude of the comforted. The sweet scent of her was in his nostrils, and her soft blond hair was warm against his neck, and so he turned his face toward her and nuzzled down, allowing his half-open lips to roam across the surface of her, and he shuddered with the alien feeling as he touched the only person who had ever felt to him like a human being.

"Oh God, I wish I could kill him," she sobbed.

Graham reached up, and his fingers brushed at the tears on her cheeks. "You know what, luv," he murmured. "I got a funny feelin' someone will."

NINE

I've been watching you."

It was far more than a statement of fact. It was an invitation to conspiracy. Caroline Kirkegaard's searchlight eyes flicked up and down the girl as if she were dusting her.

"You have?" said Jami Ramona, her voice breathless. She had been to countless Destiny meetings, but never for one second had she dared imagine she was anything more than a face in the crowd. She smiled her satisfaction—the famous Jami Ramona smile that breathed new life into the covers of *Elle* and *Vogue*; that alone guaranteed the mortgage payments on the Elan model agency's flashy Madison Avenue office; the megabuck turn-on smile that sent the cosmetics leaping from the counters of a million malls. Although she was only fifteen, they didn't come much bigger in the modeling world than sweet Jami Ramona, but all she could think was that Caroline Kirkegaard had been watching her.

"Yes, I know you well," purred Caroline.

She lay back on the cushions of the chintz chair—one leg crossed over the other—a pale python-skin, sling-back Manolo Blahnik shoe dangling from her foot. Her relaxation was so profound you could almost touch it. Her whole being vibrated with terminal truth, twitching in tune to the cosmic tremors that seemed to Jami to fill the room.

"You do?" said Jami, mystified but impressed.

Caroline allowed herself the deepest of sighs, and her magnificent chest shuddered beneath the Valentino silk-lined linen blazer. There was no acting like this. It was the best, because it hovered on the very borders of reality. The trick was to be half there, half absent. The absent part made it so completely believable, but at the same time, in order to control the process, you had to remain at least partially conscious of it. "My spirit guides have told me much, and I have asked them more, the better to know you."

The formalized, rather stilted speech was second nature now. She had stolen it from Jach Pursel, trance-channeling "Creator" of Lazaris, and grand old man of the genre. In the trance it would be amplified as the guide "took over" her vocal cords to impart the wisdom of timeless times. That at least was the public explanation. The other possibility was just as plausible: that the words and sentiments were Caroline's own—separated from the normal ones by a conscious act of dissociation that could be switched on and off at will. Sometimes even she wasn't sure which explanation to believe. But here, now, she did.

She had a job for Jami Ramona. And when it was done, she, Caroline, not Robert Hartford, would own the Sunset Hotel.

Jami moved to the edge of the sofa. For months she had been trying to arrange a private channeling and a psychic reading with the charismatic founder of the Destiny movement, but the wall of secretaries and followers had been impenetrable. The mistress did not grant private sessions on request. They were an honor she bestowed as a gift. Then, out of the blue at Greg Gorman's studio, she had received the call when she had been shooting an *Elle* cover. A person called Kanga had said Caroline Kirkegaard would see her that evening at her home on Callejuela Drive, in Coldwater Canyon. She was to be there at six sharp.

"Can you tell me what the spirits said?" Jami's eagerness was palpable.

"They will tell you directly, through me, later. But already I sense what you want to know. You are searching, aren't you, Jami, searching to find the self that you have lost."

Caroline watched and listened for the young girl's aura, damping down her intellect and tuning in her antennae to Jami Ramona's desires. What did she want? What did she need? Only when those questions were answered could she be used.

"What should you do about your mother? Yes, you must find your answer to that. And the deep doubt you feel about yourself, and the path you have taken. Why does it feel so bad, Jami, when it was supposed to feel so good? I think I know. I know, I know. The spirits have talked to me. They will talk to you."

Jami Ramona gasped. Wow! Jeez! It was scary. Double scary. How had Caroline known? How could she know? Jami had never told a soul. There had never been a soul to tell.

"Your spirit tells me of this. All your spirits, from many lives, from many ages."

The pushy mother was common knowledge in the media. It was almost a public debate. How far should you thrust a daughter? In the material world was it all right to turn looks into cash at the expense of a childhood? The hatchet-faced harridan had sat beside Jami Ramona and reeled off the justifications to Bryant Gumbel on the "Today" show as her daughter had squirmed beside her in blue jeans identical to the ones she was wearing now. Did the trust fund excuse turning a kid into a sex object? Was look-but-don't-touch cool when teddy bears were stashed behind the background paper? And what about the Arab munitions billionaire and his parties and his fleshy-faced sons, and the late nights at Boer 2 and Les Bains in Paris, in the N.Y. night fungus at M.K. and Au Bar, at the impossible to find Club O and the all-but-impossible to enter Velvet Box? Was that a fair barter for the cheerleading and chocolate of the manqué homecoming queen? Caroline smiled. The TV sound bite had defined the meaning of the term *ambivalence*. Jami Ramona would hate her powerful mom with the same intensity with which she loved her, and the problem would loom over her little life like a total eclipse of the heart.

There were tears in the aquamarine Ramona eyes. "Those . . . are the things I feel . . . the things I worry about. How did you . . ."

Caroline's hand was in the air, demanding silence. Her copper bracelet, with its fingerlike polished quartz stone, flashed in the light from the table lamp. "I asked you here for a reason. I sensed great sadness, and I feel it now, but beyond there is magnificent possibility. You are blocked, Jami Ramona, you are blocked from your future. The spirit guides can open the way. They have told me as much. They can save you for a success that the world has seldom seen before. But you must hurry. There is something to be done, and time is running out . . ."

"That's what I *feel*. I know I can do great things, but I don't know what to do, or how. I feel that something is holding me back and I don't know what it is." Jami wrung her delicate hands, and the film of tears thickened over the cover-girl eyes as she spoke.

"Be patient, Jami. You are *so* special. So unique. I don't just mean your beauty or your success—those the world recognizes even though you don't. I mean your spiritual glory. I see you astride the universe and talking with the purest spirits. I see you walking in the garden of God as his most valued and special servant . . ."

Caroline paused for the apparent throwaway that was in fact the bottom line.

"Of course, the *material* success will be fantastic. I see you moving here to L.A. and I see screens, big screens, not just television, although there will be a lot of that. Because nobody will be able to refuse you anything when you finally reach the light that you have always so deeply deserved. They will give you anything, everything. They will ask you what you want to do, and they will plead with you to name your price, and everyone who has stood in your way will bow down before you and beg the forgiveness of your mercy. And I see your mother . . . at your feet, silent at last."

Caroline stared into the misty gleaming eyes of the beautiful child she had captured. It was all there. Belief. Greed. The desperate longing for the promises to come true. Jami Ramona was sitting up straight cuddling her lovely knees, tossing her jet-black hair that way and this, and her tongue darted nervously over pale peach lips, wetting her pouting mouth as she quivered on the edge of her wonderful future.

But again the Kirkegaard hand was in the air. "If a way can be found to right the wrong. . . ." she said.

Jami stammered her response. "How can I right . . . the wrong. What can I do?"

"You must ask the spirits," Caroline replied calmly. "I will prepare my body for them."

Jami Ramona held her breath. Watching a channeler position herself for a trance was usually no big deal for her, although it always managed to quicken her pulse. After all, she'd seen most of the star turns—channeler to history's famous, Elwood Babbitt, J. Z. Knight and the spectacular Ramtha; plump Penny Torres and the bean-spilling Mafu—but this was different.

Caroline stood up. She smoothed the soft cream linen over her steel-strut body, watching the child model as she did so. Then she peered quickly around the room. The drawing room of the house that had supposedly once belonged to Hedy Lamarr stared back at her, reassuring in its Beverly Hills rented unreality. Some mock antique furniture, a few deeply indifferent hunting prints, the odd potted plant with mildewed leaves, a big screen Mitsubishi and the obligatory VCR. Only the outsize quartz crystal rock on the table in front of her was clearly not hired. It had cost Plutarch $160,000 from the Isis gallery on Rodeo Drive, and it was the key to everything.

Caroline looked at it lovingly. Impersonal and inanimate, it was her friend, because it was the source of the power she worshiped. She had possessed many stones—rubies to open the first chakra at the base of the spine and to allow the energy flow from the earth to enter the body; pink coral and pink jade to open the heart center and lift depression; carnelian, agate, and Madeira citrines to increase sexual energy—but when she had seen the mighty, clear quartz crystal she had fallen in love. It had spoken to her, as the crystals that were right for you were supposed to do, and intuitively she had known that she must own it. It wasn't just its size, its clarity, its brilliance, although all these things added to its amplifying force. It was the inclusion. Deep in its center there was an internal fracture whose prismatic light effects formed a miniature landscape with a doorway that seemed to draw you inside the crystal. Caroline could lose herself in its depths. She could climb inside it and vibrate to the heartbeat of its cold geometry. She could hide in its mystery and she could shine like a beacon from its thousand facets, from its perfect tip. It was her shelter and her springboard; her solace and her life source; it was her strength—and it asked for nothing in return. She had cleaned the crystal of all prior influences with smoke from wild sawgrass, and by immersion in sea salt for seven days and nights. Next she had recharged it by leaving it out for seven months of nights allowing the feminine moon energy and the soft light of the stars to fill it up with their subtle power. Then she had wrapped it in pure silk, and surrounded the silk with soft leather, and the leather with fine Egyptian cotton and she had stored it away, untouched by anyone else, in the wall safe, to await the work it would be called upon to perform.

That morning she had taken it out, and now she stooped to pick it up, noticing as she did so that baby Jami's blue eyes were focused tight upon it.

"Will you travel with me to another world to find out who you are?" asked Caroline, intercepting the young girl's gaze.

"Oh yes," whispered Jami. To the magical place where the cash secrets were. To the fantasy realm where Mommy dearest lost her tongue.

Caroline swept up the crystal. Cradling it against her massive bosom she walked back to her chair, sat down, and immediately closed her eyes.

Her voice was businesslike. "I will be going into a deep trance, and during that period I will have no knowledge of what the spirit guides are saying. At the beginning and at the end the trance will be lighter, and then I will have some awareness of the messages they bring. I am a clear channel—perhaps the only one—and the voices you will hear and the sentiments they express will not be influenced or filtered in any way through me. This you believe."

She paused, her eyes still closed, as if she needed confirmation.

Jami nodded at the unseeing eyes, and they seemed to sense her affirmation. She tried to hold on to the excitement bubbling inside her.

Caroline took a deep breath. The channeling process never varied. The sandalwood joss sticks burning in the circle of infinity around the room had "cleared" her. Next, she needed to "center" herself—the state of calm receptivity that was the feeling of being collected at her center. Without a proper centering it was impossible to focus correctly on the crystal. Deep breathing and concentration alone could achieve centering, but Caroline preferred to use a shortcut. She picked up the bell from the table beside her and, her eyes closed, her spine perfectly straight, she rang it once, twice, and then continuously—allowing the steady, rhythmic sound to carry her calmly toward her heart. After "centering," came "grounding." Unless you were securely tethered or grounded, it was impossible to achieve the balance that was such a vital ingredient in successful crystal work. Now, therefore, Caroline imagined a golden cord of light traveling downward, through her spine, down through the floor and into the earth. She exhaled deeply, sending energy down the cord, and as she became attached to the mass of the world, she felt the familiar heaviness in her lower body and a pleasant tingling sensation over her bottom.

She was ready. In her mind she threw the switch. As she did so, the force of her will merged with that of the crystal and together they beamed out at Jami Ramona.

She lifted the crystal above her head, holding it with both hands, and inclining it toward her target. "I am going to balance my body, aligning the energy centers to receive the spirit. When the crystal rests on my knees I will have opened myself as a trance channel."

On purpose Caroline had omitted the prayer. Most of the other channelers prayed before the trance that the gatekeeper would permit only the wise and enlightened spirits to use their bodies. But Caroline would not pray for that. Long ago she had attained a more fundamental perspective.

She was God, as much as God was God. Therefore Her will and His will were one. The spirits who would enter her body would say the things that she wanted them to say because they existed to serve her as they had always done, and in that service the cosmos would ultimately benefit as her enemies were cast down.

She took another deep breath, and her body shuddered as if shaken by a giant invisible hand. Down, down went the crystal, between her closed eyes, over her nose, brushing past the wet, parted lips to bisect her jutting chin, to run like a dagger down the white swan's neck to the rigid, mountainous breasts. For a second it paused there, sparkling with darting light, and Jami's eyes were drawn toward it, and to them, the triumvirate of the guru, who would change her life.

Caroline's breathing was heavy now, deep and rhythmic. Lower, steadily lower, sank the crystal, past the muscular midriff and the leveled stomach to the lap that was its destination.

The voice when it came was a surprise. Its accent was impossible to locate, its loudness and its pitch difficult to place on any scale. It was the voice of a woman.

"From the ancient empire of Atlantis I salute you, Jami Ramona."

Caroline Kirkegaard's head was thrown back, and her lips moved with the words that were not hers. Her eyes were tightly closed, but her hands had left the crystal in her lap and now they spread out in a strange gesture of openness that could have been some kind of a greeting.

"Who . . . are . . . you?" Jami's throat was dry as she tried the question. She had to talk to the spirit.

"I was your sister in the distant days when you were Vamara, daughter of Vanya, child of Ton. Greetings, dear one. I live in your heart, but now I can hear your voice."

"There was a wrong . . ." blurted Jami.

"You talk of the great wrong, of the sadness that surrounds your heart like a cage the sweet bird of your youth."

"Yes. Yes," stammered Jami Ramona.

"You can make it right, soul of Vamara. Now, in your age, in your place, at your time, the window of opportunity has opened. You will pass through the vale of your sorrow, and, in the wonder of the land beyond, you will become every possibility. You will be everything you have dreamed of being and far more, my beloved sister. I am here to tell you of these things, and the distant events that caused them."

Jami's mouth was open, but it didn't know what to say. Adrift on the sea of her longing, she could do nothing but wait.

"You loved Per more than your own life, and in return he worshiped you. He was older, and he was a brave warrior, but when he was with you he became the child that you were, and together you were so pure, and so strong that it seemed the sun shone from your eyes and the earth existed only as a platform for your feet. . . ."

Jami's heart thrilled as she thought of the great love that she had once experienced. Certainly the fumbling sons of the Arab billionaire didn't hold a candle to the mighty soldier of whom she was hearing for the very first time. Nor for that matter did the jaded yuppies in the Surf Club or the impoverished photographer's assistants, who sometimes made their inexpert pitches in the dressing rooms of New York studios.

"You were one with him and he with you, and your eyes belonged to each other, and you owned each other's ears and tongues and your hearts beat together. . . ."

"Like, what actually *happened?*" said Jami, unable to hide the trace of irritation in her voice.

Her celestial sister seemed totally unfazed by her sibling's earthly impatience. "You were married to Per on the eve of a great battle, and you had kept yourself for him as he had remained pure for you. That night you were to exchange the precious gifts of your bodies, but you were sad and greedy for him and fearful that he would be harmed in the coming conflict. Headstrong and selfish, you demanded that he withdraw from the combat to preserve himself for you, and until he promised to do that which he could never promise, you said your body would be forever a foreign field for him. He cried bitter tears to weaken your resolve and he pleaded with you through the restless night, but you were hard and cold when you should have been soft and warm. You withdrew from the touch of his hand, and you gambled that his desire for you was greater than his loyalty to the great Empire of Atlantis that he served. But he could not make that promise, and the great love you shared was not consummated on that wedding night, nor was it ever before the spear that found him on the morrow separated his soul from yours through light years of eternal time. . . ."

Jami Ramona blinked through the tears, and the truth pierced her as the spear had smitten her long-ago lover on that ancient battlefield. Yes, it had been like that. Now she knew it. The greatest of all loves, frozen, unconsummated, had lingered on, suspended forever on the brink of blissful union. From that moment to this in all her lives the awful blockade had held her back. She had stopped herself at the second she should have moved on to glory, and the pattern had been repeating itself ever since.

She and Per must live and love again. She must discover him somewhere on the winding roads of eternity, and the terrible wrong that she had done him must be made right at last.

"Oh, Per," she murmured. "Forgive me. Please forgive me."

Caroline Kirkegaard's hands were once again on the crystal, and Jami fought back the panic as she realized what that meant. The spirit was about to leave. The trance of the channeler was about to lighten. And nobody had told her what it was she had to do.

"Don't go yet. Please don't go. How can I meet Per? Where can I go to find him?" She blurted out the words.

"It is the reason I asked to speak with you. He is here, now in the City of the Angels. At this the crossroads of all your infinities you have a chance to meet with him and to give him the gift that in Atlantis you once denied him. But he is old in this life, and he is preparing himself for a great journey. There is not much time. . . ."

The voice was fainter. Caroline Kirkegaard's body was twitching as if struggling to be rid of the spirit that had briefly possessed her.

Jami Ramona was on her feet. "Where? Where is he? What is his name?" She howled her questions at the other world.

"I must go now. I have to leave, but you and Per will meet and love, and the gifts of a million past lives will be showered upon your head, gifts stored through eons of ultimate time are about to be released as you cement the union that once so nearly was, and once again is about to be . . ."

The voice was a whisper and the convulsions that shook Caroline's body were the curtains drawing steadily across the spirit's stage.

Jami Ramona rushed across the small space that separated them and grabbed at Caroline's massive shoulders, and she shook them as she screamed her anguish. "Who? Where? Oh, please, dear God, please tell me . . ."

"In the sunset. You will find him in the sunset . . ." murmured her spiritual sister from long ago.

Jami Ramona stood in Francisco Livingstone's Mario Buatta–designed drawing room, and she shook with desire. She moistened her dry lips with her all-but-dry tongue, and she tried to stay calm on the verge of ecstasy.

She stepped forward, fearing that she would fall, her limbs hardly hers anymore as she walked toward her destiny. On her face was a half smile of lust for her glittering future, for the lover of all her lifetimes, for the act that would transport her to the astral plane where only gods and goddesses lived.

It had been so easy, when she had feared it would be so difficult. At the channeling session an hour before, "You will find him in the sunset" had been the ultimate in enigmatic predictions. But Caroline Kirkegaard, shaking herself like a sleepy dog as she emerged from the depths of the trance, had saved the day. The spirit guide had spoken her last words in the light phase of Caroline's dissociation. She had been able to interpret the cryptic message. The sunset must be the Sunset Hotel, and the old man preparing for a journey had to be its terminally ill owner, Francisco Livingstone.

Quickly, the dominoes had slotted into space. Per, Vamara's doomed husband, lived on in the millionaire. The spirit had intervened to bring the two lovers together once again. In this life Jami could break the spell that held her in limbo. But time was moving on. The chance must be taken now. Or never.

Jami had not hesitated. She had felt more alive than at any time in her life, more certain, more bold, more single-minded. Livingstone was an old man. She was fifteen. But they were married before God, and he was her great love and she was his. The present didn't matter. Only the future mattered. Only the past.

The drive down Coldwater to the Sunset Hotel had seemed eternal, but the dry wind from the desert had plucked at her hair as the moonbeams had caught the palm trees and her heart had filled with the enormity of what was to be. The Mercedes roadster had stopped sharply in the side street that ran along one side of the hotel's grounds.

Jami had opened the car door, as she would open her heart and her body, and Caroline Kirkegaard had whispered once again the thing that she would do. "Bungalow seven, Jami. For your wedding night."

She had rung the bell, and eventually it had been answered. An ancient man, silver haired, but sweet smelling, had been wrapped in a big terry dressing gown bearing the braided legend of the Sunset Hotel on its breast pocket. He had looked like an actor auditioning for the role of God, and it was clear that he had just gotten out of the bath. He had been surprised to see her, but he had recovered quickly. When she had said, "Can I please come in?" it had seemed the shortest of times before he had answered. "Yes."

Francisco Livingstone walked before her wearing nothing but the bathrobe and an expression of bemused anticipation. Who was this marvelous-looking girl, who had presented herself at his door at bedtime? Had she been sent as a joke from a friend? Or had she simply knocked on the wrong door? The first of the two possibilities he discarded quickly. In this town, he had no such licentious acquaintances. Some variation of the second possibility was much more likely.

He turned to watch her over his shoulder and he caught his breath.

She was gorgeous. Her whole face was afire with an otherworldly animation, and her big blue eyes flashed and burned. She wore pressed 501's, a navy-blue jacket, and a cream silk shirt that struggled to handle what looked like wonderful breasts, and her mane of black hair flowed and streamed in chaotic disorder as if she had driven down from the canyons in a Mercedes roadster to meet the lover of her dreams. Her makeup looked like it had been painted by an artist. Just the minimum, restrained, delicate, immensely stylish. He cleared his throat nervously.

Jami Ramona saw herself happening in his eyes. She had a speech ready. She would welcome her ancient lover, while trying to acknowledge that her words would seem strange to him. But events were moving too fast inside her, within him. Apparently words could wait.

She saw, not an old man, but the warrior of Atlantis, soon to die, strong and brave and deeply in love with her. There was so little time to give the gift, and it must be so beautiful to sustain them both through infinity and to unlock the treasures of her future. This was the stuff of the truest lust, and in all her life Jami Ramona had not come close to it. The wet desire gripped her.

She stood there, on the Aubusson carpet, and she cocked her left leg, the knee thrown forward, the heel of her crocodile-skin loafer a half inch from the ground. As it was meant to, the professional model's pose threw her body into the shape that unleashed the dreams. Her eyes never left Livingstone's for one moment as she eased the immaculately tailored navy-blue Ralph Lauren blazer from her shoulders, allowing it to fall in an untidy heap at her ankles. The cashmere, and the bright brass buttons, wrinkled, rumpled against the pastel colors of the rich carpet, seemed to emphasize the abandonment that was to come. Next her fingers found the buttons of the cream silk shirt that was already wide open at the neck framing the outer reaches of her naked breasts. She undid them quickly to the big brass buckle of the cavalry belt, but she did not draw back the creamy silk. It stayed there, held by the buttons no longer, held only by the firm mounds of throbbing, thrusting flesh.

The Livingstone breath was on hold. The Ramona fingers were on the edges of the material. With all the time of many worlds she drew it back.

She was perfectly still, perfectly perfect, like an unveiled statue. Her breasts pointed straight ahead, browned gently by the California sun, and the pouting pink of their turned-up ends was the color of sea-washed shells on a Caribbean shore.

Jami reached up and cupped the tight flesh of her breasts in her hands, the tips of her fingers reaching for the taut nipples, and she squeezed gently, forcing the blood into the cul-de-sac, making the peach-pink cones bulge deliciously as the stretched skin fought to contain the fullness. Then the palms of her hands moved away, letting her fingers linger lightly at the very tips of her breasts, brushing the twin points, seeming to marvel at their sharpness as they swelled to the bursting point.

Almost dreamily her hands moved toward the buckle of the belt. Languidly, she flicked it open. Still her eyes never left her target. It was all for him as she unwrapped his present, and the amazement in his beaten face was confirmation that every move she made was making more certain the union that must be.

The buckle clinked against the clasp and dangled free at her waist. She reached up with her body, and wriggled once, twice, three times as she thrust down on the jeans with both hands, stripping away the soft blue denim that clung to the heat of her like a second skin. The shirt cascaded out, tenting her flat midriff, and draping the neat line of her belly button, drifting across her pulsing breasts.

Surrounded by the crumpled denim the pure whiteness of the Bloomie's bikini briefs merged delightfully with the honey-roasted skin of her taut, adolescent thighs, already streaked with desire.

"Do you like me?" asked her eyes. "Do you like the look of my body? Do you want me now as you wanted me once before in a distant life at a distant time?"

She tossed back her head, proud of the visual banquet that she was, as her thumbs found the elastic of her panties. She eased them down, allowing the dripping, shining hair to emerge with tantalizing slowness. As she did so she pushed out from her pelvis until there was nothing in the room but the perfect triangle of love and the pouting pink lips nestling at its center. Jami pushed away the panties, draping them like a rope bridge across her straining thighs, and she moved, and thrust, sending the denim jeans slipping toward her ankles. For a second or two she stood quite still as the air filled with the scent of her passion, and then her right hand moved toward the thrilling core of her. Her finger ran through the slippery, downy hair and she rested her hand against the hot, velvet softness, soothing her sensual anguish as she swayed with longing.

She pushed against herself as her eyes impaled her victim. He was hers more completely than he had been anyone's. His slumped shoulders said it, and his parted lips, his heaving chest proclaimed it.

It was time. Time to reclaim all her yesterdays and to make possible all her tomorrows.

"Come here," whispered Jami Ramona.

TEN

Paula nuzzled her chin against her white T-shirt and hunched the shoulders of her black blazer up around her neck. Carefully she studied the knees of her faded Levi's and her ice-cream-for-the-feet L.A. Gear candy-striped laceless high tops. She burrowed her back against the blue glazed Deco tiles of the wall of the Mann's Plaza cinema in Westwood, and she prayed to heaven that nobody would recognize her. The sign on the marquee above her head gave away her game. STARRING ROBERT HARTFORD . . . it read.

She had gotten there early enough to find a place to park in the lot opposite, and already the line was snaking around the side of the cinema. She breathed in deeply, steadying herself for the ordeal of the surrogate meeting with the movie star, and she looked up at the pink-and-blue mackerel sky, the clouds arranged in shoals like the aquamarine sea off the Florida Keys. Soon it would be dark, thank the Lord, and nobody would be able to watch her doing the thing she was ashamed of doing—seeing Robert Hartford again.

For the millionth time she tried to make sense of what had happened between them, before the dreadful confrontation. Something? Nothing? Not much? He had seemed far more than intrigued by her, and it had grown in intensity—in the extraordinary emotional closeness by the pool at the Sunset. While the gondolier sang, and Paula's heart leaped in her chest, Robert had made his earth-shattering prediction that they would be lovers. But his reputation as a pursuer of women was legendary. Maybe he had just been practicing on her. Maybe it had all meant zip to him. No! Paula rejected the idea out of hand. Of all the problems she had faced, self-doubt had always been toward the bottom of the list. She was beautiful, and she was good, and one day she would be wise and the world would know that she was the winner she felt herself to be. Robert Hartford had seen those things in her, and he had reacted to them.

"Paula?"

The voice cut into her thoughts, and Paula's head snapped around to find out who had spoken her name.

"Kristina?"

"Hi, what on earth are you doing here?"

Kristina Hartford was already amused, but her question wasn't unkind. She had recognized Paula Hope immediately. It wasn't the sort of face, or body, that you could easily forget.

"Oh . . . just catching a movie," Paula laughed.

"*Daddy's* movie?" Kristina cocked her head to one side. One or two of the kids in the line pricked up their ears at that, but this was L.A., and they pretended not to be listening.

Paula wasn't going to stay on the ropes for long. "Are *you* going to see it?" she countered.

She injected just enough disbelief into the question to suggest that going to see your father's movie was a little unusual, too.

"Yeah, I always do. He likes me to sample the audience reaction." Kristina admired Paula's rebound. She liked the girl. Paula was determined but not pushy, and Kristina hadn't forgotten how she had come to her rescue the night at the ball when her father had put her down. "Hey, are you alone? I am. Could I join you? Like we could see it together."

Paula tried to make sense of her ambivalence. Seeing Robert Hartford again was one thing. Doing it with his daughter was another. Yet it was always more fun with someone else, and the suggestion had come from Kristina. Their first meeting had hardly been peaceful coexistence. It would seem ungracious not to accept.

"Sure." Paula moved sideways to let Kristina join the line. "Looks like a pretty long line. If you'd had to go to the back you might not have made it."

"I could have pulled rank as the star's daughter." Kristina laughed, but she was only half joking. Then her voice went conspiratorial to show she hadn't meant to be flash. "*You* could have gotten in as the star's girlfriend."

A blush exploded all over Paula's face.

"What do you mean?" She blurted out the words.

"Just joking," said Kristina. "But aren't you?"

"Aren't I what?" asked Paula. The couple in front turned around to look at her. Behind her she could sense that the couple was already looking.

"Daddy's girlfriend." Kristina's eyes were twinkling.

"Of course I'm not. I hardly know your father."

"You could have fooled me. I was *there*, you know, at Livingstone's party. By the pool. Remember? Listen, it's no big deal. I didn't mean to embarrass you." Kristina's smile was friendly.

Paula smiled back, allowing the conspiracy. "I'd only ever met him once before that night, and I haven't seen him since."

Kristina looked relieved—then a little suspicious—then relieved again, as she studied Paula's transparently honest face and decided to believe her. Now that she knew Paula was not one of her father's conquests, she somehow wished that she were. God, he could do a lot worse. She felt a surge of warmth toward the pretty young girl.

"Well, all I can say is that I've seen most of Daddy's moves, and, boy, was he shining out to you that night. You'd better believe it."

"He was?"

"I'm *telling* you."

"I imagine he comes on strong to quite a lot of people. I don't mean to criticize, but I guess he has that reputation. . . ."

"For screwing everything that moves!"

"Kristina!" A laugh exploded from Paula's throat at the irreverence. There was a titter from the people in front. Another from those behind.

"Well, it's true. That's why this line goes around the block. But you're pretty special. Young and beautiful and sure of yourself. Daddy likes girls who are perfect."

Paula's smile faded fast at the last bit. Yes, Robert Hartford would like perfection. He would hate the things that marred it.

"You make him sound as if he thinks of women as objects."

"He does. And the funny thing is it's mutual. Sometimes I think he's a bigger sex object than Marilyn Monroe. Most girls want to score him just to say they've been there. I don't think he's ever had a grown-up relationship with anyone."

"Surely with your mother."

"*Especially* not with Mom." Kristina laughed. "The marriage was so short I sometimes wonder where they found the time to conceive me!"

"Gee, Kristina, that's your parents you're talking about."

"Oh, listen, I love Dad. It's just that he's got this one area of weakness that's also his greatest strength. Like, he's a teenager, emotionally locked in a time warp, as if nobody ever taught him how to feel. I can't imagine him falling in love like everyone else, you know, getting married, settling down, having kids. Sometimes I feel like I was a giant mistake. I call him 'Daddy' and he looks at me as if I'm absolutely crazy. It's weird!"

"Must be," said Paula, not at all sure that Robert Hartford as a father would be very nice at all, not even sure that Robert Hartford was very nice, and yet at the same time wanting to hear more and more about him.

"How's the movie doing?" Paula eased the conversation into less personal territory.

"Awesome. The opening weekend was a slam dunk, and that's how you measure a star's box-office power. It did seven and a half thousand per screen the first week. The second week was only off six percent, can you believe?"

"That's good?" asked Paula.

"That's like *totally* rad. If the second week's off anything less than twenty-five percent, it's good. Six is brilliant. It's the way you tell if a movie's going to be a hit or not. This'll do a hundred million domestic. Easy." Kristina's voice was full of infectious enthusiasm. And pride.

The line had started to move in earnest.

"Here we go," said Kristina. "Let's go see how he earns the money."

In the darkness they rearranged the food. Paula wasn't thirsty, and she certainly wasn't hungry, but to steady her nerves she had bought an outsize Cherry Coke and a cardboard box of peculiarly revolting-looking nachos with a glutinous half-cold melted cheese sauce. Over the corn chips she had ladled jalapeños, ketchup, mustard, *and* pickle relish. Kristina, who admitted to already having done a burger at Stratton's Grill, had ordered melted butter with the large carton of popcorn and a Diet Pepsi. All this junk they placed carefully at their feet, knowing as they did so that at some stage of the movie they, or the people who pushed past them, would of course spill the stickiest bits, which would then become attached to the soles of their shoes.

Robert Hartford's above-the-title credit was vast. At last the movie had begun, and the butterflies were free in Paula's stomach. Who was it up there? The man she knew, who lusted after feminine perfection with a fervor that was as crippling to his emotional life as her limp was to her body? Or the celluloid lover, as flawless as the women he sought, slinky smooth, and creamy sweet, fantasy fuel for the theaterful of

escapists who watched him. Both? Neither? A subtle amalgamation of
the two? Paula couldn't decide. At times he veered in one direction;
then he seemed to change course; alternating between nerve-racking
familiarity and equally disturbing obscurity. She tried to get a bead on
it, and slowly it dawned on her that her differing impressions of him
were not subjective. They changed with the roles he played on the
screen. It was basically a father/son AIDS movie, the first of its kind.
Robert Hartford was playing a rich conservative senator with a fading,
insecure wife and a gorgeous, focused ballet-dancer mistress, whose
whole world begins to crumble when his beloved son and potential
political heir gets ill with AIDS. What he finds impossible to come to
terms with is the implication, soon to be dramatically confirmed, that
his son is a homosexual, a way of life that the screen Robert Hartford
has spent the whole of his public life bad-mouthing. The timeless
subplot, whether or not he should break his marriage vows and leave
the wife he respects but no longer loves for the younger woman who
could light up his life, shared equal screen time with the father/son
tearjerker. Paula could sense immediately that the father/son chemistry
was a disaster. The Robert Hartford who recoiled from the exuberantly
good-looking AIDS victim was the Robert Hartford who had rushed
from the room at Livingstone's ball. In those scenes he was a star no
more. He was the man she knew—the good and the bad, the one who
had plumbed the depths of her eyes, the one who hadn't been able to
cope with her deformity. On the other hand, with the ballet dancer
and the wife he was exclusively the legend, the myth, the one-
dimensional Robert Hartford that she had never met, would never
meet. And the fascinating thing was that it was to *this* Robert Hartford
that the audience related. They squirmed almost visibly in their seats
in the father/son bits. They blossomed like flowers in sunlight at the
subplot scenes. The message was inescapable. Robert Hartford and
men was the worst possible karma. Robert Hartford and women was
sweet, fantastic dreams.

So the two sections of Paula watched the two pieces of Robert
Hartford. The public stargazer drooled over his celluloid lovemaking
as it winced at his "heavy" emotional conflict with the gay son, while
the private, infatuated girl identified wildly with his tortured reality as
it was repelled by his stylized Don Juan male/female interactions.

What neither part of her was ready for was the man in front saying,
quite loudly, "If you ask me it's the father who's the fag."

She turned to see if Kristina had heard. Her new friend's resigned
expression, eyes rolling up to the ceiling, said she had.

Paula stared daggers into the back of the bull neck in front of her, outraged that anyone beside herself was even thinking in such analytical terms about Robert Hartford. Immediately she got the picture. The big bodybuilding stiff had lost his girlfriend to the screen lover. She was stretched out beside him, feeding her face and dreaming X-rated dreams. So he had put the boot in. Not that the chick seemed to have heard him. Now he leaned over, and he said it again.

"Sssssh, Bill," she said, without taking her eyes off the screen.

Paula felt the rage well up inside her like a spring of boiling blood. Nobody could talk about Robert like that. It was disgusting. It was untrue. It was out of order. In her anger she forgot totally that he was in the public domain; that the idiot in front had paid good money and was entitled to an opinion; that he was anyway talking about the role, not the actor. She ignored the fact that she had no possible claim on Robert; that Kristina was the person, if any, who could rightfully take exception; that the remark was a private one addressed to someone who was not her. None of those things occurred to her. There was just the vast buzz of dreadful irritation, the shock of the intensely personal insult, and the absolute determination to avenge it.

Paula reached down quickly and she gathered up the Cherry Coke, and the nachos in their appalling box, swimming in the tasteless bright yellow cheese and covered with congealed relish, mustard, ketchup, and peppers. Then she scooped up Kristina's drink and her popcorn with its melted butter. For a second or two she balanced the food like a novice juggler. Then she stood up, leaned over, and emptied it all into the lap of the man in front.

His shriek of enraged surprise shot through the theater.

"Good God," said Kristina, half to herself, half out loud. "The girl's in love."

Robert Hartford sat bolt upright on the chintz sofa, and the expression on his face registered acute discomfort. It was bad enough being alone in a room with a man, but it was far worse when that man was on the verge of tears, and on the edge of revealing all sorts of dreadful personal secrets. Quite apart from anything else, it was so unexpected. Granted the old boy had sounded a bit strange when he'd asked if he could drop by for a drink, but he had given no indication that he would be bringing his amateur dramatic kit with him. So Robert coughed, and craned his neck, and crossed his corduroy-panted legs as he prayed that the unwelcome storm of sentiment would quickly blow itself out.

Francisco Livingstone sat slumped in the green upholstered Hepplewhite shield-back chair opposite, and he tried visibly to hold it all together. There was a thick film of moisture in his rheumy old eyes, and his face looked like the side of an Alp after an avalanche. It was damp and lopsided, and weirdly twisted as if one side was paralyzed, the other in spasm. He held on to the silver-headed cane propped between his legs with both hands, as if it were the precarious support on which his whole life rested, and he spoke in a quavering, reedy voice. "I've done . . . an incredibly stupid . . . thing," he said.

Robert adjusted the famous horn rims on the equally famous nose, sipped petulantly on his neat Glenfiddich, and prayed for his ordeal to be over. At least priests in the confessional didn't have to *watch* the spilling of the beans.

"Can I get you a glass of Armagnac, Francisco? I've got a bottle of Bas Armée, 1848, open. Year of revolutions and all that. Come on. Cheer you up."

Livingstone waved a hand in an ambivalent gesture, but his mind was far from brandy. "I'm afraid . . . Robert, I don't know how to say this. . . . I'm going to have to renege on our deal."

"What do you mean, Francisco?" The Hartford voice, usually soft, was hard as Sheffield steel. There was only one deal.

"I mean the hotel. I can't sell it to you. I have to sell it to Plutarch and Kirkegaard. I have no choice."

Robert Hartford could actually feel his temperature dropping. Inside it was already arctic cold, and the freeze was moving upward and outward at lightning speed. He could feel the icy frost fingers playing on his skin, on the nape of his neck, along his back, pricking like needles in the pits of his arms. Already he was in a new dimension, all fastidious homophobia on hold, all unimportant preferences and dislikes forgotten. This was reality. This was the bottom line.

"We did a deal, Francisco," he said coldly. A deal. In Hollywood, where deals were the Holy Grail. His voice emphasized that fact.

"I know we had a verbal agreement, but I want . . . you to let me out of it. If you don't I'll have to renege anyway. You'd have to sue me. . . ."

Robert shot to his feet. "Francisco! What the *hell* is all this about? What *is* all this bullshit? A deal's a deal. Of all people in this godforsaken town, you should know that. You're the only honorable man I know."

"No, it's finished, Robert. It's over. I can't sell the Sunset to you. God knows I wanted to. But something terrible has happened and it's all my fault. I've blown it. My reputation, a young girl's career. I'm going to jail, Robert, if I don't do what they say."

Robert walked across the intervening space, as he tried to calm down inside. Already the anger was receding, and into the vacuum poured the torrent of his cool, clear intelligence. Things were not as they seemed. They seldom were. All sorts of things had happened to make Livingstone change his mind. Young girls. Jail. A reputation in ruins. The one, two, three added up to blackmail. He walked across the room and placed a hand on the old man's bowed shoulder, and he squeezed gently in a gesture of solidarity.

"Tell me what's happened, Francisco. Tell me everything," Robert said quietly. But already he knew some answers. Livingstone liked young girls. How young? Perhaps, too young. And somebody had found out about it—someone who didn't want Livingstone to sell the Sunset Hotel to Robert Hartford. Someone who would do anything to get what she wanted. Someone exactly like Caroline Kirkegaard. Yes, blackmail and Caroline Kirkegaard would go together like beluga and Stolichnaya. A ray of light burst through the storm clouds as the thought cheered him. Once before he had dumped on Caroline Kirkegaard. But things had changed since then. In those days he had merely had a lease on Hollywood. These days he as good as owned it freehold—sunshine, sushi, and pseudosex. It was his village, his cabbage patch, and in it people could be made to do things, made to leave things undone. That was the whole point of being at the top of the anthill. There was no other point at all. Power was the game's name, and the trick was to *use* it.

"She just rang the door bell, around eleven o'clock last night. . . ." He paused. "I think I will have that glass of brandy, Robert."

Robert walked thoughtfully toward the Sheraton sideboard, and he poured a generous measure of Armagnac from an 1845 Dummers Jersey City works decanter into a wafer-thin balloon glass. He swirled the caramel-colored liquid around the glass once, twice, and then walked back to Francisco.

"I can't tell you how beautiful she was. All my life I don't think I've seen a young girl as lovely."

"How old *was* she, Francisco?"

"Ah, yes. How old? That's the right question, I'm afraid. She was jail bait, all right. Apparently she's fifteen."

"And you didn't know her? Didn't know where she'd come from? She just knocked on your door out of the blue?"

"Yes. Yes. I know it was madness. That's what I feel now. And that's what I felt at first last night. I was going to call security after I'd heard her pitch, but Robert, I mean, you understand things like this, she was special, out-of-this-world lovely, and she just stripped off her clothes. I mean, before I could say anything. She didn't even say her name."

Robert Hartford's eyes widened perceptibly. There were enough bullshitters in Hollywood to tell lies about what girls looked like and what they'd done, but Francisco Livingstone was not one of them. Despite his age, he was a connoisseur. Almost certainly the girl was as special as he maintained. His heart speeded imperceptibly as he contemplated that kind of beauty.

"It sounds crazy, Robert, but somehow I feel you're the only man on earth who could understand what I did. I mean, it was the *moment*. One struggles to get through life despite it, and how many times are there moments like that? You can count them on the fingers of one hand. I was crazy, but somehow I felt that nothing mattered beside the vital importance of owning that beauty, just for an hour or two. Can you begin to comprehend . . .?"

Robert nodded slowly. Yes, he understood that. Too well.

"And, you know, there was something else. She talked a lot of nonsense about being together in another world—you know the Shirley MacLaine stuff—but it felt so right one could almost believe it. Almost." He lowered his head to shield himself from the Hartford eyes.

"You made love to her?"

"Yes."

"And you didn't know how old she was? You didn't ask?"

"No."

At last he parted with the glass of brandy, handing it, almost unwillingly, to Livingstone. "And now she's filed a complaint with the BHPD?"

Livingstone took a long pull at the fiery liquid, and a deep breath before he answered. "No. It's worse than that. If that's all it was I could have brazened it out, bought her off, hushed it up. In the hotel business you do that all the time for others. There'd have been someone to do it for me. No, the awful thing is the girl was used. She's completely innocent. She was set up, and now she stands to lose even more than I do. That's what makes it so damn dreadful." The tears were in his eyes again.

"But what's the problem? You both deny it. It didn't happen. Your word against somebody else's. Easy."

"It's not as simple, Robert. They've got photographs. They sent them round to me this morning."

"Photographs? Christ, Francisco, this isn't a *movie*. This is real life.

What on earth do you mean, 'photographs'? You and the girl took photographs?"

"No, no, of course not. Oh, I don't know, Robert, but they've got some damned photographs. I screwed the girl. I wasn't looking around for bloody photographers. Someone must have got hold of a master key, and either hidden in the room earlier or let themselves in while we were in the bedroom. They shot a roll—on infrared film probably—and slunk out again. I really don't know, but I can't think of any other explanation. I *do* know they have the negatives because they sent the prints round this morning. There's absolutely no mistaking the pair of us. We're clearly identifiable."

"Who sent the photographs?"

"Caroline Kirkegaard."

Again Robert nodded, frowning as he concentrated. "Who's making the complaint? The girl's mother? If the girl's not complaining, why should the cops worry? They can't know how old she is from the photographs. All they'll know is you're a dirty old man."

He couldn't resist the oblique dig, but immediately he regretted it. Cheap shots made *you* cheap, not anyone else.

Livingstone ignored it. The things on his mind were more important. "It seems she's rather famous and that the whole world knows she's only fifteen. Apparently she's one of those hot-shot teeny-bopper models."

"What's her name?"

"Jami Ramona."

Robert Hartford's eyebrows shot up.

"*The* Jami Ramona," he said quickly, his tone incredulous.

"You've heard of her?"

Robert Hartford took a deep breath and he looked at Francisco Livingstone as if he were seeing him for the very first time. "Good *God*," he said at last, as if in the front pew at church, "*you* screwed Jami Ramona?"

Livingstone, however, didn't appreciate the nuances of what he had achieved. He plowed on. "The photographs would tell the cops that, and if they showed them to the media as well, the pressure on them to act would be enormous. They'd have to indict me. They'd have to send me down. The girl apparently has product endorsement contracts coming out of her ears. They all have morals clauses these days. Her career would be history if this came out, quite apart from what happens to me."

Robert Hartford felt the anger rushing back. Livingstone was a big boy even if an ill one and an old one. If he chose to sail close to the wind, despite all his years of experience, then there was a sense in which he deserved what was coming to him, but the girl, the beautiful young girl—Jami Ramona—ruined at fifteen by Caroline Kirkegaard in a scheme to do Robert out of the hotel he dreamed of owning. *That* was something else.

"Don't worry, Francisco. There's a way out of this. I know there is. There always is. This is our town. Between us we know everyone. Chief Terrlizese, Senator Chilton, the newspaper people. We can keep the lid on it."

Livingstone shook his head. "The story'd go nationwide. It's too big."

Again he bowed his head, as if ashamed of the words he now spoke. "I'm not proud of it, but you know, Robert, I've always *cared* what people thought of me. All my life I've had a reputation as a gentleman, and I've never really been one, not by birth, not by behavior. But it's been my vanity to create that image, and the Sunset Hotel has been a part of it. Grand, upper class, effortlessly 'correct.' Now I am exposed as a molester of children. At the end of my life I would become a disgusting joke and all the enemies through the years would have their revenge. It's too much to ask of me, Robert. I can save my reputation and a young girl's reputation by doing what they want. I know I promised you the hotel, but you're young, you have another career, a brilliant one. I'm sorry, but you have to help me."

Robert didn't answer directly.

"Has Kirkegaard contacted you, apart from sending the photographs? Was there a note?"

"She telephoned. She said that she had the negatives, and that the police and the media would get the photographs unless I agreed to sell her the Sunset Hotel. She gave me forty-eight hours to make my decision."

"How on *earth* did she get Jami Ramona to do what she did?" That was *really* worrying Robert, and not just because it was a loose end in the story. The memory of the Ramona body was fresh in his mind from the Herb Ritts photographs in the latest *Vanity Fair*, from the Bruce Weber ones in last month's *L.A. Style.*

"I just don't know. But I think it's to do with all that Destiny business. Caroline Kirkegaard has total control over some of those followers of hers. It's like Scientology, or Jim Jones, and all those Moonies. You know, cults and charismatic leaders and people looking for answers and meanings, and a way to irritate their parents. The only thing I can think is she filled her full of rubbish about us being lovers in a past life or something and the girl believed it. It's not our world, Robert, but it's Kirkegaard's and Plutarch's and apparently Jami Ramona's. That's why I never wanted to sell her the hotel in the first place."

"You're sure Ramona's not in on it."

"I'm certain. And if she is, and she's prepared to blow her entire career and be exposed to public ridicule just so that Caroline Kirkegaard can get what she wants, then she's been brainwashed and she needs help badly. Either way, it's not her fault."

"I agree." Robert seemed relieved by that. He buried his head in his hands and for a few seconds gave himself over to the contemplation of Caroline Kirkegaard's wickedness. Ripping off the gullible was one thing. This was quite another. It showed a murderous ruthlessness. In shark city that was not unheard of, but Robert Hartford didn't like it to happen around him. That was for the early days when the career was vulnerable as a newborn baby, and when the rules had to be bent by whatever tool came to hand. But now, in the rarefied echelons of haute Beverly Hills life, it was totally unacceptable. And the poor young girl, little Jami Ramona with the body of an angel and the face of a goddess. He twisted his hand up into a tight ball and he buried it in the other one, as if grinding something in a mortar.

Then slowly, like a beautiful vision forming from a vapor cloud, the idea came to him. There was a way out. A wonderful way out. One that would use the most powerful weapon that he possessed. At a stroke he would win back the hotel he coveted, save the reputation and career of a beautiful young girl, and allow a poor old man to die in peace and dignity. And once again he would cast down Caroline Kirkegaard into the dirt where she belonged. Yes, he would use his most fearsome weapon.

He would use himself.

They circled each other like gladiators in some ancient arena. But although they knew they were adversaries, locked in a battle to the death that only one could win, there was a closeness they shared: the hate that one further twist of the wheel could turn to love; the universal scorn of perennial winners for the losing lost; the common ground of those who wanted with the desperation of the obsessed.

"I wasn't sure you'd come," said Robert Hartford, his smile laden with impish charm.

"How could I refuse red roses from the latter-day Valentino?"

replied Caroline Kirkegaard. She smiled too, a ripe, sun-filled smile, that balanced the Hartford flirtation ounce for precious ounce.

Both knew that the charade was a lie, and, paradoxically and to the surprise of each, they knew, too, that it was no such thing.

She watched him as she might a lion, a healthy dose of caution mixed in with the respect, and she wondered as she did so just what it was she felt. For so long it had been so easy to loathe him. In those distant days he had destroyed her with the casual disinterest of a child pulling the wings from a fly, because she was strong and because she was a competitor. For that, and for that alone, he had capriciously ruined her movie career. In the early days of desert wound-licking, out by the Salton Sea, she had fed on her hatred, as she had discovered that her friends were impostors and her acquaintances had acquired a selective amnesia with regard to her name. Later she had learned that the open expression of anger was not the L.A. way. To become powerful you had to be cool, at least on the outside. It had been part of her growing up, and since then she had left her own victims strewn casually across the dreamscape in which only the strong survived and only the strongest triumphed.

Her smile turned inward as she took the laughing cocktail from his hand, and placed its frothing wetness against her lips. Was there anything more beautiful than an old rival setting himself up for the biggest fall of all? The roses had come straight out of the blue, and the card had said everything in the bold, straightforward handwriting of the superstar: "Dear Caroline, No hard feelings. Have dinner with me, and let's start again. Tonight at eight?" It had been signed "The new owner of the Sunset Hotel."

So Francisco Livingstone hadn't had the guts to tell him the deal was off. So he didn't know about Jami Ramona and the extraterrestrial lovemaking. So he was blissfully ignorant of the glossy photographs rubbing up against each other in her Coldwater Canyon safe, and the license they had given her to buy the hotel the idiot thought was his. Well, that was fine, because any moment now she would reveal him as being the biggest fool in Beverly Hills, where, to say the very least, the fools did not come small.

She sipped at the drink, her eyes sparkling, her tongue playing at the rim of the V-shaped cocktail glass. Already she had taken in the scene. It was to be that Hollywood institution—a Robert Hartford candlelit dinner for two—and her heart was singing as she realized what it meant.

"I hope you don't mind it being just the two of us. I should have

mentioned it before. I just thought that we had so much to discuss
. . ." He left the rest of it hanging in the air where it hung best,
allowing the glass candlesticks of the arched dining alcove, the elegant
Waterford crystal, the effortlessly patrician Limoges china to speak for
him.

The waiter hovered in the background, seen but not heard, fussing
with the table, reorganizing the cymbidium orchids, turning the
frosted white Burgundy in the silver bucket, refolding the already
immaculately folded Irish linen napkins.

"Dinner alone with Robert Hartford. Is there any other way?" She
couldn't quite hide the element of mockery, didn't really try to.

He held his glass up toward her. "To my hotel," he said, in
retaliation. "Can you drink to that?"

"Of course, Robert. Any night. Any day. To the Sunset Hotel and
its new owner." Caroline smiled mysteriously.

Both shared the identical thought. What fun it was to drink to
yourself when your audience thought you were drinking to it.

"Let's sit down for a minute or two. I asked for dinner at eight-thirty
if that's okay. It's not really cool enough for a fire, but I think they're
one of the great pleasures of life, don't you?"

He steered her toward the flickering fire. Real logs. No nonsense
with piped gas. The essence of scrub oak and eucalyptus flavored the
air. They sat down side by side on the huge sofa—black and white, oil
and water—held together by nefarious purpose. And something else?
The attraction of opposites? The mutual attraction of the stupendously
attractive?

"You've come a long way, Caroline."

"You, too, Robert."

Both smiled. Meritocrats were always proud of their journeys, in
contrast to aristocrats, who rejoiced in the lack of them.

"If I made it more difficult for you in the early days, I'm sorry." He
looked down at a perfect fingernail as he delivered the almost-apology.

"The early days are supposed to be difficult. If it hadn't been you,
it would have been someone else."

They were moving around the edges of it. The conciliation had a
purpose. Everything was occurring on two quite different levels.

It was the body that was getting to him. Somehow it defined a new
type of woman, perhaps a new age of femininity. It was a milestone,
like a Rubens *grande dame*, or an anorectic sixties model, symbolic of
things to come, and of a violent break with the immediate past. As a
connoisseur Robert Hartford wanted to see it, to feel it, to taste it, to

smell it. He wanted to hear the sounds it made when it did the things its predecessors had done—and yet there was something so dreadfully unwholesome about her, so wicked, so alarmingly "wrong." As he watched her, his whole being seemed to be split down the middle. His intellect was well aware that she was deadly, a woman who had and would stop at nothing to get what she wanted, but at the same time his emotions drew him mothlike toward her flickering flame. What did he want? The destruction of the blackmailing woman who had dared to cross him, or her superhard body melting against his? Could he allow himself to want both?

The mist of ambivalence was floating across Caroline, too. In a few hours he would know how she had triumphed over him, and her first act would be to rub his face in the dirt as he had rubbed hers so many years ago. Like a thief in the night, he would be ejected from her hotel, where he had lived for years, and she would personally supervise as her employees piled his possessions on the lawns and walkways for any passing nobody to gawk at. But right now, this minute, there was no denying the animal urgency of his attraction. The legend wafted among the liquid charm, the boyish charisma oiled the magical gestures, the scent of his sexuality insinuated itself into her nostrils. Would he take her, after dinner, as he was supposed to do—unable to resist doing the thing he was famous for doing so well? And would it be wonderful? Would he ring the bells that nobody had ever really rung, and, if not, could she then close forever the chapter of sex, that fifties, sixties, seventies thing that the eighties had been unsure about, and the nineties would do without?

He turned toward her, and his concentration was immense. She was the only woman in the room, but she was also the only person in the world. His expression said he was fascinated by her, and there was no point in hiding it.

"I'm so *glad* you came tonight," he murmured, in the voice that made womankind feel all right.

3

The finger of the flashlight poked around the darkness. At first its attention seemed random, but then its motions became more regular, the searchlight of the guardpost sweeping the blackness with remorseless efficiency. The bits of the room came together, pieces of a puzzle forming the picture—the arm of a chair, the corner of a print, the edge of an Indian dhurrie. There was total silence. Nothing moved, except the thin beam of restless light.

It was looking for something, and now the slight sound of footsteps insinuated itself into the quiet as the intruder began to move around the room. It was the walls that seemed of most interest. The beam combed them from ceiling to floor, lingering on the postage-stamp pictures, before discarding them and moving on.

The fireplace flashed into view, with its plain mahogany mantel and its cargo of engraved invitations. The light lingered hopefully, and then it moved upward. The large oil painting was less valuable than its ornate frame, and the flowers it depicted looked like they could use some water, but the beam was pleased. It steadied, and the intruder moved toward it.

A hand, gloved in black, reached up to touch the intricate carving of the wood, before running along the borders of the picture.

In the stillness, the sigh was an explosion, as breath whistled from lungs that had been holding it too long.

Caroline pushed the plate a symbolic inch toward the center of the table, and she wondered when she had last eaten so well. Succulent clams, not too big, not too small, with lemon, pepper, and the delicious shallots in vinegar that were so difficult to find outside France; a tender, juicy chicken Kiev crisp outside, soft and creamy inside with lightly cooked spinach in which she could *taste* the iron, and the newest potatoes she had ever had, painted with mint, brushed with butter, firm and round; finally, a raspberry tart, the pride of the Sunset's world-renowned pastry chef, washed down with a nectar-sweet Château Coutet from the vineyard south of Bordeaux.

It wasn't however the pleasant sensation of fullness in her tummy that was in the forefront of her consciousness. It was the far more substantial feeling deep in the depths of her.

Across the table was its cause. His face bathed in the candlelight, the twinkling eyes of the star searched hers for the evidence of his effect. All through the delicious meal he had shone out at her, and the rheostat of his attraction had been turned endlessly upward. It had been a virtuoso performance as he had run the gamut of his seductive skills, melding the different roles brilliantly, discarding one at the very point it had peaked, replacing it with another that merged in perfect harmony with the part relinquished. The enthusiasm of the child, touching in its eager simplicity, became at the very point of its maximum effect the vulnerability of the little boy lost on the sea of pointless fame. The ruthless businessman retreated at the pinnacle of his success into the altruistic philosopher, wise and kind, as the man of Mammon became in turn the artist, the pragmatist, the dreamer. He hinted of his riches as he laughed at them, and he talked of his power as he scorned it—and all the time his beauty shone on her, like the light reflecting from a many-faceted gemstone, always different, ultimately the same. Despite her valiant efforts to remain objective, Caroline Kirkegaard was hypnotized and the feeling within her said that it mattered not at all that at long last the biter had been bitten.

One thing she knew. Never again would she have a chance to sample this exotic fruit, and when he discovered what she knew, Robert Hartford would regret this evening with every fiber of his being for every second of his life. So she relaxed and allowed the wonderful feeling to build beneath the expert gaze of its creator.

The waiter seemed unnerved by the electric currents that crackled in the warm air of the room. "Can I offer you a glass of champagne, ma'am?" He held the already opened bottle, its glass misty with the cold, so that Caroline could see the label and the year.

"No, thank you," she said.

He moved around the table to Robert Hartford. "Sir?"

"No, thank you, Klaus. I think that will be everything. Oh, and Klaus, can you thank Monsieur Bosquet for me? Tell him he surpassed himself."

"Certainly, sir. Have a pleasant evening, sir. Madam."

"Thank you, Klaus. Oh, Klaus, on your way out can you leave the front door ajar. It's a little hot in here and I can't bear the air conditioning. I'll close it later."

"Of course, sir. Thank you, sir."

He was gone. They were alone.

"It was a wonderful dinner, Robert."

"It's a wonderful evening, Caroline."

"Shall we go and sit by the fire?" This time it was her suggestion. He stood up.

"Of course," he murmured.

⇉

The safe was behind the painting. The flashlight picked it out. It was small, with a combination lock, and the gloved hand moved over it eagerly, flicking the dial with the practiced ease of the expert. Two wires, two microphones emerged from the darkness, and soon their black suction caps were stuck fast to the dull bronze of the safe and the dial was spinning beneath the knowing fingers. It happened fast. A click. Another. A third, and the door was open.

The light exploded from the safe, reflected by the quartz crystal that seemed to fill the interior. But there was something else inside, and it was for the manila envelope that the hand reached.

All through dinner Robert had played her like a fine musical instrument, and he had watched her fall through cold cynicism, warmer amusement, and dawning interest into hot desire. Now, on the sofa, she was ready for him and the unescapable truth was that, despite himself, he was ready for her too.

She didn't move away as he moved nearer to her. They never did. If anything she leaned toward him like a flower toward light, inclining delicately toward his face, and his moist, inviting lips.

"Were you always as beautiful as this?" he murmured, his words wafting over her, fanning the flames that flickered in her eyes.

It wasn't a question that needed an answer. It was the delicate lubricant that would ease the slide to surrender. His hand on the back of the sofa behind Caroline's head moved imperceptibly, ready, willing, but not finally committed until the response had been received.

Caroline Kirkegaard felt herself letting go.

For the last two and a half hours she had wanted this, but she had never discarded her alternative plan. One false move, one heavy-handed gesture, and she would have struck back with the weapon of ridicule. If making love to Robert Hartford was the best way to end an evening with him, then turning him down after a clumsy advance would be its equal. So she waited to the very last moment to see how it would end.

But it never ended. One moment merged into the next. There was no actual moment when the lovemaking began. Perhaps it had started the second she had walked through his front door.

One moment they were apart. The next they were together. No decisions. No choices. Just the inevitable union.

His mouth melted against hers, and his fingers landed on the warm skin at the nape of her neck. Both touches were light, soft as the touch of a hummingbird at the face of a flower.

At first it was just his lips, millimeters apart, moving against hers, touching, ceasing to touch, touching again as they moved across the surface of hers, breathing out, breathing in. It seemed she was washed by his breath, as it rippled in waves at the gates of her nostrils. His scent was inside her, strong, and clever, full of the reassuring maleness that so very few men possessed, and, as she lay tight against him, allowing him to orchestrate the sensual dance, she felt his left hand at her breast.

It was enough. Deep inside the burning fuse reached the tinder box, and the explosion of lust shook her body. A spectator no more, she reached for him, one hand grabbing his neck, the other tearing at the breast he touched. Her mouth opened to devour him and her tongue darted out to find the wetness that his lips concealed. With her left hand she drew him into her, grinding his beautiful face against hers, and with her right she reached down into the bodice of the loose cotton dress, ripping back the flimsy material and freeing the magnificent breast for the fingers that sought it.

Paula hurried along the jasmine-scented path, clutching the folder of transparencies beneath her arm. She wasn't looking forward to this, and at the same time she was longing for it. As she walked, subconsciously trying to hide the limp that had so appalled Robert Hartford the last time they had met, she rehearsed what she would say to him: "Sorry to bother you, Mr. Hartford, but Winty wanted me to drop these transparencies around right away . . ."

She would keep it businesslike and brisk. Winthrop had been offered a whole series of the most fabulous David Hockney lithographs, but the artist wanted a quick answer. If Robert liked them, then they could be a major feature of the redecoration plan at the Sunset.

Winty had been adamant that Robert should see the transparencies right away, and he had asked Paula to drop them off at his bungalow. Reluctantly, she had agreed. Now she wondered if he could look her in the eye after the weird business at the Livingstone ball, and she wondered too, if she would be able to look him in his. She spent all her days thinking about him, but she still hadn't worked out what she felt. Above all, she remembered his beauty and his so-casual charm, the wonderful things he had said to her and the care-filled way he had said them and, although she wasn't sure she could forgive him, she was already certain she couldn't forget him.

She had arrived, and she took a deep breath as she reached for the door, noticing as she did so that it was open.

On an impulse she didn't bother with the bell. Instead she walked inside.

Her spirits rose as she tiptoed across the gray marble of the entrance hall. Where would he be? What would he be doing? Making himself some scrambled eggs in the kitchen? Catching an old movie on TV like the rest of the world? Flicking through a script with those wonderful glasses perched on the end of that wonderful nose?

The big mahogany double doors to what would be the drawing room were closed, and Paula, straining her ears for conversation, heard nothing. She took a quick look around, intrigued to find herself in the superstar's home. The walls stared back at her, giving nothing away, a reasonably good Picasso bullfight etching in a fine frame on one, and a walnut-and-gilt mirror, safe but unexciting, on the other. The stippled terra-cotta paintwork was surrounded by a bright floral-patterned orange-and-yellow material border, and the restrained, understated feel of the hallway was emphasized by the plain stone of the floor. The light, not quite enough of it, came from a run-of-the-mill china lamp with a flat, cream triangular shade.

Paula suppressed the frisson of guilt that she was trespassing. He wouldn't mind. She was there on his business, and anyway, surprising him in his own lair might help to even up the scoreboard. She crept toward the doors, and turned one of the brass knobs gently.

The visual hit her right between the eyes. Both their backs were to the door, but they were turned to face each other, and the roaring kiss had reached the critical stage. She was big and blond, and it looked like she was actually eating him. Her wide wet mouth ripped at his, and the muscles on her bare forearms stood out like ropes as she forced his head in toward her. He would certainly need dentistry to recover from the ferocious onslaught, at the very least stitches, possibly major surgery. But it was also obvious that Robert Hartford was a million miles from pain. The thing that clinched it was the vast breast overflowing from his left hand. It was a milk lake, a butter mountain, a mighty mound of smooth vanilla with a hot tip, chocolate dark, and it sent Paula's stomach on a roller-coaster churner as the nausea gripped her.

She was rooted to the spot, but inside all sorts of things were happening, all kinds of questions were being answered. Mainly anger, and frustration and disbelief and all the other myriad of human emotions that went under the umbrella heading of "jealousy."

Her voice was sharp as an icepick when at last she spoke. "Don't you just wonder where those lips have *been?*" she snarled.

He spun around, the shock all over his face, his lips bruised and wet with Caroline's saliva. "What on earth . . . ?"

"You should close your front door," she said with a sickly smile that barely disguised the murder in her heart.

Robert Hartford went through the motions of trying to stand, but his position, twisted around, off balance, his hand still locked behind Caroline's neck, was against it. He half rose, half fell back, and all the time his face changed color—pale pink, red, vermilion.

"What the *hell* are you doing in my house?" he finally managed to explode.

But already his anger lacked conviction, subdued by the pleasure he felt at seeing her.

She stood there, absolutely furious, her beautiful face beautifully twisted with rage, and he knew that she was cross because she was jealous and that made it all right. Women in Robert's world were allowed to feel such things. They were positively encouraged to do so, because it meant that they *cared*.

Paula knew she had no prior claims on Robert Hartford. At the most they had exchanged a few looks, a few meaningless phrases. It wasn't any of her business whom he kissed, and anyway she had absolutely no right at all to come barging into his home. But her emotions told her reason that Robert Hartford belonged to *her*.

"I'll tell you what the *hell* I'm doing here. I'm working for you, in case you hadn't realized. I brought these over for you to have a look at." With great deliberation she emptied the contents of the folder onto the floor. The transparencies cascaded into an untidy heap on the thick pile of the carpet.

"How was I to know you were trying to swallow Silicon Valley?" she added.

"Listen, sweetheart . . ." Caroline Kirkegaard's face was halfway between amusement and irritation as she tried to speak.

"Oh, shut up, you freak, or I'll report you to your plastic surgeon."

"Don't you dare come sneaking into my house and insulting my guests and me. Don't you know how to knock? Couldn't you ring the bell?" said Robert, his tone milder than his words.

Inside he was in love with the plastic-surgeon crack. The girl was full of spunk. She was terrific. And most of her anger seemed to be directed at Caroline.

But not, apparently, all.

"Listen, you're the one with the reputation for knocking, and ringing bells. Although from your vacuum-cleaner act it looks like you're more of a marshmallow than a stud."

His mouth dropped wide open. Nobody spoke to Robert Hartford even halfway like that. If they did, and got away with it, it would mean that his starlight was dimming.

"Don't talk to me like that. Don't talk to me like that." He was standing now, shaking with a newborn rage, and his face pulsated as he spat out the words. Who did this girl think she *was*?

Beside him on the sofa Caroline Kirkegaard's smile returned. Robert Hartford was getting his at long last.

"I'll talk to you exactly how I *want* to talk to you," said Paula quietly. "And you'd better watch what you say or maybe I'll *limp* all over you."

"Get out! Get out of here or I'll fucking throw you out!" He took a step toward her.

Paula held up her hands in mock surrender. "Okay, okay, I'm going quietly." She smirked as she backed toward the door. "Apoplexy can't be healthy at your advanced age. I wouldn't want to be responsible for that . . ."

She paused for the Parthian shot.

"*Or* the kiss of life. . . ."

ELEVEN

The canyon dawn was crisp and foggy, the mist clinging to the foothills, the soft rumble of the traffic blanketed by the moist air. Caroline shuddered in her dressing gown as she walked across the bedroom. The condensation was thick on the windows and she peered out into the early morning, her mind stiff with resolve despite the cold. It was the best time for meditation, before the day had begun and the night had ended.

She walked quickly to the bathroom and threw off the robe, allowing the icy air to touch her nakedness as she watched herself in the full-length mirror. All around the room, the walls were covered with photographs of the Sunset Hotel. They were everywhere, taped to the mirror, piled high on the marble surfaces around the basin, propped up around the bath. It was the same in the kitchen and the den, and the other rooms that people never saw. Caroline was surrounded by the thing she wanted, so that she could never forget it. The pictures kept her focused on her obsession, seeping into her mind by osmosis. She called them her treasure maps, and she encouraged her Destiny disciples to use them, too.

Maybe an actress wanted a part in a sitcom or movie. Okay, Caroline would tell her to wallpaper her house with the symbols of what she wanted—photographs of the producer, the casting guy, the writers, and the stars. She should have the name of the show made upin neon shining from the wall of her bedroom; have the theme song play on endless loop on the piped stereo system; run the repeats time after time on the VCR. That was the treasure-map trick. Live it, love it, be it, become it, until Fate surrendered and Luck gave up. Pray for it, breathe it, dream it, die for it, until they tired of resistance and welcomed you home. Aim for it, relax in it, enjoy it, experience it, until you controlled the destiny you were destined to control.

She took a deep breath and walked out, across the bedroom, along the landing, down the stairs to the den.

The crystal was always locked away in the safe, and now she pulled back the picture from the wall and reached for the combination dial. Usually the crystal was alone in there—the only truly valuable thing she possessed—but today it had company. The manila envelope and the incriminating Livingstone/Ramona photos it contained *was* the Sunset Hotel. Her hotel. The one she now effectively owned.

Caroline dialed the combination. 10123. The number of her bank account at the Crédit Suisse in Zurich.

The crystal shone back at her dully in the almost-light. But before she touched it she reached for the photographs. A quick look at the teenage raver and her heart-stopping body would be better than a six-alarm electric fire.

The smooth bottom of the safe slipped beneath her searching fingers and a shaft of panic slithered into her body as she realized that the folder was no longer there.

It had gone, but a single photograph had been left behind. The crystal swayed away to the wall of the safe as she ripped out the glossy photograph on which it rested.

In the gloom it was clear. It wasn't Jami Ramona and it wasn't Francisco Livingstone. It was a photograph of Robert Hartford, and there was writing on it. The mauve pen was quite definite. "To Caroline Kirkegaard. Thanks for an unforgettable evening. A memento from the owner of the Sunset Hotel."

Robert Hartford loved the spa at the Sunset Hotel in the early morning. It wasn't just the wall-to-wall women, although they were the main attraction. It was the high ceilings and the lack of space meanness; the immaculately clean beige carpeted sprung floor of the aerobics area; the acres of sparkling mirrored glass that allowed him to see how very beautiful he was. Of course there was Nautilus, but there was also the full range of Eagle equipment for those who preferred to torture their muscles that way, and there were hydraulic water-resistance machines for aficionados of muscle pain, and weights, and bars and swimming machines and Stairmasters, treadmills, and bicycles. Machines read your blood pressure and printed out your physiological truths, and they took your pulse through the palms of your hands, telling you when to work harder, when to relax, and how many of the dreaded calories you had actually burned. And through it all, like angels in paradise, wandered the women whose bodies he wanted to *have*. The instructresses wore identical leotards so that he could pick them out from the clients who would otherwise have resembled them. They were cut high to show lots of thigh, and the mind-bending bodies they enclosed, all strutting muscle and sleek brown skin, were out there on the surface setting the example that just had to be followed.

"Hi, Lisa," said Robert as he loped through the entrance foyer into the temple of the body beautiful.

"Good morning, Mr. Hartford. Those new towels you wanted have come in. They're real neat."

The receptionist glowed at the sight of him.

"Well done, Lisa. I'll try one out today. Is Grace in yet?"

Big and butch, a Beverly Hills police officer who worked at the Sunset gym in her spare time, Grace was the nearest thing to a man that Robert Hartford could tolerate.

"Yes, sir. She's in the staff room. I'll call through immediately and say that you're here."

He nodded briskly, pleased by the beautiful girl's deference.

He walked over to the rack and selected a pair of twenty-pound weights. "Hi, Robert. Is it true you're to be the new landlord?" said the wonderful-looking girl next to him.

He smiled enigmatically. "Would you promise to keep coming if I was, Heather? I could make it a contractual obligation of the seller to deliver you."

Heather Locklear was a star with a *really* good body. In Hollywood, mockingbird's teeth were more common than that.

"Try to keep me away from the Sunset. I want to be buried here."

"Not a bad idea. Live, love, and die at the Sunset Hotel."

The sound of a commotion wafted in from the lobby, puncturing the pleasantries. "Where *is* he? The front desk *said* he was in here. *Show* me where Robert Hartford is or I'll break your neck . . ."

Caroline Kirkegaard strode into the room close on the heels of her furious words. She wore a one piece Dance France leotard, jet black with red ankle socks. Chains were draped from a black leather band around her neck and twin thongs ran across her bondaged chest to an identical belt. Her furious searchlight eyes scanned the room and settled on Robert. The moment he saw her, a smile of beatific anticipation lit up his face.

"You cheap crook," she hissed. "You had some criminal rob my house." She rushed up to him, but two feet away she stopped, as if deflected by an invisible force field.

"What on earth can you mean, Caroline? What was stolen? What did the cops say? I thought I was having dinner with you last night."

"That's what I'm saying. You knew the house was empty," she hissed. "You arranged for someone to rob my safe. I'm going to bring charges. You're history, Robert. You're going to do time." She was trembling with a terrible anger, her lush lips, the ones he could still *taste*, working the syllables of hate.

"Money? Jewelry, Caroline? Surely not bearer bonds." He rocked backward and forward, his eyes twinkling, as he savored his moment of triumph.

"Personal things . . ." she spluttered in desperation. The defeat was all over her face. She couldn't file a complaint about the burglary of porno pix that she was intending to use in a blackmail attempt. Anyway, Robert had an alibi. And there had been no forced entry, no damage to the safe, no evidence of an intrusion of any kind, still less any information that tied Hartford to the shadowy "crime." The best she could hope for from the cops would be a polite "don't waste our time," and at worst she could open a hornets' nest if Hartford, Livingstone, and Ramona teamed up against her.

"So you lose again, Caroline. It's getting to be a habit," he said quietly.

She leered at him horribly.

"So the dear old Sunset becomes a knock shop for jaded movie stars," she said.

"At least it'll be safe from the storm troopers of the Destiny movement," he replied.

The sweat stood out on the Kirkegaard skin like dew on a Smoky Mountain morning. Her treasure maps. Her future. The future that *must* be. It suddenly looked about as certain as a sure thing in the second race.

She tried to turn the venom in her mind into liquid form as she hissed her words at Hartford. "I hate you, Robert Hartford. God, how I hate you. And I *swear*, you will be sorry you ever crossed me."

Robert reached for one of the telephones that were strategically placed around the gym. He spoke into the receiver lazily, unhurriedly, but his voice was thick with power.

"Security? Robert Hartford speaking. Get a couple of your biggest boys up to the spa, will you? There's a thing posing as a woman up here and I want you to throw it out of my hotel."

Paula slunk into the room like a thief in the night, her head held low, her spirits lower. She hadn't slept a wink. When jealousy had pushed her to one side of the bed, shame had tossed her back to the other. All night long she had wondered how she could have behaved as she had. After all, if Robert Hartford couldn't kiss who he wanted to in the sanctity of his own drawing room it wasn't much of a world. How had she summoned up the gall to think that he owed her any sort of fidelity? He probably had forgotten her name, even her face, and yet she had behaved like a wronged wife, or a crossed mistress. In retaliation, probably at this very meeting, he would blot her out as if she had never been. Thank God, he hadn't arrived yet.

"Hello, darling. Goodness, you look like you've just donated your last drop of blood. You make me feel positively 'healthy,' not at all a pleasant sensation. Are you all right?"

Winthrop Tower stood up as Paula slid into the boardroom. So did the owllike figure in the big round red plastic sunglasses.

"Sweethearts, do you know each other? This is Paula Hope, my assistant, and this, of course, is David Hockney, who actually prefers Southern California to Bradford, despite the shortage of Marmite, Weetabix and bloater paste. Shows you how perverse he is, doesn't it, dear?"

"Morning, Winty. Hi, David," said Paula, sinking down into the chair that Tower had pulled back for her as if she wanted it to swallow her whole.

The boardroom of the Sunset Hotel seemed to have been designed to enjoy the short silence that followed. The carpet was so thick it swallowed sound and threatened to drown ankles. The shining mahogany of the table was a hymn to order, as were the Sheraton dining-room chairs, and the Thomas Eakins oil of boats on a river that hung over the Adams fireplace. Only the tinkle of the coffee cups on the sideboard, receiving hot Kenyan coffee from a pear-shaped eighteenth-century silver pot, disturbed the rather aggressive calm.

"You all right, luv?" asked Hockney in an accent that sounded to Paula just like Graham's, although any Englishman would have been able to put 350 miles between them.

"Sort of," said Paula. "I didn't sleep last night," she added as explanation.

"Nights aren't for sleeping. Mornings are. That's why God made curtains—to keep out the sun while one's asleep," said Winthrop definitely.

"Is Robert Hartford coming?" asked Paula.

"That's why we're all here, dear. Waiting breathlessly for the landlord and master. Have you met him, David?"

"Course not. Otherwise I wouldn't be wearing my best sunglasses." He struck a pose, and Paula had to laugh despite herself.

"I am afraid I behaved rather badly to Robert last night," she confessed.

"Omigod. You didn't turn down one of his passes, did you? I've always maintained he'll marry the first girl that does that."

"You know, when you told me to take David's transparencies over last night? The door was open, and I caught him kissing some girl."

"Goodness, that's a bit like getting to watch the pope at his bedside prayers, isn't it," said Hockney with a laugh.

"My word, how wonderful. Is he any good at it? I mean does he *measure up?*" trilled Winthrop.

The performance of the male sex symbol was of enormous interest to the two friends.

"I behaved terribly badly. I can't figure out why, but I was rude." Somehow the understatement of the decade seemed necessary.

"You mean, you didn't applaud," said a straight-faced Hockney.

"Don't say you didn't have a ticket," said Winthrop.

Paula tried to laugh. The welcome irreverence was thick in the air. "No, seriously. When he gets here he's going to be furious. He'll splatter me all over the walls."

Winthrop peered around. "Well, that would be a great improvement on that sick-colored silk," he intoned professionally. "Brighten it up no end. Don't you think so, David?"

"Certainly would, and if we could persuade him to get a bit of her over the carpet, then bully for Robert."

Robert Hartford's arrival could be heard in the corridor outside. "They're already in the boardroom, Mr. Hartford," said an obsequious voice from behind the door. "Yes, Miss Hope is in there, too."

Around the table the joking stopped. The door opened. In the doorway stood the new owner of the Sunset Hotel.

"Good morning, gentlemen," he said. There was absolutely no acknowledgment at all that the room contained a woman. For Robert Hartford that alone was worth an entry in the *Guinness Book of Records*. He stalked over to the table and pulled back the chair at its head, motioning to the waiter that he'd have a cup of coffee.

"You know Paula, don't you," said Winthrop Tower with a broad smile. He wasn't afraid of anyone. His talent ensured that he didn't have to be.

Robert's head shot up. "Yes. I'm afraid I do." He paused. His eyes avoided Paula's when he spoke again, as hers were avoiding him.

"I wanted to say this in front of you, Winthrop, and I'm sorry that Mr. Hockney has to listen to what is essentially among the three of us. Last night Miss Hope broke into my bungalow, uninvited and unannounced, and was incredibly rude and insulting both to myself and to my guest. I want an explanation, and I want action, at the very least a verbal and a written apology." He arched his neck and peered at the ceiling, in a gesture that was supposed to be magisterial, but made it seem as if his shirt was too tight at the neck.

"Good God," said Tower. "At long last love."

"I *was* unannounced, but I didn't 'break in' because the front door was wide open, and that made me think that nothing particularly *private* was in progress. And I *was* sort of invited because Winty asked me to drop Mr. Hockney's transparencies by as a matter of urgency." Paula's voice was full of defiance. She was in the wrong, but not *that* wrong. And where was the reference to the kiss? God, he was good looking. How could he possibly want to kiss that androgynous thing on the sofa?

"Nobody asked you to drop them on my floor," said Robert with all the coldness he could muster. The girl was amazing. As far from cowardice as from dishonesty, she was a whiter shade of pale, but she wasn't intimidated by him.

"Dropped my trannies on the floor? A capital offense. Off with her head," David Hockney pitched in, ever the enemy of hypocrisy wherever he found it.

"Who was the lucky girl, Robert?" asked Winthrop shrewdly.

"That's not the point," said Robert, a speck of red high up on each cheek.

"I saw that Kirkegaard woman around eight, heading past the pool in your direction. Surely not her, Robert."

The hunted look flashed into the Hartford eyes. This was ridiculous. The topic of conversation was being changed completely. Paula was being spirited out of the dock, and he was being surreptitiously sucked into it in her place. Paula had seen Caroline. He could hardly deny it.

"Listen, stop changing the subject. Paula was extremely rude to me. She ought to apologize." He was aware as he spoke that his demands were already well watered down, and no concessions had been received from the other side. He was losing. In the ordinary way, that would have been intolerable. Somehow, now, it wasn't.

"I'm always leaving my door open," said Winthrop. "And nobody *ever* comes in. Just my luck!" An expression of monumental sadness played across his drink-ravaged features.

Robert felt the beginnings of a smile. He fought against it, but he didn't win. His three opponents saw it. Their feet were in the door of his bad mood.

"I'm sorry if I was rude," said Paula.

" 'If'?" said Robert. "You were *incredibly* rude."

"I *said* I was sorry."

He laughed. "Well, I accept your apology. I can't imagine why."

"It won't happen again," said Paula.

To Robert that suddenly sounded more like a threat than anything else.

"Thank God for that," said Winthrop. "It reminded me of Yale, and I can't *bear* to be reminded of that."

Robert craned his neck, but he made no response to the friendly jibe. "Now," he said. "Mr. Hockney's lithographs. Well, they're marvelous, aren't they?"

"It just so happens," said David Hockney in theatrical mode, "that I have brought some lithographs along with me, trannies perhaps not doing the work justice." He pulled up a portfolio from the side of his chair and began laying the lithographs out on the huge table.

For a moment or two there was silence as they sifted through them. They were all on the same side once more.

"What do you think, Paula?" said Winthrop.

"I think the tentative decorative scheme for the rooms would match them perfectly. I'm less sure about the one for the corridors."

Winthrop beamed at his star pupil. She was right of course. A disaster in the hallways. Perfection in the bedrooms.

What he was most proud of was the sensitivity with which she had handled the famous artist. Painters of Hockney's caliber were enormously wary of interior designers. Their paintings were works of art, objects in their own right, and a million miles from "decoration." Any insinuation that they were merely part of a decorative scheme, along with the color of the armchairs and the texture of the carpets, would be guaranteed to annoy. She had put it beautifully. It was a lucky coincidence that the bedroom décor would not have to be changed to accommodate the Hockney lithographs.

"Paula's right," said Winthrop, with the certainty of someone stating that two plus two equaled four. "Incidentally, Robert, do you actually *own* the hotel yet? I mean, have you signed on the dotted line?"

"Ten minutes ago. Livingstone and I tied it up at breakfast."

"Congratulations," said Paula.

"Thank you," said Robert.

For the first time since the "misunderstanding" they looked full into each other's eyes, and the crackling communication was instantly visible.

"I hope," and he smiled, "that at my 'advanced age' God will spare me for a year or two to enjoy it."

She blushed as she remembered, as she was meant to do, and she smiled back, a smile no less brilliant, no less meaningful. "If death threatens in the interim, it would be more than a pleasure to perform the kiss of life," she said.

Winthrop Tower jumped up. "Come on, gooseberry, I mean David," he said, smiling broadly. "Now that the landlord has spoken we can get off to my office and talk money, and gossip, and other boys' talk. No point sitting around here when we don't understand the private jokes."

David Hockney stopped briefly in the doorway to blow a kiss. "Bye bye, Robert. Bye, Paula. Now, you two be sure and have a very nice day."

They were alone.

Somehow that made things altogether more difficult.

For the first time in his life Robert was not quite sure what to say to a woman. The alien feeling filled him up. Doubt. Uncertainty. Goddamn it, panic. He studied his fingernails. There was an enormous tenderness inside, a great longing, all soft and gentle and full of strange emotions that he vaguely recognized but couldn't fully understand. Usually his mind was sharp, his feelings sharper. He was definition man, focused like a laser, certain of where he was going, of where he had come from. Now, inexplicably he was an unguided missile rocketing off into uncertain space, and it was wonderful while it was frightening, disturbing while it delivered the peace of which he had always dreamed. Locked tight in the grip of paradox, he did nothing, said nothing, in case the alien experience should go away.

"We drove them out," said Paula. It was the truth, but the naughty excitement in her voice was full of childlike pride. They had shared something together, something important and instantly recognizable. Two of the greatest artists in America had seen it. They wouldn't be wrong.

She wanted him to acknowledge it, too. She wanted it out in the open where the sun could warm it and the rain could nourish it and where it could grow and grow like no love had grown before.

"Yes, we did," he said, and his laugh was nervous as he stepped into the conspiracy of hearts.

It made her bolder, and her face was alive with the courage of youth. "Last night . . . I was jealous, that's why I said all those things I didn't mean." She was daring him to talk to her like a lover, or would-be lover, as he had by the pool on the night of Livingstone's party. Her face was begging for it, on fire with desire, glistening with longing. A part of him tried to respond. There was so much to explain. But speech would break the moment, and the moment was already too precious to be broken.

"You had no reason to be jealous. Perhaps I can make you understand that one day." It was as far as he could bring himself to go.

"Listen, I should have rung the beastly bell."

The sheeplike smile was magic. Robert Hartford was already halfway under its spell. It was remarkable. All these feelings, and they had scarcely touched.

He stood up, pushing the chair back gently, and Paula's heart raced in her chest as she dared to hope that it would happen. So many things were clear now. There was an intensity between them that could no longer be denied. Sometimes it had worn the mask of hatred, sometimes of attraction, now it appeared as it really was. She had no reason to, but she loved him. It was as simple and as impossible as that. The crippled orphan from nowhere, and the sexual hero of a generation who dealt in human perfection, who could choose any woman in the world. On the edge of triumph Paula could think only of failure. He had recoiled from the limp she had forgotten she had, and now, inside, he could be laughing at her extravagant presumption as he mercilessly led her on to become the greater fool.

But Robert Hartford had never been so far from laughter. At the other end of the spectrum where he was, there was only an explosion of affection, and a desire to release it.

She was only a foot or two away and he walked to her, and knelt by the side of her chair. She sat still, well aware of his presence but looking straight ahead in case she would frighten away her almost-lover. He reached out to touch her forearm, tracing a pattern on the brown skin, ruffling the blond hairs as he stared up at her profile. Then he reached up and laid his finger against her neck, as if taking the pulse of her, the temperature of the passion that lay hidden beneath the surface of her. Then he reached upward as still her face pointed away from his, and he followed the contours of her proud chin, and he lingered below the pouting lips as if afraid to be more bold without some sign of her acquiescence.

The shuddering sigh leaped from between the lips he threatened, and her breath fanned his questioning finger, but still she looked ahead, still she didn't turn toward him. So, he touched the part of her that her sigh had signaled for him to touch. The tender flesh of her lips pressed deliciously against his finger, and then at last she responded. Here in the slow dawn of commitment, she opened her mouth and gripped his finger lightly, nuzzling the explorer, her lips running along the length of it as she breathed out coating the millimeters where their bodies joined with her damp moan of longing.

More bold, he moved at the verge of her body, pressing in gently against the teeth that were closed against him. For a second he stayed there, at the gates of her, knowing that soon she would allow him to enter, soon she would beg for it. And in response to his self-confident patience, her mouth opened wider in the escalation of the war that would be love, and the dry became wet, the desert the oasis, as her tongue bathed the part of him that she could see, the only part of him she could feel.

At long last she turned to him, and their eyes met in the contract that soon their bodies would sign.

They stood together and she melted into his arms. But there was lost ground to be reclaimed. On the edges of intimacy they had hidden from each other's faces; now all must be admitted. He gazed down into the eyes of the first woman he had seen, and she gazed back into the eyes of the first man she had loved. Her face was awash with the messages of her body, and her eyes were hooded with longing, her lips parted in the half smile of desire. Above the mouth that he had touched, two tiny beads of sweat stood out, and her breath came quickly, unashamed of the raging feelings within her.

Above her, and so close, was the face they all wanted. It was covered with a mantle of gentleness she had never seen before, an otherworldly glow that spoke of angels, and of the paradise that soon she would know. He paused before the mutual surrender, as if reviewing the past life that was now ending, silent before the future that soon would unfold. Then, reverently, he bent in toward her and the lips she dreamed of sank gratefully against hers.

TWELVE

I t *can't* be economical to do all the beds with Pratesi sheets." Kristina was honestly appalled at the idea.

"Money isn't the issue here, Kristina. Excellence is. The people who stay at the new Sunset will want the best of everything. If they don't, they should go somewhere else. It's a question of getting the costing right. The sheets are three hundred dollars apiece. Work out how long they last and factor the expense into the room charge. Wilton carpets, interlined curtains shipped over from Sadlers of Pimlico, Avery Boardman sofas and chairs, four coats of paint—the rooms will be the best anywhere. They must be."

She spoke with the zeal of the fanatic, but she could see that she wasn't really carrying Kristina with her. That was the problem with a conventional background. There was always a shortfall in the imagination department. Still, that was what she had to learn. That was what Paula was teaching her. Since the day they had met by chance at the movies in Westwood the two girls had become close friends. Kristina had been fascinated by Paula's brilliance at interior design, and when she had begun to take an interest in it, Paula had immediately suggested that she work with her on the Sunset Hotel redecoration. Kristina had jumped at the chance, and Robert and Winthrop had quickly agreed.

Paula walked over to the bed and bent down to run the rose-patterned sheet between her thumb and forefinger. "Feel how soft it is, Kristina. It gets even softer the more it's washed, and it lasts four times as long as any other sheet. In the end it's probably cheaper."

"I just keep wondering if Daddy can afford all this."

Paula heard the implied criticism and rose above it. She liked Kristina and Kristina liked her. It was the way things were going to stay. It was cool that the elder girl would feel hostility. Kristina, a college kid and Hollywood "royalty," was effectively working for a nobody from nowhere with nothing but a diploma in self-confidence from the university of life, and a little thing called unlimited talent.

Their friendship was an unlikely one. Paula had never known people like Kristina. In the poverty trap they didn't exist, because there toughness was the norm and character was stripped to its basics. Kristina, however, preserved from difficulty in the aspic of ease, was infinitely complex. All the effort and energy that the Paulas of this world had spent on staying warm, or getting cool, on feeding and clothing themselves, the rich Kristinas had blown on making themselves more "interesting." On the surface self-confidence reigned supreme. But underneath the brittle heart was obviously vulnerable, conditioned by years of the casually brutal neglect that the rich pretended was "good" for their children.

Paula was intrigued by her and her automatic mistrust of the straightforward approach. She loved her world-weary pessimism and her tongue-in-cheek tendency to put herself down. Then there was the wonderful way she could use words to make smoke screens and confuse the most simple situation. All the weapons and armor that Kristina possessed were designed for wars that Paula had never had to fight. Similarly, Paula's strengths—her belief in herself, her brave honesty, her formidably useful short-fuse temper—were effective in battles that would have had no relevance at all to Kristina's looking-glass world. In short theirs was that strongest yet most volatile of mutual attractions— the attraction of opposites.

"Listen, sweetheart, your father wants the Sunset to be the envy of everyone. It will be."

"I still can't believe it, can you? It's strange that Livingstone would give up all that money just to have Daddy own the Sunset. I mean, I never really thought of Dad and Francisco as being close." She paused, lost in awe at the thought of her father's being close to *anyone*.

Paula heard what she was saying. "I think they're rather alike in some ways. Neither would be a great guest on 'Wheel of Fortune,' would he?"

They both laughed. It was true. Livingstone was a private person, hidden beneath the dense fog of his arm's-length politeness. Robert was more overtly reclusive. Both held their emotional cards close to their chests, so that nobody ever knew what they were thinking or feeling.

"Okay, I agree on the sheets. You're right. Go for bust. So how many do we need? Three sets per single and a twenty percent reserve." Kristina whipped out her calculator. "That's 432 times three equals 1,296 plus around 260 . . . God that's about a hundred eighty thousand for the single sheets, probably the same again for the kings."

"Given away," laughed Paula. "Wait till we start on the pillowcases, the shams, the bed covers, and the towels. We could blow two million bucks on the linen. Maybe more."

The model room stared back at them, unashamed in its extravagance, as far from a hotel bedroom as it was possible to be. Paula and Winthrop had avoided creeping anonymity by designing every single room in the hotel slightly differently, and the enormous amount of extra work had paid off. The room that was already finished looked as if it belonged to someone. Sleeping in it would be like sleeping in someone else's bedroom. For the night you had been lent the room of a perfect stranger, but one whose houses regularly appeared between the covers of magazines as excellent as *HG* and *Connoisseur*. Even though you could afford the price of your overnight stay you would think twice about shelling out for the Audubon bird engravings that hung over the fireplace, and you would have never thought to ask your designer to put a white terrycloth-covered sofa and an NEC color TV in the bathroom for after-tub relaxation, nor to hide the combination adjustable wall safe behind a hinged Biedermeier mirror. People were used to refrigerators in their hotel bedrooms, but the Sub-Zeros at the Sunset Hotel contained pink champagne and the nuts were macadamias, cashews, and pistachios, not the regular "mixed" variety, the bottled water Badoit, not Perrier, the chocolates from the Queen's chocolatier, Charbonnel and Walker in London, rather than the more obvious Godiva brand. They were little things in themselves, but little things that meant a lot. There was no more abused word in the English language than *luxury*, but the Sunset Hotel, paradoxically far too grand to aspire to the word, would come closest to defining it.

"It's going to be so beautiful," said Paula, the enthusiasm shining in her eyes. "Imagine the dreadful things that Kirkegaard woman would have done to it."

Kristina was standing at the window that looked out over the Sunset pool. She didn't turn around. "I like her," she said.

"Kristina! You *can't*. Nobody could. She's a monster!"

Kristina turned to face her. "I admire her. There's something so strong about her. People are frightened of her because she knows what she wants and because she's spiritual and she's wise, and she exists on so many different levels."

"Oh, bull, Kristina. She's a fake. And she's evil. Look what she tried to do to Livingstone. If it hadn't been for Robert, the old boy would have been destroyed. I can't believe what you're saying to me."

"You're too black and white, Paula. Nothing's as it seems, you know, in this life. I mean, maybe that model and he *had* met before in another life. Maybe they were meant to make love. And if Livingstone was ashamed of it afterward, then he shouldn't have done it. And if he wasn't, then why should he care so much about the world knowing? I think Caroline's pretty magnificent. I mean, she's made a whole new life for herself, and everyone lines up to dump on her. Daddy, you, everybody. It's no sin to want this hotel. My father does. Why shouldn't Caroline?"

Kristina felt the words flowing more freely as she spoke. Despite what her father had told her and Paula about the blackmail attempt, she found it impossible to blame Caroline Kirkegaard. At Livingstone's ball when she had finally met her, she had not been disappointed. Now as she thought of Caroline her mind filled with strange, warm feelings of respect, of admiration . . . and of something else, indefinable, unsettling, very far from unpleasant. It was irritating that Paula misunderstood her, but it wasn't difficult to understand why. Paula was a Taurus and both her feet were firmly planted on the ground, making her a perfect match for her father's obsessive Virgo. She didn't understand the Piscean, Aquarian world that Kristina and Caroline inhabited, the world of the seeker, the traveler, of the dreamer. But why couldn't she just admit that? Why did she have to be *right*, and Caroline wrong? Why did the blinkered realists think that they had a monopoly on wisdom?

"I didn't know you were a Destiny supporter," said Paula thoughtfully. She frowned. That was the flip side of Kristina, the vulnerability, the lack of focus, the weakness. Although they were endearing qualities, they were also dangerous. A cloud-obscured head was not the best instrument for seeing through Caroline Kirkegaard.

"I'm not a 'Destiny supporter.' I just think Caroline Kirkegaard gets a raw deal. That's all." Kristina's tone said she wanted to change the subject.

Paula walked through to the bathroom. In many ways this was the most remarkable part of the whole redecoration plan. Very few people had bathrooms as grand as the ones they found in an expensive hotel, and certainly nobody had ones as clean. It had been Paula's idea to double the size of the Sherle Wagner–fitted bathrooms and to turn them into a cross between a den and a recreation room, effectively making each single room a mini suite. They had telephones, and piped-in music, cable TV, and an intercom to the front desk. The shower doubled as a steam cabinet, and in its marble walls there were water jets for a pummeling massage. In front of the sofas were glass tables on which sat crisp copies of L.A. *Style, California Magazine,* and *Condé Nast's Traveler.* Beside the bath a marble recess contained vast jars brimful of Joy pour les Bains, and dishes were laden with Dior soap. The usual "luxury" hotel detritus of shower caps, sewing kits, spare buttons, and shampoo was conspicuous by its absence. At the Sunset people didn't do their own sewing, the women didn't do their own hair, and the something-for-nothing ambience of its "competitors" was a must to avoid. Everything that could possibly be needed was a telephone call away. No request was too outlandish, no demand sniffed at, no naïveté patronized, no ignorance punished. The guests were kings and queens for a night and a day, for the entire length of their stay. Unbeknown to them, they were watched from dawn till dusk, and more important still from dusk till dawn. The KGB would have drooled at the efficiency of the Sunset's information-gathering service, the CIA murdered to obtain it. From a thousand different directions, information on each and every guest was fed into the mainframe IBM computer. What did they like for breakfast? When did they go to sleep? When did they wake? Did they entertain "disreputable" guests, were they noisy; in what state did they leave their rooms? What did they look like in the lobby, and how much did they spend in the bar, on the telephone, in the restaurants? Their career status was monitored, and their taste in flowers noted. This secret system allowed the Sunset to excel. A hotel was only as good as its clientele. So the weeds were removed, and the trees pruned, and the survivors were nourished in a way that ensured they returned again and again to the immensely subtle welcome they had come to expect. They would be greeted by name, and the room would already be scented with their favorite flowers, the icebox packed with their favorite drinks. A persistent regular would receive the cleverest gifts—a leather-bound copy of her latest bestseller; a complimentary hour and a half's massage for the busy executive who, the computer said, had ordered one before; a dinner for two, on the house, in the hotel's restaurant, the menu already written out in italic script, the dishes chosen from past preferences stored in the infinitely knowledgeable memory bank. For others, the hotel would always be "full," and they would never fathom the reason why. How could one such former guest imagine that the computer knew about that time when, in a frantic hurry, he had cleaned his shoes on the bedroom drapes? And if another's wife didn't know about the hookers he'd entertained in the late-night Star Room, how could the hotel hold it against him? Nobody would remember that another had helped himself to a few coathangers, abused the chambermaids, and left no tip. But the Sunset did not forget . . . at least until a non grata became so successful, so famous that he or she had to be allowed a second chance.

"How much has the room cost, Kristina?"

" 'Bout seventy-five thousand."

"It looks it. Oh well, only about another two hundred and twenty to go," said Paula.

"I don't think there's going to be any time for the honeymoon," said Kristina suddenly, her face wreathed in a wicked smile.

Paula blushed and then frowned. It had been three endless days since Robert Hartford had kissed her, and she had not heard a word from him. It was driving her crazy but no way was she going to tell Kristina that. "Listen, Kristina. Your father and I are just friends." Her face relaxed in a smile. "But do you honestly think America would forgive him for not taking a honeymoon if he ever *did* get married? There'd be a revolution"—now she laughed—"led by me. . . ."

Kristina sat down on the bed, bouncing up and down as if to test its softness. "Okay, Paula. Tell the truth. What's he like? Go on. Tell me!"

"Kris*tina!*"

"No, really. Go on. I'm your best friend. Friends are allowed to talk about those things." Kristina's laughing smile was alive with fun, but there was more to it than just girl-talk. Robert's whole career was in some way based on his legendary sack-artistry. Kristina's entire school career had been a succession of endless jokes on the subject. She had constructed an encyclopedia of stock responses to the ongoing jibes, but at the end of the day she was as curious as anyone else.

"Kristina, you're gross. We're talking about your *father*." Paula laughed to show she didn't mind.

"Is it the quantity or the quality?" Kristina giggled.

Paula scooped up a Pratesi pillow. She advanced threateningly on her suddenly cowering friend.

"Or is it, 'never mind the quality, feel the width!' " Kristina laughed helplessly, falling over sideways to avoid the inevitable blow.

Thwack!

In seconds the immaculate room was in chaos as the pillow fight raged.

Robert Hartford's arrival at New York's Carlyle Hotel reminded Paula for some strange reason of the Spanish Inquisition. The limo she sat in was so stretched it looked like it had endured long hours on the rack for failing to make the right religious noises, and the green-uniformed porters hovered reverently about it like priests at a deeply significant ceremony. They made little darting motions with their hands at the still moving limo, drawing back, then swooping in again as they tried to lay their groping fingers on the door handle at the precise moment the car actually came to a stop.

Next to her on the back seat, Robert gave new meaning to the term "vehicle role," and now as the limo finally halted at the curb he melted through the door ahead of her, because he was sitting nearest to the sidewalk. Wraithlike, he drifted across the pavement, his head held low and his eyes downcast to avoid the full frontal smiles of the priest/servants. His mid-calf-length navy-blue cashmere coat swished in the crisp wind-chilled air, and his perfect features hid shyly beneath the rim of a dark brown trilby hat, the trademark tortoiseshell glasses, and the folds of the Cambridge blue tasseled scarf that was knotted casually around his neck. To Paula he looked exactly like a god, and her excitement, building steadily on the trip from Kennedy, at the sight of the Manhattan skyline, and the tense, tingling streets of New York, now kicked into overdrive.

"Hi, Peter," murmured Robert at the porter called Frank and the one called Joe as he headed for the polished brass doors of the Carlyle.

"What about the luggage?" asked Paula, smiling. She just wanted to hear his voice. She just wanted him to know she was loving every second of this, every moment of him.

"It finds its way upstairs," he said with a shy laugh and the casual wave of a black-gloved hand. Then he stood back and motioned for her to enter the already revolving door.

The lobby of the hotel opened up in front of her, slotting effortlessly and immediately into the category labeled "good taste" in her mind. The black-and-white marble here was deliciously weathered, and the stone had not seen the quarry for a good thirty years, possibly more. There were flowers, but not too many flowers, and they weren't pretentious orchids but instead white azaleas and hydrangeas. No brass. No "clever" lighting. No cheap tricks. There was no magazine stand, just a discreet hole in the wall through which you would be passed more or less anything you asked for, and the gilt mirrors, the French tapestries, and the Beauvais-style rugs were all the sorts of things that would have been completely at home in Brooke Astor's apartment on Park Avenue. The staff stood about in uniforms that clearly did not embarrass them, and they looked as if they were proud to be doing the job they were doing.

The pin-stripe-panted man hurried across the floor to greet them. "Mr. Hartford, sir. Welcome home. It must be two and a half months since we saw you last, sir."

The assistant manager was more than usually friendly. Robert Hartford had owned a pied-à-terre at the Carlyle for around seven years now, and he was always welcomed specially by the management, but in the last few days he had ceased to be "just" a movie star. Now he was the brand-new owner of the Sunset Hotel, the nearest equivalent on the West Coast to the formidably grand Carlyle. That gave cause for mild concern—would he try to poach the best staff in America? With the reticence of the first rate, he gave no hint of his thoughts, making no mention of the story that every newspaper in America had covered.

"Sullivan, may I introduce Ms. Hope, who will be staying with me. Perhaps you could arrange a key . . ."

In the elevator, he replied noncommittally to the old retainer's routine enquiry about his health. There were other things on his mind. There was Paula.

She stood beside him, tall and proud amid the unaccustomed luxury, and somehow she fitted in better than he did in her jet-black Azzedine Alaïa that clung to every molecule-moving curve of her delicious body; the wide brown crocodile belt, the silk stockings that defined eternal legs before disappearing into black Maud Frizon shoes.

He slipped his hand into hers. "I'm so glad you let me come, Paula."

"Robert, what on earth do you mean, 'let you come'!"

He smiled at her. "It's true. You're here on Tower Design business. I'm here because of you. Okay, I meet a couple of movie people for a tax write-off, but you're the reason. You know that."

It *was* true, and Paula could hardly understand the speed with which it had all happened.

Their kiss had changed everything—while it had lasted. Later, separated from him again, the doubts had come thick and fast. What did a kiss mean to Robert Hartford? It had *felt* important, but then that was part of the knack, wasn't it, the famed ability to make every woman feel like she was special.

The days had seemed like years, but there had been no call.

Nothing. For the very first time in her life Paula had experienced the unique pain of torture by telephone. Watching it, rushing back home at every possible moment to sit by it, calling the switchboard endlessly to track down hoped-for messages that might have "gone astray." Luckily there had been the work to distract her, the Coriarchi house, and Tower's arch humor and Graham's nerve-racking and increasingly hungry eyes. Just when the pain was beginning to fade, and the memory of the kiss to lose its sharp edge, the telephone did what life did, it gave her what she wanted at the very point when she didn't want it quite so badly.

"Paula? Robert."

"Hi, Robert." Oh so very casually friendly.

"I've been locked in an editing room day and night."

An excuse.

"Oh." No possible correct answer to that. "I hope you got what you wanted."

"Not yet."

Deliciously ambiguous. Paula realized he wasn't talking about the cutting room or his movie.

"Listen, Paula. I gather from Winty that you and he are going to New York next week to look at some furniture and design some apartment."

"Yes. I've never been. I'm really excited."

"Well . . ." he had paused, and Paula could almost see the little-boy gestures that defined "appealing"—the hand darting through the immaculate hair, the glasses trick, the surrogate uncertainty. "Well, I have an apartment up there, and I haven't been for a while and it would be nice to go . . ." Again the heart-melting pause. ". . . And I wondered if perhaps you would sort of 'be my guest' and I could show you New York at the times you weren't working."

There, said the voice, it's been on my mind and I've spat it out, and now, beautiful woman, I am at your mercy—poor Robert Hartford, accommodation provider, tour guide, and general gofer to the stars of the world like Paula.

"I'd love it." The words had tumbled from her.

Now they had arrived at the front door of his apartment.

"Here we are," said Hartford. "I'll let myself in," said Robert over his shoulder to the elevator man.

The door closed behind them, and in front of them the view opened up over Central Park.

She peered around the apartment with an eye that was half

professional, half looking for clues that would reveal bits of the mysterious man who fascinated her. Why did he love hotels so much? For their anonymity? Efficiency? A flight from responsibility? Didn't he want to *own* things? Or did he just want to own people? Would he be able to tell her if she asked? Could they have that kind of conversation? So many questions. So much to learn. Such joy in the learning.

"It's just beautiful, Robert. I mean, that view . . ."

The room itself was giving nothing away. Nondescript mahogany furniture, stylish Ackermann prints depicting naval battles from the Napoleonic wars, correct chintzes with a basic reddish-brown motif. There were pleasant lamps judiciously placed, a pure wool gray carpet, and a perfectly acceptable Persian runner in the small hallway. A smart black Sony TV with a matching VCR seemed the only concession to the twentieth century in what was a basically Georgian-style room—all of which served to emphasize rather than diminish the persona of its owner. Perhaps that was its real function.

"I'm glad you like it." He flopped down in an armchair and watched her as she toured the small apartment. "What do you think of New York so far?"

"Well, I think the people who live here must be the luckiest in the world. All these stretch limos and private planes and views of Central Park." She laughed as she teased him, and he, who hated to be teased, laughed back.

"You'll see the other New York, the real one, soon enough."

"When?"

"Whenever."

"You know what I've always dreamed of doing?"

"No idea."

"Going skating."

"We can do that." He paused. "Can you skate?"

She felt the hidden question. It was the time to confront the thing that must be confronted.

She sat down opposite him. "You mean with my leg?"

"No, I just meant . . . can you skate . . . ?"

"It really bothers you, doesn't it, Robert? Is it so bad? I just don't think about it. I'm so used to it. That night at Livingstone's party you really freaked, didn't you?"

He twisted around in his seat and tore his face away from hers. "I didn't freak." He hated the word and its implications. "I just hate . . . untidiness," he managed at last.

"And my limp is untidy?" She tried to feel for what he meant.

He wanted out of the conversation, but she had to get to the bottom of it.

"Not untidy . . . I mean, is it necessary? Can't you do something about it? It's such a terrible shame—you're so beautiful, Paula." He seemed suddenly irritated at being forced to fight the demons he would rather ignore.

"I think I could. I had an accident when I was very young. My leg got caught between the dock and a boat and I had something called a compound fracture of the leg bone. It was just about half an inch that was damaged but it was so badly fragmented that when it healed my left leg was just that little bit shorter than the other. It would take a lot of expensive operations to correct it, bone grafts, putting in bits of metal. . . . There was never any money for that. I just got used to it. Everyone did. I can move around as well as I want to, and yes, I can skate."

Her smile was soft, kind—seeming to say that she realized that the disability they were *really* discussing was his.

He was acutely uncomfortable. "I know it's ridiculous, but it seems so wrong. I mean, it's a crime against nature. You're so wonderful looking . . . and then there's this . . . thing. If it's only money I'd be more than glad . . ."

"To fix me up, so's I don't embarrass?"

He heard her mild rebuke. "I'm sorry, Paula. I just can't help the way I feel. I know it's crazy . . ." His voice, desolate, trailed off. How could he possibly put into words all the things he felt about beautiful women? They existed as goddesslike reflections in the eyes of a little boy in his father's suite at the Sunset Hotel. They weren't just people, they were symbols of life's perfection, of its possibility. He loved women. He loved everything about them, and he dreamed of a manless world in which only he existed to worship them. Every flaw they possessed was an insult to the natural order, because they were meant to be unblemished, untarnished, undefiled. But how could he say all that without sounding like a madman?

"You can't just love me as I am? *I* think I'm pretty special."

"I don't want to change you, Paula."

"What do you want to do with me?"

Her voice was husky.

She took one step toward him. And another.

The breath crept from him like a thief in the night. He didn't want to disturb the moment, but his body was saying the things it loved to say. She stood between his open legs, her leg was against his, and the scent of her was in his nostrils. Her lips opened as her eyes widened. She was there to be touched. She expected it. She wanted it. The permission was in her eyes. The command was in them.

He sat stock still. He was mesmerized by the promise of what she would do. His coat was still on, his scarf, everything, and yet he was wide open to her.

For a second he paused. In past lives he had not had to think about this. Instinct had guided him. Now, in the alien world called love, he was frighteningly responsible.

His hand was on her stomach, his other against her hip. Hardly touching her, he signaled her toward him. She sank down, her eyes not leaving his, and, as she did so, her skirt slid upward to reveal the brown skin at the top of her black-stockinged legs. Her lips were parted and her breath came fast. Her fingers found the bone buttons of his coat. She freed the material and pushed it away from his body.

Together they crossed the dangerous divide into intimacy. Now their collusion translated into longing, as his desire took physical form. He reached forward to touch the side of her head, in awe of her beauty. He stroked at her silky, soft hair, feeling the warmth of her beneath his fingers, and he moaned quietly in anticipation of the pleasure to come.

She smiled at his acquiescence, and the love flowed freely from her face to his as she reached down to unloose the buttons that strained to restrain him.

He closed his eyes as she freed him, and she sighed as she reached for him, holding it gently, clasping the fingers of her right hand around its base, running those of her left up and down the shaft of it, amazed by the beauty of the symbol of his need for her. With both hands she held it, then, letting go, she tortured him with the soft touch of her fingertips, exploring him, as she grew more bold and the wonderful sensation soared within her. She reached down to the depths, and her hand pushed beneath him, gamboling in the secret places, before reemerging to stoke the flames of his lust. Up and down and around about her fingers moved, prowling like a tiger in the night fires of the forest, sometimes hurrying, sometimes stealthy, always tantalizingly unpredictable. And she watched him, as each precious touch, each deliciously threatened absence, winged to the fevered forefront of his mind.

"Paula, Paula," he murmured and he reached out to hold her, crushing her to him, as he dedicated his life to her. Then, slowly, he stood up, and he drew her up with him. They stood there, their bodies painted against each other, locked tight in the embrace from which there could be only release.

Still she held him, and he was alive against her hand, expanding, thrusting, growing, becoming, and she sighed as she pressed harder against him at the eagerness she could feel. Her lips parted, and her teeth bared as she knew that she must have him, and his eyes flashed and his head moved from side to side as he, too, surrendered to the union that must be. Now her mouth closed across his neck, and her tongue snaked out to taste his flesh, as below he bucked and reared against her hand. Tenderly yet jealously she kissed him, standing up on the tips of her toes to reach him, and as she did so she thrust her pelvis out and guided the rock hardness of him to the place where stocking and garter met, to the baby-soft skin of her upper thigh. All the time her eyes questioned him, and told him all the truths they had waited so long to tell. He heard her, and his, too, had messages for her as the moan gathered at the back of his throat, and his throbbing blood rushed like a waterfall so near to the core of her.

Nuzzling in against his neck, she soaked him with her saturated breath and still she held him, tightening her grip on him as he expanded, relaxing it as he ebbed, loving the life she could feel in her hand, against her leg, in the howling center of her mind. She moved him against her, pointing him at the subtly different parts of her upper leg, rubbing him against the sheer silk of her stocking tops, pushing him daringly against the elastic edge of her panties. There at the brink of her she played with him, allowing him to rest briefly among the downy, wet hairs before guiding him back once more to the outside.

"Oh, Paula. Oh God, I love you," he whispered.

But she reached up higher and her lips trembled before his as they told of her own love. He bent down toward her, and his tongue slipped out to the tip of her chin. For a moment it lingered there, and then rhythmically it began to move. It traveled upward to her lower lip, brushing across her teeth, then hooking beneath her upper lip, pulling it away and allowing it to fall back, before resuming its journey. It traced a wonderful, wet pattern at the edge of her nostril, flirting lazily with the borders of the entrance before hurrying on to the bridge of her nose. It was a brush, softer and finer and more laden with sweet wetness than any had ever been, and it moved with deft strokes to paint the beauty of Paula's face. It sank daringly into the valleys of her now closed eyes. It roamed free across cheek and forehead and chin, and it drank shamelessly from her eager lips.

The groan of abandonment broke in Paula's throat. Before she had been an explorer in the foreign country of passion, but now she was a veteran in the love war. Her lips merged with his, and she fanned his mouth with her breath as her tongue invaded him, taunting his with the sharpness of her teeth. All the time she shared the universal predicament of lovers. How far? How fast? How to capture the elusive physical moment so that the wonder would never die? Only one thing was certain. They must become each other. They must fuse. They must merge. Later, in marriage, but now in the commitment of total ecstasy. Afterward, during forever, there would be time for tenderness and bittersweet words and for all the promises and poetry of the romance they would create. But here was reality: two bodies sizzling with the heat they had made for each other. She wanted him to take her, standing up, before any words were spoken. She wanted him to fill her with his love, and spray her with the purity of his intentions because words were liars that had kept them apart and must do so no longer. It was what he wanted, too.

She arched her back and braced herself, and she thrust up at him, reaching into the kiss as she pushed her hips forward. At the same time she eased down her panties and she guided him to the wetness of her. Now his hands looped down behind her and his palms cupped her buttocks, drawing them toward him, as he positioned himself for the sublime moment. She felt the pressure and her hand moved to place him at her entry as she opened up to give him the gift that would always be his.

There was a void within her, a vacuum of dripping, boiling need, and the lips of her love were pink petals of longing in the rain-soaked jungle of desire. So she reached up once again for precious height, and he bent down low and the tip of him strained at the shy entrance, and it closed over him, touching him with its velvet promise. Then he pushed out at her and she at him and his fingers sank into the firm flesh of her bottom, and he drew her in and she enclosed him.

Deep within her she could feel him. She drew back and she watched him as he invaded her, the half smile of desire all over her face. She was pinned against him, his strong hands on her buttocks as he thrust into the heart of her body, hard and high and deep. Paula cried out in happiness. She felt light, and lighter and lightest as her feet parted from the floor and suddenly she was in midair, held on the spear of his longing. She wrapped her legs around his waist and drew them tight together, using them to force him even farther inside her. Tight against the roof of her, he waited and they lived for pleasure, existing for the seconds that seemed like light years on the pinnacle of passion. Then he moved across the narrow hallway, carrying her with him to the bedroom, and he laid her down on the bed.

Now the length of him began to move within her and the wet sounds where their bodies touched made music for the celebration of their love. Even before he had found a rhythm, she knew that she couldn't hold back her orgasm. It was too much, too soon, after far too long. Her whole body was poised for the moment. Beneath her breasts, in her stomach, in her wide-open heartland, she felt the muscles tense. Inside she was wet like a river around the invader. She could feel the fountain spraying down the inside of her legs, falling back into the divide of her buttocks. The fresh musk of her need was hot in the air, and she reached down with both hands to feel the place where he surged into her, where his sweat-soaked hair rubbed deliciously against her melting, sliding mound of love.

But it was hopeless. She was lost. It was running away from her toward the inevitable conclusion. She tried to warn him, her damp hands pushing gently against his heaving chest, her eyes telling him, her lips murmuring soundlessly the great truth of what was to come. But he wanted it, too, because he, too, was ready—poised to melt down his heart and his mind and his soul and to feed it into her forever. She heard the thickening of his breathing as his lungs raced to fuel his coursing blood, and she watched him hungrily as his expression signaled the ecstasy of despair at the brink of bliss. I love you. I love you, she told him with her heart, and he heard her on that wild plain where lovers spoke. I love you, too, my darling, said his faraway eyes.

So they leaned in together, bathed in sweat and swathed in love, as they sought the strength for the sweet communion. He had pulled out from her, almost all the way, and he hovered there in the entrance of her, caught between the slippery pink fingers that framed his pulsating heat. Neither dared to move, eager not to disturb the intensity of the moment, eager to contrast the stillness now with the explosion that was to come. In the silence they were together, floating high above the canyon of the orgasm like hawks on the wind, stalking it, hunting it, waiting to possess it. How long could they stay there, untouched by it? It was a glorious game as they flirted with the ultimate ecstasy, easy lovers in flight above the abyss.

She felt it first in his hands. They tightened, they tensed, and then they reached for what they must have.

She felt her whole pelvis being dragged into him, as his fingers dived down into the depths of her buttocks as if they would draw her inside his body. At the same time he launched himself forward and plunged into the heart of her.

Like an arrow quivering in the target, she felt his shuddering surrender at the sublime moment of his conquest. The dammed-up torrent of longing cascaded from him, soaking the silken walls of her with endless ribbons of love. It was a jumping, rearing feeling of total satisfaction as his body shook against hers and still it came, ceaselessly abundant, filling her, falling from her, whipping her senses into a frenzy as the tropical tempest drowned her in the flood of crazy joy. His whole body was a fountain, existing only to bathe her in love and he pushed against her, and she pushed back, as his desire collided with her excitement and their world changed forever in the truth of the orgasm. The walls of her clamped down over him, and pleasure fell on them like hard rain on a lonely road as she milked him of his precious gift. And now her waterfall was added to the sensual sea, and together they poured into each other, drowning as they had meant to drown in the beauty of eternal love.

In the quaking aftermath, deep inside her still, Robert leaned forward to find her lips and Paula leaned forward to find his. Nuzzling into each other they kissed, full of happiness and the sure knowledge that what had passed between them was the end of nothing but the beginning.

THIRTEEN

obert Hartford was watching Paula, and she was almost, but not quite, oblivious to him. In the Peter Purcell showrooms in the D & D Building, the beating heart of the chic New York decorator scene, the action was hotting up and Paula was in the thick of it. She stood there, in the simple sand-colored Christina de Castelnau dress, its formal lines in love with the curves of her body, as she argued her point with the fervor of someone who knew she was correct.

"This furniture *is* right, Winty. In fact, it's perfect. More than perfect. It's just what the Montmorencys need. I know you're off trompe l'oeil and the distressed look, but try to separate the furniture from the rest of it. It's the *association* that's throwing you off course."

The rounded, avuncular figure at the end of the table chuckled at the irreverence. As pioneer of the Maxwell Parrish-meets-Magritte style of intellectual, Mediterranean-influenced design, Peter Purcell was the colossus of New York interior decoration. In L.A. people died for a Tower-designed house. In the Big Apple they were equally happy to lay down their lives for a Purcell apartment. Like Winthrop, he picked and he chose. Mere money was not enough. He had to like you. And now, despite her shortage of tact, he very much liked Paula Hope.

Robert smiled as he watched her. Purcell and Tower were rivals. They respected each other, but they couldn't afford to actually *like* each other, although each was scrupulously careful to avoid anything at all that would bring that out into the open. However, there were points that each wanted to make, and as the pressure of irritation built up a head of steam beneath the surface, outright confrontation remained a distinct possibility. Paula, Robert realized, was in the middle, and he had never seen anything more magnificent.

Tower tugged at his spaniel's earlobe and peered around the cluttered but immaculate showroom. "You see, Paula, you have to remember that the Montmorencys are basically as old as France, which has been around for a year or two. That means that all their European houses are not exactly new, and it also means, despite their loot, that they know what a damp wall looks like. They're not Rothschilds, you know. They're aristocrats."

"Yes?" Paula, in full spate, and in love with the fabulous Purcell furniture, was impatient to get to Winthrop's point.

He ignored her exasperation, although when he spoke again, there was a new I'm-talking-as-slowly-as-I-can-so-that-you'll-understand quality to his voice.

"What I'm getting at is that the Montmorencys don't really need their New York apartment to be done up at great expense to look like the west wing of the château after the leaves have blocked the gutter in the heavy rains. It's fine for the nouvelle society people—they're sick and tired of everything looking brand new and working perfectly—but the Montmorencys like the idea of having something a bit slick and sleek for a change. That's why they've chosen a penthouse at the Metropolitan Tower, rather than some stuffy triplex in a coop on Fifth. They'll tell all their friends that of course they realize it's frightfully common, but actually they'll be tickled to bits with it."

Robert drew in his breath. So did Purcell. Battle lines were being drawn. Paula, however, knew what she wanted.

Purcell spoke up. "I think Ms. Hope's point, Paula's point, Winthrop, is that the furniture can and does exist perfectly well in isolation from my particular design point of view. If the 'Montmorencys', or anyone else for that matter, finds *that* laughable in any way, then it doesn't of necessity extend to the furniture."

"Precisely," said Paula.

Tower scowled. Paula had committed a cardinal sin. She had sided with a rival against him, and in public. "Mr. Purcell is not the only person in New York designing 'excellent' furniture, Paula. There's Jay Spectre and Mario Buatta and Juan Montoya. Maybe you'll fall in love with them, too." He flicked an eye over at Robert in the corner. "At your age you're young enough to fall in love with everyone."

"Isn't she lucky," jousted Purcell. "At our age we're too old to fall in love with *anyone*."

"Except ourselves," said Winthrop.

An uneasy silence descended.

Robert caught Paula's eye. She caught his. At last she seemed to realize that hornets were shifting about in their nest and that somehow, unwittingly, it was she who had stirred them up.

"Well, I know I'm just the casual observer," said Robert diplomatically, "and I find it all terribly interesting, but what I'm longing to do is to see the actual apartment. Is the plan that we go there now, and then I get to take Paula out to lunch?"

Winthrop Tower raised an eyebrow. "On the principle that in America and India designers defer to movie stars, I suppose we should fall in with your plan," he said dryly, and stood up. "Yes, I think we've seen just about everything," he added. The "worth seeing" was very nearly said. "Thanks a lot, Peter. We must break bread sometime."

"Open a bottle, anyway," said Purcell with a smirk.

Break it over your cheap little toupee, dear, thought Tower.

"Listen, I really enjoyed meeting you. I think your furniture is divine," said Paula.

"Yes, and when she's taken over my firm I expect she'll be buying lots of it."

A pained expression rushed across Paula's face.

In the limo outside she came out with it. "Winty, I'm sorry, have I upset you in some way?"

He capitulated immediately. "No, darling. Of course not. You know me. Couldn't bear you going on and on about his furniture. The smug old tart looked like he'd had his first orgasm in years."

She laughed, but she still couldn't give up. "But it *is* wonderful."

"Seen worse," conceded Winthrop.

She punched at his arm and laughed to show it was all over.

"Believe it or not, I was your age once," he responded ruefully.

"Stick around and you will be again," said Paula.

"Can I stick around too?" asked Robert. She was right. She did make time go backward. There was ozone in the air around her, and sparkling electricity. She made the colors sing, the smells more real, and the sounds vibrate. If that wasn't an elixir of youth, what was?

She snuggled into him, and he could feel her breast firm, infinitely appealing, against his chest, and he could smell the sweetness of her breath as she laughed up into his eyes. "You can stick as close as you like for as long as you like."

"Now come along, children, not in front of the adult," admonished Winthrop Tower as the limo swept past the Plaza and onto Central Park South.

But they didn't hear the joke. They were together in the private world of lovers. They knew each other now, not each other's minds, each other's souls, but far more significant, each other's bodies. In the love furnace of the night they had bathed in passion and the memory of ecstasy lived on. She slipped her hand into his and he squeezed it hard as he savored the intense excitement. He had watched her in Purcell's office, and she had taken his breath away. Her bravery, her self-confidence, the accuracy of her taste. She had confronted the two famous designers as an equal and emerged unscathed from the contest. Before she had always been just a beautiful little girl in his eyes—the goddess from the backwoods who had burst into his world, but who remained a lesser mortal to be humored, and patronized perhaps, before the shuddering surrender. Now she was an equal, a superior in what was to him an alien scene, and it made his conquest more poignant. That was part of it. The other part was more important. To achieve the ultimate conquest you had to be conquered yourself. He hadn't known that before. Last night he had learned the lesson.

As she fell Paula could feel him falling. She could see it in his tender eyes, she could feel it against her breast in his speeding heart. So she crept nearer, plastering herself tight to his body, and he leaned back toward her in the conspiracy of closeness as they both dreamed of the skin beneath the clothes, of the lust and love just under the surface.

"I'm thinking of last night," she whispered softly.

"I'm thinking of tonight," he whispered back.

At the Metropolitan Tower they were expected.

The doorman leaped forward and two or three people who had just lunched at the Russian Tea Room next door stopped to see if the limo contained any "faces." The "look-isn't-that-Robert-Hartford?" chorus erupted around the trio as they went inside.

"Mr. Tower for the Count de Montmorency," said Winthrop to the pretty girl behind the reception desk. "What do you think of the Léger?" he said over his shoulder to Paula and Robert. A vast Léger black-and-white tapestry dominated the exquisite entrance hall, with its understated azaleas, and minimalist black leather armchairs.

"It's great. I love the whole look."

"Andrée Putnam. Works out of Paris. Very big in the sixties. Coming back now. Did Rubell's Morgans. The Léger belongs to Harry Macklowe, who built the building. There's another one, in color, at the Fifty-sixth Street entrance. We'll catch it on the way out."

The receptionist was talking into the intercom. "Yes, sir, I'll send them up."

A tall, diffident Frenchman was waiting for them in the foyer of the penthouse apartment. He pushed forward a ramrod hand. "Edouard de Montmorency."

Winthrop made the introductions. "And this is Robert Hartford," he paused for effect. "He's my assistant's assistant."

The aristocrat looked a bit confused at what was clearly a private joke. "I can't offer you anything . . ." He made a feeble gesture at the totally empty space that stretched out for acres, seventy-five stories above New York.

"That's fine. We just wanted to get an impression of the apartment. Obviously we have floor plans and photographs, but seeing is believing, touching is the truth."

Paula and Robert wandered over to the glass wall, a mural of the best view in New York. "God, this is magnificent," said Robert. "Both rivers, the Park, New Jersey, La Guardia. What a skyline."

"Paula. What do you think?" said Winthrop. "What would old Emily Carstairs have thought of this? Actually, we're so high up, we could probably ask her." He looked at his watch. "Perhaps better not. The sun's over the yardarm. She'll be plastered by now if paradise lives up to its name."

Paula snapped into action. She talked fast, as if plugging into some stream of consciousness. "Obviously the view is the main attraction, but I think we should avoid maximizing it. It would be too much. It's so strong all by itself that to point chairs and things at it would be to detract from the living space. The thing to do is to aim everything in that direction so you balance the inside against the outside and end up with some harmony."

Robert watched in awe as she set off on a lightning tour of the five-thousand-square-foot apartment. Walls crashed down, new ones sprang up as she bulldozed through the space, dreaming of what it could be, what it could mean. Colors rushed from her mouth and textures danced in her eyes as she painted the verbal picture of the beauty that was screaming to be created. Occasionally she would turn to an at first confused and then progressively enchanted Montmorency to ask him how he liked to live, what his family consisted of, their ages, their hobbies, his preoccupations. As they all listened, mouths half open in bewildered admiration, the dream apartment came together before their eyes. It was a visible thing, and it bore as much relation to the rooms in which they stood as space appeared to have to time.

Even Winthrop Tower was astounded. "Dear me, I think she's got it," he said, Professor Higgins-like, from the ranks of the spectators.

"Wonderful," said Montmorency, his eyes shining. "I accept," he added enigmatically, in an utterance that sounded suspiciously like the "I do" of the marriage ceremony.

"How on earth can you *do* that, Paula?" said an impressed Robert, oblivious to the presence of the others in the room.

"Did you like it?" she said.

"I loved it."

Do you like *me*, asked her eyes.

I love you, howled his.

Mmmmmmmmmmm, said her body.

He moved toward her.

"Listen, you two. I'm sure that it's around time for that lunch or whatever you were both planning. Why don't you hop off, and I'll stay and sort out a few of the boring details with the count," said Winthrop quickly. He gave them an enormous wink.

Almost before the wink was over, the two lovers were gone.

There was an almost unbearable pain somewhere at the bottom of Robert Hartford's legs.

None of the other skaters seemed to be suffering as he was. They glided by, contented smiles on their faces, and their cheeks were ruddy as they waved their arms in time to the waltz that blared gaudily from the loudspeakers. But Robert wanted to rest, and so he swerved clumsily to the red barrier that surrounded the Wollman rink.

When they had erupted out of the Metropolitan Tower, onto 57th Street, Paula had had the idea. "Oh, Robert, let's go try the skating rink we could see from the penthouse. Please."

He had immediately succumbed to her enthusiasm.

Now, the roar of skates, a blur of color, and the shout of enthusiastic welcome signaled Paula's arrival.

"Christ, where did you learn how to do that?"

"My dad taught me when I was very young. There was a rink in Miami. He'd drive me over on the weekends sometimes. I haven't done it for years, but it seems like yesterday."

His face veiled over with a sudden sadness as she spoke. "How old were you when your old man died?"

"Fifteen." She pushed the reply out fast as if she hoped that would end it.

Robert lay across the barrier like a beaten prizefighter, but even in his skating getup he looked like someone from a superior planet. Blue jeans, the thick lambswool sweater, black as night, and the trilby hat of the day before, softly folded, yet as crisp and as neat as any that Lock's of St. James's could produce. His face was alight with the cold and the exertion, and Paula's closeness was filling him up with a sense of power and grandeur that he had never felt before.

All his life he had considered himself a connoisseur of lovemaking. Sometimes he felt he had invented it. Now however, he realized that he knew nothing at all about it. Bertrand Russell had once said that to recognize that was the beginnings of wisdom. If so, then Robert's life so far had been blissfully ignorant. In retrospect it was simple. The vital ingredient in the mix had always been absent. He had left out the love. Now, with this girl, the fatal deficiency had been rectified. He loved her, but he hardly knew the person he loved, and now every time she spoke he would learn more of her. Her body he had explored, but that, too, had mysteries in reserve, to be revealed in breathtaking installments over passion-filled years. And there was her past—the family, the strange void, the aura of tragedy that hung around her like a phantom of the night. What had made her as wonderful as she was, and what could he do to ease the pain that summoned up a tenderness within him he had never known he possessed?

"You loved your father very much, didn't you? I can see it in your eyes."

"Yes, oh yes. I loved him." Paula leaned over the balustrade. She cupped her chin on her red woolen mittens, and tears filled her eyes. "Do you know what he did?" she said, and her voice caught as she spoke. She swallowed and then she patted her chest with her right hand. "He reached inside . . . and he put a string of fairy lights around my heart."

He reached for her, his hand useless on her arm but there for her, in the gesture that said he always would be. "But not your mother?"

How did he know that? The leap of intuition was effortless, as if she was speaking to him on several levels all at once. Was this what love was like? Shorthand? "No, not my mother. Poor Mama. Somehow she never measured up to Dad. He was my man."

She gave a little half laugh of disbelief, and a tear dislodged itself, tracing an uneasy pattern down her flushed cheek.

Robert reached for it, wiping it away. "I'm looking after you now."

His words said more than that. Your problems are over, sweet Paula. Those days are gone. Anything you want now you will have. Because you are with me, and I am strong, and I have power and I control the people who control this world of ours. Let me please you. Name what you want. Let me show you my strength.

She smiled up at him, hearing what he was saying, grateful for it,

despite the fact that she knew he could not right the ultimate wrong
that tortured her.

"I loved last night," she said simply.

"So did I."

She moved toward him on the barrier and pressed her shoulder
against his.

"I want to do it again."

She peered up at him, and her smile was no longer sad, but it was
teasing, full of affection, hovering on the borders of desire.

"Here?"

"We could skate real close," she murmured. "I mean *real* close."

"Paula!" His voice registered mock shock. "I've got cramps in my
legs." He laughed.

"Beats a headache!" She dug him in the ribs, laughing too.

"Omigod. Is it Robert Hartford?"

A huge girl with zits more or less crashed into them as she went into
recognition mode. "It is. Oh it *is*," she spluttered. "Marie!" she
screamed over her shoulder.

Robert cursed the fame he loved. Most of his life was spent avoiding
this in public, even as he schemed and worked for it in private. His
neck seemed to shorten and his face retreated beneath the brim of his
hat. Celebrity recognition took several forms, each as inexplicably
weird as the others. Some people were just plain rude, believing that
to insult fame was a good method of preserving precarious self-respect.
"Hated your last movie." "You don't look so hot in the flesh." "Is it
really true what they say in the *Enquirer,* that you've made arrangements to be preserved in ice when you die?" Others went mute, staring
with baleful eyes. Some demanded autographs, but possessed no pen
or paper and ended up with a scrawled "hello" in lipstick on the back
of their hand. Some, mercifully few, played amateur critic and ran
through the plots of several movies, only a few of which he had
actually starred in. All started from the assumption that he was a
creature so far removed from them, that the ordinary conventions of
polite human intercourse could and should be suspended. In the
absence of rules, anything could happen, and that made Robert
Hartford extremely nervous.

The fan stuck out an accusatory finger at Paula. "Is that the actress
who played the hooker in *Past Master?*"

"If you'll excuse us," mumbled Robert. He grabbed Paula's arm and
pulled her toward the nearby exit.

Over his shoulder wafted an excitable, "I had a dream about you
once."

"Did you hear that? You had her in her dream." Paula giggled at her accusation.

"On that basis, I'm afraid there have been several others!"

"On *any* basis there have been several others." Again she laughed to show that it was another joke. Somehow the laughter this time wasn't *quite* so spontaneous.

"And now there's you." He turned to look at her, and his eyes were full of concern as he surprised himself. "There's *only* you," he added.

She looked at him quizzically; then she slipped her hand into his.

"Let's take it minute by minute," she said at last, wondering what on earth she meant.

"Let's," he said, and his arms were around her. Then his mouth crushed down on hers and he kissed her as if he were never going to be allowed to touch her again. She tried to gasp but his hungry lips had other ideas and so she just tingled with the thrill of it as her feet reached up on tiptoe so that she could be that little bit closer than close to him.

"Let's go back to the Carlyle." Robert's voice was thick.

"Please," she murmured.

They hurried from the rink, but the skates and the cramp had made Robert's walk stiff and awkward.

"Who's limping now?" whispered Paula.

The telephone was ringing when they walked into the apartment.

"Let's leave it," said Robert.

"No, you can't," said Paula.

The really young could never do that. He smiled, indulging her. The desk would have taken a message.

"Hello," he said.

"Mr. Robert Hartford?" said the bright voice of a young woman.

"Yes."

"Can you please hold the line while I pass you on to Mr. William Kentucky, personal assistant to Mr. Hank Marvel." She spoke the names in a very definite, very careful way, as if they were deeply impressive.

Robert Hartford groaned. It was bad enough that the call was from Marvel, but this sort of corporate game playing drove him crazy. He wasn't against ego building, but he liked the bricks to be made of something substantial, like Oscars or box-office returns. Anybody with a mill or two could hire an army of wet-knickered, hair-lacquered, overmanicured bimbos to keep people waiting on the telephone. He sent his eyes up to the ceiling to tell Paula it was a bore, that he wanted to be with her, and she smiled back as she began to unpeel the layers of clothes that wrapped her.

The male voice that came on the line now was full of self-importance. "I'm sorry to keep you waiting, but the president of Moviecom International wishes to speak with you, and he is presently on a call to the Coast."

"Tell Marvel," said Robert Hartford in the voice he reserved for out-of-line males, the lowest species in the evolutionary hierarchy, "to call me back, in *person* please, when he is finished with his call to 'the Coast.' "

He slammed the telephone down. "Asshole," he said, as Paula watched him. He didn't move from the telephone. It rang almost immediately.

"Hartford? Marvel."

"Yes," barked Robert rudely.

"*Hank* Marvel," said the gravelly voice, chastened, but irritated by the Hartford response to the most valuable thing he had, his name. "I believe we're having dinner tonight."

Robert winced, as he beheld, albeit at the end of the telephone, the nastiness of Hank Marvel. He was the classic Napoleon type, a short man with a shorter fuse who had fought his way from the gutter, piled up the bodies, and then climbed on top of them to reach the pot of gold he was now plundering. He was no longer small in the eyes of the world, but as he pulled the covers over him at night he would *feel* small and he would be forever on the lookout for those who had sensed his *real* net worth—people like Robert Hartford, whose patrician vision could peer effortlessly into the dark recesses of the Marvel poisonality.

"My people booked a table at Le Cirque." He sounded quite pleased about that. Very nouvelle society. Kravis and Roehm. Erteguns and Trumps, Steinbergs and Kluges. It was where they all went when they felt like something a little grander than Mortimer's. A very rich man like Marvel would be at home in Le Cirque, where he could be sure of meeting a person or two who was quite a bit richer than he. Marvel would probably have his own table there.

"Can't stand the place," said Robert in a definite voice.

"Why on earth not? It's a very good restaurant."

"Oh, you know how it is. One has one's likes and dislikes."

"Well, where do *you* want to go?" Marvel was thoroughly disgruntled. The yes-men he surrounded himself with didn't have likes and dislikes. He had them on their behalf.

"What about the Russian Tea Room?"

Since the distant days when he had been a struggling actor Robert had always loved the beautiful restaurant next to Carnegie Hall on West 57th Street. The fact that it had always been Hollywood's home away from home in New York was almost incidental. It was a marvelous no-nonsense restaurant that had never made the fatal mistake of allowing its age-old trendiness to go to its head. It seemed to be open all day and all night, and anyone with the price of its meals could and would get a table there. Perhaps alone in New York it was where middle America could actually hear the dreary things that celebrities said to each other. The food was safe, not brilliant, with a few notable exceptions, but the ambience, the luscious red leather chairs, the enormously well framed, well-hung paintings, and the attentive but far from overzealous service made it a classic that had never lost the cutting edge of its chic.

Marvel laughed a nasty patronizing laugh. "Ha! I should have guessed. That's where all you movie stars hang out, isn't it? They make a big fuss of you there, do they?"

"Sort of. You might bump into the odd studio owner as well. You know, the *mainstream* ones."

Marvel had deserved that. Moviecom was a pushy little studio that was traveling fast but hadn't yet arrived. They made commercial movies but they had a reputation for cutting corners and double dealing. Robert had accepted Marvel's invitation out of basic curiosity. A dealer like Marvel, a businessman rather than a moviemaker, had to want something.

"Listen, Moviecom's on its way up. It'll be there," said Marvel bluntly, cutting down into the deeper layers of the conversation. "I have plans for the company. That's why I wanted to meet up with you tonight."

Robert paused. To cancel or not to cancel. That was the question. Curiosity versus pleasure. Curiosity won. "Well, I look forward very much to hearing any of your business proposals." Robert managed to emphasize the word *business*. What he meant was, "Stay away from the artistic side, philistine. The nearest thing you get to creativity is in the morning when you dump."

"Yeah," growled Marvel. "Okay, you book a table at your place. See you at seven."

"Seven-thirty."

"Whatever!" Marvel slammed down the phone as if he were crushing it into Robert's face.

"What was *that* all about?" said Paula.

"I'm afraid," said Robert moving toward her, "we're in for a terrible evening."

"But that's not till tonight."

Paula's message was unmistakable.

Robert spirited Paula under the blood-red canopy through the polished-brass and carved-wood doors of the Russian Tea Room, past the line that waited patiently for a table, to the place where the suited manager hovered.

"Hello, Mr. Hartford. How kind of you to come and see us. Your guests have arrived." He turned around and made little ushering gestures toward the number-one semicircular banquette just inside the main room, the place where all the real stars sat. Three people were there already. Two, Robert Hartford had expected. Hank Marvel, charming as genocide, and a bleached, birdlike thing that was obviously his wife. The third man was a total surprise. It was David Plutarch.

Robert's cool was his most valuable asset after his looks. He didn't lose it now, even though his mind was on red alert. Plutarch! Caroline's Plutarch. There was only one thing that was certain. His presence here, despite any bullshit excuses, would be no accident at all.

Marvel rose like scum to the surface to greet them. "Ah, Robert. There you are. Good to see you. Yes, good." He seemed to be trying to convince himself. "You don't know my wife. This is Marie-Lee, a big fan of your 'work,' and I hope you don't mind my bringing along my great friend, David Plutarch. David was at loose ends in New York, if you can believe that, and I insisted he join us."

The Plutarch expression was a mystery wrapped in an enigma inside a question mark. He raised himself an inch or two from the seat, in a gesture that said he didn't stand for anyone, and he extended a tentative hand toward Robert. An inscrutable half smile played across his lips. "Robert, how nice," he said. "Not since Livingstone's black ball."

"Hello, David," said Robert, taking his hand. Then he turned his dazzling smile on Marie-Lee Marvel. "I'm very pleased to meet you," he said, investing the *you* with a special emphasis that brought a blush to Mrs. Marvel's cheeks. He stood back to reveal his prized possession. "And this is Paula Hope."

Paula felt the eyes rake her. Robert had briefed her about the Marvels. The roughly good-looking man in the dark suit called Plutarch she didn't know, although his name seemed vaguely familiar. God, they were really giving her a going over. She fought back the desire to look down and check her dress. Inside, she was still making love. Did it show!

They all stood up and moved about, working out some unspoken placement, and then they were huddled around the table, the massive egos rubbing up against each other, fighting for space.

"David was the underbidder on the Sunset Hotel, darling," said Robert, turning quickly toward Paula who sat close by his side. She must know that fast. It would be an evening for careful conversation.

"Hardly the *under*bidder," said Plutarch sharply. "Let's just say the losing bidder."

Robert just smiled.

"Well, it's a great pleasure meeting you at last, Robert," said Marvel with the sincerity of a sociopath.

"It's a great honor, dear," said the wife.

Marie-Lee Marvel had seen better days, but she could still remember them. Her beauty, or rather her prettiness, had long since fled, but it had left traces behind, hints in the bone structure, insinuations in the almost stylish cut of the bleached brittle hair, faint suggestions around the hard mouth and the heavily mascaraed eyes. She had married the pushy Hank Marvel when he was less than nothing and had stood by him on the harrowing journey from crass via cash to some pale imitation of class. The secret they shared was that they were the only two people alive who knew just exactly how awful he was.

"It's not an 'honor,' " said Marvel crossly, contradicting his wife and annoyed by the implications of her excessive humility. "It's a pleasure, as I said."

"I wonder if you'd mind not smoking that cigar," said Hartford calmly, ignoring the undercurrents of the conversation completely. "It would spoil my food and I don't think it would be fair to the other diners either."

Hank Marvel looked down at the unlit Montecristo No. 2 cigar that sat like a torpedo between his fat fingers. He seemed surprised to see it there. He looked up at Robert, at his wife, at Paula, at Plutarch, at the restaurant where the "other diners" were, and his small eyes narrowed to keyhole slits. Slowly, deliberately, he reached for his inside pocket and pulled out a leather cigar case. He stowed the offending weed away beside its after-dinner fellow, and his lips were tight against his uneven teeth.

"Thank you," said Robert coolly. "I hope you didn't mind my asking."

Paula pushed her knee hard against his in the gesture that said "well done." She felt the little thrill inside, and the warmth of her lover's leg pushing against her.

"Do you come here often, Mr. Hartford? I know it has a reputation

as a watering hole for the movie industry. Publishing, too, I think,"
said Marie-Lee.

"Call him Robert," said Marvel rudely.

"Yes, please do, Mrs. Marvel, Marie-Lee," said Robert smiling
suavely into the heavily made-up face.

"Good Lord," said Paula suddenly, "look at that marvelous Picasso."

Four heads shot around to follow the direction of her pointed finger.
The painting she referred to was on the opposite wall. A red-haired
lady sat in profile, and at the same time head on, holding in her lap
a cage in which two small birds cavorted. Her right breast, large and
round, formed the dead center of the canvas, while her left breast
simply didn't exist at all. Instead, the viewer's eye was drawn to a
muscular forearm of dubious anatomical accuracy. The vivid red of
her dress matched the red leather of the banquette below her, and was
relieved by two cunningly placed stripes of jet black. The background,
arranged in layers of progressively darkened green, wandered away to
the plain gilt frame in waves whose shape suggested the outline of the
lady herself.

"That's not a Picasso," said Hank Marvel.

They all looked at him, Robert and Paula and his wife in horror,
Plutarch with a kind of detached fascination.

"I've just been reading that Stassinopu-what's-it's book on Picasso,
and that's not one," he added by way of explanation.

Hartford's arm flicked out and a waiter materialized out of thin air.
"Ask Gregory to slip over for a second would you."

The manager was there immediately.

"Who painted the picture over there? The one of the lady in red."

"That's a Picasso, sir."

"It doesn't look like a fucking Picasso," said Marvel truculently.

"Oh, but it does. It couldn't possibly be by anyone else," said Paula
firmly.

"I gather from the reviews that Arianna's book is mainly about
Picasso's sex life. Thinking of turning it into a skin flick, Hank?" added
Robert.

"Can I get you all something to drink," said the waiter into the ugly
silence.

"Champagne," said Marvel as if it were a response in church. Then,
realizing that this was not a sufficient response, he cranked out, "Dom
Pérignon or Cristal?" as he peered crossly around the table for
dissension. In the Marvel world there was only one kind of
champagne—the kind that cost the most.

"I think you'll find," said Robert carefully, "that they don't have the Cristal, and the Dom Pérignon is a little old, I see. Nothing the matter with that, but what I always do is have a carafe of champagne. I don't know anywhere else they do that, and it's rather good. It's French nonvintage, but totally acceptable, dry and not too acid. I think you'd like it."

"That sounds nice," said Marie-Lee Marvel, intrigued by the rubber necks that were zeroing in on her table, on Robert Hartford. However rich Hank and she got, nobody ever looked at *them.*

"Great," said Paula, adding her vote to the majority. Plutarch's nod was noncommittal, signaling that it was of no consequence at all to him what he drank. Three to one. Marvel looked like he was going to explode with anger.

"Shall I bring a carafe of the house champagne?" The waiter looked first to Robert, second to Marvel.

"Yes. And bring me a bottle of Dom, and make sure the damn thing's cold, okay?" barked Marvel. His face was on fire with fury but he fought to stay calm. Don't get mad. Get even. Forget even, get ahead. Way ahead.

"Hello luv," said Dudley Moore. Moore had walked across the room from superagent Sam Cohn's banquette opposite, where the two were dining with RTR regulars David Mamet and Joe Mantegna.

"Hi, Dudley," said Robert warmly. "Do you know Marie-Lee Marvel, Paula Hope, Hank Marvel, David Plutarch?"

Hank Marvel jumped up. Moore was a star with staying power. The audiences loved him, and they would forgive him anything. Even failures. That was real stardom. "I hope you will work for my studio someday," he said pompously.

Dudley caught the Hartford eye, but he was far too well trained in the Hollywood game to send up the studio head's pomposity. In England powerful people expected to be ridiculed. It was the national pastime, the price you paid for wanting a thing as disreputable as success. Here in America where success was godly, and where failure was frowned upon rather than celebrated, the famous expected to be taken very seriously indeed.

"I'd certainly like that, Mr. Marvel. I've heard Moviecom has some very good things in the pipeline."

"A few, a few," chuckled Marvel, his mood to some extent restored by the ego massage. *His* studio had some good things in development. The star had said so.

Robert couldn't resist it. Moore was big, but *he* was the biggest. He didn't have to play the Hollywood game. He was above it, and he liked Hank Marvel like he liked nuclear war.

"Mr. Marvel is a *business* genius," was what he said. "Mr. Marvel can take no artistic credit at all for any good things in the Moviecom pipeline," was what he meant.

Dudley Moore smiled nervously. "Well, anyway. Good luck. Good luck," he said, backing away from the table.

Marvel had been hot inside; now he was cold as the icy fingers of hatred plucked at his innards. He wondered if he should say it now, this minute, when he felt like saying it. Plutarch's voice, sharp, concerned, preempted him. "How's the picture deal with Galaxy going, Robert? You must be busy. Brave of you to take on the Sunset as well."

Robert watched him like a mongoose watches a snake. He sat there, so tight and so deadly, with his billions in his pocket—and all around him, hovering like an aura, was the fatal presence of Caroline Kirkegaard. He could sense her. Like Banquo's ghost, she was there at the feast.

Plutarch wasn't talking about the shortage of Robert's time. He was talking about the relative shortage in Robert's bank balance. He'd just paid $11.5 million into escrow as the ten percent deposit on the sale, with the balance due on closing in three months' time. The bank financing was in place, but his liquid assets were just about cleaned out, until he could complete the deal and get his hands on the Sunset's cash flow. In the meantime the income from the Galaxy contract would barely pay the mortgage and the borrowing costs. At the end of the eighties it was the American way. It was called gearing. Robert hadn't done a deal like this before. He was worried about it. He'd even lost a little sleep. There was very little margin for error.

"Oh, you know, David. There's only one life."

"Are you sure?" said David Plutarch, the wintery smile flicking around his cold-fish eyes.

Robert turned to Paula, and his laugh was dismissive. "David's into reincarnation, darling. He's very trendy, you know. I'm a little old for it myself."

"I'd never have guessed it." Again she pushed her leg against his under the table. The reference was to this afternoon. Everyone sensed that.

Hank Marvel's eyes were narrow as he watched Robert. He opened his mouth to say something but again from across the table the Plutarch eyes silenced him, his head moving almost imperceptibly from side to side.

"Are you ready to order, or would you like a few more minutes?" said the waiter. Dressed in a red Cossack-style tunic and black pants, he hovered solicitously by the number-one table.

"Are you all ready to order? Perhaps, Robert you would suggest dinner for us. Obviously you are the regular here." The totally unexpected charm suddenly dripped from the Marvel lips.

Robert's head flipped back, on instant alert. "Well, everyone ought to try the borscht. You can have it cold but hot is best, and they serve it with delicious pastries, filled with meat. They call them 'pirojok.' It's a much better start than the caviar, which is the same as it is everywhere else. Otherwise the chicken Kiev is good, unusually moist inside. That's if you're not on a diet . . . or what about a good, traditional stroganoff? The beef is mixed with crunchy mushrooms in a terrific cream sauce . . ."

"Sounds wonderful," beamed the brand-new Hank Marvel.

"Delicious," twittered his wife.

Plutarch was silent.

"Mmmmmm," said Paula, squeezing Robert's leg.

They settled back in the new pseudoharmony and prepared to survive the evening. Then David Plutarch cleared his throat. "I think that perhaps this is the moment for my little announcement," he said. He leaned back in his chair, quiet, deadly. The loudest thing about him was his rather unfortunate tie.

Robert felt the surge of adrenaline. Next to him Paula felt him feel it. They both knew at once. Plutarch's prior detachment now suddenly made sense. He had been watching Robert and Paula dig holes. Now he was going to push them in.

"Hank and I are going to become partners, which is, I suppose, a way of saying that I have taken a controlling interest in Moviecom International."

That wasn't it. Robert knew that. A lot of superrich people put money into the movies. Hollywood was one of the few places on earth where cash could still be transferred into instant status of sorts. It meant that the two enemies he had at the table were now revealed as a team. But Plutarch's presence there had suggested that anyway. "How nice," he said.

Plutarch leaned forward into the patronization, his eyes narrow now, his face a killer's face.

Marvel's breath was coming faster. He'd wanted to do this himself, but at least it was getting done at last.

"The second half of my foray into Hollywood is Moviecom's agreed bid for control of Galaxy. I signed the papers this afternoon."

Robert felt the color leave his face. He tried to keep it there but it just drained away.

"So, basically, Robert, from today on you're working for me."

He paused before he added the fatal rider. "For now, that is."

All Robert knew was that a terrible thing had happened to him, and that it was impossible to remain sitting at the table in the face of it. He stood up slowly, his remote-control cool covering his retreat. His mouth was tight shut, a bloodless line of lips bisecting his jutting jaw. He said nothing. There was nothing that could, with dignity, be said.

He reached for Paula's hand and he pulled her up with him, and together they pushed into the body of the room.

The two men, wreathed in malicious smiles, watched them go.

"Oh, I almost forgot," said Plutarch as Robert backed away from him. "Caroline said to say hello."

Paula lay across the sofa of Robert's Carlyle apartment, slumped against the petitpoint cushions. She knew something dreadful had happened, but she couldn't understand its dimensions. Across the table, sunk in gloom against the Clarence House chintz of a fine Chippendale lug chair, Robert Hartford clearly could. He sipped pensively on a caramel-colored scotch.

"I can't tell you how bad the vibrations were. It was awful," said Paula, more to murder the nervous silence than for any other reason.

"Sounds like a *wonderful* evening," trilled Winthrop Tower valiantly. "My evenings never vibrate these days. Anyway, I love self-made billionaires. They're so . . . *raw*. And they do nothing but talk about money. Such a relief from art, don't you think?"

Robert smiled wanly, Paula bravely.

"The trouble was that Robert kept putting them down in this incredibly subtle way—so that they couldn't take offense openly. It drove them crazy." Her voice was full of admiration as she watched him. It seemed to cheer him. He straightened himself up in the chair, and this time his smile had body.

"The only point in reaching the top in this goddamn country is not having to sniff around the guys who think they've made it. You don't see Winty brown-nosing the heavy hitters."

Winthrop paused as if in serious thought.

"There was a *certain* amount of sniffing around that milk-carton heir up on Laurel. He was *so* cute, stuck irretrievably in the closet door, not sure whether he was in or out. He changed the color of his drawing room three times in four weeks, or was it four times in three weeks. Anyway, I took it lying down. I *wish!*"

Robert scooped up the receiver and punched the numbers, reading them from the pad next to the telephone.

"It's Robert Hartford again. Is Mr. Liebowitz back yet?" His eyes narrowed and he leaned forward intently. He'd tried four times to reach the Galaxy CEO since they'd gotten back from the Russian Tea Room, but his car phone had been permanently engaged. Now, at last Liebowitz was home. He was being put through. "Bos? Robert."

"Robert, for chrissakes, where are you? I've left a hundred messages at the Sunset. We've got to meet. Like now." There was panic in Liebowitz's voice. It had happened. Robert had prayed, but never believed, that Plutarch had been bluffing.

"I'm in New York, at the Carlyle. What's up?" He knew, of course, but old habits died hard. Always hear the other man's information before you volunteered your own.

"You've got to get back here, Robert. What the hell's going on? It's chaos here. The whole thing's falling apart." He was babbling, his voice thick with fear.

"Bos, calm down. What is all this?"

"There's nothing to be fucking calm about," shouted Liebowitz. "For crying out loud, what has Marvel got against you? I'm fucking history around here, and the word is it's your fault."

Robert slipped into more gentle mode as he tried to pry the information from the studio head. "So it's true that Galaxy has been reversed into Moviecom? That's final, is it?"

"You'd better believe it's final, and do you know how I heard about it—me, the guy who's supposed to run Galaxy? George Christy calls me up from the *Reporter* and tells me his inside man at Reuters says the wires are running the story in forty-five minutes. I call Hank Marvel and he confirms, and oh-by-the-way he says, the first thing they're going to do is junk your contract and the second thing they're going to do is to junk me. What's going down, Robert? What the hell's going down?"

"Try not to get upset, Bos. . . . I've just had dinner with . . ."

"I *am* upset, Robert. I'm on the street with nothing, and I've got payments, and Rachel won't understand. You've fucking destroyed me, Robert, and it's pissing me off . . . it's really pissing me off. . . ."

Robert waited. Across the room Paula's eyes were wide. Winthrop's head was cocked to one side, like a wise old owl's.

The broken voice at the end of the telephone was small now, like the career of its owner. "I've been sitting next to the fax, Robert. The documents are coming in nonstop. David Plutarch, the Stellar

Communications guy, bought Marvel's sixty-two percent of Movie-com. As part of the same deal Moviecom bought the Wayco share of Galaxy, which gives it control. Marvel takes over the presidency and my job at Galaxy. The legal department has instructions to void the Galaxy deal with you, whatever it takes. They want you dead, Robert. It's almost as if the whole thing is about you. What did you do, Robert? What have you done to me . . . ?"

He started to whine, but Robert Hartford was no longer listening. He was thinking. As if in a dream, he put down the telephone in the middle of a Liebowitz sentence. Whatever details Bos had still to tell him were incidental. The deed had been done, as Plutarch had promised. The billionaire had paid maybe 150 million bucks for Moviecom and probably the best part of five hundred big ones for the controlling interest in Galaxy. And he had done it with the sole purpose of screwing Robert's career and finances. For the very first time in his life Robert saw a vision of the scenery on the other side of the hill.

He laughed the hollowest laugh in history. "He's done it," he said. "Plutarch's torn up my movie contract." There was an expression of total disbelief on his face.

"He can't do that. It was a legal contract. Galaxy signed it," said Paula, equally incredulous. She leaned forward—her eyes full of hurt and frustration at the affront to her lover.

Robert's voice was quiet. He had thought about that already. "I couldn't afford the court battle. Plutarch'd love it. His studio could bleed me white with every delaying tactic in the book. At the end of the day you can't make someone employ you if it's the last thing in the world he wants to do. The contract's just paper. Galaxy'll lose a fortune in potential profits when they blow this deal, and all the prestige that went with it. But the guy doesn't mind. He's more than happy to take a financial hit to get at me. Caroline Kirkegaard got him to do it, to pay me back for screwing up her blackmail attempt on Francisco. I can't believe she's got that much power over him. It's weird. It's frightening."

"Can't the studio management stand up to him? I mean, they wanted this deal. They were crazy for it," said Paula.

Robert smiled tenderly at her. There was so much she didn't know about Hollywood.

"The studio management," said Winthrop Tower, his voice laden with double entendre, "have been unable to stand for years."

Mist welled up in Paula's eyes. She jumped up and she walked slowly across to Robert. Kneeling down beside him, she threaded her hand into his in a gesture of solidarity that was also mixed with apology, as if to say, "I hope you don't think I'm bad luck." In answer, he squeezed her hand. "I know what you're thinking. Don't. This is my problem. You make it easier to bear," said his gentle touch.

"I think I might have another glass of whiskey," said Tower, more to himself than to anyone else as he moved toward the ship's decanter on the amboyna-inlaid library table. "I suppose," he added almost as an afterthought, "that the loss of the cash flow on the Galaxy contract might complicate the financing of the Sunset Hotel."

"That," said Robert simply, "is what the whole thing is about."

It was true. It was the double whammy. His career had suffered a major setback, but so had his finances. Without the income from the movie deal there was no way he could afford to borrow the money to buy the Sunset. Plutarch knew that. Caroline knew that. Together they had spent around 650 million dollars to get both their revenge and their own way. Now, with Robert an impoverished spectator on the sidelines, Livingstone would almost certainly have to sell them the hotel.

Winthrop sloshed the scotch into the thick crystal glass. "Let's hope Francisco gives you back your deposit," he said, his voice quietly ominous.

"What?"

Winthrop Tower's remark arrowed into Robert's brain. The deposit. There were eleven and a half million dollars sitting in escrow. Francisco Livingstone was not legally obliged to return his deposit if, as now seemed certain, he would have to back out of his commitment to buy the Sunset Hotel.

Robert's voice shook as he spoke. "I hadn't thought of that. He doesn't have to give me the money back, does he? That was the deal. Would you? Would I?"

Tower didn't know the answer to either question. There was friendship; there was honor; and there was decency. And there were eleven and a half million bucks.

"I'm sure he'd do the right thing," said Winthrop doubtfully.

Robert wasn't sure either. He'd always worked on the principle that nobody could be relied upon to "do the right thing," especially in Hollywood. That way occasionally you were pleasantly surprised. His mouth was dry. "He might. He's a good man, and he owes me one. But he's not a fool, and it wouldn't be a sensible thing to do, would it?"

He pushed back in the chair, his hand slipping from Paula's. He murmured to himself, to them. "If he takes the deposit, I'll have nothing left."

Winthrop walked over with the decanter. Without saying anything he poured four fingers of Glenfiddich into Robert's glass. No ice. No soda. Just sympathy. Robert lifted the malt whiskey to his lips, but he didn't drink it.

"Robert, it's not the end of the world." Paula reached out for his shoulder. "You can earn a fortune anywhere. If Galaxy wanted you, then Paramount will, and Universal, and all the others."

He looked up at her, but it was as if he wasn't really seeing her. Was it mere coincidence that his first love had coincided with the collapse of his life? Perhaps some people were just not meant to live in the world of emotions. When he spoke, the irritation coursed through the words, reflecting the illogical desire to hit out, to harm someone, to push part of the blame onto the only person in the world he was close to. "You don't understand these things, Paula," he said sharply. "Hollywood is sheep town. They follow each other. They'll all want to know why Galaxy pulled the contract, and nobody will guess or believe the real reason. The studio's new management will start a KGB-style disinformation service that'll fuel the rumor factory for months, coast to coast. Bits in Liz Smith, the trades out here—*Variety* and the *Reporter*, the celebrity mags like *Premiere* and *Us*. They'll say I'm over the hill, that I've peaked. They'll suggest I'm a megalomaniac, unreasonable in my demands, impossible to satisfy, a royal pain in the butt. You name it, they'll say it, up to and over the borders of libel, as long as it's damaging enough. They'll even pull in the Sunset deal. You can imagine the kind of thing . . . some crazy idea to buy a hotel he could never really afford . . . a sign of instability, of losing contact with reality. They might even bring you into it. . . ." His eyes glinted with the cruelty of the deeply wounded. "You know, involving himself with someone young enough to be his daughter. . . ."

He buried his head in his hands. Would the studio be so very wrong in all the things they would say?

Paula looked at Winthrop in desperation, wanting him to tell her that it wasn't true. But he just nodded at her. Up and down. Affirmative.

Robert's voice seemed to come from far away. ". . . I'm going down. That's the truth of it. My fee takes a nosedive, and second chances in that town are rarer than overnight success." Again he looked up at her, and this time there were tears in his eyes, tears of anger, of frustration as much as fear for his suddenly uncertain future. All he had worked for, all he had built, the extraordinary edifice of his brilliant career stood teetering above the abyss.

His reputation was in the bloodstained hands of a latter-day Jack the

Ripper, and the witch who controlled him, and his food, warmth, and shelter were at the disposal of a capricious old man. And then there was Paula.

He had fallen in love with her. Brilliant! Perfect timing. At the height of his fame, poised for greater glory than he had ever known, he had met the only girl to whom he had ever opened his heart. And she loved him, too. He could see it in her eyes. He could feel it in the warmth of her tender heart. And *whom* did she love? The movie star, of course. The myth. Paula loved the man who dined with presidents and was courted by the candidates for his legendary fund-raising abilities. She loved the biggest name in the industry that epitomized America, the man who could charm women because of his beauty, self-confidence, and power. She hadn't fallen for a fading has-been. Few of those survived the rocket-ship reentry on the journey back from the stars. What was left of them was picked up at the Betty Ford, on "Hollywood Squares," in guest-star roles on the dreaded "Love Boat." No, Paula would not love him then, and he wouldn't blame her. He wouldn't even like himself.

"What will you do?" said Winthrop softly.

Robert splayed out his hands. "There's nothing for me to do. The others are in the driver's seat. Kirkegaard. Plutarch. Livingstone. Whoever. I can't change anything, and sure as hell I'm not going to beg. Who knows? Maybe Plutarch will be struck by lightning. God can't like him a whole lot." Robert laughed bitterly.

"Robert." Paula's voice was sharp, urgent. "This doesn't change anything, does it?" The "about us" was left hanging.

"I don't know," he said.

FOURTEEN

The moonlight danced across the Pacific Ocean, picking out the dark rocks just off the shore, and the late gulls that scurried among them searching for food. The salmon sunset was over, but a pink-blue light stained the distant horizon and the line of the Malibu Hills still separated earth from sky. The desert wind moaned gently across the rapidly cooling sand, and the lights of the mainland across the Santa Monica bay and the distant planes rising from LAX were a frame for the picture of the lovers.

Hand in hand, Robert and Paula nuzzled close, protecting each other from a thousand make-believe demons, as they walked on the deserted private beach of the Malibu Colony toward the pier. They kicked contentedly at mounds of seaweed, they rolled up the legs of their jeans to ford the shallow rivulets that criss-crossed the sand, and they admired the myriad moonlit sandcastles left hostage by happy children to the ravages of the wind and sea. "It's so beautiful here. So perfect," she murmured, her words almost lost in the salt-stained breeze. He didn't answer but he held her tighter, and the strength of his arms said yes, he felt that. Despite everything. Despite the danger to the only world he had. The only world that had existed . . . before Paula.

Yesterday, in New York, when everything had been turned upside down, he had been unable to get things into perspective. Like a hound at bay, he had turned against the girl who loved him as instinct had told him to discard anything that might slow him down in the battle to preserve what he was in danger of losing.

Then, on the long flight back to L.A. lying beside her, high in the

223

night sky, he had realized that nothing mattered to him except this girl, this strange beautiful waif who had entered his life so late, and who had captured it so completely. Somewhere over the heartland of America he had discovered the extraordinary truth. Robert Hartford, the screen idol, was no longer alone—and he never need be again. The moment the plane had landed they had gone to the beach—some lunch at Michael's, drinks with Goldie Hawn and Kurt Russell at Broad Beach—and now here they were, on the potent sands of Malibu.

She looked up into his eyes and smiled. "Nothing matters except us," she said. "There isn't anything else."

Paula had come to realize that he was like a Russian doll. Layer upon layer of carefully crafted sophistication had produced a lacquered exterior whose sole purpose was to hide the man inside. Slippery smooth, he wafted through life on the cloud of his own charisma, and no one had ever before plumbed the depths of him except her. She knew and loved the inner core. She loved the gentle child who had been starved of his parents' love, and who had fought and won the world's sham adoration as a pale substitute. She loved the loneliness of the superstar and the vulnerability of the lover who didn't know how to love, and she was sucked into his naïveté as it clutched so desperately at the blanket of worldly wisdom. Paula loved the delicious paradox of him. Nothing was as it seemed, the outward persona at war with the inner being.

"You know, before I met you, today would have been the worst day of my life. You've made it the best," he said. He bent toward her and for long seconds their breaths mingled, the scent of them exchanged with the happiness they shared, merging in the magic moonlight of the Pacific beach.

Then he kissed her. It was not the kiss of passion. Not the kiss of exploration, that first nervous step to the feast of bodies. Instead it was the kiss of love. His lips moved against hers in the twilight, reverently, as if he was taking the sacrament. It was a moment of shared wholeness, a holy moment of truth that only true lovers could feel. His lips brushed hers, too caring to crush them as he talked to her with his kiss. "I love you," it said. "I will always love you," it vowed. "All my life I will exist for you. You have made everything new again. You have given me a second chance."

Paula fought to stop time in its tracks and suspend the moment forever. All she had ever wanted was to be loved like this. Now, at last, she was fulfilled. Her lips were melting with the passivity of total love.

She was his, and she was telling him that with the ultimate eloquence, more beautiful, more true by far than all the lies of language.

He pulled back, not because he wanted to stop but because more than that he wanted to watch her. He must fix her in his memory, now, at this precious time.

Like a frightened doe, infinitely vulnerable on the mighty plain of love, she stared up at him, her lips painted with moisture, her mouth parted to let the warm breath escape. Her eyes were wide with the glorious fear of decision, as she surrendered to him, body and soul, heart and mind, this day, and tomorrow and forever more.

"I love you, Paula," he said, his words thick on the night air, as he peered into her essence, plundering it of its sweet generosity, of its purity, its innocent strength.

A shuddering sigh rushed from her and her breasts thrust against his chest as she hugged him tight and the joy coursed through her. "Oh Robert, I love you too. God, how much. How very much," she whispered.

There were tears in his eyes as he heard her, and he fought to make sense of the crazy feelings. No longer was he Robert Hartford, the great lover. He was a child again, experiencing the awesome feeling of global newness, the thrill and the fear that came with the realization that everything would have to be learned. Here was the man who knew how to please a woman. And here on the cooling sand, with the wind in his hair and the so young girl in his arms was a teenage novice, lost in the mad glory of his own first love.

"Love me always. Whatever happens. Love only me," he said.

He could have laughed as he heard what he was asking, but he had never been more serious in his life. Never before had he revealed the desperate insecurity lurking beneath the superstar veneer.

"I do. I will. Of course I will."

She clung to him limpet tight as she promised the strange promise. She didn't hate his sudden doubt. She loved it. She didn't care that he was the movie star, or the millionaire. The first time she had met him she had felt the tug at her heart, and then he had been the busboy, the guy with the "hello" eyes she had tipped on that faraway first evening at the Sunset Hotel. It was wonderful that he wanted her to be faithful to him, because it meant that he cared, this supposedly casual, careless, carefree myth whose body was plastered warm against hers on the Malibu sand. How could he doubt her? How could he need to ask her about forever? But she understood, because those were the questions on *her* lips, asked and answered and asked yet again in the beauty of their kiss, and in all the kisses they would share. "Do you love me?" "Will you always love me?" "Promise never to love another." There would never be any escape from the fears that measured the strength of the feelings. The loss of such sublime happiness was too terrible to contemplate. Only when the flame flickered, and began to die would the timeless questions at last become irrelevant.

But the intensity had not left his face. He needed more than her breathless agreement. "I want you to promise, Paula. Promise now that you will never be unfaithful to me. From this moment on. Promise."

The old Robert Hartford stood back shocked and shaken as he contemplated the new. Where did this terror come from? Had it all started with his father's casual promiscuity when he had learned the lessons of female infidelity, and had, at the same time, fallen in collective love with the unfaithful? Those soft sirens of long ago, romping silkily around the bungalows of the Sunset Hotel, had defined the impermanence of sexuality. They had been the stuff of it, and they had filled him up with it as they had turned him on, and molded him into the man he had become. His father had loved them and left them, and so had he. Left the leavers. Done it first. Stuck in the daggers that were planned for his own back. But what if you dared to care? What if you *loved?* What if you gave yourself to those unworthy of the gift? It had been far too awful to contemplate and so, through the long years, he had insulated himself from that, and instead perfected the skills of sterile lovemaking in the void where love itself was a stranger.

Now, it had happened, and with the cruelty of fate it had happened on the eve of his own destruction. With his riches stripped away and his fame in ruins, the "expert" was about to become a novice locked in the terminal angst of those who dared to put themselves on the line. In the affair of the heart, Robert Hartford was a gambler at last. And it scared the living daylights out of him.

So around his brain the word kept winging around and around. *Promise. Promise. Promise.*

He knelt down and his arms held her tight so that she knelt before him, too, and they faced each other, solemn, close.

Paula reached out and touched his cheek as if to soothe away the pain of doubt. "I promise you, Robert Hartford. On my life I promise I will always be faithful to you."

A tear rolled down the famous cheek.

"Make love to me," he said.

* * *

It was the end of a long day, but Francisco Livingstone's tiredness was not the normal kind. His illness was draining his energy.

He walked over to the Benjamin Burnham Connecticut block-front cherry desk and the typewritten document stared up at him. Thank God, his beloved hotel would be in good hands. Robert Hartford would make all sorts of mistakes, but then so had he in the early days. It didn't matter. It would be good for the Sunset to go through a few dramas. At least Robert's heart was in the right place, and most of all he had good taste, and the wisdom to hire people whose taste was better than his. The problems he would engineer would result from his standards being too high rather than too low, and at the end of the day those could always be overcome.

He brightened a little. At least he would get to see the Winthrop Tower–designed Sunset. That would be some memorial.

He sat down, pulled the silk dressing gown tightly around him, and picked up the telephone.

"Front desk? Whom am I speaking to?"

"John, Mr. Livingstone." They all recognized his voice.

"Oh, John, be a good fellow and send a bellboy down to my bungalow, will you? I want him to witness a signature. He'll bring you back a sealed envelope. Could you put it in the night safe and give it to the manager in the morning? Tell Brough I want it transferred to my own document safe tomorrow. Is that clear?"

"Quite clear, Mr. Livingstone."

Everyone knew that the hotel was in escrow and that Robert Hartford was the new owner, but equally everyone knew that while he was alive the Sunset would always belong to Francisco Livingstone.

"And, sir, there's a message just come in for you. Your masseuse telephoned to say she was sick. She's arranged a replacement who she says is very good indeed. If it's okay, she'll be there at the usual time. That's in about half an hour, sir."

Livingstone put down the receiver, irritated. His weekly massage was a ritual that he relied upon for its total regularity. Karen, the usual girl, knew exactly what he liked and disliked and they had evolved a clockwork procedure that reduced to a minimum all potential for discord. On the first day she had visited him she had asked how he liked to be massaged. "In total silence," he had replied, and that was how it had always occurred. Over the years they had refined the procedure. Knowing that he could set his watch by the punctuality of her arrival, he would have a ten-minute sauna, a twenty-minute bath, and would then take up his position on the permanent marble slab that was a feature of his cavernous bathroom. The sweating and the heat would relax him completely, and sometimes he would even doze off to awaken to the soothing caresses of Karen's practiced fingers. One hour's massage was always followed by a facial, manicure, pedicure, and a vigorous rubdown with a rough towel bathed in cologne. The whole business took about three hours, and it was the best part of Francisco Livingstone's week. On the very few occasions when Karen had canceled before, she had provided a replacement and briefed her on the plot of the massage. He hoped she'd done so this time.

The doorbell rang. He walked over and let the bellboy in.

"I just wanted you to witness my signature on this document." He scrawled his name in a spidery hand. The bellboy wrote his in big round letters beneath, purposefully not asking what it was he was signing. "Thank you. Now you be sure to give that to John and make sure he remembers to put it in the night safe. What's your name?"

"Walter."

To ask an employee's name was the equivalent of a tip. The impression was given that Walter would not be forgotten.

Well, that was one thing out of the way. Far better to be safe than sorry.

Now what should he do about the masseuse? Karen had a key. Had she given it to the new girl? Almost certainly not. Should he disrupt his usual schedule? No. He walked quickly to the door and placed it on the latch. The girl could let herself in. By that stage he'd be totally relaxed on the slab. That was the whole point of it all.

He had switched the sauna on earlier and it was creaking with heat when he opened the door, the scrubbed, faded wood hot to the touch, the coals glowing radiantly in the spotless, stainless-steel furnace. He reached inside and ladled some green-pine essence onto the coals, watching the steam heat hiss into the dry atmosphere. Quickly he checked the inventory. Six or seven crisp, clean towels, *The New Yorker*, *The Economist*, and *Vogue*, a Thermos of crushed ice for the delicious merger of heat and cold that was perhaps the best part of the sauna. He slipped off the dressing gown and stepped inside, being careful to avoid contact with any of the burning wooden surfaces. He stretched out full length and flicked the switch that controlled the piped music, a little Beethoven for the jangled nerves. Beneath him the towel sopped up the moisture springing from his back. He had to be careful at his age. Dehydration was a problem, and the heart was always threatening unpleasant surprises. Still, he breathed in deeply and sighed his contentment. Then, quite suddenly, there was a shift deep within him. In the middle of the carefully orchestrated comfort he felt the premonition. It tickled at the back of his spine where the sweat gathered, and it speeded his already racing heart. He hadn't the faintest idea what had caused it. He was wrapped in sensuous comfort, and yet suddenly he was thoroughly disturbed. It made no sense at all, and if there was one thing that Francisco Livingstone couldn't stand it was nonsense. He closed his eyes and hoped it would go away, as the timer ticked and the wooden walls of the sauna expanded and contracted to the conductor's baton of the thermostat.

He picked up a copy of *Vogue*, thumbed past an article on spa burn-out, and settled on a photospread of Jami Ramona! Her beauty and his memories wiped his mind clean. Had it really happened? He looked down at his own body, and a smile softened his crinkled features. The little girl had nearly destroyed him, but it had been worth it. Absentmindedly, he ladled some more pine essence onto the coals.

The small glass window in the wooden door of the sauna steamed up as he threw the pine liquid onto the coals. What made him think of *Psycho?* God, what a creepy film that was. The knife falling, falling, the outflow of the tub, the rusty water and poor Janet Leigh's lifeless eye. On an impulse he reached out to wipe the window clear with the corner of the towel, but only the tan marble of the bathroom wall stared back at him. Livingstone had had enough. Maybe the warm bubbles in the bath would help restore his equilibrium. But in the bath the silly mood persisted. He ladled out a more than generous quantity of Dior bath oil into the water, tipping it with abandon from the twenties cut-glass decanter. It was a superstitious gesture of sorts, as if conspicuous consumption would somehow protect him from the evil spirits that seemed to dance around the room. Livingstone sighed. He got out of the bath, pulled the Sunset Hotel bathrobe around him, and patted himself dry. Then he let the robe fall to the floor, walked to the massage table, and climbed on top of it. He lay face downward, adjusting a large towel over his lower back. The exertion of it all had exhausted him, as it was supposed to. He looked at his watch. Half past. The girl would be here any moment.

Good. That was better. The tension was easing at last.

He heard the girl then—soft, muffled sounds as she let herself in. She would be orienting herself from Karen's instructions, working out which door led to the hallway, which to the massage area that separated the vast clothes closet from the bathroom. He heard the door open, heard it close. The unseen girl walked toward him and stood by the side of his bed. A hand, cool, its touch light but knowing, landed in the small of his back.

"Hi," she said quietly.

He twisted around and peered upward, up the neat thighs, the short white skirt of the uniform, past the angled breasts to the girl's face. She smiled down at him, very pretty, very friendly, eager to please from the milk-white teeth to the retroussé nose, from the square dimpled chin to the gorgeous flame-red hair.

"Hi," grunted Livingstone. That should about do it for the conversation. He had no need whatsoever to know her name.

He could smell the almond oil as she poured it on her hands, and his skin waited in anticipation for the fingers that would charm him into the reverie of the no-man's-land between sleep and wakefulness.

She dug deep into his back, firm yet gentle in the perfect combination, up to the shoulders, thumbs to the base of the neck, kneading, testing, exploring his body as she felt for the right pace, the optimum degree of hardness.

Francisco Livingstone wafted in and out of sleep as he was supposed to do, unsure whether dropping off or coming around was more blissful. All life should be like this—responsibility banished; sensuality with no recriminations; nothing to catch, nobody to catch you. It must feel like this to be a violin, milked of your music, vibrating at the whim of another's fingers. How wonderfully passive he felt, and yet, paradoxically, it was he who was in control. With his barked command, the pace would slow or quicken, the hands reach deeper or less deep.

"Could you turn over, Mr. Livingstone." The request was a caress.

He rolled over, like an old log on a young river, adjusting immediately to his new position, and only marginally aware that he had exposed his nakedness to the young girl. He felt her hands reorganize the towel to cover his front, and once more he was flirting with sleep.

She bent in close to his ear and her breath went inside it with her words. "You just relax, Mr. Livingstone. I'll start your facial right after I finish the massage."

But Francisco Livingstone was already asleep.

The girl stopped. Her hands slipped away from him, and noiselessly she stood back from the table, watching him, gauging how far gone he was into sleep. For a minute or two she stood motionless in the quiet room, until his snores became stronger. Then, suddenly she seemed to decide. She walked quickly to the door, and she opened it carefully, her eyes never leaving her sleeping client.

A woman stood in the doorway, like an angel of death. She filled it

up, from floor to ceiling, legs apart, hands on hips, her face hidden
beneath the brim of a black leather peaked cap. Claude Montana
clothed the broad shoulders, and the soft leather of the micro-skirt
clung like wallpaper to the curves of her bottom. She wore leather
boots, black as the devil's heart. A belt of wound thongs strangled her
waspish waist, and a black cashmere polo-necked sweater hugged her
tall white neck. Lit from the back she stood there, surrounded by the
aura of her terrible vengeance.

"He's asleep," said Kanga.

"Good," said Caroline Kirkegaard.

They passed each other, speaking no more, and the redhead's eyes
fixed on the floor as she walked by the woman who owned her.

Caroline Kirkegaard glided into the room. He was snoring on the
massage table, this puny obstacle to her purpose. Francisco Livingstone had tried to deliver up the Sunset to the man she loathed. Once
Hartford had slithered from her trap. He would not do so again. For
two delicious days she had reveled in Plutarch's and her revenge on
Robert Hartford and the wonderful fact that he would no longer be
able to afford the hotel that Livingstone so desperately wanted to sell to
him. Once more she was so near. Yet nothing could be left to chance.
Who could predict the caprice of a rich and dying man? Despite
Hartford's cash crisis Livingstone might still find a way for his friend to
buy the Sunset—at the very least he would search the ends of the earth
for an acceptable alternative. But with Francisco dead, and Hartford
unable to complete his deal, the Livingstone executors would sell
immediately to the highest and most convenient bidder—to David
Plutarch. And Robert Hartford would never see his eleven and a half
million dollar deposit again. He would be penniless, in Beverly Hills,
where poverty was a serious felony.

So she walked quietly toward the table and her heart laughed as she
contemplated the marvelous thing she would do.

He wanted a facial. That was what he always had, according to the
hotel gossip. He would get one. It had been simple to find the number
of his masseuse, and no problem at all to cancel her. "Mr. Livingstone
has asked me to cancel his appointment for this evening as he has an
important business meeting. His secretary will call you tomorrow to
reschedule." The message left at the reception had been equally
straightforward. "This is Karen, Mr. Livingstone's masseuse. I'm
unable to keep my appointment this evening, but I have organized a
replacement in the usual way. Can you please pass the message on to
Mr. Livingstone, as his private line has been engaged?"

She reached into her bag as she took up her position at the head of the table. A good facial should always begin with a thorough cleaning of the pores, shouldn't it? She drew out the bottle of astringent lotion and splashed some onto her hands, filling the room with the smell of jasmine.

She smoothed the lotion onto his parchment skin, taking care not to get it near his lips, his eyes, his nose. No sting must wake him.

Again she reached into her bag, but this time no potion, no sweet-smelling lotion, no soothing cream emerged. The tube was big and ugly, and it was painted a garish green. The letters in red were quite clear about its contents. CYANOACRYLATE, they said.

It was super glue.

She unscrewed the top, and she moved the tube toward Francisco Livingstone's jasmine-scented face. The pungent aroma of the industrial glue was lost, as it was supposed to be, in the heavy perfume.

First the mouth, parted a little as his meager breath escaped it. The dollops of clear liquid ran all over it, cascading between his thin lips, bonding eagerly onto his teeth. Quick, so quick the tube raced to his nose, and her hands squeezed tight as the glue invaded the nostrils, running, racing, sliding to fill the twin voids. And then, of course, his eyes. Not necessary, but such fun to block them up. One. Two. So easy as they wept the innocent liquid that was not tears. Nor ever would be.

She stood back, and a smile lit up her beautiful face as she surveyed her handiwork. The bits of him where the air entered, where the breath left him, were awash with the glue. The manufacturers were adamant about it. That was why it was "super." It set in seconds. And it bonded stronger than tempered steel.

She reached forward with her finger and thumb and she placed them on each side of the patrician nose. Then, as if picking a delicate flower, she nipped it tight.

Francisco Livingstone's dream was turning sour. The carpet on which he floated over the scented valley had turned into a bed of sharp nails. And now, worse, it was falling precipitously from the sky toward a black, dark lake he had not seen before. Down, down he went, and he braced himself for impact, and readied himself to swim for his life as the waters threatened to swallow him up. Splash. He must hold his breath in this foul-smelling water. He must get out of this suffocating blackness to the surface and the sunlight.

He sat bolt upright and fire filled his throat, as agony burned in his eyes and his nose. He tried to breathe in, but he couldn't breathe and he tried to open his eyes, but he couldn't see. His hands raced to his face to find out why. But his searching fingers found no answers. There was concrete at his lips, at his nostrils, in his eyes. He was blocked up with some strange substance that seared and burned at him, but the pain didn't matter because he couldn't *breathe,* and his world was deathly dark. A massage. A masseuse. There would be someone there to help him and he tried to scream in the soundless void as his lungs howled their protest in his chest and the panic squeezed the toothpaste of his brain. He tore at his mouth, ripping at his sealed lips, and he tried to push his fingers into the blocked nostrils, but there were no holes anymore. He was all stopped up. There was cement in his vital places, and, oh God, his eyes! Red pokers of white heat were stuck in them, but they merged with the rest of his face when he tried to find them. They were gone, lost in a featureless expanse of smooth, plastic nothingness. He fell sideways in the soundless chaos and his hand scratched at the air, his fingers brushing briefly at the hair of the person who had murdered him. Then he crashed headlong toward the marble floor.

Only his ears were still open. That she knew. That she intended. "Good-bye, Francisco Livingstone," she said. "When you get to wherever you're going, tell them that Caroline Kirkegaard sent you."

FIFTEEN

Limousines were lined up outside the Church of the Good Shepherd like Russian tanks at a May Day parade. They stretched back down Bedford Drive as far as the eye could see, and they seemed to be disgorging their contents all at once.

Robert Hartford stood on the breezy sidewalk in front of the main doors of the church on Santa Monica Boulevard and shrank from the crowds that swirled all around him. He had never been to this particular church before, nor even known that Livingstone was a Catholic, but as he looked around, it appeared that God shared the preoccupations of all the other proprietors of Beverly Hills real estate. The United Artists building was just across the street, and so was the Wells Fargo bank, while outside the church a bright sign announced that it was protected by Selective Security. Clearly the Almighty was leaving nothing to either chance or the morals of those He had created, and He had taken care to position His house as close to Mammon and the movie industry as was decently possible in La-la Land.

Robert suppressed a bitter smile. He couldn't afford such cynicism. He had a more pressing problem. Two days before, the Galaxy press conference announcing the rescinding of his movie contract had cleaned the other news off the front page of every show-biz paper in America, and now the press was in a feeding frenzy.

The side streets around the Sunset Hotel were packed with paparazzi, and everywhere he went they lined up to humiliate him. In the whole of his life he had never experienced anything like it. Fame and money made you soft. You withdrew from the world behind your cash mountain and you threw bucks at your problems until all paths were smooth. Mentally flabby on the diet of sycophancy and luxury, you grew weak. Then the walls were ripped away. Like now. And the icy blast of cruel reality zipped through your unprepared body to freeze your heart. He should have been ready for the legendary impermanence of superstardom. Apparently he wasn't.

David Plutarch loomed up, welcome as an iceberg on a lonely sea at night. "Ah, Robert. My people have been trying to reach you. So sad about poor Francisco. Still, what a way to go! No pain. No misery. They found him in the tub, apparently. Out like a light." He flicked his fingers in the air. On his face was a mocking smile.

Robert stared back at him, the hatred blazing in his expression. Yet he knew he had to take it. The world was watching him. They wanted to know whether he would lose his cool along with everything else.

"Of course, it's an ill wind, isn't it, Robert? I mean, Livingstone being so implacably opposed to my buying the Sunset, and then this business . . . and your 'cash flow' problem on top . . ." He tailed off. What he was saying was that Robert Hartford was bust and that he, Plutarch, had done the busting. He smiled an oily smile, and he stood back to watch the effect on Robert.

"Closing isn't until the day after tomorrow," Robert replied, trying to make his voice sound relaxed and steely all at the same time. But this wasn't the movies, and Plutarch knew his way around a deal like a roach around a kitchen.

"Yes," Plutarch continued, "not really enough time to find someone to take you out of the contract by closing, so it's good-bye to your deposit, I imagine. I suppose the Livingstone estate will look quite kindly on my offer now." His eyes glinted. "Still, not to worry, Robert. It's only eleven-point-five that you lose. That's small change to you movie stars, isn't it? But I remember the days when I *thought* it was quite a lot of money, don't you?" He paused, allowing the irony to burn deep; then he turned and walked toward the church. "See you inside," he said cheerfully over his shoulder. "Oh, and watch out for Caroline. She'll be here soon, and she's just *dying* to see you."

Robert didn't often feel like a drink, but he did now. He shouldn't have come, let alone take it on himself to arrange the funeral. But there had been no one else to do it, and it had to be done. Why had Francisco chosen this time to die? At the back of his mind he had felt that the old boy would do the right thing by him and let him off the hook by paying him back his deposit. No way in a million light years would the Livingstone executors—some hatchet-faced attorneys from

Century City with shifting sand for souls and time clocks for hearts. Yet, even in his frustration at the timing of it, there was room for genuine sorrow. He had liked the old boy. They went back a long way, they were polite to each other, and when they met by chance each looked pleased. In Robert Hartford's book that just about defined friendship, but he was hardly an expert on the subject. In this life people were divided into those who worked on their careers, those who concentrated on their families, and those whose efforts went into their friends. Only one thing was certain. Juggling all three ended in balls on the floor.

He peered over the heads of the milling crowd. Where was Paula, and Kristina, and dear old Winty? Robert was already regretting that he had come on ahead to make sure that the Sunset Hotel people were organizing things properly.

"Robert Hartford, we meet again."

Hank Marvel was standing in front of Robert and apparently he, too, wanted to collect his pound of flesh.

"I've got nothing to say to you. Talk to my lawyers," snapped Robert. "We're here for a funeral, not a fight."

Hank Marvel was the sort of man who did not come singly. His entourage clustered around him like greedy puppies at a bitch's teat. Robert scanned them quickly. They were quite a high-powered bunch for hangers-on.

"Nobody's fighting. Nobody's fighting," lied a hot-shot agent who had been courting Robert Hartford for the last five years, but whose face was alight with the realization that he would have to court him no more. "We're just businesspeople trying to turn a buck."

Robert Hartford was there in a flash. Being an agent who doubled as an attorney was the preferred path to running a studio these days.

"Congratulations, Sam. I gather that you get to sit on the board at Galaxy. Wasn't it lucky I didn't sign with you, like you kept asking me to. I'd be clean out of an agent now, wouldn't I?"

"But will you be needing one?" barked Marvel.

They all laughed at that. Status changed fast in Beverly Hills. A week before and they'd have been clustering around the Hartford table at Spago like priests around a pope.

Robert bit his lip. Damn. He'd walked right into that one.

"So it's business as usual at Galaxy, is it? Making more bombs for the Pentagon!" Robert sneered the insult.

The agent-turned-studio-executive could cope with that one. "Oh, I think we'll be all right from now on. Poor old Bos lost the plot, I'm afraid. Your contract would have bled the studio white. Best to junk it. No point putting all one's eggs in one bastard," he said.

"Why on earth not?" blasted the icy tones of Winthrop Tower. "I mean, after all, you've crammed all the bastards into one Galaxy."

Robert spun around as Tower arrived, and the Marvel entourage took a metaphorical collective step backward. Open season might have been declared on Robert Hartford. It had certainly *not* been declared on Winthrop Tower. He was an intact Hollywood legend, standing foresquare on the crossroads where business met art; where money, often for the first time, met taste; and where the slow of tongue and the feeble of mind invariably met their Waterloo.

"I see the drinking men stand together," tried Hank, without conviction.

"Yes, better watch out in the gutter when we piss," said Winthrop cheerfully. Billionaires, studio heads, powerful attorneys meant nothing to him. The harder they fell.

They backed off at that. Nobody wanted to alienate Tower to the point of no return. One fine day he might be prevailed upon to make their homes look like they didn't own them, that ultimate signal of social arrival.

"See you in court," Robert shot at the retreating Marvel.

"If you can find a contingency lawyer," said Marvel loudly over his shoulder as he walked away.

"Where's Paula?" asked Robert.

"She's coming. She was driving with Kristina," said Winthrop.

Robert felt the relief run through him. "Thanks for the support there, Winty," he said, squeezing the Tower arm.

"Anytime, dear. Sitting ducks are *such* good sport, aren't they? Funny thing, isn't it, that the very last thing you need to make money in Beverly Hills is *brains*."

Suddenly Paula was by his side. Her hand slipped into his, and she squeezed it tight.

"Well I think this is a *wonderful* funeral," Tower chimed in. "Haven't had so much fun at a Livingstone party for years. Come on, let's go and bury the dear old thing. I'm told the choirboys are a *dream*." Tower shepherded them inside, his gimlet eyes frightening off any would-be Robert baiters who might be littering the steps of the church.

All around them the glorious sadness of Mozart's Requiem Mass filled the air. The fragrant melody, heavy with heartache, burdened with grief, floated free. It rose to the high ceiling, climbed to the spires, and flew like a message to God through the Giorgio-scented air. But all the sorrow was in the music. Among the rubber-necking, lipo-sucked, tummy-tucked crowd there was only the mild exhilaration of finding themselves in the right place at the right time. As if aware it was carrying the entire burden of the mourning, the music crashed to a climax and stopped. In the loud silence that followed, Robert led the way down the long aisle toward the front pew. Arranging the funeral had given him a choice of a seat at it, and all around the tongues were murmuring that he had better enjoy his last shot at being first.

The Beverly Hills crowd saw the bravado of his stride. He was walking as if he wanted the world to know that he still knew where he was going, and his jaw was set pugnaciously like the sails of a small ship on a rough sea—defiant, proud, and worried all at the same time. It was a high-profile, stiff walk, too aware of the eyes that watched him, too determined not to care. The old Robert Hartford had padded about like a loose leopard, and the surrogate shyness, that potent signal of his temporal power, had beamed off him to cow the world and deter the would-be intimate. Now, the paradox was the giveaway to the finely tuned antennae of the congregation. The word was out. Robert Hartford had peaked, and the valley yawned on the other side of the hill.

It wasn't totally certain, of course. Nothing in Hollywood was. But Galaxy had not only pulled the picture deal, they had gone out of their way to bad mouth him, both privately and publicly. So the cognoscenti hurried to count him out, to start the trend of the self-fulfilling prophecy.

The stage whisper over to the right was hissingly sibilant. "God!" said somebody. "Nobody told me that Robert's new girl was a cripple."

Robert almost stopped as the verbal missile struck home. He faltered, and next to him he felt Paula shake suddenly as the vicious words roared into her brain. But the gauntlet had to be run. They both knew that. There could be no public response. Not now. So they marched on toward the front pew and the pain welled up inside along with the anger and the frustration and the mutual tenderness.

Into the breach of unnatural quiet, the priest moved toward the lectern. His voice—frail but rich, its accent softened by the hint of an Irish brogue—winged out over the scattered loudspeakers into the packed church. "Fellow mourners, we are gathered here today to say good-bye to someone we all loved. A servant of God, a child of America. In this time of great sadness words can seldom help, but I urge you today to remember that Francisco lives on, safe in the arms

of Jesus. It is we who bear the burden of his passing. It is we who
suffer . . ."

Robert Hartford wasn't listening, but he *was* suffering. How could
he reach out to her, and tell her it was all right? How could he blot out
the insult to her very essence, the wickedness that had basically been
aimed at him and not at her? It felt as if his heart were bleeding. The
sadness welled out of it, and the pool of pure love built within him,
filling him up with desire for the woman he loved, and the need to
comfort her.

And then he knew. It wasn't the first time that the idea had occurred
to him, but it was the only time that it had seemed to be joined to
action. He didn't think about it. He didn't have to. It was just so
effortlessly right. He was on his knees. She was kneeling, too.

He leaned toward her, and there were tears in his eyes as he spoke.
"Paula, will you marry me?" he said.

Paula's eyes opened wide as she watched him, and she traveled from
the depths of despair to the sublime. The tracks of her tears were there
already. Now it was joy, not pain, that fathered them.

"What?" she whispered back, her voice quivering with excitement.

He smiled at her, at himself, at the wonderful thing that was
happening to them.

"Marry me!" It was a command, and he said it louder, not caring
that this was a man's funeral, caring only that it was the future he
wanted, the one he needed, the one he must have.

"Oh, Robert. Oh, Robert," she breathed his name, unsure how to
respond. To say simply yes seemed so banal at this precious moment.

He didn't mind. Her eyes were saying all the things he wanted her
to say. Her face, her body, her voice were joined in the chorus of
commitment.

So he moved toward her, and his lips reached for hers to seal the life
they would spend together.

At the lectern the priest, oblivious to the pocket of sudden happiness
in the sea of surrogate sorrow, droned on. "Francisco Livingstone was
above all a gentleman, a gentle man, courteous, chivalrous in an age
when those qualities are so very hard to find . . ." He paused to allow
the congregation to ponder the passage of chivalry, to contemplate its
isolated existence in the persona of Francisco Livingstone. Then he
began to warm to his theme. "Today, unfortunately, good manners are
almost nonexistent, the elderly are no longer respected. . . ."

The crash from the back of the church stopped him in mid-cliché.
Everyone turned to see what had happened.

Caroline Kirkegaard was what had happened. She had arrived. Flinging open the carved oak doors of the church as if they were papier-mâché stage furniture, she posed in the entrance, head flung back, lips parted in anticipation, as she gratefully received the eyes of the congregation. Silhouetted against the harsh vertical light of the early Beverly Hills afternoon, she was a Valkyrie from some Wagnerian opera, an Amazonian warrior hot from the hunting field, an avenging horseman posthaste from Hades. Everyone recognized her, but many had never really "seen" her until now. It was her moment. The ultimate arrival. Caroline Kirkegaard, queen of the New Age, paramour of the billionaire, and, it was rumored among those who knew, the brand-new owner-to-be of the Sunset Hotel.

With the majestic inevitability of a rocket blasting from the Cape, Caroline Kirkegaard set off down the aisle. She was huge, more than formidable, far more impressive than statuesque. She sailed, glided, poured herself toward the front of the church and the rustling of her viscose velour silk-satin Marc Bohan black tiered dress was the only sound that anyone could hear. In each ear a black satin bow was threaded through the black pearl-and-diamond earrings that had been given to the duchess of Windsor by the duke, and on her head a rakish, wide-brimmed felt fedora reached to the line of the pads at her powerful shoulders.

A force field of Dior's Poison preceded her and she licked full, voluptuous lips as she basked in the almost palpable fascination of the mourners. On her face she wore a half smile, something between humility and graciousness, because although this was a funeral, it was also a coronation. As if to emphasize that fact, David Plutarch walked Prince Philip–style two paces behind her.

All around the wagging tongues told the story.

"Mistress . . . Moviecom and Galaxy . . . he's buying her the Sunset . . . power over him . . . Destiny cult . . . ruthless people . . ."

Like an arrow to the bull Caroline Kirkegaard made for the front pew across the aisle from the Hartford group. She didn't permit herself to think that there would be no place for her there. It was a trick she had learned early in life. Great expectations alone delivered greatness. Unto them that hath, it shall be given. Who dared, won.

The occupants of the front pew, ancient Southern California royalty, folded up before the Kirkegaard assault like a tattered concertina. "Hello, we're so sorry to disturb you," she lied, shoving the social heavy hitters up against each other like dates in a box.

The Pasadena family who'd been Livingstone's distant cousins grinned as they bore it. They weren't used to being exposed to people like Caroline. The whole of their sheltered lives was dedicated to the avoidance of that. It was what the old money was for, a moat against the meritocrats, a hedge against the horrible. "Quite all right," they muttered unconvincingly through stiffened upper lips as they crammed up to accommodate the interlopers in their midst.

Caroline stood back to allow Plutarch to enter the pew first. She wanted to be on the outside, where she could see and be seen, where Robert Hartford would be available to her.

On the outside of the Hartford pew, Kristina, like the rest of the congregation, had been submerged in the drama of Caroline Kirke-gaard's theatrical entry. On her it had a special impact. In her life so far there had been few heroes, fewer heroines, but Caroline Kirkegaard was one. Kristina couldn't quite remember when she had begun to take the spiritual path. There had been no blinding light, no born-again experience, but gradually she had found herself gravitating toward the mystical and away from the material. It had started with a book or two from the Bodhi Tree, and progressed through Forum, Life Spring, and an Insight weekend, to a Destiny desert retreat via a couple of channelings and a private "reading." She had given up booze and learned to sneer at drugs, and slowly but surely she had dropped her old friends, knee deep in materialism, and acquired new ones with their heads in the clouds. Bit by bit, Kristina had begun to accept not only that reality was unreal, but that the bizarre was in fact common-place, the unusual not extraordinary at all. Truth, at a stroke, was reassigned to the realm of the emotions rather than the intellect, which made it infinitely more fun. This New Age world had its own gurus, and standing head and shoulders above them all—both literally and metaphorically—was Caroline Kirkegaard.

Now, from across the aisle, Caroline Kirkegaard was smiling directly at her.

It was an extraordinary smile, much deeper and more interesting than the normal smiles you might expect from someone you had met briefly at a party a few weeks before. Her ripe lips were pulled back from her fine teeth, and Kristina couldn't help noticing that they were damp, moist, wet actually. There was a quizzical component to the expression—as if Caroline Kirkegaard were questioning her. Her eyes sparkled and shone with an unmistakable warmth, and Kristina couldn't escape the feeling that this was the smile of an old friend, one that . . . you were rather attracted to, although you hadn't really worked out why. Had Caroline Kirkegaard remembered the evening of poor Livingstone's black ball, when they had sat at the same table and had a brief conversation beforehand about the power of amethysts?

Certainly she could not know of the Destiny meetings that Kristina had attended—a fascinated disciple vibrating with wonder in the darkness of the room.

One thing, however, was clear. There was a contact between them at a spiritual level, and on a physical level, too. New and disturbing realities were taking shape.

The smile was going on too long. It was time to look away. It was like walking toward a stranger on a lonely street. Your eyes met his, untangled, hooked up again. It might be long seconds till you passed by him, but now you and he had made some tenuous contact and it was your decision, his too, whether you would nod and smile, and say hello—not because you wanted to but because it was difficult to do otherwise.

Kristina couldn't break the link of the smile. Instead, suddenly and inexplicably helpless in its bondage, she returned it—the silly, bemused expression sitting all over her own face like a fat cat on a baby.

At the very moment Kristina was about to give up her effort to interpret what she was feeling, her body began to speak. The whole of her seemed suddenly sensitized, the peculiar awareness that she possessed bodily parts that one seldom thought about in church, at funerals, while psychics smiled at you across the aisle. It started as a sensation of warmth, of fullness, and it proceeded to take on electrical form, a tingling, tickling feeling that was on the move, creeping, crawling, slowly at first then faster between her skin and the soft silk of her Dior panties. If she had a geographical center then it had begun there, but now it was wherever her blood was, rushing hither and thither, as if it couldn't make up its mind where to go or what to do. Only one thing was completely certain. It was mothered by Caroline Kirkegaard's deeply unsettling smile.

Kristina breathed in deeply as the weird feeling took her, and her breath shuddered out again. The church was disappearing, and Caroline's face was getting bigger, filling her mind with its sweet seduction, and crowding out all thought as it conjured up the ghostly music in her body. She was being played like an instrument, her heartstrings caressed by a silken bow, her tense skin stroked by a steady touch of deepening strength, and there was nothing at all that she could do about it, and still less that she wanted to do. She was sinking in the whirlpools of Caroline's eyes.

In the back of the parked limo outside the church on the corner of Bedford and Santa Monica, Graham stared moodily at the TV and wondered if he could be bothered to switch the channels. Which brand of soap would best clean off the depression that had settled over him like a fine layer of dust since his recent return from London. Maybe he should do a drink instead, something thoroughly British like warm lager, sticky-sweet sherry, or scotch and soda with no ice. He reached forward to the drinks tray and splashed a double measure of twelve-year-old Chivas Regal whiskey into the heavy Orrefors tumbler. Then he leaned back into the aggressively comfortable cushions as he sipped petulantly at the unappetizing drink. Was he glad to be back in Beverly Hills? It was impossible to say. One thing was for sure. The thing he had gone away to forget hadn't been forgotten.

And that was the problem. Paula wasn't a thing at all. Things could be got. They could be had. They could be bought and sold. In Graham's odd life people were categorized as "things." In the East End of London where he had been dragged up, there had never been time for the finer nuances of "feeling." Those, and the other luxuries of life, had been in short supply among the jellied eels, the creeping cold, and the mean streets of his cockney fish-and-chips childhood. Back then, within the sound of Bow Bells' chimes, sentiment was singing "Danny Boy" half pissed with your mates on the way back from the boozer at closing time. Politeness was not hitting a man with glasses. Sensitivity was bothering to get out of the tin tub by the fire to piss in the outside khazi. In the slums of East Ham there had been no crash course in romance. Everyone had been far too busy surviving.

It was funny how he felt about her, if *felt* was the right word. He wanted her, he desired her, and that meant that he must have her—in his bed, in his life, in his debt—doing the things he told her to do, saying the words he wanted to hear. She must think only about him, not recognizing others. She must come when he called, do what pleased him; and of course she should be loyal to him, because she would be his mistress and he would be her master, as proper men were to their proper women. In return he would take her as his wife, and he would fight any man that crossed her, and break the teeth and the arms and the legs of those who insulted him through her. In his fashion he would be faithful—in his own way he would be true to her—but when the time came to scratch the itch of maleness it would not threaten what they had, because he would never flaunt it, and what the eye didn't see . . . A man knew where he was in a relationship like that. It was how things were in the Old World, and it would have to be like that in the new one.

Deep down, however, he knew it was pure fantasy. Paula would never be that kind of a person, and it wasn't just because she was American. It was worse than that. On paper she should share his philosophy, but for some reason she was beyond him and his working-class attitudes and expectations. Her neck wasn't red and she had effortlessly transcended the world of the bumper sticker and the pickup truck, because, despite her small-town upbringing, there was nothing small about her dreams. In the ordinary way that wouldn't have mattered. It should have been simple. They were wrong for each other, so he should forget her. It was what he had gone to England to do—Tower had owed him a holiday and he had taken it—but it hadn't worked out as planned.

On his short vacation he had found that the old haunts hadn't changed much, and neither had the sharp-tongued, bleached-blond bints of Barking. They had laughed at his jokes and mocked the mid-Atlantic accent he'd developed and their brittle good humor and straightforward, no-nonsense sexual appetites had provided a test of sorts for his feelings for Paula. He had stood his rounds and slashed in the car parks, and he had indulged in knee tremblers outside the pubs in the old Kent Road, and slightly more upmarket liaisons on half a dozen couches with sparky Aryan girls whose chirpy self-confidence papered over the sad limitations of their lives. But at night when he tumbled into bed through the bitter beer haze and wondered if the electric blanket would make it through the night, he could think only of Paula's angelic beauty, and her bright brilliance, and the terrible tragedies she had survived. He would fall asleep and his dreams would be alive with California and Paula.

So now he was back in L.A., and the evil mood persisted, knotting up his insides beneath the hard, flat stomach and poisoning his mind. He placed the glass on the steel muscle of his thigh and his face tightened and his body tensed as he thought of what he had discovered on his return.

Robert and Paula had gone to New York, and they had become lovers. Not for one second did he doubt it. Their every gesture, their every word, confirmed it. And it was eating away at his soul.

His mind roamed around like a hungry hyena on a snow-covered steppe. It wasn't the first time he had thought of it, but now the former daydream had the substance of a plan. Paula herself had given him the vital information, in the sweet-scented garden on the night of Livingstone's party, as the tears had bathed her beauty and she had told of the terrible night in a place called Placid when a man called Seth Baker had raped and murdered her friend and burned the twin brothers she worshiped. A powerless woman with an awesome desire for vengeance would look with all the favor in the world on an avenging angel. A girl would live for the man who killed for her. A girl would love the man that she lived for. It was so straightforward in his simple mind. Yes, Seth Baker was the open sesame to the future he wanted.

The knock on the window was sharp, and Graham reached forward to wind it down.

"Can you move the limo forward to the front entrance please, sir? They'll be out in a minute or two." The cop wasn't usually so deferential, but then limos weren't usually that long. Over the policeman's shoulder the ubiquitous Beverly Hills palm trees, fat ones alternating with thin, lined the street, their manicured orderliness a dramatic contrast to Graham's dangerous emotions.

"Okay," said Graham, thrusting the drink out of sight.

Mentally he braced himself. Paula had gone in with Robert Hartford. Soon she would be coming out with him, and the superstar's supercilious eyes would be all over him. "Hello, servant," they would say. "You dared to lust after my girl, didn't you? And you don't like me, do you, because I'm rich and successful, and I'm even better looking than you and I don't work for *anybody* but myself." It was small consolation that Hartford's career was in free fall. It would take a lifetime for it to reach the lowly level where Graham's bumped along.

He cleaned the glass quickly and opened the door, smoothing down the gray worsted of the uniform that was nearly a suit. He slipped into the driver's seat and did what the cop wanted. Then he was outside again, his peaked cap stuck awkwardly beneath his arm where it was less noticeable. Next he adjusted the Revo sunglasses for greater anonymity, and he leaned casually against the spit-and-polished coachwork of the stretch Mercedes.

The doors to the church were opening. From his position by the number-one car Graham could see right inside. The first few pews were disgorging their contents steadily into the aisle, as the organ ground and the mourners beamed and everyone wondered how long Livingstone would do in purgatory before they allowed the old lecher upstairs.

Robert Hartford and Paula seemed completely insulated from the tense group that had now arrived at the top of the steps. Wrapped in a cellophane of transcendent happiness, they stared into each other's eyes, their hands intertwined, their bodies so close that walking seemed a miracle. Hovering about them, like Indians around a well-defended wagon train, were a malevolent blond beauty and, swooping and darting at her side, the billionaire David Plutarch. Kristina, a dreamy, trancelike expression on her face, seemed locked in the blonde's gravitational field. Winthrop Tower and five classically dressed aristocrats made up the remainder of the extraordinary group. The blonde's voice floated toward Graham like a cloud of nuclear dust. "Robert. Robert! We'd just love to have you stay on at the Sunset, but we'd have to move you into something a little less spacious. Probably suit you now."

Robert Hartford didn't seem to hear her. Her sour sarcasm floated harmlessly over his head as he looked down tenderly at Paula.

Stung by his indifference, Caroline tried again, louder this time. "Perhaps you could move in with Mr. Tower. Yes, that's the best thing. The odd couple. A pair of 'confirmed bachelors.' We could use it in the advertising. Turn it into a tourist attraction. Isn't that a wonderful idea, David?"

Robert turned to look at her as if he was seeing her for the very first time. There was no hatred on his face. There was only undiluted pleasure. "Sorry to disappoint you, Caroline, but that wouldn't do at all. You see I won't *be* a bachelor, confirmed or otherwise."

Some got there faster than others. Tower was the first of all.

"Robert. Paula. That's *wonderful!*" he boomed.

Caroline Kirkegaard froze as the penny dropped. Her eyes, wide, incredulous, shot back and forth from Robert to Paula. Kristina, stunned, could say nothing at all. Graham had reached them now, but as he walked the information had been pouring into his protesting mind. The lovers, indecently happy on the steps of the church, were joined together, their postures emphasizing the closeness of their commitment. He was shut out. He didn't exist. They didn't even know he was there. He opened his mouth to say something—anything—to turn them away, however briefly, from each other, but the big blonde was talking and now Robert Hartford had just said the words that had stopped Graham's world in its tracks.

"Yes," said Robert. "Paula and I are going to get married."

"No!" said Graham. His voice was sharp, the desperate shout of the man who interrupted the reading of the banns in church. Robert couldn't marry her, because he wanted Paula for himself.

Everyone saw him for the very first time. Robert looked at him in intense surprise, and then his lip began to curl around the edges of the happiness on his face. "What do you mean 'no'?" he asked.

"I mean, you can't . . . get married . . . to Paula," Graham stammered, his face drained of blood, his hands clenched at his side.

The silence gathered strength. Robert's eyes were flashing.

Caroline Kirkegaard saw it in a second. The angelic-looking
chauffeur loved Paula himself. The lord of the manor had pulled
seignurial rank on the vassal. It was a drama as old as life, and for a
brief moment it sustained her in the midst of her disappointment.

"Who on *earth* says so?"

Graham was cornered. Caroline watched the Englishman carefully.
He seemed to be undergoing an extraordinary change. He was
shrinking, crouching down low, but at the same time his chest was
expanding and his shoulders seemed to be broadening beneath her
gaze. His eyes were small and his lips thin and the baby face was flat,
the pale skin plastered tight across the perfect bone structure. His
nostrils were flared and his fists were tight, and he was coiled up like
a spring forced into a box, the one whose lid the child's fingers were
beginning to loosen. . . .

"That's right, Graham," said Paula quickly. "This *is* a Tower
Design corporate decision, isn't it Winty? Only the full board can give
me away. . . ." She laughed easily into the unbearable tension.

"Absolutely right. Board meeting convened. Over drinks. At the
Sunset Hotel. Marriage motion to be laid before the board." Winthrop
Tower backed her up, and the fuse spluttered out, millimeters from the
bomb.

Graham backed away, unwinding slowly, and the furious fires died
down in Robert's eyes. Paula and Winthrop exchanged lightning
glances. Caroline Kirkegaard smiled as she made careful note of the
incident.

"Come on, Paula. You're coming in my car," said Robert.

But apparently the Livingstone funeral was not quite over.

The two men who now approached looked like lawyers.

"Mr. Hartford?" said one.

Robert spun around, irritated, desperate to be out of it. "Yes, what
is it?"

"I am Enthoven of Emory, Quiddick, Marshall, Maverick, Nolan
and Enthoven. We are the attorneys for Mr. Livingstone's estate."

David Plutarch cut in rudely. "Why haven't you been answering my
letters?" he barked.

The lawyer ignored him. It was to Robert Hartford that he
continued to speak. "We need to discuss with you the contents of Mr.
Livingstone's will."

"Livingstone's *will?*" said Caroline Kirkegaard in a voice that
sounded as if it came from another world.

"Yes," said Enthoven. "We've found a new will. A very recent

one." Now he turned to Plutarch. "I know, sir, that you've written
letters expressing a willingness to buy the Sunset Hotel should Mr.
Hartford's offer not be completed. I think it is important that you
attend the reading of the will, along with Mr. Hartford. Would
tomorrow morning be suitable for you all? Say at ten? Mr. Tower, too,
sir, and Miss Kirkegaard, if it is at all convenient." The lawyer looked
supremely doubtful. It seemed unlikely that everyone would have the
time or inclination to attend the meeting he had suggested.

But Enthoven had overlooked one of the most powerful and least
visible of human emotions—curiosity. The giant question mark hung
over the group. One by one, quite quickly, they said that yes, why not,
ten o'clock would be just fine.

"Coffee. Black."

Somehow it wasn't the kind of place you said please.

The waitress didn't seem at all put out. Plain, her face pocked like
a pineapple, she splashed the coffee into an almost clean cup, allowing
it to overflow into a chipped saucer. Her movements were brisk, the
irritation just beneath the surface. Folks who drifted in ten minutes
before closing time were popular as palmetto bugs.

Graham shifted on the scuffed plastic of the bar stool and peered
around the diner. It was "Happy Days" gone sour, all messed up by
dirt, neglect, and by an unmistakable sense of all-pervasive gloom that
hung over the restaurant. It was even possible to pinpoint the place the
bad vibrations were coming from. They were beaming out from the
corner. From the table at which the fat man sat. They were coming
from the man who would be Seth Baker.

He was monumentally ugly, his stomach hanging over the edge of
the table like a filthy cloth. A big pitcher of beer in front of him was
nearly empty. His eyes were lost in the fleshy, parchment-colored folds
of his face, and the stubble of his uneven beard, sometimes gray,
sometimes black, was dotted with beads of booze and sweat. Graham
wasn't near enough to smell him, but he knew from twenty feet what
the smell would be. Sour, decaying, beer and body.

He turned back to face the front, and the music started somewhere
in the depths of his brain. "Seth Baker?" he said quietly to the girl
behind the bar, nodding his head backward over his shoulder.

She tried to summon up the energy to make a problem. "Who's
askin'," something like that. He could see it in her irritable eyes. But
she couldn't make it. In the Everglades problem creation took effort.

"Yeah," she mumbled.

Seth Baker. Graham could see him through the back of his head. This piece of human rubbish that had raped and killed Paula's friend—who had murdered Paula's beloved brothers in an attempt to kill her. He smiled at the grotesqueness of the thought, allowing it to stoke the fires of wrath that flickered deep within him. This diseased creature had raped a woman. He had tried to set Paula on fire to protect his foul secret. He wasn't a human being. He was a thing—but a thing that would make noises when the time came for it to be broken. He smiled, and this time a strange laugh slipped from the back of his throat.

The waitress watched him, suddenly in tune with the aura of menace that clung to him. "Just passin' through?" she said. He talked funny. Like an out-of-state trucker. There were a few of those.

He didn't reply. He just looked through her, as if she didn't exist. She shrugged. "Better finish your coffee. We're closin' in a minute or two," she managed in retaliation.

Graham felt the familiar chill in his fingers, the itch in the muscles of his forearms. It was wonderful, this, the heightened awareness, as the world danced in new colors, and his thoughts came crystal clear, and his nostrils flared to sniff at the adrenaline reality.

He reached inside the scruffy anorak and he pulled out his wallet. From it he took five single hundred-dollar bills. They were crisp, ironed, and he laid them on the counter like soldiers on the paradeground, perfectly symmetrical, side by side. The eyes of the waitress zeroed in on them.

"Step outside for ten minutes, honey, will you," said Graham. "Somethin' I got to talk about to the boss."

He could see the bills reflected in her pupils, and inside her brain the bells were ringing as the cash registered. One, two, three, four, five across the neurone mass, up and down and around the tangled undergrowth on the slow voyage to understanding. Before she arrived at the destination of meaning her fingers were reaching toward the money, drawn by a magnet far more powerful than the intellect. She placed them one on top of each other, carefully, and she drew them toward her with the reverence of the communicant placing the wafer to her lips. "You want me to get lost?" she said as the five hundred disappeared into the pocket of her Levi's. "You got it." She didn't bother to do any tidying up around the bar. The look on her face said she wasn't ever coming back. She was junk labor in a junk bar in a junk town, and she'd never been as close to five hundred as she was right now, nor would she ever be again. If walking was what the gentleman wanted then walking was what he was going to get. An' the stranger looked like bad news to Seth Baker, and that was the second best news today.

"Where you goin'?" The gravelly roar cut through the gloom. It wasn't closing time. The girl owed him another five minutes. Some loser was still propping up the bar.

But she didn't turn to look at him. The slam of the door was all she left behind.

Baker growled to himself and reached for the beer. What the heck! They came and they went. He changed his pants less often.

Graham stood up and he ambled to the door. He reached for the sign marked OPEN and he twisted it around till it read CLOSED. Then he slipped the bolt across the door, and he turned, and very slowly he walked across the diner to the corner where Seth Baker sat.

Seth Baker stuck a fat finger inside his mouth and dislodged a piece of chili that was wedged beneath tooth and gum up there at the back. He swallowed it. Good chili. Fartin' burpin' good chili. What did the drifter want? A job most like. Well, if he could get into the dress he could wait the tables. Ha! Ha! Then the laughter died. Because now he could see the eyes of the stranger.

They were the eyes of winter. Not of the pale apology for a winter they had down here, but a real one, bleak, and angry, ice-cold cruel, a winter that could kill, a winter that loved nothing more. They were blue, the bluest blue he had ever seen, but there was no spark of life, nothing swimming in their clear, frozen depths. And they were deep, endlessly deep, passing through twin infinities and beyond, to the end of other worlds. They were forever eyes, unswervingly eternal, and suddenly the gas in his guts was exploding and the prickly heat was sizzling around the fat folds of his neck where the nape had once been.

Closer, he came closer, until he was on the edge of Seth Baker's space, where any more intrusion would be invasion. He stopped.

"What you want?" Baker's voice was nervous.

But Graham didn't answer. All around the loneliness was loud, amplifying the dread that built around the two men.

Graham watched him, and inside he played the heat against the cool, the flames of his hatred searing the freezing blocks of his resolve. Exterminators didn't feel. They walked among the creepy crawly things and they killed dispassionately, efficiently, fast. But this hideous thing was so very ugly and all his life he would have done horrible deeds. Like to Paula, the girl who would be his. And he laughed then, when he thought of that, because this filthy flesh mountain had wounded *him* by wounding her. It was personal. Not like the rivals of

long ago on the wet streets, in the damp alleyways, in the cavernous
lofts of the East End. He'd twisted flesh then in the business
relationship that had sometimes been death, and the pain had been
incidental, uninteresting, like the howling of the wind or the crackling
of a fire. But this time it would be sweet music. Blissful music.
Wedding music. Because of what would happen now, he would be
given the key to Paula's heart. After this, she could refuse him nothing.

"Do you remember Paula?" His voice was featureless, matter-
of-fact.

Seth Baker's head flipped back as he heard the name, and he knew
he must lie as he knew that the eyes would not believe him. The name
dried in his mouth, and his lips stuck firm together as he tried to force
them apart. Paula! Paula, who'd frightened him, who he'd tried to kill.
Paula, whose little brothers had died in the fire he'd started. "I don'
know no Paula."

Graham smiled at that, and his head moved slowly from side to side
in the gesture of denial. "It doesn't matter," he said. It was true. It
didn't matter, because for Seth Baker nothing mattered anymore.
Soon, so soon, nothing would ever matter again.

He reached behind him, and the neon glow fell across the
matte-black blade of the knife. He put it out in front of him, where
Seth Baker could see it, and he turned it around slowly like a pig on
a spit.

The threat was not in the action. The threat was everywhere. It
hung in the still air, and it lurked in the foul smell that sprang in panic
from beneath Seth Baker's arms. It clung to the ceiling and it sprang
up from the floor, but mostly it lurked in the place where it had always
been. In the terrible eyes of the stranger.

Seth Baker tried to get up. His knees, his legs could usually manage
that, but not this time. He was halfway there when they let him down
and so he sank back like a paralyzed man, and the sweat leaped to his
forehead, and bubbled at his upper lip as his mind tumbled over itself
in its rush for the exit.

"I never laid no finger on Paula," he babbled. No finger on the girl
he didn't know. What would it take to close the eyes that watched him
from the depths of his grave? He could see every detail of the knife.
With the clarity of super-vision he knew it. It was a flat, dull thing, so
undramatic for the horror it conjured up, and he could feel it on his
skin as he focused on the space that separated him from it, as the cries
for a mercy he wouldn't receive formed in his throat. Once more he
tried to stand. He pressed down on the table with both hands, and one
slid on a pool of beer sending the pitcher crashing to the floor, but the

diversion meant nothing, like the sound in the forest unheard. At last
he was upright, his enormous belly weighing him down as his
fear-weakened legs bowed beneath the strain. His hands made little
pleading motions, funny, unambitious gestures, his pudgy fingers
going around in circles as they sought to communicate with the
emptiness in the stranger's head.

Graham took one step toward him. He did not draw back his arm.
He did not push out with it. He simply laid the tip of the blade against
the stomach of Seth Baker, right up against the grubby T-shirt, and for
a second or two he did not move. There they stood, waiting for the
music to start, waiting for the dance of death to begin.

A big tear squeezed from Seth Baker's eyes and rolled down his
cheek, parting the grime, conquering the stubble.

"Please," he murmured.

"Okay," said Graham.

The knife seemed to have a life of its own. A magic knife, it sank
sedately into the folds of fat, dragging the arm of the killer along with
it. The blood rushed out to greet it, but it didn't stay for its warm
welcome. It had embarked on a journey. Off it went, slowly,
gracefully, like a sailing ship caught by a sudden breeze on a brisk sea.
Once, twice it tacked as it sped through the yielding skin, and once,
twice it shuddered as if catching a glancing blow on some submerged
obstacle. But it didn't stop. On, on it went, the blood rushing past its
bows, oozing, cascading as it hurried to form the bright, bubbling wake
of the vessel that was the knife.

Seth Baker's features were still set in the look of supplication. Mercy
was what he wanted, and it had hardly registered that it was too late.
But there was a weird feeling in his gut, a tugging, a pulling, an
experience that was on the verge of pain but not yet there. Should he
continue his plea to the eyes that couldn't see him? Should he
investigate the source of discomfort down below?

He looked down. Oh, the blood! Oh! Oh! Oh, the blood was all
over him. He was a Jacuzzi spouting it, and the shark fin of the knife,
that black knife, was swimming around in his guts. He heard himself
screaming and he looked back to find the face laughing in his as he
tried to make sense of it all. Paula. It had something to do with Paula,
and the fire he'd set.

He sank down to the floor, because this was not something that
should take place standing up, and the man who held the knife sank
down with him.

"I'm bleeding," said Seth Baker.

"Oh yes, you are," agreed Graham. He drew his arm back, and the blade came with it, making a little sucking noise as it jumped from its temporary home. Graham laid it, dripping, on the scuffed linoleum floor of the diner.

Once again, his face wrapped in disbelief, Seth checked the place where his belly had been. It wasn't there anymore. His guts were. They had spilled out of him, and they showed no sign at all of wanting to stop. On and on they came, like the baloney he talked, great coils of them, bright brown and blood red, steaming in a growing pile on the floor.

Now, his mind said *pain*. It howled the message to his lungs and his lips drew back and his teeth bared as the roar of anguish cascaded from him. He threw back his head and he screamed the scream of the damned.

Graham moved with lightning speed. He scooped up a length of Seth Baker's bowel and he looped it around his exposed neck, once, twice. Then he pulled it tight.

In front of him, the scream died as he turned the tourniquet. Now Seth Baker's eyes were the eyes of fishes, popping, so big, in the blood-red face.

His hands tore at his misplaced guts, and the battle to express pain was now the struggle to breathe.

Tighter and tighter drew the noose. It bit into his neck, slippery, unyielding, and his head seemed to bulge as it filled with blood that could not escape. There was no room for his brain in the closed box, no room for thought, no place for the future. If only he could breathe. If he could do that then all the horror would go away. But there was no breath. No life. No nothing. There were only the eyes still peering into his, and a strange booming sound that seemed to be saying . . . Paula . . .

SIXTEEN

The two teams faced each other across the shining mahogany of the Sunset Hotel's boardroom table, beneath the full-length portrait of Francisco Livingstone. He beamed down on them, and today the enigmatic, Mona Lisa smile on his face had a new significance.

"Let's get on with it," said Caroline Kirkegaard.

She wasn't dressed to be disobeyed. The Jean-Paul Gaultier sleek black molded leather "torso" jumpsuit was future shock. A black jersey top transformed at the nipples into front and back panels of softly dangerous black leather, held together at the side by an intricate wool cable weave. She wore short black PVC ankle boots, elbow-length black gloves, and a black leather skullcap pulled down over her forehead in the style of an Olympic swimmer.

Beside her, David Plutarch contributed to the tense atmosphere. His nervous eyes roamed the room. The aura of angst had already enveloped the three well-fed attorneys he had brought along to the meeting.

Enthoven, from the prestigious Century City law firm, sat at the head of the table. He arranged the papers into two neat rows in front of him, and he looked up solemnly in response to Caroline's suggestion.

"Are we all here?" he said.

Robert Hartford could not escape the feeling that this was in some way a deeply philosophical question. Were they all here? Or were they all somewhere else? With an effort he straightened up his mind for the business at hand, and beneath the table his leg moved out to rest

254

against Paula's knee, glad that it pushed back at his. He lay back in the chair, detached from the formality of the lawyers, in an open-neck Brooks Brothers shirt and loose navy-blue poplin pants that were distinctly more Palm Beach than Beverly Hills. For the first time in his life he found himself agreeing with Caroline Kirkegaard. His irritable cough said so.

"Ladies and gentlemen, it is very kind of you to spare us a little of your valuable time . . ." Enthoven paused as if calculating just how valuable that time actually was. Plutarch's hour was probably worth more than *he* would earn in an entire year. "I hope you won't feel that it has been wasted. As you already know, Mr. Livingstone has appointed the trust department of my firm to administer his estate. It is in that capacity that I appear before you today. It goes without saying that this is a very sad occasion. Mr. Livingstone was, I am proud to say, a personal friend of mine as well as a client, so I share your feelings. . . ." He lowered his head, rather dramatically, as if he felt that a tear might be appropriate at this point.

Why was it, thought Winthrop Tower, that even the supporting players in L.A.—the butchers, the bakers, and the candlestick makers—all wanted to be actors? God, the attorney was ugly. There should be a law against people looking like that. Perhaps one of the million lawyers on his letterhead could help draft it. He put both his hands up to his throbbing temples and wished he'd passed on the wine at Cha Cha Cha. The transcendent beauty of the owner had hardly made up for it. He couldn't for the life of him think why he was there. Presumably dear old Francisco had left him something personal. Hopefully not his dreadful collection of neckties in Gatsbyesque colors from increasingly garish Turnbull and Asser. Superrich old men, with or without relatives, left anything valuable to obscure charities. It was baked in the cake. You spent the rest of your days wondering what strange bond had been formed in his lifetime between Francisco Livingstone and the Bellringers Benevolent Society, or why at some moment of doubt he had imagined he had Von Recklinghausen's disease and in consequence left millions to the remote institute where they struggled to find a cure for it.

Winthrop groaned out loud and wished that his hangover would go away. And he wondered where the *hell* Graham had got to. He hadn't showed up for work that morning and Tower needed to be a hundred places later in the day. That meant some tired limo driver pitching him scripts despite Winthrop's disbelieved protestations that he had nothing to do with the movie business.

"But life must go on. Business must go on, and that's why Francisco

hired us, and that's why we are here today." Enthoven brightened
visibly to show that he had made a successful passage through the
valley of the shadow of his personal grief, and that, brave and resilient,
he was now able to carry on. "It's really a very simple will. Quite
straightforward, and it has been carefully drafted, so I don't think there
can be any doubts as to intention, nor . . ."—and he laughed now—
"as to soundness of mind . . ."

The lawyer looked up quickly at the nest of Plutarch legal eagles.
They looked evenly back at him. "So, if I may, I'll just read away. It
is a new will, drafted, signed, and witnessed last Thursday, I think, yes,
that's right."

"What?" said Caroline Kirkegaard. Her face was pale, and her
question shot out across the table like a bullet from a gun. Her mind
was racing. Livingstone had made a will on the day he had died. On
the day of his last massage.

"Is there any problem with that?" asked Enthoven.

She climbed down fast, as she realized that there was nothing she
could say. Plutarch's eyes were on her. "Oh no, I just didn't hear you
properly. Last Thursday, you said."

"Last Thursday."

Paula watched her in fascination. She was so big, so deadly, and
Robert had kissed her. Now she knew the whole story, of Caroline's
attempted blackmail of Livingstone, of Jami Ramona, and of Robert's
diversionary candlelit dinner for two while the incriminating photographs were being recovered. But still they had kissed. Had they *needed*
to do that? Had Robert needed to? She tried to push the nasty thought
out of her mind, and she wondered instead how Caroline had *dared*
come to Livingstone's funeral. What in God's name could he possibly
have left her in his will? One thing was certain. Kirkegaard was not her
usual calm, evil self.

Pressing herself secretly against her lover, against her fiancé, Paula
looked down happily at the beautiful ring. The single emerald was
totally perfect, large but not too large, the classic marquise cut
complementing its antique setting. Despite herself she had mixed
feelings about the tearing-up of the Galaxy contract. Obviously she
cared desperately about his happiness, but strangely it seemed to have
survived the misfortune. She had been his safety net, and now on the
edge of an eternity together she had picked him up and put him back
on top, not of Hollywood, but of life. Nothing else mattered. Nothing
except the Sunset Hotel. That had been a dream they had both shared.
Together it would have been their life's work, as it had been

Livingstone's, and she tried to suppress the sadness that bubbled up as she thought about how they had lost it.

At the table's head Enthoven was off and running. " 'I, Francisco Livingstone, being of sound mind, hereby declare this to be my last will and testament superseding all others. I have made this will because of the circumstances that have arisen during the last few months with regard to my principal asset, my one hundred percent holding in the private corporation, Sunset Hotel, Inc. On the first day of November of this year I signed a contract of sale in which I agreed to sell my shareholding to Robert Hartford. The contract stated that completion was to take place on the last day of January, of next year.' "

Caroline Kirkegaard began to settle down. This wasn't as bad as she thought. Livingstone was going to tell everyone that in the event of the deal not being completed then the lawyers were to sell it to the highest bidder, or perhaps he was even going to specify that the sale should be to Plutarch. The glint in Plutarch's eye said that was what he thought, too.

Robert Hartford sighed. It was so sad. So unnecessary. So terribly wrong. He, too, was wondering why he was there. Obviously Livingstone had left him something. Wine, maybe. The Canaletto of Westminster Bridge that was his pride and joy and which Robert had so often admired?

" 'It occurs to me as I write this document that I am in poor health. Death is a factor that should be taken into account in making my dispositions.' "

But you didn't know how soon, did you, Francisco Livingstone? thought Caroline. You didn't know that you had only hours to live as you wrote your boring will. I beat you, didn't I? If you had known Robert couldn't afford your precious hotel you might have given him back his deposit and left him a relatively rich man. And you might have hawked your hotel around until you found another buyer, some effete loser with more money than sense who shared your ancient ideas about class, your pretension and your hypocrisy.

Enthoven droned on. " 'In the event of my dying between the time of the signing of the contract and the completion of the sale, and in the event of Mr. Hartford for some unforeseen reason being unable to complete the purchase of my aforementioned shares, it occurs to me that the contract would become null and void and my executors would be legally bound, in the absence of any guidance from me, to sell to the highest bidder.' "

Tower pricked up his ears. Only one phrase so far had promised any fireworks at all. "In the absence of any guidance from me." Where would the executors be guided? He sat forward in his chair. Good old Livingstone. This was turning out to be quite fun. He must have one of these himself one day, but not just yet.

" 'It seems likely, given the interest already shown in the hotel, that the highest bidder would, in this situation, be David Plutarch, acting for and on behalf of his friend, Caroline Kirkegaard.' "

The lawyer managed to put question marks on either side of the word *friend*. As a professional actor, Robert had to admit it was quite well done.

The attorney paused. He looked up at Plutarch. At Livingstone's portrait. He turned to look at Robert Hartford. He looked down again. " 'Under no circumstances could I die in peace thinking that the Sunset Hotel might end up in the hands of Plutarch and Kirkegaard.' "

Not a muscle moved, not a face twitched as the news sank in.

" 'It is the purpose of this document to ensure that this dreadful hypothetical situation will never come to pass.' "

Fire burned high on David Plutarch's cheeks. The trio of his attorneys began to scribble on their yellow legal pads.

Caroline Kirkegaard stood up. Then she sat down. Then she stood up again. Her mouth opened, closed, opened once more. No sound came out. She looked like the Method acting school's prize-winning depiction of "shock."

Robert Hartford, too, fought back the desire to jump to his feet. It didn't matter that he had lost. At least Plutarch and Kirkegaard had been denied the prize.

"Bravo, Francisco," said Tower out loud.

But Livingstone was still speaking. " 'Because simple things work best, this is my solution. If I die before completion of the above-mentioned contract, I hereby will and bequeath my entire shareholding in the Sunset Hotel Corporation free and gratis and unencumbered to Robert Byron Hartford of the Sunset Hotel, Sunset Boulevard, Beverly Hills.' "

The Sunset Hotel. It was his. He had been given it. For nothing. One hundred and fifty million dollars. Maybe more.

He jumped up, and Paula, too, was on her feet. She rushed toward him and fell into his arms. "Darling, oh, my darling. You've won. You've *won*." He ran his fingers through her hair, and he looked down at her tenderly.

Then Robert turned toward Caroline Kirkegaard. At the other end of the table she stood facing him. The full length of the gleaming table separated them, but in reality they stood eyeball to eyeball, locked in a hatred that glued them together.

Paula took a deep breath. Never in her whole life had she seen a woman so dangerous. Caroline stood, vibrating her wrath, her huge chest rising and falling beneath the wicked jumpsuit. Around her muscular neck several single platinum chains nestled against the throbbing carotid arteries, and the cargo they carried, a cluster of assorted crystals, sparkled and shone beneath the bright boardroom lights. So much for the healing power of crystals. So much for their calming, soothing influence, the mystical ability they gave the wearer to transcend life's tricky moments. She was not cool. She was hot, hotter than the fires of hell, and she hadn't even *started* to burn. Paula watched in wonder as the natural rouge bloodied her cheeks, and she caught the twitching, clenching hands at the ends of arms that looked like they could kill. Instinctively Paula looked for missiles, ashtrays, anything that might be hurled at the man she loved. But there was none within range of Caroline Kirkegaard, and it didn't look as if it were earthly missiles she was after. She was searching for thunderbolts, weapons of awesome complexity and fiendish destruction, that could be used for the once-and-for-all demolition of the Teflon man.

Through the mist of her fury Caroline Kirkegaard saw him. He was standing before her, and he was laughing as he loathed her, smiling as he despised her. Around and around in her mind ran the words of the will. If she hadn't murdered Livingstone this would never have happened. Robert didn't know it, but it was *she* who had just handed him the Sunset Hotel. What he couldn't pay for she had given him for nothing.

"We shall contest this will," barked Plutarch.

"On what grounds?" drawled Robert Hartford.

Plutarch, cold and deadly, turned to his lawyers. Lawyers could always find "grounds" even when there weren't any.

"We shall want to interview the witness to the signature. Also, at Mr. Livingstone's advanced age there is the question of competency. Mr. Hartford is not a relative. It may be that undue influence . . ."

The lead Plutarch attorney talked fast, but not fast enough. Enthoven trumped his cards as he played them. Like a cardsharp on a Mississippi riverboat he floated his aces onto the table, throwing the documents so that they skidded along the smooth surface.

"One affidavit signed by the witness to the will and notarized . . . the report of two independent handwriting experts stating that the signature is indeed Francisco Livingstone's . . . a medical report signed by a board-certified neuropsychiatrist that at his last checkup one month ago Mr. Livingstone's mental status was normal in every way . . . a copy of a letter from Mr. Livingstone to Mr. Hartford saying how pleased he was that Mr. Hartford was the buyer of the Sunset Hotel because he could think of no one in whose hands the hotel would be safer. . . ."

Plutarch stood too. There was a time to give up. He nodded at his team and flicked his head toward the door. They were leaving. They had lost.

"Enjoy it while you can, Robert," Caroline snarled.

"Get the *hell* out of my hotel," he ordered. There was venom in his voice.

"Caroline!" Plutarch's voice was sharp. There would be other days, other times for revenge. Right now, they were beaten, and in enemy territory.

Caroline moved toward Plutarch, but her mind was roaring. Inside, she made the solemn promise. She would take his toy away from him. Whatever it took. Whatever price had to be paid. But in the meantime there was his happiness. How could she destroy that? She looked at Paula, and already she was thinking about the love-struck chauffeur at the funeral, with the vicious, haunted, hurting eyes. And, as it did at times like these, when the little people made her angry and the silly world messed up her brilliant schemes, her mind was already planning a terrible retribution.

Paula lay back on the sofa, yawned and stretched. She was in Robert's bungalow, watching MTV, and she had fallen fast asleep, all tubed out, after an incredible room-service dinner. She looked at her watch and rubbed sleep from her eyes. It was nearly midnight. She should drag herself into the bedroom and crash properly. Robert would be back tomorrow, and she wanted to look as good for him as she possibly could.

The thought of him finished the job of waking her up, and she smiled to his empty room—the one that so soon would be hers as well as his. He was in New York. Right now he would be all tucked up in the Carlyle double bed, the place where first they had made love, and tomorrow he would be back with her again. She hadn't realized until now that Hollywood had invented the roller-coaster ride. She and Robert had just ridden it. The news of Livingstone's will and Robert's windfall had traveled the grapevine at breakneck speed, and quite suddenly his injured career had staged a dramatic recovery. How many movie stars were worth a hundred and fifty big ones? How many strato-celebrities owned the best hotel in the world? Suddenly everyone believed the Hartford counterrumors, the ones that gave the lie to the Galaxy/Plutarch misinformation. Galaxy had dumped Robert because he had crossed the star-struck corporate Monopoly man and his sinister lover, and for no other reason. Well, good for Robert, Hollywood had concluded. In tearing up the Hartford contract the billionaire had been childishly cutting off his nose to spite his face.

Three studios had called to pick up the contract that Galaxy had dropped, and right now Robert was in New York discussing a new deal. When he had called earlier that day, the renegotiation with Horizon Pictures had been coming together like peaches and cream. By now it might even be signed, and the man she loved would be back in the pilot's seat.

In three short weeks they would be married. Christian Lacroix had designed the dress, an extravaganza of fluffy lightness and scintillating romance and, Kristina, who understood such things, was helping her with the arrangements for the wedding.

She shivered with delight and she leaped up, smoothing down the crumpled Georges Marciano denim skirt so that it just about covered what it was designed to just about cover, as the exhilaration coursed through her. She ran over to the full-length mirror in the entrance hall, the one that checked the legend on his forays into the outside world, and she pirouetted happily in front of it. She had never felt more beautiful. Her skin was glowing with a mad joy and her breasts pushed out straight against the navy-blue pullover, her hair shining with vitality, her teeth gleaming in the center of her smile.

She twirled around. "I feel pretty, oh, so pretty," she sang to herself and to the lover who couldn't hear her. "It's alarming how charming I feel." She was bubbling, a dancing caldron of pure bliss as she wondered if anyone, ever, had had such a perfect life, and if there was anything that could possibly make it better.

There was.

The telephone warbled its greeting. Eleven forty-five P.M. It was way past Beverly Hills' bedtime. It could only be one person. Leaping across the big sofa, dancing deliriously on the cushions, she ran toward it.

She would surprise him.

"Hello darling," she whispered provocatively. "I love you."

"Allo, luv," said Graham's flat, featureless voice.

"Graham? Goodness, I thought you were Robert." Her voice was full of irrational reproach. He *should* have been Robert.

"Yeah, I thought that's what you thought."

"It's nearly midnight," she said, irritated.

"Yeah."

"What do you want, Graham?"

Her fabulous mood was going, going, gone.

"Listen, luv, I've got to talk to you."

"I was just going to bed. It'll have to wait until tomorrow."

"No!" His voice was suddenly sharp. "It's important, Paula. I need to see you now. Right away. Can I come on over? I'm calling from a phone on the Strip."

"No, you can't come over. This is Robert's home. I'm just staying here. He's in New York."

Graham got the picture. He wasn't welcome in Robert's house. Robert didn't like him. And it would be deeply inappropriate for Paula to entertain men of any sort in the middle of the night three weeks before her wedding—especially when it was an open secret that Graham had a crush on her.

"You gotta hear what I gotta say, luv. I mean you've *got* to."

It wasn't the desperate plea of a lovesick suitor. It was a plain statement of fact. Quite suddenly Paula picked up on the underlying vibrations. Graham had some bad news.

"Okay, we can talk now. You can't come over."

"I can't talk on the phone, luv."

"Oh, Graham, stop being so *dramatic*. What's so urgent in the middle of the night? I was just about to get into bed."

"I just got back from Florida. I been to Placid, luv."

Paula's heart stopped. When it started again, it was beating far faster than before. "What? Why? Why did you go to Placid, Graham?" Oh no! Oh dear *God* no! Not now. It was all *over*.

"I 'ad to see someone, didn't I? I 'ad to see someone 'bout somefink."

Paula's voice was quiet. "You'd better come on over," she said.

He put the telephone down quickly, as if worried that she'd change her mind.

She stood up and walked in a daze to the bathroom to splash some cold water on her face. Graham had gone to Placid. There was only one person he could have gone to see. Seth Baker, who had killed poor Laura and murdered her brothers. Seth Baker, whom she had hated with such a desperate loathing in those far-off days before she had fallen in love.

Almost before she had dared to dread it, the doorbell rang.

When she opened the door he was standing there, wreathed in

shadows, and there was a look on his face that Paula had never seen before. For a second they stood watching each other, sizing each other up, like wild animals prepared to fight for their needs, to defend their territory whatever the cost. She didn't say "come in," but she stood back, and he slid past her into the bungalow, his movements somehow furtive, strangely threatening.

"I 'ad to see you Paula. I know it's late, but you'll understand."

She led the way into the drawing room, uncertain how best to do this. She had to hear the news he brought, and then she had to neutralize it. But at the same time she didn't want to hear it. Instead, she wanted it to be like the old times when she had laughed and joked with him, even relied on him. "What were you doing in Placid, Graham?"

" 'e was slime, Paula. 'e was rubbish."

He wasn't ashamed as he spoke. He was proud. He smiled to show her that.

Paula's hand flew to her mouth.

"I done 'im in, Paula. For wot 'e did to you an' your little ones. 'An 'e didn't die nice—trust me—I gave 'im a right bad time." He sank down on the sofa and he watched her for her reaction as he delivered his gift, neatly wrapped, in the packet marked "vengeance."

"You killed him? You murdered Seth Baker?"

"I executed him, luv. 'e 'ad no right to be on the same planet as you."

"Oh, Graham, you *didn't!*" It was clear what had happened. In his crazed mind he expected her to be grateful. All the time her premonitions about him had been correct. There was a screw missing behind his impenetrable eyes. Immediately the thick fog of foreboding descended. She knew instinctively that a terrible thing was about to happen. She stood there, rigid with fright. Please God, she murmured to herself. I've suffered enough. Must I suffer more? Incredibly there was no part of her that was glad, despite all the nights she had lain awake and prayed to God for this moment. The thought that one day she might engineer the destruction of the man she loathed had given her the strength to carry on, and once she had been prepared to trade her life for his, in the knowledge that she would be meting out justice that the law would never provide. But now, as she heard of the revolting man's death, there was no pleasure in it. Her love for Robert had healed her hating heart, and in the love land there was no place for loathing and revenge. It was different because *she* was different. She was about to be married, and her past had melted away, bleached into insignificance by the bright sunlight of her future. In the slow fade, the scars had dimmed, and the brilliant colors of her pain, her hurt, and her hatred had metamorphosed into the uniform sepia of an old photograph. Before, she had nothing to lose but her own miserable life. Now all the happiness in the world was suddenly at risk. Graham had killed for her. How far was that from killing at her command? At the very least she was an accomplice to his crime. She would be guilty before the law, if and when the murder was discovered.

Graham tried to understand her feelings so that he could move on to the other things, to the claiming of the reward he was there to claim.

"Don't worry. They won't pin it on me . . . on us, Paula."

His reassurance shuddered against the implied threat.

"Why? Why did you kill him, Graham?" It was a ridiculous question, because of course she knew. She was playing for time. She had to know what all this meant to him. She had to understand what was going down in the vacant lot behind his eyes.

"I done 'im in for you, Paula. You told me 'ow much you wanted to 'urt 'im for wot 'e done. I did it for you, luv. I did it for us."

Again the "us." The conspiracy. She splayed out her hands and the tears sprang to her eyes as she realized the hopelessness of her position. He wanted something, this killer who sat with her in the dead of night. He wanted her! He had killed Seth Baker to get her.

"But, Graham, you're crazy!" The exasperation spilled out of her. "You're mad. I'm going to be married. I'm in love with Robert. I never wanted you to kill him. People don't kill people." The words were tumbling over themselves as she tried to deny the deed she knew had been performed.

"I love you, girl. You can learn to love me."

"I can't love you. I don't love you. What the hell are you talking about, Graham? You're mad. Do you hear? I love Robert. We're going to be married. Can't you understand that?" She was shouting at him, her voice breaking with the strain.

He stood up, quickly, and his face was changing. Anger scurried across it. He took hold of her arms, roughly, and his fingers closed tightly around them.

"Listen to me! Listen to me! Forget Robert bleedin' 'artford. 'e's over. 'e's 'istory. Talk like that again an' I'll 'urt 'im, too. You're not getting married to 'im. You're gettin' married to me! You got a choice. Live with me, or burn with me. Understand, darlin'. You 'earin wot I'm sayin'?"

Paula was terrified. This man who held her was no longer Graham, her cockney friend. He was a cold-blooded psychopathic killer. Now at last her mind slowed down as she began to think. What she did now, what she said now, mattered more than thought and action had ever mattered before.

"Don't hurt me, Graham. I'm just confused, that's all," she said carefully. He would understand that: a poor confused woman, shocked and shaken by the violence of the all-male world.

"I won't 'urt you, doll. Just do right by me. Just 'ear me out. See it my way. I love you, doll."

His hands relaxed their steely grip, and she rubbed at the marks they left as her mind whirred on, and she tried to avoid his cold blue gaze. "Graham, we've got to talk," she said into the sudden quiet.

"Yeah, we can talk."

She sat down beside him on the sofa. Paula knew that she had to get rid of him. Nothing else was important. Once he had gone she could call Robert in New York. He would know what to do. He would get in touch with hotel security, call Winty, call the police, whatever. He would make it all right. But first she had to get rid of Graham. How? What would make him go? What did he have to hear before he would leave? Only lies could save her.

She turned toward him, and she prayed for her words to ring true. "I can't believe what you did for me. I just can't believe it." Stay as close to the truth as possible. Tears poured down her cheeks, fear posing as gratitude. "I hated him so much. He destroyed my life."

Graham waited and watched with the gutter cunning of his species. There was no trust in him. His life was lived in enemy territory. Even those he desired, especially those he desired, had the power to harm him.

"How could I possibly stop loving Robert and start loving you? I *like* you, Graham. I'm fond of you, but I'm not in love with you. And this whole thing. It's such a shock. I'm just so *confused*. I can't make any sense out of it."

The words said that she would never love him, but her confusion injected doubt into her message, and the liking she had for him would be a base on which to build. His expression said he had wanted more. But she had given him hope. It said that, too. "It'll just take time, girl. That's all." He sat there, not reaching for her, prim and proper on the edge of the sofa, like some suitor in a Victorian melodrama. If he'd had a hat it would have been on his knees, his fingers fiddling with its brim.

Paula leaped into the opportunity he had provided for her. "You're right. That's what I need, Graham. I need time to think. I'm tired. It's late. I need to sleep. I need to make sense of it all. Of what you say. Of what you've done for me."

"Come away with me now. To my place. We can send for your things in the morning." His voice was insistent, and he leaned forward.

"No! I have to be alone. I have to get my feelings straightened out. You can understand that, can't you? I must be alone."

Graham looked at her carefully, suspicion heavy on his face. His eyes roamed the room, taking in the heavy door, the shutters on the windows. If he left he would not be allowed to return. Where was Robert? Would she try to tell him what had happened? If so, his reaction would be violent and effective. No, she couldn't be trusted. She wanted him outside. She was playing for time. The hope she was giving him was counterfeit hope.

"You gotta come with me," he said.

The panic rushed up in the back of Paula's throat as she saw the door slamming shut on her plan. If she went with him anything might happen. He could kill her, when it sank in that she would never be his. He might go to the police and confess the murder, implicating her. He could rape her.

She had to get rid of him. Only then would Robert be able to save her. Paula's eyes flicked toward the telephone, and the number of the Carlyle flashed in her mind. He would be asleep, and she would wake him and all her troubles would be over as Robert Hartford roared into action.

But he had seen her eyes on the telephone, and he knew what she was thinking. "Come on," he said, and he stood up.

Again a surge of terror rushed through Paula. She had no weapon to fight him, and any resistance would make him angry. She must avoid that at all costs.

Then, at the moment of hopelessness, she remembered. She did have a weapon. The oldest one of all. The one that women had used against men since the dawn of time. She had her body. And he wanted it.

"Graham!" Her voice was husky, low pitched.

He paused, and his mind registered the new development as his body was caught in the tangled web of instant desire. She was going to give herself to him—in gratitude, perhaps; in lust possibly, if not in love. It was a victory that he had not dared to hope for. If they became lovers now, just once, here in Robert Hartford's home, everything would change. On Robert's sofa—in the lair of the man who despised him—he would make love to the woman he would marry and at a stroke all the jealousy and the hatred would melt away. He smiled at the thought of so much pleasure. Paula's sweet body, a mighty rival humiliated, his own way so comprehensively achieved. In the act of love the ghosts would be exorcised, and Paula would be pulled from the pedestal from which she taunted him, down low into the world of grunts and groans and taut, slippery flesh. And maybe then her spell over him would be broken, and the fatal attraction that plagued him would melt away in the groveling surrender of her hungry body.

He pushed his head to one side to indicate that he heard her message and that he wanted confirmation of it, and he smiled the cocky cockney smile of the small-time winner.

Paula swallowed hard. Was it the only way? If she allowed him this, he would have to trust her. In the lazy aftermath she would make him leave her, because he would believe that he could not lose her. Then, with the doors closed against him, she could be as unfair as he had been. Then she could fight him, accuse him of rape, of threatening her, expose him as the murderer he was, and throw herself on Robert's mercy. In one way or another he could be handled, but only if she survived this night.

So she stood up, and she watched him with what she hoped was a look of awakening desire and she pleaded with her body to help her do this thing. "Make love to me," she said.

Graham laughed. Already he could feel a new lightness inside him. At the end of the day she was just a doll like all the rest. The uncomfortable tenderness he had felt, the aching longing, all the bad times in London and before and since were beginning to blow away like a mist in a wind and he was glad. So he laughed again as he saw the subservience in her eyes, and at the moment of his triumph he wanted more. He wanted vengeance, too, as she had been avenged on Seth Baker. He wanted to be repaid for Robert Hartford's snotty looks and patronizing remarks, and he wanted to be recompensed for the misery of the past few weeks when he had felt an odd love so alien to his nature.

"Get undressed," he said.

Paula heard the new harshness in his voice and paradoxically it made it easier for her to do what had to be done. She reached for the edges of the sweater, and she tried to push the horror from her eyes.

"Take off your skirt first," he ordered, the dreamy expression of triumph and lust all mixed up with the cruelty on his face.

She moved quickly to obey him, as the hurry to be done with it masqueraded as enthusiasm.

He watched her as she unloosed her belt and wriggled free of the denim micro-skirt. It fell like a crumpled blue handkerchief around her ankle boots.

"That's better, ain't it, darlin'," he said, and she closed her eyes so as not to see him as he moved toward her. Greedily his hand reached for her, slipping roughly into her panties, ripping them away from her, defiling the desert dry heart of her with his rough fingers. At the same time, his mouth bowed down and his lips crushed against hers.

"Paula!"

Robert Hartford's voice exploded into the dreadful moment, freezing it in time, catching it forever in the photograph of his memory. He stood in the entrance of the room, and his face was already white. A dozen red roses drooped from his left hand and the key to his own front door stuck up from his right. Behind him was a single suitcase. He was no longer in New York.

Paula opened her eyes as Graham's face raced back from hers, as his hand fought to disentangle itself from her. Her mouth flew open, and she tried to speak, knowing as she did so that there was nothing to say. Her seminakedness spoke for her. Graham's hand was gabbling its message, her crushed lips, unmoving, were describing every detail of the disaster. On the floor, the crumpled skirt screamed its reproach, and her long legs, quivering with surprise, howled their complicity in the betrayal. In fascination she watched the pain splatter over Robert's face. His fists were clenched tight, his knuckles white with anguish, and still he was only halfway to the realization that his fiancée was making love, in his home, to a man who wasn't him.

Graham stepped back. The surprise on his face was fading fast. " 'Allo, Robert," he said. "We wasn't 'spectin' you back so soon." There was a cheerfulness in his voice, absolutely horrible in its self-centered superiority. At last he had the drop on the man he hated. He had screwed the screwer. He, the lowly Graham, had shown the legend just who the real man was.

Paula felt the nausea well up within her—at what she'd done, at what had happened, at what would happen.

"Robert," she said, as her hands reached in vain to cover herself. But her voice died away. What could she possibly say? Later, when light years had passed, there might be some way to make this right. First there would have to be hell on this earth, the hell that was starting now.

Robert's blazing eyes tore themselves away from the vision that was his wife-to-be, and they carried with them the portrait of treachery. Her naked legs were trembling, her panties lewdly askew as the alien fingers milked at her privacy, at the place that was his alone, that had been pledged to him forever. Her skirt was lying on the floor where it had been kicked down as lust had run too fast for decency.

Now his furious gaze centered on Graham and he dropped the roses, and he dropped the key, and he launched himself body and soul at the man he must kill.

The street fighter in Graham saw him move before Robert himself knew what he would do, and pleasure flickered in his ghostly eyes. He ducked, hardly seeming to do so, and Robert's flailing arms flew above his head. Then he hit him, hard, so hard, where his chest met his stomach, and the breath crunched out of the older man as he stopped in midair, impaled hopelessly on the spear of Graham's fist.

For a second he hung there. Then Graham's left hand smashed like a hard wave into the proud cliff of Robert Hartford's cheek. He staggered back, straightened up by the force of the blow, and then he fell backward, his legs leaderless, his mind scrambled.

"No! Graham, don't hurt him. Don't *hurt* him!" screamed Paula. But she was too late. Graham had hurt him more thoroughly and completely than he had ever been hurt before, than he ever would be again.

The desk hit Robert hard in the small of his back and his momentum sent him up and over it. For a second he hovered there, his legs pointing toward the ceiling, and then down he went, landing hard on his shoulder, his fall broken only by the waste-paper basket that crumpled like a beer can beneath his weight.

Graham had won, but he hadn't finished. He walked quickly to the prostrate figure of Robert Hartford and he kicked him, casually, once, twice and a third time in his side, in his ribs, and the last, contemptuously, on his rump. He turned once again to Paula. "Rude not to knock," he said. "Now, where was we?"

She screamed now with all the fury and the anguish and the horror of the death of her life. It was loud, the scream, so loud that it blocked out her mind as it went on, and on, and on.

Graham's back was toward his defeated rival. He had dismissed him, because he had beaten him and he had humiliated him. The movie weakling would not attack him again. All he could do now was watch the fun.

Robert hauled himself to his feet, his fingers grabbing at the edge of the desk. The room was spinning around him to the music of Paula's screams, and the nausea gripped at his stomach as he fought to stand. His eyes swam in his head and he tried desperately to focus, to stop the mad ringing in his ears. Then an awful roar of rage exploded in his throat and once again he threw himself at his mortal enemy.

Graham half turned, but slowly, languidly, and a smile of condescension flashed across his face.

Robert Hartford had ceased to be a human being. He had become a missile. In the core of him the demon had been unleashed and all the anger had jelled into a quivering mass of venomous hatred. Here were all his rivals for all the sweet goddesses, wrapped up in the disgusting form of a single man, his lewd fingers plucking at the embodiment of feminine beauty—the one who had promised herself so solemnly to him. From the bottom of the low life his essence was being insulted, and the terrible desire for revenge ran like high-octane fuel in his broken body, filling him up with mad energy and the strength of the damned. The power surged in his quadriceps, and flowed free in the muscles of his calves, and, both his hands rigid with fury, he flew like the spear he had become at Graham.

Both palms landed in the small of Graham's back, and behind them was the total mass of Robert's body. Graham flew forward, off balance, trying too late to push his feet forward to maintain equilibrium. They caught in the edge of the rug, and he pitched forward toward the thick glass coffee table that stood in front of the fireplace. Both shins hit the three-quarter-inch-thick glass at the same time, and the sickening sound of the collision cut the air like the crack of a bullwhip. But the awful blow didn't stop Graham. On and on he went, crashing down now on the slippery glass as he slid head first across the ice rink that was the table, scattering the blue-covered scripts, the art books, and the African sculptures in his wake. Still he didn't stop, and the pain from his legs and the surprise at his extraordinary predicament fought for control of the expression on his speeding face.

At the end of the table, to one side of the sofa, stood the Advent television. Black and superb, big and beautiful, it loomed like a sculpture from the hydraulic mahogany cabinet that was its home. It had always been Robert's pride and joy. The touch of a button and it sank gracefully from sight. The flick of another and it rose serenely to view and be viewed. Beneath it was the cavernous hole that was supposed to hold the video tapes that Robert had never bothered to collect. The studio sent over the movies he wanted to see, and later someone would pick them up. So the space beneath the forty-two-inch monitor screen was empty, a glistening black hole just longing to be filled.

Like a limo gliding into a garage, Graham's rocket-tip head, face

down, aimed itself toward the beckoning void. It was a tight fit. Not
really technically a "fit" at all. His head collided with the opening, and
the sharp edge of the cabinet smashed effortlessly through his nose and
crushed up against his forehead as the bottom of the television casually
scalped the back of his head. He was half in, half out, wedged tight
where the tapes should be, and his scream of shock and agony was
muffled in the enclosed space. At last he had stopped, and apart from
his hands, which pried frantically at the opening of the hole that
trapped him, he was still.

Suddenly the room was quiet, the peace interrupted only by a
regular, insistent drip, drip, drip. It was blood falling with the
regularity of a metronome onto the immaculate glass table. Graham
was not speaking, but he was bleeding.

Crouched like a wild animal where he had fallen from the force of
his forward momentum, Robert Hartford watched the thing he had
done. His eyes stared from his head, and on the famous cheek the red
of the bruise was spreading upward, downward, sideways toward his
pencil-thin mouth. The air rasped through flared nostrils and his chest
rose and fell in heaving lurches as he struggled to get his breath. His
head darted to Paula, frozen in horror and her seminakedness, and
then to Graham, lying half conscious amidst the wreckage of the
table—his damaged head wedged tight in the hydraulic TV console.
Robert's eyes glinted their fury, and then deep in the depths of them,
there was another emotion. It was only a spark at first, but a tiny flame
in a scrubland of potential fire. It was the flame of pleasure. Brightly
now it burned in the forests of Robert's eyes, and the light from it
fanned outward to illuminate his face. The smile was small, growing,
big, bigger, a horrible leering thing that mocked his beauty as it hinted
at a new and terrible purpose. His lips relaxed over his teeth, and what
had been thin and mean with hatred were suddenly full and voluptuous
with the joy of cruelty to come. He crawled forward, and with his right
hand he searched among the coffee-table detritus. He was looking for
something, and he laughed now as he looked, and the maniacal sound
filled up the room, background music to the devil's pact he had already
signed in his heart. There it was. He'd found it, and his fingers
clutched at it, drawing it toward his chest like a mother a newborn
child. Small and flat it lay, innocent, in the palm of his hand, and he
didn't even have to look closely at it to know how to use it. It was the
remote-control device that operated his television set—the one that
lifted it up from its box . . . the one that sent it sinking down, so
smoothly, so gently, with such irresistible force.

He held it up high, at arm's length, like the magic sword of He-Man, Master of the Universe, and, still laughing, he pressed down hard on the button.

It was an old Whitney Houston video, on MTV, and although the sound was turned way down low, it was just possible to learn that she wanted to dance with somebody, wanted to feel the heat of somebody, needed only someone to love her. But now Whitney Houston was descending like a coffin at a cremation. The initial sound was something in between a crack and a crunch but almost immediately it merged into the noise of heavy feet marching relentlessly across softly packed gravel. At first it was all so effortless, so inexorable, but quite suddenly there were sounds of protest, of mechanical protest, of human protest. The TV seemed to realize that there was an obstacle to its sedate disappearing act, and in the bowels of the cabinetry the smooth hum of the engine turned nervous, high pitched, as it lost its rhythm. Now it whined and whirred and strained, but its noises were drowned by the gurgling, muffled, liquid scream that came from what was left of Graham's mouth. Whitney Houston reared in the middle of her song, up an inch, down two, as she shuddered sideways, her brilliant brown sugary legs dancing, dancing, dancing on the back of Graham's crushed and bleeding head.

For milliseconds the battle raged. The eggshell of Graham's skull, his slippery soft brain within, against the brute force of the expensive machine. Would Whitney Houston dance into the very center of Graham's mind? Was that where she would find the heat of somebody? In the mud of his gray matter would there be someone to love her?

Robert's thumb was white on the button as he vibrated to the wonderful music. His hand danced up and down as if he was conducting it, orchestrating the terror, the ultimate downfall of every man in the cosmos who wasn't him. He was all but oblivious to hands that wrestled with his, to the voice shouting in his ear for him to turn off the spigot of murder that spurted in his heart.

Paula tore at his knuckles, her naked legs brushing against his bleeding cheek as she tried to get him to stop the dreadful thing he was doing. Already she had forgotten herself. She was existing at a deeper level of humanity, the place where death was evil and life was sacred. Robert's blood was on her thigh, and his acrid sweat was in her nostrils as she fought with him to spare what was left of the life of the man who had destroyed hers.

"Robert, stop it. Stop it. For God's sake, stop it," she screamed.

And he did, eventually. His hand relaxed and the color returned to his snow-white knuckles, as his thumb lifted from the button at last.

There was a faraway look in Robert's eyes, the look of postcoital ecstasy that she had learned to love before, in the far distant land that was now her past. Then she turned to look at Graham. At what was left of him. He lay there, his mangled head stuffed into the inverted V of Whitney Houston's endless legs, and there was only one part of him that moved.

His left leg had a life of its own. It twitched convulsively, and the toe of his shoe beat out a truncated rhythm on the shiny glass. Slower, then more slowly and with less force, the limb kept up its inaccurate dance, scattering a book, an obelisk, a headhunter's dagger from West Irian. *Rat-a-tat-tat-a-tat* it went . . . before, at last, the silly mindless sound trailed off into the stillness of an apocalyptic silence.

SEVENTEEN

Winthrop Tower scurried along the path, his head down, and the folds of his sky-blue silk Alfred Dunhill dressing gown flared out in the cold night air. His hair stood up in uneven tufts and he screwed up his eyes in concentration as he tried to wake up, to make sense of the telephone conversation he had just had. Robert had been short, his voice clipped. There had been a terrible accident at his bungalow. For some extraordinary reason Graham had been badly injured and had already been taken to the hospital. The police were there now. Could Winthrop get over as soon as possible? At the interface of sleep and wakefulness, of drunkenness and sobriety, he had slammed down the telephone and thrown on the dressing gown over his pajamas. In the Sunset lobby the clock had said three in the morning, but the electricity in the atmosphere had hinted that the time was high noon. There had been all sorts of movement at the desk, a couple of tight knots of people, and two or three uniformed policemen standing about with the casual unconcern that hinted that something important had happened.

The policeman guarding the front door of the bungalow seemed to have been expecting him.

"Mr. Winthrop Tower?"

"I think so. I think so," muttered Winthrop, pushing past him. Hoping that curiosity would not kill the cat, he wondered what he would find. He could probably deal with anything but blood.

First he found Robert.

"God, Robert are you all right? You look as bad as I feel. What the hell's going on?"

"I caught Graham and Paula making love," he said with the suave calm of a matinee idol pouring tea. "On the carpet, in front of the fire," he added.

"Good God!"

Robert peered at him carefully. "Do you know Barton, from the Beverly Hills P.D.?" asked Robert suddenly. "Captain Barton, this is Winthrop Tower, he's . . . the . . . uh . . . the employer." He clearly couldn't bring himself to mention Graham's name.

"Making love?" said Winthrop Tower. It hadn't really sunk in.

"Mr. Hartford returned from New York unexpectedly," said the man called Barton. "It appears that Miss Hope, his fiancée, was in uh . . . uh . . . a compromising position with Ovenden, who works for you. Mr. Hartford asked the man to leave. He was attacked. There was a scuffle, and in the course of it, Mr. Ovenden's head was badly damaged in the hydraulic mechanism of the television over there." He pointed at the TV. It was covered with white dust and white masking tape and toward its base where it met the cabinet the laminated plastic had suffered some kind of trauma. That was where the red stuff was, rusty, flaky, caked. Winthrop's stomach did a practice roll.

"Is Graham going to be all right?"

"Not necessarily," said Robert.

Winthrop looked at him, a stupid expression of incredulity all over his face. God, he looked wonderful. Absolutely *tragic*. And his weird choice of words seemed to emphasize the utter transcendence of his grief.

"Mr. Ovenden's been taken to Cedars-Sinai, sir," the policeman said smoothly. "The paramedics seem to think he's suffered a serious head injury. A very serious one."

"He *attacked* you, Robert?"

"Yes, he did, sir, as you can see," said the policeman. "There was a struggle, and Ovenden fell across the table and collided with the underside of the television. The impact started up the mechanism that lowers the television into the cabinet. Ovenden's head got caught inside. Miss Hope confirmed the facts. She works for you, too, I think, sir. Is that right?"

"Yes. Yes, they both do," agreed Winthrop.

"Did," said Robert.

Winthrop suddenly realized he was going to have to take sides. He ran the unedited tape through his mind, trying to make sense of the disjointed plot. Graham and Paula had been caught two-timing Robert Hartford in the drawing room of his own home. In the fight that followed, his servant had been all but killed, and Paula had confirmed the story to the police. The fiancée had admitted the infidelity. The marriage was over before it had started.

But Paula simply couldn't have behaved like that. It wasn't just out of character; it was totally bizarre. Yet it seemed impossible to argue with the facts, and it was certainly true that Graham had wanted to be Paula's lover. At least one of the conspirators had the right motive.

"Did you know that your two employees were having a relationship, Mr. Tower?"

"No. Certainly not. I mean, I think I recognized that Graham was taken with Paula Hope. As far as I knew it certainly wasn't reciprocated. She regarded him as a friend. She was a very attractive woman. Men liked her." Winthrop was surprised to hear himself talking in the past tense. "Where is she now?" he asked.

"Back in the gutter where she belongs." Robert's lip curled with aggression as he spoke. He paced over to the window and stared out into the blackness as if searching for Paula among the streets to which he had consigned her.

He turned back toward them. "Is there anything else I can help you with, Captain Barton?"

"No, I think we have everything we need. Obviously we'd like a statement from Ovenden, but it may be we won't be getting that. Otherwise we'll be collating the fingerprint and photographic evidence, but I think yours and Ms. Hope's statements will be more than enough for the file. Of course if Ovenden dies then there would have to be an inquest, and a medical examiner's verdict, but as far as I'm concerned that's it for now. You maintain that the batteries in the remote-control device had been dead for at least three days?"

"At least."

"Well, Ms. Hope confirms that, and she had been using the television, and the batteries we removed from the remote *are* nonfunctioning. So it really just remains for me to say how very sorry I am, sir, that this unfortunate business has happened."

"Thank you for your courtesy and your efficiency," said Robert with the forced charm of a minor royal on a tour of the factory.

The policeman hovered, unwilling to take the ultimate step of actually leaving. It wasn't every day he got to investigate the domestic violence of the Robert Hartfords of this world, and he would have liked to linger. But there was nothing else to do. The story just had to be true, for one reason and one alone. The girl had corroborated the movie star's version. If he had killed her lover in a fit of jealous rage she would hardly have allowed herself to become an accomplice to the cover-up. And if she still loved Robert and was risking jail to protect him, then there was no way she would have been so enthusiastically cheating on him in the first place. Her testimony had allowed Barton to do professionally what he had wanted to do emotionally—to believe the man it was so easy to believe.

"I'll do my best to keep the lid on this one, Mr. Hartford."

"I'd be extremely grateful if you could." Robert Hartford drooped with weariness. His shoulders were bowed, his voice heavy, his lids hovering leadlike over the amazing eyes.

"I'll let myself out. Good-bye, Mr. Tower."

He was gone.

Winthrop walked quickly over to his old friend and put out a hand to his shoulder. "Robert, I'm most terribly sorry."

Robert smiled back wanly.

"Not your fault, Winty. Mine. I trusted her. She was so easy to trust. I've never done it before."

"Can't there be any other explanation? I mean, she wasn't drunk or anything. Sort of a horseplay thing?"

Robert shook his head slowly. He walked to the sofa and flung himself down on it. Then he fixed Winthrop with his eyes. When he spoke his voice was far away, the tone plaintive. "I came back from New York and I didn't tell her I was coming because I wanted to surprise her. I wanted to wake her up, and make love to her, and tell her about the new deal I'd just done because I was so happy and I wanted her to be happy for me. They were standing there"—and he nodded to the middle of the room by the fireplace—"and she was naked, more or less, below the waist and he had his fingers . . . inside her . . . while he was kissing her."

Winthrop Tower took a deep breath and winced as he imagined it—Graham, his hard body the stuff of countless of Winthrop's own fantasies, and Paula, the angelic daughter he had never had—the pair of them traitors, mocking and shaming the grownups who had dared to love them.

"I wanted to kill him," said Robert's defeated voice, "the little limey with his chirpy tongue and his cheap suits, and he turned around and he smiled, and do you know what he said? 'We weren't expecting you.' 'We,' Winty. 'We weren't expecting you.' " Robert's face struggled with disbelief, and he propped himself up against the cushions as a shuddering sigh escaped him. He screwed up his eyes in pain.

"I tried to beat his brains out, but of course he was better at that sort of thing, wasn't he? He was walking back toward Paula, and he said something like, 'Let's finish it off.' . . . I don't know . . . and I . . . I just ran at him and he sort of fell forward and that thing just . . . swallowed him up."

Again Winthrop Tower twisted his eyes away from Robert's. There was a very nasty feeling inside his head—the one called responsibility, the one he always tried so hard to avoid. He had been the prime mover in all this. Graham was a Tower production. So was Paula. He had more or less invented them, and then injected them into Robert Hartford's world. Now Graham was fighting for his life on some operating table, and Paula, on whom all his hopes for the future had been pinned, was now a pariah. He tried to digest the last part. Yes, Paula would have to go. His loyalty to Robert demanded it. He had known Hartford for twenty years. He had known Paula for one. Then there was the design of the Sunset. Robert would never allow her near the place after his humiliation at her hands. Last but not least, there was Paula's extraordinary mind-bending lapse of taste. Standing up! With an employee! Without double locking the door from the inside! One expected more from protégés. Very much more. There was no doubt at all about it. Paula Hope had let him down badly.

"I mean," said Robert, and Winthrop couldn't help noticing the mist that had sprung up in the famous eyes, "she just took my feelings, in the palm of her hand . . . and she crushed them . . . just like that."

"It goes without saying, Robert, that Paula no longer works for me, and I can be pretty sure that she won't work for anyone else either. I imagine she won't hang around for long." Winthrop fought back the regret. The girl had revealed herself to be serious trouble. Nothing wrong with that in small doses—they were rather stimulating—but there was a limit, and she had leaped over it. And yet . . . and yet . . .

For a second or two Robert pondered Paula's fate. His face was inscrutable. It was impossible to know whether he wanted further revenge or whether, already, he, too, was beginning to miss her. And when at last he spoke his meaning was very far from clear. "I can't stop thinking about her limp," he said.

Graham lay quite still, his face and head swathed in bandages, the plastic tubes with their straw-colored liquid disappearing into the folds of crepe around the flat area where his nose should have been.

Winthrop Tower picked up the pale hand of his servant and squeezed it. "Can you hear me, Graham?" he said. "Not with this fucking bandage on, mate," was the answer for which he half hoped.

"I am afraid he can't," said the quiet voice from behind.

Winthrop turned around. The neurosurgeon's green smock was

covered with blood, but his hand, lily white and talcum powdered, was clean. He held it out for Winthrop to shake. "I gather from the nurse you're Winthrop Tower, Ovenden's employer," he added.

Tower took a deep breath at the sight of the doctor's gory appearance. His hand flew to his suddenly sweat-soaked brow, and he staggered sideways.

"Are you all right?" asked the doctor sharply in the tone of voice the medical profession reserves for unreliable friends of the family.

"Sorry. Yes, I'm fine. Never very good with blood. Not even very fond of the color red," muttered Winthrop weakly.

"Oh," said the surgeon, looking down absentmindedly at his stained smock. "I think you'd better sit down," he added, his voice more kindly now.

Winthrop sat down in the chair next to the bed. Beside his face the EKG machine traced the regular pattern of Graham's heartbeat.

"How is he?"

"He's had a terrible injury to the head. Multiple compound fractures of the skull. Bone injected into the gray matter. Brain compression. Tearing of the arteries in the cerebral and cerebellar areas. I'm not sure he's going to make it. I'm not sure it would be the best thing in the world if he did."

"You mean, he'd . . ."

"Well, it's difficult to say. He's throwing off EEG activity. He's not brain dead, but he's in a deep coma. If we can keep his vital signs stable for the next few days, he might survive. But he might never regain consciousness. If he did, he might not be able to speak or move."

"Like poor Sunny Von Bülow."

"That's more than a possibility."

"If it came to that, I'd be happy to pay for it," said Winthrop. "I don't want anyone switching him off." He wanted that absolutely clear. Quite suddenly he felt sadness well up within him. Dear Graham, who'd made him laugh, who'd eased his life, who'd looked like wild dreams. What would he look like now, behind the crepe mask, after being eaten by a television? God, what a way to go! Graham had always thought of himself as being up-to-date, but that was ridiculous. Winthrop smiled wryly as he felt the sadness recede. If life was ridiculous, why couldn't death be? Any minute now it would be his turn. Graham might actually outlast him, locked in the twilight of his ruinously expensive coma.

"Well, I'll certainly make a note of that in the medical file. So, you're going to be financially responsible for him?"

"Yes, certainly."

"Good. Look, I've got to go. We'll talk again. In the meantime there's nothing to do but wait and hope, I'm afraid."

"Yes, thank you. Thank you very much." Alone in the dim religious light of the intensive care cubicle, Winthrop Tower buried his head in his hands, and he realized exactly what he needed—a great big drink.

The hand on his shoulder was light, tentative.

"Hello, Winty," said Paula.

He started up.

"Paula! What the *hell* are you doing here?"

She stood before him, proud and defiant, and she looked him straight in his bloodshot eyes. "I came to find out how Graham was."

"He's a fucking vegetable, and it's your fault," blurted Winthrop, conscious of the cruelty, meaning to be cruel.

Her face was white, drained of blood, but it didn't change when he spoke. She didn't flinch at his terrible words. "It's not my fault, Winty. I hoped I could make you believe that."

Again she looked at him, straight in the eye, and Winthrop had to admire her brazenness. "How can you talk like that, Paula? How can you have done what you did to Robert? How long had it been going on?"

She looked desperate now, at the mention of Robert's name. Her lips trembled, her eyes widened. She was pleading with him, but he knew that she wasn't going to beg. "Graham could tell you what happened."

"He's never going to be able to, Paula."

"You believed what Robert told you, I suppose. He didn't want to hear my side of the story. I thought you would." There was despair in her voice.

Winthrop tried to tell himself that she was a counterfeit, a forger of emotions. After all, she had misled him, cheated his friend, and enslaved poor Graham, and now here she was trying to escape the consequences of her actions. What explanation *could* there be? She herself had confirmed to the police Robert's story of her infidelity.

He thundered when he spoke, the violence of his expressed sentiment partly disguising the strange ambivalence he felt. "How dare you stand in front of me, here in this hospital, with Graham fighting for his life, and tell me you have a 'side of the story'? What possible side could there be? I fear you're a tramp, Paula Hope, who took us all for a ride. Well, from now on you're a nobody all over again. I say so. Robert says so. And that means *everybody* says so." He jumped up, and he thrust out his chin as his belligerence burst over her.

For a long time she held his gaze. She didn't look away, and she was silent. She made no attempt to justify herself in the face of his anger.

Quietly, and quite firmly, she said, "Fuck *you*, Winthrop Tower," and then she turned quickly and strode from the room.

In the Bel-Air Hotel, Paula Hope was falling apart. All around her lay the wreck of the once immaculate room—half-empty coffee cups, the dirty towels piled high on the floor, the unmade bed. She hadn't allowed housekeeping in for at least three days, nor room service to take away the old trays, and the congealed food—greasy burgers, exhausted lettuce, melted ice cream—gave off a smell that reminded her of the diner in Placid on the Sunday morning after a Saturday night. The Bel-Air, haughtily aristocratic, had understood. Their guests were always indulged, however outlandish their requests.

It had been a terrible three weeks since the night in the Sunset Hotel when first Robert, then Winty, had become her enemy. Since then she had had no more contact with her old world than had poor Graham, sunk deep in his coma. She had crashed out of their lives on a raging sea of anger and disappointment, furious that the man she loved and the friend she trusted had trusted and loved her so little in return. Even a common criminal had the right to be heard, but they hadn't allowed her to explain, and in the face of their prejudice she had told them both to go to hell. But it was she who had gone there. She had moved into the Bel-Air, and the depression had settled over her like a black cloud as she had wandered around the curtained room in the robe they provided, unable to wash, to eat, or to sleep. The flickering TV, tuned in to MTV with the sound turned down low, had been the backdrop to her sorrow, and her thoughts had slowed down, sinking into numbness, way past tears, into the unreality of nothingness.

Paula sat down on the end of the bed. They had won. The world had beaten her. She had traveled on a magic carpet from hell to heaven, and she had found the happiness she deserved in beautiful Beverly Hills. Now it was gone. And so, at five hundred bucks a night, was the money she'd saved. In the hotel lot, just beyond the bridge and the swans, was the rest of her capital—the 1966 classic convertible Mustang that would carry her away from the place and the people she had dared to love.

Then, quite suddenly, a molecular shift occurred. Was it thinking about the car? Or escape? Or her lack of money? No. It was the contemplation of losing. She was not prepared to be defeated. Others had gotten their own way when she wanted hers. It was intolerable, said her heart. It was disgusting said her guts. It was impossible, screamed her newly discovered will. She stood up.

"Screw *you!*" she said.

"Screw *you*, Robert Hartford! Screw you, Winthrop Tower! Screw YOU, Beverly Hills!"

She ran to the bathroom, the cleanest part of her suite, and she threw off the bathrobe and turned on the COLD tap. The water shocked her, and her thoughts were speeding as she soaped away the sweat and the tears. She jumped out, turned up the MTV, and let the clean music blast at her, reminding her that she was still *alive*. She scooped up a bathing suit and climbed into it, and she ran out of the door into the sunshine, her eyes blinking at the light. She wasn't even sure what time of day it was, though it was early morning certainly from the cold and the dew on the grass. In the pale blue sky, the underside of the shallow clouds were painted pink by the rising sun, and the air was crisp as she hurried along the path toward the pool.

When she reached it, she threw off the gown and she dived in, and once again the fresh water baptized her. She broke the surface, reborn, her whole body tingling. She looked up as she swam, toward the pencil-thin petticoat palms and the tall cypresses that ringed the oval pool, and she vowed that from now on she would only look forward and never look back. Her muscles rejoiced and her heart sang as she planned her future. They wouldn't drive her away from Beverly Hills, as they had driven her from Placid. She would find a job. Her Filofax was full of numbers—rival designers, suppliers, clients, would-be clients, and just plain strangers who passed in the plutocratic night of uptown L.A. One of them would come up trumps for her. It was just a matter of trying. It was simply a question of not losing faith. She swam for half an hour, and then she hurried back to her room and opened the drawer of the desk. She sketched out her plans on the Bel-Air writing paper. At nine o'clock the telephone would open up her brand-new world.

"No way José, Paula love. What did you do to them, dear? I mean, I had some bird-brain girl on the line from Tower Design saying that you'd been fired and that you were bad news. She actually said that the old boy would consider it a personal favor if we failed to help out should you make a call like this. You didn't hide his whiskey bottle did you, honey, or bad mouth his English taste? Well, I told her to mind her own business, darling, didn't I, but it wouldn't really be minding mine to give you a job. Not that you'd enjoy mincing around with my lot. The camp around here's not so much 'haute' as stratospheric. If the wrists get any limper they'll fall off! Anyway, *fantastic* talking to you, and good luck, darling. Have you thought about Alaska? No, no, just joking, sweetheart. One's got to laugh, lovely. It's only life."

Paula put the phone down. There had been all sorts of different ways of saying it, but the message had been the same. Thanks, but no thanks. They had closed the town on her. She had never imagined it was possible. Now she knew it was. She'd made thirty calls, but Winty and Robert had apparently made more. She was an untouchable in the place in which she'd vowed to succeed.

But Paula had had enough of pessimism. She had one chance and she picked it up from the desk, running her thumb absentmindedly over the raised italic script of the invitation. Unlike those who sent it, it was a very stylish thing, totally correct in the tradition of understatement—black on the finest white cardboard, no color, no drawings, no mindless colloquial chatter. *Mrs. Antoine Coriarchi*, it read. *At home. Black tie.* And the date? Tonight. At the top of Benedict Canyon, in the sky above Beverly Hills.

Paula swung the wheel of the Mustang and took the turn off Sunset by the Beverly Hills Hotel. Soon she was speeding through the flats up into the canyon. The houses looked grander at night, as the floodlights picked out the plants that God created rather than the houses that the humans had made. She fed the Bob Seger tape into the deck and cranked up the volume of the Blaupunkt a notch or two, allowing the hard-rock music to merge with the night air. The singer was going on about diamonds and frills in the Hollywood Hills. She laughed out loud at the lyrics. The black Anouska Hempel evening dress would do for the frills, but forget the diamonds. For now! Up ahead were the hills, and on the scuffed plastic of the seat beside her was the invitation to the Coriarchi party. She glanced down at it, as her heart beat faster in time to the frantic rhythm of the Silver Bullet band. It seemed light years since the time when the Coriarchis had played the role of doormat to Winty's Stanislavsky interpretation of filthy feet. Since that day their star had risen. Maybe the house she designed for them had helped. Anyway, someone had given them a proper movie to make— Patrick Swayze had said yes to a Bo Goldman script, which meant that tonight's party would be far from the social desert it would otherwise have been. That was lucky, because it would be her last chance to salvage something from the wreckage of her career.

On either side the houses flashed by—great stone estates, displaced Mediterranean villas, contemporary masterpieces glossy wall by mossy jowl with somebody's idea of French châteaux. She climbed the twisting, turning road, and the adrenaline began to pump inside her, as the breeze plucked at her hair, sending it streaming out into the darkness. It was going to be all right. Nowhere this beautiful could be that bad. She had felt it on Melrose on the day she'd arrived. She was feeling it now. The angst of L.A. was coursing in her blood, all mixed up with hope, and optimism, and a reckless determination to win, here on the edge of the world where the dreamers dreamed.

The torches blazed at the entrance to the Coriarchi driveway, and Paula sent the gravel blasting from the Mustang's tires as she screeched to a halt in front of the valet parkers' station.

The blond boy, whose hand was on the handle of the door, looked almost too good to eat. His California "hello" smile was wide open. Paula smiled back. He was her age, but he wasn't her speed. "Great car," he said. "Great owner," he added.

"Thanks," she said, smiling back. She knew L.A. well enough to know that compliments like that got passed around a *lot*.

Encouraged by her attitude he tried again. "Hey, you wanna take in Camp Hollywood soon as this shit is over?" he tried, deepening the smile.

"Bail out, dork dick," said Paula cheerfully, heading toward the front door of the house, and smiling over her shoulder at him to show that there were no hard feelings. The heavy-metal video and barbecue bar might have been fun.

In the Coriarchi hallway she had herself designed, people were standing patiently before a gilt desk at which an elderly lady checked their invitations against a list. God, how awful, thought Paula. It was fine at some charity ball where people were paying $250 a pop for the tickets, but at a private party it was unbearably pretentious, insinuating both that people would actually want to crash a Coriarchi function, and that the hosts didn't know the people they had invited. In Hollywood, however, nobody liked to step out of line for fear of insulting someone, so all were submitting gracefully to the interrogation.

In front of her in the line a Tower client, who had never before missed an opportunity to say hello, twisted and turned her head like an ostrich to avoid eye contact with Paula. Her bony back, draped in shimmering Adolfo, was arranged in Paula's face like a shield and she chattered away to her surprised husband of the moment as if she actually enjoyed talking to him.

"Winthrop did this house, Michael. Did you know that? Isn't it wonderful? Really he is *so* clever."

The carrot-shredder voice wafted back over the skeletal shoulders.

Paula fought back the desire to tap her on the arm, introduce herself, and lay claim to the decorative scheme that the Coriarchi cow had attributed to Tower. But there wasn't time. Paula was at the desk. Her invitation floated down onto the table.

"Paula Hope," said Paula.

The social secretary peered at the list. She looked at Paula. Then she stared once more at the list. "I don't have any Paula Hope here," she said in a definite voice.

"But this is my invitation." The line behind Paula had gone deathly quiet.

The guardian of the gate picked it up like a bank cashier inspecting a dubious hundred. "And you *are* Paula Hope?" she said at last.

"Yes, of course I am," said Paula. She was getting angry and nervous. Weird things were beginning to occur to her. Could this have been done on purpose, as some kind of cruel social punishment?

"I'm afraid my instructions are to admit no one who isn't on this list, whether they have an invitation or not." It was the voice of the universal bureaucrat.

"This is ridiculous," said Paula. "I worked for Winthrop Tower. I *designed* this house." The irritation rushed out of her. Watch it, or I'll redesign you, said her threatening eyes.

"I don't make the rules, I just carry them out," said the narc with the self-satisfaction of her species. It was the umbrella excuse of the led as they basked in their little moment of power, their brief excursion into the otherwise forbidden land of the leader.

"At Nuremberg they hanged people who said that," said Paula.

"Can't you just step aside and let the rest of us join the party?" said someone loudly from behind.

"I don't think she works for Tower any more," said somebody else.

"What seems to be the problem?" said Antoine Coriarchi. He had emerged as if from nowhere, and now he hovered at the shoulder of his minion.

"Ms. Hope has an invitation but she isn't on my list, and Mrs. Coriarchi told me specifically that no one who isn't on the list . . ." mumbled the woman, hurrying to cover herself in case she seemed to be doing the wrong thing.

"Please explain that I should have been on the list," said Paula. Her voice was sharp, not placatory at all. She didn't bother to say hello to her host.

For a second Antoine Coriarchi smiled his greasy Levantine smile.

He knew what had happened, of course. His wife had mentioned it to him. This was a party unlike any he had given before. His newfound success meant that he had graduated from the Z team to the A one, and, in Hollywood style, it had happened overnight as it was meant to. Somewhere along the line one of the power people had declared through their offices that Paula Hope, the pretty young designer who'd done their house and then graduated briefly to Robert Hartford live-in status, was no longer persona grata. Therefore, she had been removed from the list. Simple. QED. Quite easily done. But now he seemed to remember that the shaker who'd wanted the girl scrubbed was in fact Tower, her former employer—Tower, who'd humiliated him when he was merely another Arab semipornographer; Tower, who'd said things that in any civilized country would have had a man reaching for his knife.

"Miss Hope is always an honored guest in my home," he said, and he bowed and he smiled as he contemplated his little act of revenge.

"*Thank* you," said Paula, and she swept into the bowels of the party that she already knew would be a battleground.

Paula helped herself to a glass of champagne and wandered out toward the swimming pool, where people seemed to be congregating. All around her the spectacular landscape lighting that she had organized merged with the light from flickering Malibu torches to bathe the partygoers in a flattering, luminescent glow. She recognized an actress she'd met with Robert.

"Hello, Martha," said Paula.

The girl looked at her in horror, the expression she had used when the vampire was about to do the business on her neck in a Cannon movie. "God! Paula," she said. She peered around quickly. "What are you *doing* here?" she stage-whispered.

"What do you mean 'What am I doing here'? I was invited, just like you."

"Well . . . I just think . . . you're incredibly brave," said Martha, making *brave* sound exactly like *stupid*. Then she turned and scurried away into the safety of the crowd.

Paula took a deep breath. She looked around. How had the Coriarchis handled the hot potato of a noncharity Beverly Hills party? Well. The flowers were definitely David Jones and somehow they'd managed to get Wolfgang Puck to do the catering. The groaning buffet had his fingerprints all over it—smoked salmon pizza, cheesecakes, big bowls of crème brulée. That scored points. The only other viable alternatives would have been Party Planners, overused Rococo, or safe but unexciting Chasens. She'd already heard someone say the poolside ivories were to be tinkled by hot Michael Feinstein rather than the more usual Marvin Hamlisch. Then there were the two or three uniformed Beverly Hills policemen dotted strategically around the house and gardens. That was a first-tier party touch. The guests, too, were far from a disaster. Beverly Hills supporting cast, mainly, but with the odd truffle scattered among the pâté. She noticed psychiatrist to the stars and former president of the American Psychiatric Association, Judd Marmor, chatting animatedly to numerologist Michael Kassett, yogi Alan Finger, and psychic nutritionist Eileen Poole, in a poolside meeting of the minds. There were no "go" studio people, but Columbia mini-moguls Rob Fried and Amy Pascal were working the crowd, as was Lois Bonfiglio of Fonda Films. Sharp divorce lawyer Gary Hendler circled; wide-eyed, charismatic Insight guru and actress Leigh Taylor Young hovered; Marilyn Grabowski, Hollywood insider and power behind Playboy, was surrounded by three or four of the youngest and most beautiful women at the party.

That was the knot that Paula wandered toward.

"Hi, darling," said Marilyn as she approached, and Paula smiled in gratitude that there was someone there who was not afraid to talk to her.

"Hi, Marilyn. Did you ever find that house down in Malibu?"

"Not yet, but apparently when I do you're not allowed to design it." Marilyn laughed to show that she'd heard but she didn't care, that she didn't take orders from the Hartfords and Towers of this world. Playboy was an insulated world within the world of Hollywood, and that was the way Hef liked to keep it.

"Boy, I'm glad you're here. They tried to throw me out at the door. Wow, they sure marked my card in this town. Like the old 'you'll-never-work-again' is alive and *well*."

Marilyn laughed. "Don't worry, honey. You've got the talent. They've just got the egos."

The teenager with the part on the hottest soap had had enough of Marilyn's attention being distracted. "If you could get someone like Bruce Weber, and it wasn't *total* nudity, I mean, like, it was tasteful, I *might* be interested. . . ."

Marilyn rolled her eyes toward the sky and turned toward the pouting beauty.

Paula wandered on.

She approached an outlying group, recognizing a packager from Creative Artists Agency whose house she'd helped do. "Hi, Mr.

Stieglitz, how's that fabulous Jack Russell terrier of yours? Has he eaten the drapes yet?"

The man next to the agent spun around at the sound of her voice. His back had been toward her. The up-lighter at the base of a nearby royal palm lit his face from below.

"Paula!" exploded Robert Hartford.

Paula took one step back. She stopped breathing. Her heart sprinted.

Shadows flickered around Robert's cheekbones, the angle of the light bathing him in Boris Karloff shades. Even in the diffuse glow it was quite apparent that initial shock was already turning into white-hot fury. He clenched his fists by the side of his immaculate dinner jacket and his neck pulsated above the floppy black velvet of his double bow tie. His eyes, seemingly sunk in dark trenches, blazed their anger. His whole body leaned toward her like a tree on some blasted heath.

"Hello, Robert," said Paula's mangled voice.

"What the *hell* are you. . . . How *dare* you come here. . . ." He spluttered his rage.

Paula managed to swallow. How many emotions could you feel at once? She loved him. Still. That was number one, and there was no doubt about it. You had to love him. He was an infinitely wayward child who could be forgiven everything because of the divinity of his face and the wonder of his body. His fame, his reputation, his cool power, the laser of his concentration, his absolute desire to give pleasure, his inventive single-mindedness in receiving it; all were good reasons to love him, and for all of them, she hated him, too.

"I didn't know this was your party," she said. "I wouldn't have come if it was." Sarcasm dripped from her words.

The four other people in the conversational knot acquired glacial smiles, but to Paula and Robert they had ceased to exist.

"You . . . shouldn't be allowed to . . . *mix* with decent people. Do you hear me? Do you hear me?"

Everybody did. The babble of poolside conversation stilled as the realization filtered into a couple of hundred minds. There was going to be a spectacular row.

"And where," said Paula evenly, "are the 'decent' people?"

She looked into the twin blazes that were his eyes. They were as close now as they had ever been, locked in loathing as they had been locked in love. Both wanted desperately to hurt; both knew that they would be hurt in return.

"You little . . . hooker," shouted Robert.

"I've never thought of myself as that, but coming from the expert on hookers I suppose I ought to give it some consideration. Perhaps it was the quality that made you want to marry me."

"Just *what* do you mean by that?" Robert's voice was still loud, but now it was superconductor cold.

"I'm merely saying what everyone knows already, Robert, that if it's female and between sixteen and sixty you screw it, or try to."

A buzz of excitement zipped around the Coriarchi pool. Cabaret like this could not be bought with mere money. Poor Michael Feinstein, scheduled to perform later, had already been upstaged.

Robert shuddered beneath the blow like an oak ship receiving a broadside at sea. She stood so still and defiant before him, unafraid, brimful of courage. He must punish her.

"You," he hissed the words, "were the first and the very last time I have ever screwed a cripple."

The oohs and the aahs that rumbled around the pool were Richter-scale strength. It wasn't just the viciousness of the insult. It was much more than that. Most of the listeners had been in therapy. They spoke psychobabble as a second language. Already the theories were forming, all of them different, all of them arriving at the same destination. Hartford was overreacting because, for the very first time in his life, somebody had lit his flame, and that same somebody/ nobody had also blown it out. But a cripple, no less. Name calling had taken on a new dimension. Hell, was it *true?* Who cared? It was deeply, meaningfully wonderful.

The tears sprang to Paula's eyes, and she shook her head in disbelief. She clenched her fists and battled against the sadness as she tried to think of a reply.

"Only a crippled mind could possibly say anything so cruel," Paula said.

She turned around, and she walked away from him, the stunned, delighted onlookers parting silently like the Red Sea to let her by. She half ran to the drawing room in a silence so thick that her own steps rattled like castanets. The tears poured down her cheeks, and all the time she could think of only one thing. She was limping. From the back he could see that. They all could. Now they knew what he was talking about, and in Hollywood, where they dealt in physical perfection, they would know that Robert Hartford was right. At the end of the day she was not merely a nothing; not just another maid come to town to milk the dream; not just another loose screw in the sleek machinery of the L.A. scene machine— Oh no, when the day became the night, what Paula Hope *really* was, was a cripple.

EIGHTEEN

The breeze that was trying to be a wind sent the swallows curling in a night sky still ablaze with the memory of the marmalade sun. On Melrose the lights of the cars merged with the glow of the sodium vapor street lamps, the man-made brightness at war with the after-burn of the Beverly Hills sunset. The hum of the traffic filtered through the thick glass and merged with the other mating calls of the city at the left edge of heaven—the siren of a cop car, the shriek of brakes, the raucous music from the stereos of the designer macho machines, open Jeeps, Samurais, Mitsubishis, and all the other latter-day horses of the endlessly wild west.

In the queen's chair, the place where it had all started, Paula curled her legs up beneath her, and wondered where on earth it would end. She shouldn't be here. It was a crazy idea, but in crazy city where only the weird was real, it was okay to act on impulse—*if* you were out of the mainstream. Anyway, tonight she would be leaving L.A., and she wanted to leave from the place where she had arrived.

She sighed loudly in the dark of the Tower emporium, and all around the beauty wrapped her up. She still had her keys, and they had neglected to change the locks, so she had waited until she knew the showrooms would be deserted before slipping in, switching off the alarm, and then wandering alone in the place that had been so briefly the rich backdrop to her life. She had checked out of the Bel-Air at lunchtime and had spent the afternoon driving around Beverly Hills, her mind numbed by Robert's terrible words at the party the night before. As evening descended, she had had the idea of going back to

Tower Design to say good-bye—not to him, but to the magical things they had both loved. Then? God knew. A ride to the desert? To Arizona? To some place south?

The big tear grew in Paula's eye, and she blinked as she thought of all the leaving that went by the name of life. Dear Daddy; poor, sad Laura; Cool Hand Luke and little Jake; and now Winty and Robert, who had learned how to love her, but who had never learned to forgive. Was it like this for all the Los Angelenos behind the masks they wore on the freeways, on the Santa Monica sands, in all the humdrum places of the dreamland? Or did the drabness of their thoughts mirror the ordinariness of their outward appearance, and were the highs and lows hers alone, to be suffered and enjoyed in the roller-coaster ride between the warm womb and the grave's cold? There were no answers to questions like that. Instead there was just the ticking of the clock, the countdown to good-bye, and the brave hello to a storm-clouded future.

"I'll miss you all," she said out loud, and her words conjured up a bigger tear as her heart lurched in her chest. There was no good reason to miss them, godlike Robert with his angel's face and his hideous words; sharp-tongued Winty, who had revealed a bizarre talent for betrayal; and Graham, who had so casually destroyed her and paid for her destruction with his brain—but she *would* miss them, because she still loved them. Still loved *him*. Could she ever forget the man who had predicted with such accuracy that they would be lovers but failed to mention that he would break her heart?

The end and the new beginning were creeping nearer, and Paula crouched back against the upholstery to draw strength from the memories for the long journey into the night.

A new noise thrust into the muted sounds of evening L.A. A key was turning in the lock of the store. Paula sat up as a thrill of alarm rushed through her. Immediately she knew it wasn't a break-in. For some odd reason, it was Winthrop Tower. Crumpled and crouched, looking just like the Savile Row scarecrow she remembered so well, he shambled into the showroom.

She stood up, anxious, but at the same time strangely pleased that she would see him one last time. "Winty?" she said.

"Good God, who is it? Paula?" He peered through the gloom, advancing into the shop. "What on earth are you doing here?"

"Don't worry, Winty. I'm not stealing anything. I came here to say good-bye." There was weariness in her words.

"Good-bye, Paula," said Winthrop Tower.

"Just 'Good-bye.' No 'Good luck'? Is that all I deserve?"

"Damn it, Paula, don't you realize what you've done?" There was exasperation in Winthrop's voice.

"I know what you've all done to *me*. You've worked overtime to make sure that I can never do anything in this town. Maybe I can understand Robert, but you . . ." The aching sense of loss was alive in her voice.

"I simply took back what I gave you, Paula. The first time you sat in that chair you had nothing either."

His eyes seemed to mist over as he remembered. Like Robert, Paula had turned him into a giver, had taught his heart to love. Like Robert she had made him see that to trust was dangerous. It was why he, too, had reacted so violently to her betrayal.

"Do you know why Graham was in the bungalow that night?" She would try just once, only once, to explain.

"Spare me the tearjerker about the heart overriding the head. I don't want to hear how it was bigger than both of you. The soaps on TV are bad enough."

The bitterness was everywhere, but he hadn't choked her off. He was still standing in front of her. Still listening.

"He murdered someone he thought I wanted dead."

The Tower eyebrows shot upward. He hadn't expected anything so inventive. It was a good line. He could never resist those. "Oh?"

"He went to Florida, to Placid where I lived, and he killed a man called Seth Baker. He said he loved me, and he wanted to take me away with him, and that if I didn't go then he'd say I had planned the killing with him."

"And why did this poor Mr. Baker have to die at Graham's hand?" The sarcasm was ladled over the Tower words, yet in the wise old eyes there was the spark of interest.

Paula stood still, her leaden words still ringing in her ears. She knew it sounded impossibly unbelievable. Only a lunatic would imagine murder to be the way to a young girl's heart, and Graham had never seemed to be crazy.

Winty was the nearest thing she had to a friend on earth, and she could see from his whole demeanor that he thought she was lying. The surge tide of despair crashed headlong into the flood of memories. Why had Baker died, Winty had asked.

"Because he raped my friend, and he murdered my little brothers," she howled at him, and she sank down to her knees as the tears came and the great white-topped waves of grief rolled over her. All the fighting and the struggling, all the desire and the ambition, all the hurt

and the heartache flowed from her in a raging torrent of anguish. Her
head fell forward onto her chest and she held it in her hands in a
gesture of prayer as the tears oozed through her fingers and the sobs
burst from her lips. Her chest heaved as she battled for air to fuel her
sorrow, and the sounds of her misery filled up the room. All around
the tapestries watched her, the eyes of the famous, the ancient Romans
at whom she had once dared to stick out her tongue. Now they had
their revenge. Paula was finished. The emotion was draining from her
before their marbled gaze, the life blood of feeling seeping steadily
from her broken heart. In the darkness beneath the ocean of tears she
felt the rock bottom of her life, but, as she touched it, there was
something else.

Around her shoulders there were arms, in her ears there was a dear
old voice. "Darling, I believe you. Of course I believe you. It's going
to be all right," said Winthrop Tower.

Winthrop Tower watched Robert closely over the rim of the glass of
Glenlivet. Would he believe the story he had just heard? Paula's and
Robert's own future happiness depended on it. Winthrop had left
nothing out. He had told it, as Paula had told him—the rape of her
friend, the murder of her little brothers, Graham's free-lance revenge
on Seth Baker. He had spelled out the hitherto invisible details of
Paula's seeming betrayal, and now he could only wait to see how
Robert would react.

Robert shifted in the armchair, his face expressionless, only his
clenched fists giving away the strength of his feelings. He crossed one
leg over the other, saying nothing.

"So we're asked to believe that your servant Graham is some sort of
a freak psychopath?" he asked in a detached voice.

Winthrop's heart sank. He had half hoped for a joyous reaction—
the enthusiasm of the lover on learning that the loved had not been
unfaithful after all. But he had only *half* hoped. Robert Hartford had
been badly wounded. The injury would not heal overnight. "Well,
yes, it seems I got him wrong. It seems we all did." Winthrop
suppressed the frisson of guilt. How wrong had he really got Graham?
He had always known that there was a violent element to him. It was
what he had been attracted to in the first place, the out-to-lunch eyes
in the angel's face, the ropelike muscles and angular bones at odds with
the cheerful cockney-sparrow demeanor. It had been fun to have a
chauffeur like that, almost like having your own personal bodyguard
while avoiding the L.A. cliché of hiring the real thing.

"So I suppose now you'll be thinking about having him switched off that life-support system you're paying through the nose for." The cruel edge to Robert's voice was totally unexpected, the viciousness of his words doubly so.

Winthrop coughed nervously. The conversation was not going as he had planned. Robert preoccupied had given way to Robert in vengeance mode. "I hadn't really thought about that," he said.

"I think you should. Either way, he'd be better off dead."

There was color now high up on Robert's cheeks, near the yellowing bruises. He sipped determinedly on a tall glass of Corona.

" 'Either way' . . . ?" said Winthrop as a request for clarification. But Robert cut in. "Why do you believe her, Winty?" It was a schoolmaster's question of a lowly pupil.

Winthrop could feel himself warming up inside. Robert had been his friend for twenty years. They had always treated each other as equals. Now he was being patronized. He had been told what to do with Graham. He was being asked to justify his faith in Paula. It was becoming irritating.

"If you'd heard her tell her story you'd have believed her, Robert. You loved her. You wanted to marry her. You weren't wrong about her."

Robert cocked his head to one side and allowed himself a sad smile. "I wasn't wrong about her?" His tone was mildly incredulous, the kindly teacher surprised and a little hurt that a star pupil had let him down. "Winty, I'm not a man who trusts easily. Some might call that a weakness. I've always regarded it as a strength. Everything I've ever achieved, I've done on my own. You know better than most how difficult it is to make the dreams come true. With Paula I broke the golden rule. I loved her. I actually *loved* her." He shook his head from side to side as his whole face registered the disbelief at his own stupidity.

"I mean . . . there are the feelings . . ." He waved a dismissive hand to register the global unimportance of *those*. "And then there are the other inconveniences. Can you have any *idea*, Winty, what a thing like this does to an image like mine? The rumors are everywhere. The studio hears them. The public hear them. And they get magnified in the telling, don't they . . . not that the actual truth needs much magnification. The point is that a thing like this could have destroyed my *career*." He leaned forward and thrust the last word at Winthrop like an ace of trumps.

Winthrop wasn't buying. He knew Robert's apparent concern with his image was an attempt to disguise his hurt pride.

"But if it wasn't her *fault*, Robert, then you have to forgive her. I mean, she did it for you. What would you have done in her position? She was just trying to get rid of Graham so that she could call you in New York, and get you to protect her." Winthrop's voice was patient now, its tone humoring, sad that anyone could be so desperately naïve.

"It's all lies, Winty. She's made it up. Can't you see what's happening? She's trying to get back, and she's dreamed up this . . . *incredible* story, and she's actually made you believe it." Suddenly, he was tired of all the meaningless words that would never alter the bottom line. "Anyway, whatever you care to believe, I don't want her in this hotel. Understood? So get rid of her, Winty. Do I make myself clear?" His voice had sharpened. His eyes had narrowed. His jaw jutted.

So did Winthrop's. "You don't tell me what to do, Robert."

"I do in this hotel. I own it, remember? And I don't want Paula Hope anywhere near it. Another thing . . . if you choose to believe her nonsense and take her back into your company then I suggest that we rethink our plans to work together on the redecoration of the Sunset."

Winthrop felt the bile rise within him. Nobody talked to him like that. Not *anybody*. For Paula's sake, he tried to hold on to his temper. "It hurt you that badly, did it, Robert? You can't forget the sight of it, and the pain has screwed up your thinking."

"Cut the psychojargon, Winthrop!" he exploded. "Just get her out of my hotel. Do you hear? Just do it!" Robert drew himself up in the chair as if it were a throne, wrapping himself in an aura of kingly arrogance.

"Robert Hartford, you are a self-centered, emotionally ugly, narcissistic bastard, and I suggest that by far the best person for you to go screw is yourself."

The color sprang to Robert's cheeks.

"I suggest you get out of here, Tower, and out of the Sunset as well. You're history, okay? You understand me?" His voice was quiet.

Winthrop pumped himself up. "If I'm history, Robert, then you, my love, are *ancient* history. People are going to have to learn an entirely new language just to *study* you, dear. And without Livingstone and without me, your precious Sunset Hotel is going to become a monument. You won't have guests, you'll have sightseers. Behold the glory that was Rome until the mad emperor blew it all away. Good-bye, darling, and, oh, try to stay 'up' without us all. I mean your *mood*, sweetheart. After all, we mustn't ask for miracles." He jumped up and headed for the door as the cluster bomb of abuse rained down on Robert Hartford's astonished head.

On the path outside he walked fast. Already he knew exactly what he would do. He rushed along the walkways and he pushed past room-service trolleys and hurrying waiters, past pink-aproned maids, green-clad Mexican gardeners, and the odd scurrying guest late for a Star Room power lunch. He swam past the pool on a cloud of fearsome resolve, and he bustled through the lobby to the bank of elevators.

He was furious with Robert, but he was also furious with himself. If only he had listened to Paula in the first place. Instead, he and Robert had been so full of their inflated importance that they had never bothered to get to know the angel they both loved. Her past had remained a mystery to them, because *they* had not been a part of it, and therefore it was by definition uninteresting. They had played along with her reticence, not out of delicacy, but because, in typical Hollywood style, it suited them to pose and strut and joke and play at the center of the stage, oblivious to the feelings of lesser mortals—to their sorrow, their sadness, the horror of their memories. Last night as she had sobbed in his arms and poured out the dreadful details of her story there and then he had taken her back into his life, his home, and his heart.

He had driven her to the Sunset and put her to bed, with a gallon of tea and an ocean of sympathy, but he had hardly been able to stop the tears. He couldn't believe there could be so much moisture in a human being. Immediately he had wanted to go to Robert to tell him the extraordinary news, but he had been unwilling to leave her, and he had eventually asked one of the maids he knew well to sit with her while he went to arrange the reconciliation. Well, so much for *that* plan. Now Winthrop was a messenger bearing the worst news of all.

The elevator door opened and his irritable finger jabbed at the P. God *damn* it. In what mood of mischief had the Good Lord dreamed up sex?

He searched for his key in the high-class junkyard of his pocket, and he burst into the apartment. The maid Maria jumped up as he hurried into the bedroom. On the bed, Paula, pale and all cried out, sat up. Her eyes searched Winthrop's face for clues.

"You and I, darling, are leaving this dreadful hotel, and we are never, ever coming back," he said. He didn't stop. He made straight for the telephone and grabbed at it like an important letter in a high wind.

"Roger, Mr. Tower. Roger, I'm checking out. Yes, that's exactly what I'm doing, leaving, and if you have any sense at all you yourself will check out. King Lear has flipped. I want an army of valets up here to pack, cases, crates—the works."

He banged the telephone down, and he turned to face the incredulous Paula. "Now you, Paula, are going to have to be brave. And you are going to have to trust me. Both at the same time."

"What did he say?" asked Paula.

"This isn't the time to go into that. The important thing is we're leaving and we're leaving now."

"What did he *say*, Winty?"

"He didn't believe your story. He's drowning in ego. I think his nuts have fallen off."

Paula started to get out of bed. "I'm going to see him. I'm going to set this straight. He'll listen to me."

"Paula! For*get* it. Listen to *me*. He's going crazy in there. Trust me."

"He'll take it from me. He loved me. He still loves me."

Winthrop took a deep breath. He would have to be cruel to be kind. That was usually *enormous* fun. It wasn't going to be now. "He doesn't love you, Paula. He *hates* you. He can't deal with what he saw. He's like a vicious, wounded animal. He wants to destroy you. That's all he wants."

Her shoulders began to shake, the tears squeezing from her eyes all over again.

But Tower's voice was diamond hard as he spoke. "Listen, Paula. *Listen* to me! There's no time for this. Not now. Maybe not ever. A terrible thing has happened. The worst. Now you have two options. You can use it, or you can let it use you. You can be the victim or you can make someone else be a victim. It's your choice. You've only got one thing in this life. Yourself and your pride in yourself. Lose that, and you lose everything. Robert Hartford is a bastard, and a cheap bastard. Don't chase him. Let him go. Don't let him humiliate you. Humiliate him. I'll help you. I promise. Just pick yourself up off the floor, and toughen up, and get the *hell* on with your life."

Her sobs died down as the words sank in. He was right. She was too poor, too alone to wallow in the luxury of going to pieces. She had no army of friends who would enjoy her tragedy on condition that she in turn enjoyed theirs. There would be no audience for her nervous breakdown, and without one of those nothing in Hollywood meant anything at all.

Slowly she stood up, and she brushed away the dust of pain, and she fought the tears back. "What are we going to do?"

Winthrop, tutor in adversity, beamed at his star pupil. "We're going to have *fun*," he promised. He picked up the telephone, flipped through the battered black Asprey Filofax, and punched out a long distance number. "Mr. Tower calling for Mr. Adam Partridge."

He was through in seconds. "Mr. Partridge? Winthrop Tower. Very well indeed, thank you. Good. Good. Yes, I know, I have been a little slow in answering your letters. Well, I'll tell you."

He smiled reassuringly at Paula. "I wondered if the deal you offered was still open. Really? Good. Well, I accept it. Yes. Just like that. I propose that this telephone conversation constitute an agreement between gentlemen to proceed on the basis of your lawyer's letter—the one you sent toward the end of last year. Yes, Mr. Partridge, I share your opinion of lawyers, but once our minds meet then they can be told what to do. Precisely. Exactly. Now there is just one additional condition, which shouldn't be a problem—I want to move into the Château tomorrow morning—first thing. If you could have a penthouse or one of the bungalows prepared, and I'll need a personal office, and a construction office, and the architects will want somewhere to do their drawings or whatever it is they do . . . yes, yes. Good. Then we have a deal. Yes, you'll have a long, dull letter confirming it tomorrow, and doubtless you will send me an even more boring one in return. Good-bye, Mr. Partridge. Good-bye, Adam . . ."

He put down the telephone.

"There," he said. "Now we have a roof over our heads. And do you know what we are going to do? You and I, sweet Paula, are going to take over the Château Madrid."

The Château Madrid had seen the very best days of all, but it was so ancient it had forgotten them. It stood half a mile back from the Strip, nestled among the foothills, and it reached up to scratch the sky like an old, decaying tooth. Lost in its dreamy detachment, its mildly anxious disorientation, the Château creaked and crumbled and lost bits in the high winds as it waited in resignation for death by demolition. Time had not so much passed it by as blown through it, covering everything with the dust of ages, and loosening the cement of elegance that once held it together.

The Partridge family had owned the Madrid for as long as anyone could remember. As if it were an elderly relative in an old people's home, they visited from time to time and made the right noises, and they brought fruit and flowers in the form of the occasional coat of paint, the odd roof tile replaced, the odder sofa recovered. Then they hurried back to Pasadena where their real world was, to their gigantic family trusts, their prize azaleas, their charitable foundations, and of course to the serious business of murdering things that flew, and several other inoffensive animals that didn't. They had held on to the

Madrid because one didn't sell one's things. So there it remained, a broken toy in the attic of the Partridge dynasty, like that awful, common aeroplane that Uncle Freddie had bought, which now stood rusting in some hangar up north.

Adam Partridge sat on the board of the Met in New York. A Partridge usually did, and Adam had been selected for the job because he had once taken a fine arts course at Yale, and had bothered to amass the finest collection of Jasper Johns in America. This set him apart as the family member with modern "taste." One fine day he had had an *idea*, and there were some in the family who had not yet forgiven him this departure from Partridge tradition. The more aggressive family members, however—the ones who paid lip service to the existence of an outside world and as a result administered the family money—had been rather taken with Adam's plan. It had been suggested that the enormously respected Winthrop Tower, the rare designing bird that was taken as seriously on the East Coast as on the West, be asked to rebuild and redecorate the Madrid in return for a slice of its equity. The beauty of the scheme was that it did not require the Partridge family to spend a single cent of their indecently large fortune, and *that* was how the old money stayed old. The revamped hotel, presently worth nothing apart from the real estate on which it sat, could be turned into a money spinner under the clever guidance of the most fashionable designer in America. The Partridges had been impressed most of all by the fact that Tower was the black sheep of a family to which they were distantly related, and also by the very large sum of money it was rumored he had been left by his disappointed father. They had agreed that he should be approached.

But Tower had told them he did not "do" hotels. With the bemused incredulity of their class that anybody, anywhere would refuse them anything, the Partridges redoubled their efforts to persuade him. True aristocrats, they courted mercilessly those who wanted nothing to do with them, while reserving their scorn and disdain for those unfortunate outsiders who aspired to their ranks. As a result Winthrop had come under siege from the Pasadena law firm that existed primarily to administer the Partridge family affairs. Like spoiled rich children unable to have their own way, they had progressively sweetened their offer, secure in the knowledge that everyone but they had a "price," and that it was just a question of finding out what it was. Their most recent offer, which Tower had not even bothered to answer, was that he would do up the hotel at his own expense in return for a twenty-five percent share of the equity. He would also be given the option to buy out the Partridge seventy-five percent stake at any time during a five-year period at a price twenty percent higher than the prevailing value of the real estate. Thus, in a worst-case scenario, with Tower buying them out, they would receive twenty percent more than the present value of their investment, and, if real estate continued its upward spiral, perhaps very much more. However, if Tower succeeded in turning the Madrid around and didn't exercise his option to buy them out, then they would own three-quarters of a valuable, successful hotel instead of a hundred percent of a worthless one. Either way they would retain their real-estate play, and it would cost them nothing.

Now, quite suddenly, Tower had telephoned out of the blue and changed his mind, and he had just signed the ultimately binding agreement, a gentleman's agreement between genuine gentlemen.

The limo that swept Winthrop and Paula up to the baroque entrance to the Château seemed to sense the importance of its cargo. It swooped down like a hawk on the deserted forecourt of the hotel and crunched to a halt, seemingly appalled by the lack of ceremony that greeted its arrival. The "valet parker" did not speak English. It was a forlorn entrance, no flowers, no doorman, and the carpet that led into the somber reception hall was so dirty that the newer stains looked clean.

Winthrop erupted from the back seat, unfazed by the enormity of the task ahead. "Whatever we do to it, Paula," he pronounced, "whatever we do, we must not banish entirely the marvelous *depression* of this entry." He charged inside, and Paula, brightening, followed in his wake.

"I see granite. Granite everywhere. Marble is over. Marble is dead," he warbled. "Black granite, gray granite, cream granite. My word," he sighed, "I feel a granite jag coming on."

At the reception desk they were almost ready for him.

"Welcome to the Château Madrid," said the old man behind the desk, his uniform shiny as black ice. "We have bungalow 4 reserved for you, Mr. Tower. That's the Jean Harlow bungalow, out by the pool."

"I hope they've changed the sheets since her day," muttered Tower. "I was always worried about the state of her underwear."

"Winty!" said Paula, beginning to lose herself in the excitement. She looked around with the eye of the professional stranger. First impressions were vital.

The proportions were perfect: high ceilings, a good strong rectangular shape, well-placed windows. Winty was right. It could take granite.

"Minimalist," said Winthrop. "Let the architecture do the talking. It needs some very good paintings, light but traditional. Boucher. Fragonard. Poussin. Isn't it *romantic?*"

Paula didn't let the word upset her. This could be made absolutely wonderful. "God, look at that ceiling. That mural's out of this world. Restore it, light it. Maybe even repeat it. Say in the restaurant. We could fly Willie Feilding over from London. He'd do it perfectly. Just his style."

Paula clapped her hands in glee. "Oh, Winty, I can't believe this. I see ancient and modern in perfect harmony. Yes, your granite, but perhaps Ron Rezek lamps, over monolithic boxlike sofas in strong, dark colors in something no-nonsense durable like sail cloth. Spotlit oils on the walls, I agree, but tapestries, too. Marvelous Morris floss-silk-on-damask tapestries over pale pink magnolia walls—a five-to-one white to pink, very subtle, very quiet. Those cornices need rebuilding, and the reception desk has to go, and that awful newsstand, and the porter's desk, and something must be made of those stairs. . . ."

He smiled gently at her, and again the wave of guilt broke over him. How could he have doubted her? He, Winthrop Tower, had played the alien roles of sheep, hypocrite, and Victorian moralist as if to the manner born, and yet Paula's undiluted talent alone should have been enough to convince him that she would never stoop to the kind of callous infidelity of which he had accused her. A part of him had always wanted to believe her, but that was a coward's excuse. He had allowed himself to be overruled by the force of Robert Hartford's personality, by the conventional response, by the insider's traditional mistrust for the outsider. Paula had been L.A.-ed, and he had done the L.A.-ing. So much for the Yale motto, *Lux et Veritas*. Light and Truth.

Well, now he had amends to make. He would see Paula through this one last tragedy, the one called Robert Hartford, and he would help her rebuild her broken life brick by brick. Already, thank God, the thrill of the work was beginning to damp down her misery, as he had hoped that it would.

"I told you we were going to have fun," he said. "And you ain't seen nuthin' yet."

N I N E T E E N

Robert Hartford looked down at the open copy of *Interior Design* magazine on his desk and once again anger rushed into the back of his throat. The timing was so perfect it had to have been done on purpose. On the very day that he was launching the revamped Sunset Hotel to the press of America, he had been scooped. The Château Madrid had gotten there first. The endless, gushing article in the intellectual *Interior Design*, the most sophisticated of the shelter magazines, declared the new Madrid a triumph. Tower and his brilliant young protégé Paula Hope had performed a miracle. It was a glittering example of understated good taste, a masterpiece of interior decoration that had the writer scurrying around his thesaurus to discover appropriate superlatives. Everywhere the obvious had been avoided for the innovative, and safety had been left behind in a celebration of artistic vision, bold and sure, dramatic yet practical, a perfect melding of the old and the new. The last paragraph had been the worst of all. Winthrop Tower had given the credit to Paula. "I merely held her hand," he said. "If I'd let it go, the Madrid would look even better than it does today." Then the writer had written the paragraph that had had Robert spinning sleepless in his bed for the last week.

It is rare to see such beauty in a redesigned building. For years the Madrid was an architectural gem waiting to be discovered. Now, the touch of the true artist has wakened it from its Rip Van Winkle sleep. And this was a gentle kiss, accurate, sensitive, effortlessly sure of its purpose. The extraordinary design triumph of the Château has at a stroke catapulted Paula Hope into the first rank of young designers. It is the beginning of what can only be a stupendously successful career. One last thought. We were lucky to have something with which to compare the new Madrid. This month Robert Hartford's famed Sunset Hotel has completed *its* refurbishment. What a disaster it has been. The design firm of Tanker, Voos and Foster, usually reliable if seldom exciting, have produced a monument to mediocrity. They have never fallen beneath a standard of universal dullness in their work on the Sunset. Nor have they ever risen above it. The student of late-twentieth-century design would do well to ponder these two rival hotels. In traveling from the one to the other he will come to understand the true meaning of the phrase "from the sublime to the ridiculous."

Robert wondered how the hell he was going to get through the press conference. Some bright spark would have read the *Interior Design* piece, and he would be closely questioned about it. What could he say? It was true. The Madrid looked like God's house in heaven. The Sunset's "new" look was about as visually interesting as a shopping mall in Wisconsin. Would they have found out that Tower and Paula had been his first-choice designers and that he had thrown them off the job?

He stared down at the article but he wasn't seeing it. He was thinking as he always thought—about Paula, and the night she had betrayed him. His hand moved up to his face and he stroked the small scar he had never bothered to get the surgeons to remove. It lingered on, an aide to memory, and a backbone to resolve. He could still feel Graham's fist exploding against his cheek, but it was the vision in his eyes that hurt him. That hand. That dreadful, lewd hand roaming free where only his was allowed to be. What had she been feeling as those fingers had invaded her? Had she been hot for the Englishman's street body, and his gutter mind? Had she been thinking of him, Robert, safe in New York, as she readied herself to receive his rival? Had she been laughing inside at the treachery as she rushed to do it, standing up, like some cheap Strip hustler in a back alley. For a year and three months he had whipped himself with the questions that could never be adequately answered. Graham was sealed off from the world. Paula was gone. And why, anyway, should she ever tell him the truth? He shook his head to make the memories go away, but they didn't obey him. That skirt, so squalid on the floor, and her panties, pulled away from her, yet not removed. God, the horror of it. The betrayal. It was a cliché that love could turn to hate, but he hated her. So much. So strong. So deep. So wide. And now, beyond his reach, in the Winthrop Tower firmament, she continued to taunt him with her talent.

Kristina didn't bother to knock. She came in fast, and the look on her face said "more bad news." "André's leaving." She blurted it out fast. "He's just been to see me. Mason's has poached him, and he's taking Paul and Michelle with him."

Robert groaned out loud. His chef. His under-chef. His pastry chef. It was a disaster, but it was not the first disaster. "You offered them more?"

"Yes, of course. I told him to name it. He wouldn't. Same old thing. He says the atmosphere here is a nightmare. He says everybody's worried about the falling occupancy. Nobody believes the management's on top of it, and he's still bitter about you calling him a jumped-up frog."

"How long did they give?"

"A month."

"Christ. We can't get anyone good in that time."

"I've already put out ads in Paris and Brussels. I guess I ought to try New York, too."

"Well, pay them anything. We've got to keep the Century at the top. That and the Star Room are the only things holding the place together."

"It's not the money, Dad. You know that. It's the tension. Everyone's unhappy. Everyone's nervous."

Robert slammed his fist down on the color photographs of the new Château. "Goddamn it, they've got no *right* to be nervous. I'm not selling the place. I'll die here."

"It's your temper, Dad. That's what makes them nervous. You fired Von Hofstader and they liked him and trusted him. He was the link with Livingstone."

"The kraut was on the take. He was raiding the wine cellar."

"Who cares, Dad? In offices you take the paperclips and the Bics. It's called perks. The new guy's got the personality of a sheep on Valium. Morale is falling out of bed. The staff are snapping at the guests and the guests are complaining to the staff. It's a vicious circle. Now that the occupancy's down to fifty percent it's ten below break even, and it's trending lower."

"Maybe I should get them all together and talk to them again."

"No way. The malcontents leak it to the press, and they start up all those 'trouble at the Sunset' rumors. Then the staff gets even more anxious. Personally, I don't think it helped last time when you told everybody that you were Big Brother and you were watching them. I thought that was a little confrontational."

"Oh, so now you're the world's hot-shot hotelier, are you?"

"No, of course I'm not, but they'd rather deal with me than you. André came to me, didn't he?"

"He came to you because you're marshmallow soft, Kristina. That French creep wouldn't have had the balls to come in here and tell me he was walking out with my entire kitchen leadership. I'd have threatened to sue him for breach of contract. He'd have to have flambéed a few frog's legs to finance that little action."

"He didn't *have* a contract, Dad. He and Livingstone had been friends for years. He used to cook the old guy dinner in his bungalow once a month, and then they'd sit down and eat it. They tried out new recipes for the menu. He actually wept when he told me about it."

"You're right, Kristina. I'm sorry. I'm just not very good at this."

"The Madrid hasn't helped," she said, her eyes wandering down to the open magazine on her father's desk.

"You'd better believe it hasn't helped," he growled. "They're filling their beds with Sunset guests. Your friend Hope has really stuck it to us."

The thunder cloud floated across his brow.

Kristina watched him quizzically. It had all started to unravel from that long-ago night in her father's bungalow. She had believed his story of course, of Paula's infidelity and Graham's accidental injury and of Winthrop Tower's extraordinary decision to side with the cheating lovers. She had cut Paula out of her life, not that her former friend had ever tried to contact her, but in her heart she had found it difficult to believe the story of her treachery. Her father had been devastated by the ending of the only real relationship he had ever experienced, and now the Sunset was slowly sinking below the horizon, while the faded Château was fast rising in the Hollywood Hills.

Kristina wondered if her father was ready for the next bit of bad news. "I heard that the Madrid hired Alfredo."

"What?"

"He gave notice. Said he wanted to go to Santa Barbara. Now I hear he's running the bar at the Château."

"They poached him?"

"It's difficult to say. Anyway, he's there now. And he's taken a lot of the regulars. Business in the Star Room is way down, and a lot of the screenwriters have apparently gone with Alfredo. He actually used to *listen* to their sob stories about what the studios had done to their scripts. The gossip says he used to get them women to make them feel better. The new guy wouldn't know a woman if she sat on his face. You'd think twice about telling him the time of day, let alone pouring out your sorrows."

"Well, fire him for God's sake, Kristina."

"Listen, at least he knows a mimosa from a screwdriver, even if he is psychotoxic. The next guy'd probably be a dealer, or worse."

Robert let out a weary sigh. That was it in a nutshell. Kristina was the realist. He dealt in the raw emotion. She was right, of course. For now it was probably better to have the devil they knew behind the bar. At least people could still get a drink, even if sympathy was off the menu.

"Sometimes I wonder if I've got the right temperament for this. Of course, you're right, darling. Do whatever you think is best. The bar is the least of my problems." He massaged invisible furrows on his smooth brow.

"You look tired."

"Yeah, I guess I am. I go on location tomorrow, and the script's a mess."

"How long will you be away?"

"Oh God, I don't know. They've been shooting around me. I guess it could be a wrap in six weeks, if there are no ego problems." He watched Kristina closely. She looked relieved. No doubt about it. "So you'll be able to get on with running the place with no interference," he added to show that he knew.

"I'll keep you in touch with developments. For God's sake, give Suki Marlowe a night or two off. She's pale enough as it is, and you look as if you've given your last pint of blood. Remember it's supposed to be a horse opera, not a ghost movie."

He laughed at her irreverence, and Suki Marlowe's face, pixie sweet, wafted across his mind's eye. Yes, she would be a distraction of sorts. They usually were. It would be a relief to get back to the game he was really good at. Thank God the police and his litigious reputation had managed to keep the lid on the Graham thing. Horizon, the studio that had picked up the Galaxy contract, had been skittish as wild mustangs while the rumors had multiplied but they'd hung in there, and now the contracted movies were beginning to get made. Somehow the Sunset would struggle through. It could probably live for years on the fat of its former glory, until Kristina and her dull manager, the one who made the dial tone sound like Lloyd Webber in full flood, learned the ropes. And one fine day, somewhere out there in the misty future, he'd probably be able to forget Paula Hope.

He stood up. "Listen, darling. I've got to pack. What the hell do they all wear in Arizona?"

The three or four people in the packed bar who had actually been born in Southern California could remember the Château from their childhood. It had been the place where Auntie stayed on her annual visit from Boston, and it had smelled a bit like her—fusty, musty, and dusty. It had been spooky to have tea in the vast reception hall, and later that night the Madrid would provide an appropriate backdrop for ghostly fantasies and nervous dreams at bedtime. Now, however, it had been born again, and the zealous light in the trendy eyes of 150 guests said so. If you were out with the in crowd, at this very second you were drinking in the Kennedy Room at the Château Madrid.

Like a modern-day Régine, Paula sat at the corner table and sipped on a spritzer as they lined up to pay homage. Residents of the City of Angels prided themselves on their ability to recognize new talent, and the word was out. Paula was the Tower heir apparent. She would have to do their houses—despite the fact that they had just been "done."

They had reacted to her rehabilitation in exactly the same way they had to her downfall—with lemminglike enthusiasm, with Gadarene gusto, and now that the once waned star was bright in the heavens, they fell over each other to follow it. Wisemen, Bethlehem.

Paula looked around, and the success smiled back. It was funny how you could tell. There were crowded bars from the redwood forests to the New York island but this was different. These people had dedicated their lives and their vast talents to "knowing" and their presence there, at six o'clock on an ordinary day, with nothing special going on, was like a message from God. Certainly the press coverage had helped, but it was much more than that. All over the city the telephones were ringing off their hooks as it was casually dropped that the meeting should be at the Madrid, rather than the Sunset—"So dull, dear, now that Livingstone's gone—and while we're there why not let's try the restaurant. Carl's organized a table, and I hear they're quite busy." So Carl had managed a table at the Madrid, had he? The movie must be doing well, better than the returns hinted. Was there an Oscar in the air? Paula was learning every minute, and she found that she was as good at running a hotel as she was at designing one. In the end it required the same skills—a commitment to excellence, an unfailingly accurate sense of good taste, a certain showman's panache. If you had those three, then everything else fitted into place. The staff, seeing themselves part of something superb, became pussycats overnight. They didn't need top dollar, because they were getting top job satisfaction, and they pulled together as part of a winning team, forgetting petty jealousies and nit-picking demarcation disputes as they concentrated instead on the greater good, the success of the Château Madrid. The best people at the other hotels were flooding her offices with their résumés, like Alfredo, the head bartender at the Sunset. Right now he stood there like a king behind the polished mahogany dispensing cocktails, sublime mixtures of spirits and equal parts wisdom, laced with an acid wit, and topped with a heartwarming smile. That was brilliance. That was art. How the hell could Robert have let him go?

A frown flew across Paula's face as she thought of him. He had seldom been out of her mind, but she had walled him off in his own private cell and now he was a prisoner there, unable to escape. Each day, each minute, she added another brick to the wall that surrounded him, as she fortified herself against him and the harm he could do. From that dreadful night at the Coriarchi party to this moment she had not set eyes on him, and it was difficult to know anymore what she felt about him because she had taught herself not to confront that. But he was there, in chains in the prison of her mind, and occasionally the clanking sound would remind her of the disturbing presence.

In the frenzied excitement of the Château she had been reborn. It seemed the Madrid was on the other end of the scales from the Sunset. While the Château had risen the Sunset, fat and heavy and out of condition, had fallen. It wasn't done on purpose. She hadn't tried to poach Alfredo, for instance. He had just been drawn to the magnet of the Madrid's success. The design had been one factor. The papers had been full of the innovative brilliance of the Madrid's décor, and gleefully they had contrasted it with the pedestrian design of Robert's hotel. In his crumbling tower, Robert would not be thanking her for her victory. He would be cursing her for it. Part of her cared about that. The other part didn't give a damn.

Winthrop Tower was the diversion from the unsettling thoughts. He pushed through the crowd and headed straight for Paula's table. His eyes were wide and his hair was tousled and it was clear from forty feet that he was both sober and in an enormously good mood. From ten feet away, he boomed his greeting. "I've exercised," he shouted. "For the first time in my life I've exercised and I feel bloody *marvelous*."

Paula leaped up in mock alarm, and she pulled out a chair for him as someone at the bar actually began to clap and twenty or thirty people nearby joined in.

"Sit down before you fall down, Winty. What on earth have you been doing? You don't look as if you're dressed for aerobics. Are you sure you're wise at your age? Aren't you supposed to start gently?"

Winthrop collapsed into the chair. "I have exercised," he said. "I have exercised my option."

"Your *option?*"

"Yes, darling. I've just bought the rest of the sodding hotel." He beamed at her proudly.

"You *haven't*, Winty."

"I have. I've just this second completed the contract. The Partridges are sulking in a pear tree. They didn't believe I was the silk-purse-from-sow's-ear guru. It's mine. The whole thing. I can blow it up if I like." His face brightened at the thought.

"God, that's the deal of the century."

"Yes, I suppose it is," said Winthrop. The idea of doing something as unoriginal as making money seemed momentarily to depress him. "Well, never mind that. Let's celebrate. At least I'll never have to see Adam Partridge again. He's a very decent fellow, and I couldn't begin to kick him as far as I trust him, but he keeps talking about the responsibilities of his position, and family tradition and all that bullshit. I'd have thought that the only responsibility the Partridges had was to spread it about like muck so that the rest of us can wallow in it."

"What does it feel like to be a hotelier?"

"A bloody site better than it feels to poor old Robert." He watched her as he said that, but her enigmatic smile told him nothing. "Goodness, this joint is jumping, isn't it? These people actually look as if they're enjoying themselves. God knows how they do that on the Perrier they all drink."

"What made it happen? Why the Madrid? Why not the Sunset?" Paula was genuinely bemused by it all.

"It's all to do with old age, sweetheart. West Coast folk pretend to love anything that's old, but they don't really. While they like the *idea* of old things they can't stand the disadvantages that come with old age—the plumbing and water-works problems, the dilapidations of the exterior, the deteriorating electrical circuits—I'm talking about the *people* of course. . . ."

He giggled, full of wicked malice, as he plowed on. "So you take somewhere like the Château that has the cachet of being old and you make it modern and fix it up and presto, you have a success. And it helps that one has a certain reputation on the *East* Coast. Westerners love nothing more than to impress Easterners with their taste, in the same way that Easterners love to flaunt their virility in front of Westerners. It isn't often that each gets a chance to do either."

"Winty, you don't have a drink. How can we celebrate without one of those?" Paula caught a passing waiter. "Stoli on the rocks, and hold the rocks," she said.

"Good girl," agreed Winthrop. He pushed himself back in the chair, and he smiled around the room. It was going to be a wonderful evening. Dinner with Paula in *his* restaurant. The shortest possible distance to bed afterward. And everyone within earshot desperate to be there, every servant in his personal employ. He felt the thrill course through him, a little adrenaline surge of pure pleasure.

"What on earth shall I do for an encore?" he said.

There were lots of possibilities on his list. Having a heart attack was not at the top of it.

It was a strange feeling. Like heartburn at first, high up in the chest. Then it changed. It was lower, in the middle, and it hurt. The pain struck him a crushing central blow in the chest that stayed and didn't go away. It was as if someone had lowered a weight onto him, and that someone else had decided to sit on it. A band tightened around him, tighter, and tighter, and he opened his mouth to breathe because his nose wasn't doing the job properly anymore. With the pain came the feeling of panic, and his brain started to jabber to him—"heart attack, heart attack, you're having a heart attack."

The panic made the pain worse and the increased pain deepened the panic, and both made breathing more difficult as the room swam around and he stiffened in his chair, both his fists clasped to the center of his chest where the agony was.

Paula was standing, and her face was in shock and he could hear her saying, "Winty, Winty. What is it? What's the matter?" And he couldn't tell her, but he knew that she knew. She knew everything. His Paula. She would look after him.

They were crowding around him now, and one mustached face was pushed up against his as a hand clasped his wrist, and another tore at his necktie. Winthrop recognized him. He knew this man. From the deep somewhere he managed a throaty stage whisper. "This man's not a doctor. He's a plastic surgeon."

The Beverly Hills face restorer was not put off by the vote of no confidence from the victim. "Call for an ambulance," he barked. He fished in his pocket for some keys. "There's a matte-black Ferrari Testarossa outside. On the back seat there's a Louis Vuitton briefcase. Somebody run and get it. Fast. I need some IV heroin."

"Drug addict!" Somehow Winthrop managed the joke through the waves of pain that engulfed him.

Paula stood quite still. She was praying as she had never prayed before. In front of her, cradled in a semisitting position in the doctor's arms, Winthrop Tower was white as winter snow. Sweat stood out on his face, which was twisted terribly. His eyes were screwed shut and his clenched fists were little balls at his chest as the doctor wrestled to take off his coat, to free the arm vein for the needle.

Suddenly the Vuitton case was there, and the diamorphine was bubbling into the syringe. The doctor didn't bother to clean the surface of the arm. He just jammed the needle in, pulling back first on the plunger to send the smoky wisp of blood into the clear liquid. Thank God the veins hadn't collapsed, and thank God he'd brought the vials of Omnopon back from England where they realized that it was the only stuff for situations like this. In America, heroin was still unavailable to doctors.

At the end of the needle there was a dramatic change in Winthrop Tower, as the most powerful painkiller in the world cut into the vicious circle of pain-anxiety-anxiety-pain. Winthrop felt the steel band that encircled him loosen a notch, and he managed to fill his lungs with air. He was soaked with sweat, his skin was clammy and cold, and the fingers of nausea pushed and pulled in his stomach. But the pain was going and the relief was a new life. He was going to be all right. The tummy tucker had saved him. He managed the faintest of smiles as he tried to speak. "Don't worry, Paula. It was the exercise . . . the exercise."

"Oh, Winty, oh, Winty . . ." She knelt by his side. "Don't speak. Don't say anything. I'm here. You're going to be all right."

The paramedics pushed through the crowd, and the doctor stood up to greet them. "He's had a coronary. I've given him five milligrams of intravenous diamorphine and he's got a regular tachycardia of one ten. I haven't got a cuff but he's got perfusion pressure. He'll need an open line for access—I guess some dextrose. I'll come with you. Where does he go? ICU at Cedars? I'm on the staff there."

They carried Winthrop through the lobby he had so brilliantly designed, the drip attached to his arm, the defibrillator pack and the oxygen cylinders following him.

"Don't leave me, Paula." He held her hand tightly as she walked beside the stretcher, and she blinked back the tears.

"I'm not going to leave you. I'm coming with you in the ambulance."

They squeezed inside it, Paula, the doctor, the seen-it-all-before paramedics, and Winthrop cocooned in the red blanket, his dear face poking out at the top, determined to find something to laugh about in the middle of the tragedy.

"I wouldn't be seen dead in red," he muttered, "but won't it be *lovely* to start collecting on all that Blue Cross."

"Try not to speak too much, Mr. Tower," said the doctor.

The wail of the ambulance siren underlined the seriousness of it all, as they sped down the winding roads toward Sunset Boulevard.

"Paula. Paula!" Winthrop's voice was suddenly urgent as he called out to her and she leaned in close to comfort him.

"It's all right, Winthrop. Just relax. You're going to be all right."

The paramedic and the doctor exchanged glances, but said nothing.

"Listen, Paula. I'm sure this is a false alarm, but if it isn't there are some things you should know. First, you're my heir. I've left you everything, and it's quite a lot."

She shook her head, not wanting to hear him talk like that, and a tear broke out and started a drunken journey down her cheek.

"I never could think of anything to spend it on, and it just accumulated in all sorts of dull things like apartment blocks, and dreadful things called bonds. Someone told me it was about fifty million a little while ago, and of course now there's the Château and Tower Design. They'll be yours when I go, and I couldn't care less what you do with them as long as you have *fun* with them and always remember not to take them too seriously. It's all a joke, you know, Paula. The one thing God has is a sense of humor. Not a very *kind* sense of humor, but a sense of it nonetheless."

"Oh, please don't say things like that, Winty. Please don't. You're making me cry. You're not going anywhere."

"Nonsense, darling. We all are. We're just haggling over the time and place. And the second thing is much more important. You're the kindest, loveliest, most talented person I have ever met in my entire life and you're also far and away the most beautiful. There. How about that. And I didn't need any vino for the veritas."

She bent down and kissed him gently on the cheek, as the tears poured silently down hers. They looked at each other, and the knowledge came to each at the same time. The time for jokes was nearly over. It was almost the time for sorrow, the time, so soon, for mourning.

His voice was clear as a bell when he spoke. "I hope to heaven," he said, "that there's a bloody good barman in hell."

And then, quite suddenly, he was gone.

He didn't move. No sigh escaped him. No pain tormented him. Inside him, something that had been hanging by a thread gave way. So close to him, she felt his spirit slip away, its wings fluttering in relief at the endless freedom. And she rested her head down, on his dear cheek, and she whispered low, "Good-bye, my darling."

Graham didn't look beautiful anymore. He looked like a badly broken doll, and he lay motionless against the crisp white sheets. His eyes were closed, and someone had combed his hair, its fashionless tidiness mocking the memory of the man who had hummed with life. All the wires came out of him at one point, and it was easy to imagine the spaghetti junction of terminals feeding them beneath the plain hospital blankets that wrapped him in the cocoon of the living dead. Beside the bed was a bank of machinery, the center point of which were the two screens tracing the patterns of both brain and heart. The bedside table was bare. No fruit, no magazines, no photographs of the friends and loved ones that Graham had never had.

"Hello, Graham," said Paula.

How did you speak to someone who couldn't hear, who couldn't feel, who didn't care? It wasn't the first time she had visited him, and so the problem was not new, but it didn't go away. She tried to visualize Graham in the old days, before the night of madness when he had so wantonly destroyed her world. She remembered that first night, when he had carried poor Winty across the parking lot at Morton's. "Never separate 'im from 'is drink," he'd said and he'd winked at her, beginning the conspiracy she had treasured, before it had turned to tragedy.

"I came to tell you that Winty died last night," she said. "It was very quick, and he was joking all the time. A heart attack, we think."

She swallowed as the lump in her throat pushed up against her pointless words. Who was she telling? What was she talking to? But of course she knew. She was talking to the only living friend she had in the entire world. There was no one else with whom she could share her sorrow. Just this broken collection of flesh and blood whose heart ticked meaninglessly in his chest.

"He was so lovely, Graham, wasn't he? You knew that. We both did. And he loved us. We were the only ones he loved, and he was so beastly to everyone else." She laughed in the middle of the tears, summoning up the vision of Winty and his whiplash tongue, the Winty who had left her his fortune, his talent, and the warmth of his memory.

She moved closer to the bed and she held the cool hand, its flesh flaccid against hers. "I'm all alone again now, Graham. It's just me, but I have all Winty's work to do, and I have the Château." She squeezed his hand to tell him that she was brave, and she chewed on her lower lip as she plowed on.

"I want you to see our Château Madrid someday, Graham. It's a marvelous hotel, and it's doing much better than the Sunset. Everybody says so. It must be driving poor Robert mad."

If on some astral plane he could understand, the news that Robert was having a bad time would please him. "He's always hated me since that night, you know, when the devil got into you. He never believed me when I told him what happened. And we loved each other *so* much, *so* much, and yet he didn't believe me. Can you understand that? *I've* never been able to." With her free hand she plucked distractedly at the blanket, as her sigh of despair filled the room.

"But I shouldn't moan on about myself. Look at you. Poor, poor Graham. All you did was love me. I wish I could have loved you back."

The big tear hurried out onto the lower lid of her eye. Then, like a suicide on the ledge of a skyscraper, it jumped, cascading down her cheek. "We were both outsiders, weren't we, and Winty took us in, and now he's gone. . . . So it's just us against everyone, and we'll *win*, Graham, won't we. We'll win."

A cough came from behind her shoulder, the announcement of someone's presence rather than the clearing of a throat.

The doctor was standing close behind her. "Miss Hope? I'm so sorry to hear the news about Mr. Tower."

She smiled wanly and wiped hard at her face, well aware that he would have seen her tears. "I can't really believe it yet," she said simply.

"There's a period of shock, when you feel like that," he replied, his voice kind.

"How's Mr. Ovenden?" She tried to change the subject.

"Oh, there's no change. There won't be, I'm afraid. He's completely stable, but deep in his coma. He could go on like this for years."

He looked down and studied his feet. There was a question hidden among his words. Tower had paid the bills. Tower was dead. What would happen now? Was Miss Hope the right person to ask?

She heard his thoughts. "I'm Mr. Tower's sole heir," she said. "I want everything to go on as before."

"It's my duty to tell you that the prognosis is very poor. His brain has some activity, but I'm all but certain he'll never regain consciousness. It'll cost a fortune to . . ."

"That doesn't matter," said Paula quickly. She waved a suddenly impatient hand. "There's a ton of money, a *ton* of it."

"Well, that's a very caring attitude. He's a . . . a very lucky . . ." The doctor trailed off as he looked down at the luckless Graham, then back at Paula. Somehow his sentence had gone wrong.

"He's the only one I have left," she said.

She had turned fully to face the doctor, determined to let him know how much his damaged patient meant to her. Keep him alive, said her earnest expression. Don't cut off the last lifeline to my past.

She didn't see the movement behind her, because her body was between the doctor and the bed. So neither of them saw Graham's hand—saw it clasp once, twice; saw it hover above the blanket like a wounded bird trying for flight; saw it fall back exhausted into the stillness of his coma.

"Listen, forget the small-print script bullshit, is the high concept 'fish-out-of-water' or not?"

In the ice-cold interior of his personal converted Winnebago, rented to the production company as a "perk," Robert Hartford's voice smashed into the moviebabble like a fist into flesh.

For a second or two there was silence.

"I think Robert's right," said Suki Marlowe, uncoiling the best legs in the business as she licked her lips and thought of the night before, of the night to come. The fact that Robert had asked a question rather than made a statement meant nothing. He was the bankable name. His was the bunkable bed. That made him right, even when he was wrong.

"Well, it *is* fish-out-of-water, Robert, but we can't make the guy a *complete* hick. I mean, by the end of the movie he's got to be swimming on land like he's never even *heard* of the fucking sea."

Robert Hartford's fingers stopped their drumming on the mahogany table beside his chair. "I wish you wouldn't use words like that in front of Suki," he said.

The brand-name scriptwriter looked sorry, at the rebuke from the star, at the mess they were making of his script, at the fact that he hadn't won the state lottery and therefore couldn't afford to tell this roomful of idiots what to do with their artistic presumption.

The director, in the referee role, pitched in on what would be the winning side. "I'm inclined to agree with Robert and Suki," he said slowly, as if he had bothered to think about it for more than a nanosecond. "Can you write it that way?"

The "If you can't, we can find someone who will" hung in the cold air, the eternal Damoclean sword hovering over the heads of all movie writers.

"Yes, of course I can write it that way. I can turn it around to a musical S.F. 'buddy' movie set in ancient Rome if you want, but I just wonder if they'd want to come and see it."

"One or two of us in this room have a little experience of what they want to come and see," Robert drawled.

Somehow he managed to wrap the word *what* in a question mark. It filtered through to everyone in the room that only modesty had prevented him using the word *who*. And it was true. *He* was the guarantee the movie would open, and open big. Compared to the power of his name the script was blowing in the wind.

"The only thing I know to be true about the future is that it is essentially unpredictable, especially where movies are concerned," said the writer. He was angry, and enough of an idealist, and more important with enough of a track record, to stand up to a star of Hartford's magnitude.

The temperature in the trailer notched down a point or two. It made everyone uncomfortable when someone offered up "the great truth."

Robert Hartford's voice was very quiet. "If you're right, then presumably you know nothing either."

There was a long silence.

"So in the absence of divine guidance and laying aside contractual rights, perhaps in this little democracy we could let the majority decide." The sarcasm dripped from his lips. He flicked a look at Suki. Another at the director.

"Robert's right," pouted his costar on cue. Actually she thought the writer was quite cute, but in the industry you balled busters if you wanted to get on, writers if you wanted to get off.

"So that's settled then, David. You let us have some 'make like a nerd' pages, and later we graft the underdog-becomes-overdog theme onto the original high concept. That was what you envisaged, wasn't it, Robert?" said the director.

Robert had won. He peered out of the window at the battleship-gray mountains through the sparkling champagne-clear air. It was about 110 out there in the high desert, but inside the trailer he was wearing his baby-blue cashmere Scotch House cardigan. He looked over toward Suki Marlowe, impossibly pretty in an all-black leotard, pink leggings, and beautiful bare brown feet. Then he turned back to the little group of courtiers who were waiting for his assent.

Script approval. That was what it was all about. And all the other approvals, too. Who was hired, fired, booed, sued; who was praised, hazed, raised, fazed.

Why couldn't it be like that at the Sunset? Why didn't the staff behave like these yes-men? They had for Livingstone. They'd fed from the hand of the decrepit old bird, the minions bowing and scraping before him, and in his entire life Robert had never heard him raise his voice. Here he could make or break careers; in the Sunset he couldn't even get the bartender to make a decent martini. At the last meal he'd eaten in the Century Room, the whole place had the feel of a terminal illness, the flowers not actually wilted but certainly no longer fresh; the tablecloths white, but not pristine; the cutlery clean but not gleaming. Nobody had laughed and the conversation had been low pitched, as the guests had muttered gloomily to themselves and wondered why on earth they'd come. The waiters had dispensed the thoroughly mediocre food and drink as if it was the absolution, gliding reverentially between the tables like priests officiating at some solemn last rite.

"Robert?"

"What? Oh yes, yeah. That's the way to do it."

Damn! He had to concentrate. He always gave himself totally to a movie during shooting. The brooding single-mindedness went straight onto the film stock. If it wasn't there the public would miss it. But the Sunset was distracting him. All week he had burned up the lines to L.A. as Kristina had given him the blow by blow of the hotel's ongoing dissolution, and the worry was getting to him. He was only half there, in the world where he needed to be one hundred percent present.

"This is tomorrow's shooting schedule, Robert. It's an early call, I'm afraid. Four o'clock wake-up, makeup, but the scene's got to be in the can by sunup. These desert dawns are really something. Better than L.A. sunsets."

The director leaned forward and passed the mimeographed schedule to Robert. "We'll need Suki, too," he added. Please, please don't keep her up all night, was the unspoken request.

He took the pages but he was thinking of the maddening impossibility of running the Sunset Hotel. How *had* Livingstone managed it? Robert had never seen *him* struggling. He had floated above the whole thing like the conductor of a well-drilled orchestra. The martinis had never been less than perfect in Livingstone's day and it was impossible to imagine him sitting down to a dinner of the inferior quality that he and Kristina had endured on the night before he'd left for location. A raised eyebrow would have given the chef a nervous breakdown, a frown would have sent the bartender crying to his drink. Yet Robert could rant and rave and they looked at him as if *he* were crazy, as they continued to provide service, food, and drink about which the only thing first class was price.

"That okay for you, Robert? The start tomorrow?"

Again he snapped back into the here and now. "Yes, of course it is. No problem." But even as he spoke he knew that there *was* a problem—the oil-and-water mix of his movie career and the Sunset Hotel.

The telephone on the table next to him rang once. He reached for it.

"Mr. Hartford. Your daughter Kristina is here, at the main set office. I told her you were in conference but she wants to see you right away. She says it's important."

"Bring her over," snapped Robert. He put down the telephone carefully, in an effort to control the frustration that was already building inside him. Okay, so he'd had enough of the toads in his trailer, but Kristina, in *Arizona*, unannounced and unexpected and with a bagful of undreamed-of disasters from the Sunset Hotel—that he could do without.

He stood up. "I'm afraid I must ask you all to leave. I have a visitor from L.A. I think we've basically wrapped up all the outstanding points."

They hurried to obey, the writer and the director eager to leave the demanding presence of the superstar, Suki Marlowe signaling her disappointment and irritation at the arrival of the "visitor" from L.A.

Kristina came in fast, talking from the hip. "I'm sorry, Dad. I'm really sorry, but this wasn't a phone-call thing."

He offered her a distracted embrace.

"Roosevelt left," she said simply. "He walked yesterday. He's got a job as assistant manager, *assistant* manager, can you believe, at the Four Seasons."

"He wouldn't have the nerve," said Robert, his mouth quivering in disbelief. Roosevelt had made soggy pasta look like high-tensile steel wire.

"He's done it. He's history, packed and gone. He said it was a personality conflict with you."

"He didn't *have* a fucking personality!" shouted Robert.

Kristina looked away in exasperation. There was only one problem with the Sunset Hotel. Her father. "Maybe we should discuss what we do about it." She threw herself down into a chair.

"Listen, Kristina, believe it or not, I'm trying to make a movie here. It's big budget purely and simply because they are having to pay *me*. I had to throw the entire creative team out of here to make space for you and the Sunset. I can't handle this any longer. I'm an actor. I've got to *act*. It's not as easy as I make it look."

"Maybe you should have thought of that before you bid for the Sunset."

Robert weaved an elegant hand through immaculate hair. Yes, Kristina was right. His childhood obsession was turning into a nightmare. "Okay, what are we going to do? Advertise, I guess."

"The trade journals are carrying nothing else but help-wanted ads for the Sunset. Any minute now they're going to come out with a special Sunset classified section. People leaving are a symptom, Dad. You don't treat a bacterial infection with blood transfusions."

There was a silence. Something had definitely been said.

"And *I* am the bacterial infection?"

Kristina said nothing.

Robert Hartford sat quite still, as he adjusted to being a disease.

"Dad, maybe we should get in a management company and let them run things. We're out of our depth here."

"I'm not having outsiders fiddling around with the Sunset," snapped Robert. In his mind he could see them, all the ugly men in their boxlike suits sniffing around the hotel that he loved as much as beautiful women. Better by far that it should die than that it should suffer the fate far more terrible than death as the filthy fingers of the faceless ones rummaged through its secret places, breaking its quivering heart.

"We've got to do *something*," said Kristina.

He fixed her with the killer eyes. There *was* a way out.

"You run it, Kristina. Take over the whole thing. Run it yourself. I'll be in the background in an advisory capacity."

" 'Advisory capacity'?" Kristina's heart quickened. The idea had not been far from the center of her mind, but the suggestion had had to come from her father.

"Yes, a consultant, a sort of chairman of the board." He waved a hand to suggest that his actual title was of no importance, and he looked at her intently as he wondered why she hadn't jumped at his suggestion.

"If I'm going to run things, I think I should have the votes." Kristina's tone was determined. She didn't want her father criticizing, complaining, moaning, groaning. It would be worse than the status quo. At least now the responsibility for his own mess was his, not hers.

Robert's eyebrows shot upward. "You mean shares? A controlling interest?"

"Whatever."

Kristina set her Hartford jaw. If there was to be a battle, let it be now. Her father was ruining the hotel she was trying to run, and the atmosphere of uncertainty was poisoning the Sunset. There was only one chance. He must back out before it was too late. Either he had to hire someone else and give that person some sort of tenure, or he had to let her do the job. Either way he would have to give up *control*.

Robert laughed, and he shook his head. He was amazed yet not angered by her request. He had always loved Kristina, despite her mystical preoccupations and her tendency to float about in a high wind. Now she was giving him something to respect. There was actually something to be said for her brave, not to say foolhardy, suggestion. The staff liked her and trusted her, and she was learning fast. It was he who was making it all go wrong. He undercut her authority, and his nerve-racking hands-on/hands-off management style played havoc with that most delicate of flowers, employee confidence. The atmosphere of mistrust had seeped into the fabric of the Sunset Hotel. They thought of him as Lear, the mad, sad, unpredictable king, and now here, before him, was his daughter asking for a slice of the kingdom.

His voice was dreamily reflective, when at last he spoke. "And what guarantee would I have, if I was to give you fifty-one percent of the Sunset, that you would not use it against me at some unforeseeable time in the future?"

Lear had never thought of that. Robert just had.

"I wouldn't do anything to upset you, Dad. Surely you know that. I love you."

"Ah, love," he said, "the thing that herpes outlasts."

But despite his words he was in tune with Kristina's thinking. He needed psychologically to be free of the Sunset, and yet he wanted the cake to be there after he had consumed it. It was a human enough desire, and Kristina had suggested a way of achieving it. The hotel had after all been a gift, and where else would it eventually end up but in his only daughter's hands? By giving her control now, he would get rid of the responsibility, and yet still retain forty-nine percent of the shares. The world would still consider it "his" hotel, while the staff would know that he had zero control over their destinies. He would "save" the Sunset by giving it away to the only person in the world that he loved, and he would continue to live there into a ripe old . . . He forced the alien thought from his mind.

"Have you ever heard of Wittgenstein?" he said.

"Vaguely."

"He was perhaps the greatest philosopher of the twentieth century, and he lived in Cambridge. He was walking in a public park one day with a friend, and he 'gave' his friend one of the trees. Only he made the gift subject to all sorts of conditions. For instance his friend was never to climb the tree, never to cut it down, never to tell anyone else that he owned it, etc. He was a linguistic philosopher and he was making a point about language, and its meaning. When you took into account all the restrictions, he wasn't really giving the tree away at all. Genuine ownership implies the right to be able to dispose of the things you own."

"I don't get it," said Kristina, but she did.

Robert leaned forward in his chair. "I'll give you fifty-one percent of the Sunset on the single condition that you never, ever sell any of the shares and that in the unlikely event of your dying before me then I get them back."

"And I get to prune the tree, fertilize it, water it, spray it for pests—with no interference from you?"

"All of the above."

"You'd draw up a contract. . . ."

"Why, certainly we'd sign a contract."

She stood up. So did he.

They didn't shake hands on the deal, they hugged on it, and this time all the warmth in the world was in the embrace.

TWENTY

In David Plutarch's tennis-court-size office the glass walls gave him views over the whole of Los Angeles, but what he could really see was the world. He didn't look out much. He looked in. That was where the high visibility was. On the flickering Quotron screens; on the New York Stock Exchange tape that ran the full length of the only wall that wasn't see-through; on the four clocks, their hands set to West Coast, East Coast, Tokyo and London time and with thick red bands showing the timing of the opening and closing of the major exchanges.

He sat at a monolithic desk, and his feet were up on the faded green leather, as he clipped immaculate nails, sending the chips spinning out to be lost in the inch-deep pile of the carpet.

"Lose those Chicago calls," he shouted suddenly. "I don't like them. Don't be careful about it. Be brutal. Christ, why the hell isn't there any decent way to short Tokyo direct?"

Across the room the tape recorder caught it. Everything in this room was recorded. Millions of dollars flew in and out of this office. Later, if there was a difference of opinion over what had been said, the tape could decide who got fired. But the recorder wasn't the only person listening. Management of the around two billion in liquid assets that were left after his movie deals was a twenty-four-hour business. Most of it went through Morgan Stanley in New York, the best-run bank in America, but Plutarch liked to do a little dealing himself, hence the hometown operation in Beverly Hills. In the room with the money hero were a Japanese-speaking dealer, a young attorney specializing in the tax law of mergers and acquisitions, and a secretary whose job it was to monitor the wire services—Reuters, Dow Jones, and the financial press generally—for bits of information that pertained to Plutarch and his actual or possible business dealings. Throughout the day Financial News Network and CNN ran permanently, as did other programs, recorded on VHS during the previous twenty-four hours— Louis Rukeyser's "Wall Street Week," "Moneyline," and "The Nightly Business Report." Nothing in the public domain passed Plutarch by, and not much in the private one either. The banks of telephones surrounding his desk like a stockade saw to that.

"Difficult to short Japan," the dealer shouted back. "They don't like foreigners selling shares they don't own."

"Can't we try it?" asked Plutarch. "Dump some Sony we haven't got, and wait for the tariff barriers to go up. There'll be blood on the walls in Tokyo when they figure out that gravity works for stocks, too. My Congress people don't want to solve the trade deficit by raising taxes. They want to do it the popular way and nix the Nissans and the Hondas and tailspin the dollar. Who the hell cares about the currency when only one in ten Americans have a passport?"

"You're right on the fundamentals, Taipan, but forget shorting Japan. We tried it before. They just close out the positions without consulting us whenever it suits them. The Finance Ministry gives the order. *Free market* is something they pretend not to understand."

"All I say is, when they go, they blow. We're zero Jap exposure, aren't we?"

The dealer picked up the phone. In seconds he was through to the duty CPA. "What's our Japanese exposure?"

"Securities, yen, and real estate?"

"Yup."

"Zero direct stocks. Around five million in Euroyen year maturities. Nil real estate. Ten million in Bank of Tokyo Eurobonds, five-year maturity. Minimal exposure."

Plutarch waved a dismissive arm, as the dealer repeated the information. "Yeah, it's peanuts and it's safe peanuts. Forget it."

He stood up. It was a dull market. Nil action. He should make some. Greenmail a sleepy industrial. Shake up a teetering S and L. Dream up a leveraged buyout of a food company, and put a spike in the Pepto Bismol sales.

He walked moodily to the window, and he peered down at the pool beneath. The site was balm for the billionaire's jaded eyes. Kanga was massaging Caroline Kirkegaard's back.

*   *   *

Caroline breathed in deeply. It was called Shiatsu, and it felt sublime. Poolside at Plutarch's, the Kirkegaard mood was good. She lay back on the sun bed and let the rays soak through her as the clever fingers kneaded her rippling muscles. Mmmmmmmm! Things were almost better again. Destiny was growing explosively, the members pouring in, donating outrageous gifts to the movement in exchange for the cradle-to-grave/grave-to-infinity guidance and protection it offered in return. Who needed an L.A. tract home in the cosmic blot that was this lifetime when it could be traded in for an eternal ticket to ride? Who cared about cash, about jewelry (apart from crystals), about cars, when there was the possibility of happiness without end on the millennial journey that Destiny promised? Nobody who had seen the light in the Kirkegaard eyes, shining like a beacon to the true believer, gave a damn about those mundane things. The Destiny funds, played brilliantly by Plutarch, were soaring giddily to heights of which Caroline had never dreamed. Already there was a Destiny building on Wilshire, and a brownstone in New York, a branch office in London, and another in Paris. And there was no stopping it. New Age was getting bigger, but it hadn't really started, and now there was Destiny incense, Destiny herb tea, Destiny music, and Destiny crystal jewelry, quite apart from the bestseller *March to Destiny*, and the videotapes of Kirkegaard channeling spirits, and preaching charismatic Destiny themes to the ecstatic faithful. Yes, she was a guru now, but she had built only the ground floor. One fine day she would raise the roof, and then go through the roof, and up into the heavens where God lived, and where she, Caroline Kirkegaard, would rule.

One thought killed her joy. Robert Hartford and the Sunset Hotel. When there was nothing left to want she would still want it. When there was nothing left to dream of she would dream of his destruction. The rumor that it was running down under his erratic management was beside the point. If revenge was to mean anything at all it would have to be *she* who caused his downfall. But he would never part with the hotel. He would demolish it rather than let it fall into her hands.

She looked up, aware suddenly that he was watching her from the window of his office, and she smiled at Destiny's most important member.

He smiled at her, aware that she had seen him. Maybe he should wander down, and watch them together, the two beautiful girls, and their two beautiful bodies. . . .

An assistant with a Harvard MBA wandered into the Plutarch office. "Are we still interested in the Sunset Hotel?" she asked.

Plutarch spun around. "For sure," he said quickly. "What you got?"

She held out a piece of Reuters tape. "Reuters is saying Robert Hartford's made over a controlling interest in the Sunset to his daughter, Kristina. He's called a press conference for sometime next week. Want me to check it out? Sunset Corporation is private, but if Reuters has it, it's no secret. Should be able to confirm or deny, no problem."

Plutarch walked over to her and tore the piece of tape from her hand. His greedy eyes devoured it. "Confirm it," he barked. "And if it's true I want an in-depth profile on the daughter. Twenty-four-hour surveillance. History. Everything. Okay?"

He ran from the room, taking the marble stairs two at a time, and he nearly tripped as he darted across the cavernous hall. As he erupted onto the terrace, he was already calling Caroline's name.

She sat up and twisted around to face him.

"Hartford's given the Sunset to his daughter," he blurted out as he cascaded across the patio.

"What!" It wasn't a question. She'd heard. She just needed a second or two for her mind to catch up with the explosive news.

"Her name's Kristina. I think we met at Livingstone's black ball."

A radiant smile lit up the Kirkegaard face.

"Oh yes, we did, David. And at the Livingstone funeral, too."

"Well, she owns the Sunset now."

"But for how long?" said Caroline.

"Would you like some tea?" said Caroline.

"Oh no, I don't think so, thank you," said Kristina.

"Please do. Join me. It's special herb tea. No caffeine. It's very soothing."

"Oh, okay, I'll try it. Thanks."

She felt it again. That feeling at the funeral. Caroline Kirkegaard could not be resisted—not because she was so powerful, so strong, so dictatorial—but because you didn't *want* to resist her. Instead, Kristina wanted to please her. Being with her reminded Kristina of school, when she had developed a crush on the teacher. She wanted to be her pet. She wanted to be clever for her. She wanted to behave really well.

"I'm glad you came, Kristina. I'm not surprised you did, but I'm glad."

Kristina couldn't think of a reply. Caroline was right. There was an inevitability about it, even though she had waited until the last minute before deciding definitely to come. The telephone call had arrived out of the blue, and there had been no real reason given for it.

"Hello, Kristina? This is Caroline Kirkegaard."

The voice, relaxed, self-confident, had been totally natural. Kristina's nervous reply had not been. "Oh, goodness! Caroline! Hello."

"I've been thinking about you a lot since Francisco's funeral. I want to find out why."

"Oh."

"Can we meet?"

Kristina's throat had gone dry. Her fingers had tingled. At the other end of the telephone she had sensed the full lips, the compelling eyes.

" 'Meet'?"

"Come and have tea with me. Say tomorrow. At four. It's the last house on Callejuela Drive off Coldwater. We can talk."

Refusal hadn't seemed an option. Caroline's voice had been heavy with destiny.

"Okay," Kristina had mumbled. Too late she had remembered the restaurant staff meeting scheduled for three-fifteen—the one that would hardly have started by four o'clock. The line had gone dead and she was glad there hadn't been time for the excuse.

From that moment to this she had thought of nothing else except Caroline Kirkegaard. The straight world couldn't make up its mind about her and the Destiny movement. Some saw it as a band of harmless hippies, lost in an airhead sixties time warp, albeit a mercifully drug-free one. Others believed it to be a sinister cult— shades of Satanism and the worst excesses of Synanon, with the ghost of Manson hovering overhead for good measure. Either way they were suspicious of it, fearing its antifamily, antiestablishment bias, and worst of all its antieighties materialism—that prize that conservative America had worked so hard and so long to win.

The straight world's antipathy toward Destiny was for Kristina a powerful argument in its favor. Her grudge against conventional wisdom had been conditioned by a lifetime as the victim of her mother's shape-up-or-ship-out nastiness. But it was not the strongest reason for keeping an open mind. *That* was Caroline Kirkegaard herself. As the personification of Destiny she transcended it in the way that Christ transcended Christianity, Buddha Buddhism. Her whole startling personality challenged the observer to make the leap of faith onto her strong shoulders. Oh, there were words, but she *was* the word, and the way and the truth and the light, too. Kristina had read the book, seen the video, and even bought the incense—all available at the Bodhi Tree, and now at Waldenbooks and B. Dalton as well—and though she had been impressed by the tantalizing mysticism, it had been when she had stared into the Kirkegaard eyes at Livingstone's funeral that things had begun to happen. It hadn't been the light at the Damascus roadside, but it had been a turning point. There was the feeling that her life might easily divide into a before and after, if she would just allow herself to embrace the truth.

From that moment on the phrases of Destiny had begun to roll around like ripe seeds in her mind. "God is in the Good but God is also in the Evil because he created all things and he lives in them." "Through eternal lives we can perfect ourselves, but we must trust the Guide that first we must find." "Our lives are little, our lives are short, but there is time to put one foot upon the path of Destiny." "We must cast away possessions to make room for the belief in the eternal that alone we can carry from this life to the next."

"Kanga, can you get us some of the new herb tea? We'll sit in the bay window."

It was all so normal. The room was like a thousand others in Beverly Hills, but as Kristina followed her toward the window her heart was thumping in her chest.

"Sit down, Kristina."

Kristina did as she was told, unable to escape the feeling that this was not merely a polite invitation but a life-or-death command.

Caroline's eyes peered at her and she smiled nervously back at them, letting her own eyes fall away when the intensity got too great. It seemed Caroline was already inside her.

"You are afraid of yourself. You are fearful of the great power I sense within you."

Kristina swallowed. There was something incredibly personal about the remark. At a stroke the conversation had moved to a far deeper level of communication. She had been invited for tea, for no very clear reason except the odd one that since the funeral she had been on Caroline's mind. Now here she was, unsure what to expect, but expectant nonetheless.

" 'Great power'?" said Kristina.

"I know you, Kristina. I have watched you and known you through many lifetimes. We have been friends. We have been enemies. We have been lovers . . ."

A blush exploded over Kristina's cheeks at Caroline's words. Suddenly she understood the feeling inside her. It had been there at the funeral, and it had hovered in the atmosphere ever since. She hadn't faced it. She hadn't named it. Caroline had. She looked away, as the blush deepened. Caroline's lips were parted, and her eyes were questioning, pleased with the color her words had painted on Kristina's cheeks.

"Lovers," she repeated, and her hand reached out across the space that separated them and she touched Kristina's knee. "Lovers across time and space and in dimensions that you cannot understand."

Kristina looked helplessly at the fingers resting on her knee. She didn't move away. The mesmeric quality of Caroline's voice, and the hypnotic thought of supernatural love combined to paralyze her. But the feelings were not still. They raged and roared inside her and the Kirkegaard fingers could feel them, that she knew, that she was afraid, that she wanted.

"You are so nearly open. So nearly open to the truth. When you embrace it, it will make you invincible. But you are afraid. You are afraid to claim the power that will be yours."

"I don't really understand," said Kristina's distant voice.

Caroline laughed. She threw back her head so that the sunlight caught the sculpted head, the chiseled hair, the jutting chin.

"There is no understanding of Destiny," she said. "Touch it with reason and it is gone. The truths we know are our truths. They are our reality. Our creation. As gods of our infinite soul we master our Destiny. We have no need of understanding."

"I see," said Kristina.

"But I will teach you to feel." She leaned forward, far forward, "And I will teach you how to be, and how to become."

Her face filled up Kristina's visual field.

"And your worries and fears will fade on the horizon of many lives. I will travel with you through endless worlds and I will be your guide and you will be my companion on the journey toward perfect happiness. Will you come with me, Kristina, to the end of the future, and the beginning that starts there?"

Kristina could see Caroline's lips and the words they spoke, but the two were existing on separate levels. The words spoke to her mind, and there was frantic sense in them. She believed in reincarnation. The circle of rebirth. Each new life a refining of the previous one. Perfection, found on the endless path, through the seeing eyes of the spirit guide. Yes, she wanted that. She wanted Caroline Kirkegaard to banish the insecurities, and the misery, and the lack of self-confidence and to exchange it for the bright light of infinite bliss. But the lips had meaning apart from the words they spoke. It was to them that her body responded. They were alluring, softly voluptuous, daringly sensuous. They spoke the truth but they *were* the truth, and suddenly Kristina realized she wanted to kiss them.

They leaned in closer, and Kristina felt herself drawn to them.

In the kiss there would be so many answers. She would be filled up—body and mind—with the sweet messages of Caroline's mouth. There she would find the pieces that had always been missing in her life. In those lips she would find her destiny.

So she moved forward, and her eyes were big as she watched herself flirting on the edge of intimacy.

"Shall I pour the tea now?" said Kanga.

Like a glass shattered into a thousand pieces by the blow of a hammer, the illusion vanished with the words.

Kanga knew what she had done and her shamed face said that she was not able to help it. The tea had been ordered, but light years had passed since then. The whole room was full of the subtle rhythms of cosmic seduction and she more than anyone could sense them. Long ago, Kanga had starred in the leading role, and she had never forgotten the magic of the drama or its sublime conclusion.

In the slavery that had begun that day, she had found freedom from self. She had ceased to exist as a person, and she had become the creature of Caroline Kirkegaard. Now she was merely a body, a brain, an instrument, a tool. Orders were the substitute for motivation, commands the replacement for voluntary acts. But inside the shell that looked like a person, the random sparks of emotion could still crackle and dart. Like now, when another threatened to usurp her place.

"Leave it on the table," said Caroline. In her jealousy, Kanga had willfully sabotaged the moment. Now she placed the tray on the table and backed away, her eyes wide with panic as she contemplated her punishment.

"Drive over to Sherman Oaks. Do some shopping," said Caroline, the words sharp as a chilled wind, as she banished her assistant. The end of the earth was not farther than the shops of the San Fernando Valley that moment, and Kanga knew it, but she hurried to obey.

Caroline took a deep breath, as if composing herself after hearing of some terrible tragedy. Then she reached forward for the pot, and she poured the tea that had broken the spell. "You know of Destiny?" she said.

"Yes, I've read your book. I've seen the tape of you channeling. . . . I've been to the meetings and one of the seminars in the desert."

Caroline replaced the pot on the tray, and suddenly she reached across it, taking up Kristina's hands in hers and staring deep into her eyes.

"Oh, Kristina. How can I make you understand how strong you are going to be? You are full of doubt, but you will walk with gods. You will be among them, as an equal. If you could harness one iota of your future greatness in this life, you would rule this world that knows you not. You would walk across it like a Titan, and the people would bow down before you and pray to you for the salvation that you could provide. I know it seems impossible to you. I am inside your mind and I feel the disbelief, but I promise you this is your destiny. Let your heart believe me. Let your body trust what your brain cannot. You must have faith to liberate your power. Believe in me. Trust in me, so that your faith can move the mountains of the world."

Kristina could feel the fervor. It could be touched. It was an incredible outpouring of certainty that melted puny doubt and groveling intellect. The words did not fit Kristina's experience of herself. She had always been a nobody. Oh, she had been Robert Hartford's daughter, and her body was great, and there had been little triumphs dotted along the roadside of her unremarkable life, but basically she was a nothing like everyone else. So the words seemed to lie, but the words did not exist alone. They had become more than objects. They rolled over her, melting her insignificance and painting her in the proud colors of glory. Now, before her, this strange, wonderful woman was drawing pictures of a future more brilliant than she had dared to imagine, a future that could somehow trickle down to her present and change her life.

She wanted to believe so badly. It would be so easy. Only the thin thread of common sense separated her from the spiritual riches that were rightfully hers.

She was being asked to cut that thread. It was an offer that she could hardly refuse. "What do I have to do?" she said.

The triumph that blazed in Caroline's eyes wore the mask of pleasure.

"You only have to surrender. You have to surrender your old self to Destiny. Give away your fear and doubt. Cast off your uncertainty. Open the doors that are closed. Let the word into your life. Let me inside you, Kristina. Let me come in."

Again her face filled up Kristina's. The face of a savior; the face of a goddess; the face of a lover.

I want to be inside you, said the lips. I want to live inside your body, and I want you to live in mine.

"Ohhhhhhh!" Kristina's soft sound was the moan of acquiescence. There was no way of saying yes to the inevitable. There was only the bowing down before it. The bended knee. The surrendered heart. The whole of her body was full of the sound of trumpets as she passed over to the other side. This was it. Her life had changed. Now she walked with Destiny.

"Kiss me, Kristina," said Caroline Kirkegaard.

"Magic, Magic, Magic."

The chant filled the Forum and Robert Hartford, sitting on the extreme edge of the cheap metal orange chair, was sucked into it. It wasn't remotely his style to be cheering somebody, cheering a *man* and in public, but a Lakers game was different. Earvin "Magic" Johnson, Lakers' guard and spearhead of the team's fast-break offense, was different.

Johnson, tapeworm tall, shimmied down the court as if he were slam dancing at On the Rox. The fact that the entire Celtics team was there to take the ball away from him didn't seem to figure in his equation. The opposition scurried about like fourth-graders whose coach had decided on a whim to show them how it was *really* done. The ball yo-yoed from his sensitive fingers, seemingly attached to them by an invisible string, and the drumbeat of rubber on polished wood had a rhythm all of its own. The NBA's highest-paid player, with his own billboard on the Boulevard, and now signed by Mike Ovitz, Hollywood's ultimate dealmonger, Johnson defined the word *star* and in the heavens where he shone the other luminaries were not ashamed to applaud him.

There were enough of them to do it. Ringside at the Forum, the industry was out in force, and they were just about the only people who could afford to be there. If you knew a friend of God's you could buy a season seat for around ten thousand dollars. If you were merely an acquaintance of St. Peter you could be scalped a thousand a game, more for the playoffs. Of course you didn't have to sit at courtside, but then you didn't *have* to breathe. Robert had been given the tickets by John McEnroe and Tatum O'Neal, season ticket holders up by the Laker bench, and McEnroe had gotten them from Dr. Buss, the Forum owner, in exchange for playing a demonstration match for which he would normally have charged a hundred grand. So there they were, he and Suki Marlowe, who didn't know a basketball from a testicle, where the "now" L.A. action was, screaming for Magic and getting it. Last night they had gone to the movie wrap party at Spago, and today, blinking in the arc lights, the two filmmaking hermits were back at last in what passed for the real world.

Out on the court Johnson deigned to score, but before he did so
there was a beautiful moment when his stiltlike legs were set in
cement. They were the only part of him that wasn't a ballet of liquid
motion. He was a limbo dancer; a charmed snake; he was the belly
button of some sinuous Turkish delight. He was a candle in a low
wind, the rushes of a weaved basket, the leather thong of a cracking
whip. He never got where he was going, and he never returned from
where he had come, and the dizzy eyes of the Celtics and their darting,
ineffectual arms were always seconds behind him, inches in front of
the place where once he had been. For an age and an instant he
tortured them, and then at last he tired of the mice to whom he had
become the cat. His arm-without-end arced behind him, the ball
superglued to the palm of his hand. Then it bowled forward on its
pendulum course, and as it reached the level of his shoulders the glue
dissolved. The ball sailed, impossibly high, over the heads of the
defenders, up, up, up, down, down, down. As it made the basket it
hardly seemed to touch the sides, so central was its triumphal entry.

Over to the right of Robert, Nicholson was on his feet and so were
his guests, Harry Dean Stanton and Timothy Hutton. To the left,
Walter Matthau, another season ticket holder, had jumped up, as had
father and son Douglases and Sheens, who had been lent the Lorimar
block of seats. In the president's box directly opposite, the boxers, too,
were jumping for joy—Sugar Ray Leonard and Mike Tyson sandwich-
ing Mike's date, Michael Jackson's sister LaToya. Whoopi Goldberg
and Dyan Cannon bounced up and down in delight in their regular
seats opposite the Celtics bench, while behind it Ovitz clients Dustin
Hoffman and Bill Murray went quietly wild with glee. On the bench,
Pat Riley, better looking by far than most of his actor fans, smiled the
sexy soft smile of a star on the daytime soaps. Dapper in a sharp
business suit, his hair slicked back with gel, he looked more like a
gun-slinging bond trader on Wall Street than the head coach of the
best basketball team in the world.

"How much longer?" whispered Suki Marlowe.

Robert Hartford was probably the only man in the 17,500-seat
stadium who didn't mind her asking. The reason was simple. It was a
woman's remark, and he was the man who loved women. All around,
the superstars—with varying degrees of enthusiasm—would have
considered themselves fond of the opposite sex, but they had other
loves too, like male camaraderie, and one-of-a-kind athletes, and the
L.A. Lakers on a winning streak. Those, except possibly the last,
Robert did not share. It was right and fitting that Suki Marlowe would
be bored out of her microscopic mind by basketball, because it meant

that what she liked far more was to step out of the confines of her microscopic skirt. Here in this arena she was nothing but a gorgeous prop, a brilliantly colored umbrella in the male rain.

"Not long now," he said simply, smiling to himself at her irreverence.

He looked at her surreptitiously out of the corner of his eye. She had made the movie bearable, and he had used her for the chemistry in the love scenes, as he had used all the others. In the sealed world of the location you needed a partner. The shoot was like a mini-lifetime with its births and deaths, its spring and its winter, its Borgia subplots and Machiavellian conspiracies. So for two short months in the heat of the desert he had "married" Suki Marlowe, and she, poor thing, was already falling into the role of wife just days away from the divorce. Maybe tomorrow he'd dump her. Maybe tonight. The old speech would do—the one about "We've shared something beautiful. Don't let's spoil it by not being able to let go." It never went down particularly well, but the "You can always count on me to help you with your career" invariably dried the tears and brought out the thin, silver-medal smiles. That was the good and the bad news about Hollywood. The girls were the real tough guys. They had to be.

The unwelcome thought suddenly lanced into his mind. Tough girls like Paula, the ragamuffin to riches, who had traveled from anonymity to fame and fortune with just a little help from her friends . . . and lovers. Would he *ever* be able to forget her? Tower's death and the emergence of Paula as his heir had been a media feast of gluttonous proportions. Oh, Tower had left his mark, but the Paula Hope inheritance had provided a topspin to the story that had lifted it bodily from the arts section to the entertainment pages. The articles had starred Paula and the extraordinary story of Winthrop Tower's undreamed-of cash mountain. Lip service was paid to his place in the design hierarchy, his East Coast reputation, and there were snippets of conversation with the odd celebrity whose houses he had designed, but the L.A. bottom line had been the money that he'd salted away and the beautiful nobody from nowhere who'd scored it. How had it been possible to keep so much money hidden in this material world? Had it been honestly obtained? Had taxes been paid on it? And who was Paula Hope, the girl with the limp and the beauty, who had somehow escaped the movies and the sexual magnetism of none other than Robert Hartford, to whom she had briefly been engaged? What had been her hold on Tower, the "confirmed bachelor"—nudge, nudge, wink, wink—and what had precipitated the row between Tower and Hartford around the time of the mysterious accident to the chauffeur who still lingered on at Cedars-Sinai? The pieces had always concluded with the immediate present, the only thing Tinsel Town cared about more than the maddeningly unpredictable future. Paula Hope was chatelaine of the intriguing Château, having mouth-to-mouthed it back from the dead, and now the tunes of her pied-piper pipes were emptying the bedrooms and the ballrooms of the fast-fading Sunset Hotel—to the almost certain fury of the reclusive superstar who had once loved her.

"Magic, Magic, Magic," chanted the crowd.

"You want, we'll split right now," said Robert suddenly.

Suki Marlowe beamed her pleasure. Had she just controlled the controller? She was doing better than she'd thought. In this town you judged people by the quality of the people they walked out on, and *nobody* walked on the Lakers.

She jumped up in case he changed his mind. "Yeah, my ass went to sleep," she said.

The McEnroe seats were next to the gangway. Ducking down low to avoid obscuring the view of the lesser fans, they began their escape.

The Horizon production veep five rows back had other ideas. He had been working on the movie, and it was too recently over for Robert to ignore him. His hand snaked out for the Hartford sleeve. "Hi, Robert. You *leaving?*"

Robert cursed silently as he slipped his arm away from the unwanted embrace. "Suki's not feeling too good," he muttered.

"Great party last night, no?"

Robert knew the game. This was maximum industry visibility. The studio nobody was scoring more points than Magic Johnson by being seen talking to Robert Hartford. The longer the conversation lasted, the more points he would run up. Touching and holding on to Hartford flesh was bonus goodies. A bear hug would have been a knockout career move.

"It was fine," said Robert.

He was moving away. The executive's moment in the sun was nearly over. His mind worked overtime for something that would hold the movie star in his orbit. You could all but hear the grinding of his mental gears. "I saw your daughter, Kristina, at lunch yesterday," he blurted out, wondering if he'd found the flypaper that would make Hartford stick. "She was in Le Dôme with that guru figure, Caroline Kirkegaard. *What* a great-looking couple!" He squeezed on the compliment like icing on a cake.

"Are you coming, Robert?" said Suki, reveling in her unaccustomed role as prime mover of immovable objects.

But Robert had stopped. His body had stopped. His mind had stopped. His soul had stopped.

He sat down in the gangway, and the eyes of the studio executive opened wide as he caught a glimpse of paradise on earth.

"*What* did you just say?" asked Robert.

"Kristina. Caroline Kirkegaard. Eating in the Dôme. Didn't you know she was in town, or something?"

"Are you sure about that?" barked Robert.

"Yeah, sure I'm sure. My son goes to those Destiny seminars. He's got pictures of Caroline Kirkegaard all over his room. And I know Kristina. I've seen her at the Sunset several times." The studio exec was puzzled, but he was making out. The front people were turning around to watch them, that guy from Carson Productions, another from CBS. Christ, there was Irving Azoff, the MCA president, eyeballing the pair of them.

Slowly Robert Hartford stood up, and his face looked like he had seen not a loser but a ghost.

Kristina had been eating with Caroline Kirkegaard. His daughter and his enemy. The one who owned the Sunset Hotel, and the one who wanted it. It was as innocent and as appetizing as a Jonestown picnic. The worst thing of all was that it made sense of things that had been puzzling him. For the last two months since he had signed the controlling interest over to Kristina, he had hardly spoken to her. She had sent some profit-and-loss schedules, some occupancy rates, a few notes on this and that, and from them he had gained the impression that there had been a marginal improvement in the Sunset's fortunes. When he had telephoned to congratulate her, he had not been able to reach her, except once when she had been unusually distant and evasive. He hadn't thought much about it. After all, it had been what he wanted—to be allowed to get on with making his movie in relative peace, untroubled by the goings-on at the hotel. He'd imagined she was as preoccupied as he was, and that had been just fine. Or had it? Now he was far from sure, and a hideous thought kept bubbling to the surface of his mind. Thank God, he had tied up the shares.

Whatever Kristina was up to she wouldn't be able to sell them, anymore than Wittgenstein's friend could have sold his miserable tree.

He powered up the gangway, overtaking Suki Marlowe as he headed for the exit. "Where are we going?" she wailed at his wake.

"I'm going back to the Sunset," said Robert Hartford, without bothering to turn around.

✳   ✳   ✳

Robert stormed into his drawing room. It had not been made up. The cushions had not been plumped. An empty glass on a side table had not been cleared away. The curtains had not been drawn for the evening. He stalked through to the bedroom, his mind on red alert. Nobody had made the bed, changed the sheets, replaced the flowers. In the bathroom, a pile of towels lay on the still-wet floor, the bathwater in situ, the shaving paraphernalia, the Royal Yacht aftershave, the tube of toothpaste all exactly as he'd left them. A copy of the L.A. *Herald Examiner* had soaked up a puddle from the floor and now it lay in a nasty papier-mâché heap on the twisted bathmat. Even the bathroom television, its sound turned down low, still warbled on.

As he reached for the telephone, it rang.

"Mr. Hartford?"

"Who is it?" he barked.

"Front desk, Mr. Hartford . . ."

"My place hasn't been cleaned!" he exploded.

There was a silence.

"We have you down as a checkout, sir . . . twelve noon today . . . that was why I was ringing."

"Checkout? Checkout? What the *hell* are you talking about? This is Robert Hartford. I live here. This is *my* hotel."

Again, a pause. "It's quite clear, this note, sir. It says, 'Mr. Robert Hartford will be checking out at noon today.' That's why the room hasn't been done, sir. It's done after the guest leaves."

"I'm not a *guest*! Who the *fuck* are you? What's your name?"

"I'm Dale, sir. Front desk duty assistant manager."

"I don't know you. Who hired you?" rasped Robert.

"Miss Kristina, sir, three weeks ago."

"And who was the joker who wrote this ridiculous 'note'?"

"It's signed by Mr. Vierteli, sir, the new manager. I'm sorry if there's been some mistake, sir. We're all new around here. But the problem is a little difficult, sir, because your bungalow has been rebooked . . . to a Mr. Ben Gazi, sir, and the gentleman has just arrived with his family. They're waiting in the lobby."

Robert Hartford spoke very slowly. "Listen, Dale, you may be new, but get wise. I'm Robert Hartford. *The* Robert Hartford, not some unlucky namesake. I *own* this hotel, and you ought to know that. I live here. I've always lived here. I'm always going to live here. I am not—repeat not—a guest and I never, repeat never, 'check out.' So I suggest you pitch Mr. Ben Gazi *and* his family right out on their asses if you haven't got anywhere to put them, and I suggest you put me through to the manager so that he can explain personally to me just what the *hell* is going on around here. Then maybe, just maybe, we can try to forgive you for being the new kid on the block."

There was definite fear in the quiet at the other end of the telephone. Rocks and hard places, devils and deep blue seas—the unfortunate Dale was sandwiched between them.

"Mr. Vierteli is at a meeting, sir."

"Put me THROUGH to him!"

"I can't, sir. I had specific instructions not to disturb him."

Robert's voice was ice cold. It was true. It had happened. Or at least it was trying to happen. "Put me through to my daughter," he said.

"She's not here this evening, sir."

"Put me through to her office. *Do* it, Dale. Do it now." He dared the minion to disobey him. There was a long pause and then the extension began ringing.

Robert gripped the receiver tight in his fist as if it were a blunt instrument.

"Hello," said a woman's voice.

"Who *is* this?" he yelled down the line.

"Hello, Robert," said Caroline Kirkegaard.

Robert Hartford stood in the office that had once been Kristina's, in the office that before then had been his. He fought for breath because he had just run all the way from his bungalow and his rage made speech difficult.

"What are you doing in my hotel?" he screamed.

Caroline Kirkegaard, razor sharp in a Valentino double-breasted suit, didn't bother to get up from the desk at which she sat. She just looked at him, in frank amazement, a smile playing at the corners of her mouth.

"*Your* hotel?" she said.

"My hotel. Kristina's hotel. What in God's name are you doing here? I told you if you ever set foot in this place again . . ."

"You'd have me thrown out. Well, Robert, guess who's going to be doing the throwing."

He paused. He had gotten this far on a surge tide of adrenaline, but there were things he had to know. "Did Kristina give you permission to come here?"

"I don't get permission. I give it." Her voice was threatening, totally in control.

Robert Hartford felt the fingers of doubt probing at him. He leaned forward, menacing, his jaw pushing out at her. "Are you telling me you think you've bought Kristina's share in the Sunset?" he thundered.

"Because you can't. She's not allowed to sell it. Any contract you've signed with her is null and void."

He smiled bitterly through his fury. Was it possible that yet once again Caroline Kirkegaard had underestimated him? If so it would be the last time. By God he swore it.

" 'Bought'?" said Caroline quietly. "Sold? Who mentioned buying and selling?"

He watched her, the understanding creeping into his eyes from the corners.

"No!" he gasped.

"Yes," said Caroline.

"Kristina *gave* me her fifty-one percent share in the Sunset Hotel, and this . . ."—she pushed a piece of paper across the desk at him—"is the deed of gift."

Robert Hartford stared down at it as if it were his own bleeding heart.

There would be no point reading it. Plutarch's lawyers would have done that, time and time again. A gift. A present. It was a Wittgenstein condition he hadn't thought to include in the contract with Kristina. It had never occurred to him. How could he have conceived of the impossible?

"What did you do to her?" His voice was breaking.

Caroline threw back her head and laughed. "It was more what she did to me."

The insinuation crawled through the words.

"I'll fight you, Caroline. No court will uphold this."

Her smile was the purest patronization now. "Fight me by all means, Robert, but I wouldn't bother with the courts. The 'understanding' that Kristina and I have is unshakable. There was no duress. All the 'persuasion' came exclusively from your daughter. So, this is my hotel now, Robert Hartford, which reminds me . . . I think my people have told you that we need your room and you're way past checkout time. I'm afraid we're going to have to charge you for a whole extra day."

He backed away from her, but already she was reaching for the telephone, talking into it, and as she did so her eyes locked onto his.

"Yes, Mr. Hartford will be leaving. Have security supervise it. Yes, now. This minute. No, I'm not at all sure where he's going. Just stack it up in the lobby. Wherever. That's right. And report back to me when it's done. Okay. Good. Yes, that's right. The Sunset won't be at *all* the same place without him."

✻   ✻   ✻

Smog had closed in on Los Angeles, a hazy layer of unfocused yellow, swathing the city in an acrid blanket of surreptitious poison. The Hollywood Hills, above and beyond it, shone bright in the late afternoon sun. From the position where Robert stood, his nose pushed close to the inch-thick glass of the Century City skyscraper, it seemed that he was peering across a sea of ocher cotton wool to the distant mountains.

He had stood up, because he couldn't sit down any longer, and because he could no longer endure the drip, drip, drip of undiluted pessimism that was costing him a thousand dollars an hour. In this mini-Manhattan with palm trees four top attorneys at $250 each would be at least that, without the extras. Not that money was the problem. Kristina was.

"We'd have to prove that her mental capacities were diminished at the time of the deed of gift. Not now, but then. That's notoriously difficult. It's the problem with the insanity defense. How do you prove a compromised mental state a year or two ago?"

Robert turned from the window. It had all been said before. Now it would all be said again.

"Listen, for God's sake. We're not talking a year ago. We're talking six weeks ago. And anyway the nature of the deed tells you she was out of her mind. She just gave away a fifty-one percent share in a hotel that's worth a hundred and fifty million bucks. For nothing. A gift. If that isn't crazy, what the hell is?"

"People give that sort of money away all the time. It's called charity," said one of the lawyers.

"Destiny is *not* a charity. It's a cult. My daughter has been brainwashed, and you'd better find a way to make some judge believe it, and you'd better start by believing it yourselves."

"I suppose we could ask for an injunction, or at least a restraining order preventing Kirkegaard from taking control of the hotel pending a hearing, but we'd still have to present evidence at this stage, and the problem is we haven't got any."

The senior partner tried to inject a little optimism into the proceedings. "The trouble is," he continued, "Plutarch's lawyers are on top of all this. Thom Craddock wasn't born yesterday. They could countersue. I can think of half a dozen grounds for a complaint. I don't suppose there's any way we can get to your daughter, Robert?"

"She won't speak to me, and I can't get into the Sunset. They've got more security people in there than waiters and maids. It's like a fortress," he said bitterly.

"I guess we could subpoena her if we bring suit, but it guarantees her hostility. The bottom line is that if we don't have Kristina, we don't have a case. If they've got her in their pockets, and it looks as if they have, we'll have a devil of a time trying to prove her incompetence," said the attorney.

Robert turned back to the window and stared out morosely at the city. He couldn't see the Sunset, but he could see the Château Madrid. The top of its roof stuck up toward the sky like a finger raised in disdain.

The telephone warbled in the background.

One of the lawyers picked it up. "Yes, he's here. Hang on." He turned to Robert and held out the phone. "Mr. Hartford, it's for you. A doctor from Cedars-Sinai. Says it's very urgent that he speak to you."

Robert took the receiver. "Mr. Hartford. This is Dr. Peel. I believe you know of a patient here, a Mr. Graham Ovenden. He's been in a coma here for over a year."

"I know who you mean," said Robert irritably.

"Well, he's come out of his coma. I've never seen it happen before. He's talking, and he seems to be making sense, and he wants to see you."

"I have absolutely no interest in seeing him," said Robert dismissively.

"He has a remarkable story to tell, Mr. Hartford. I think you should hear it. It appears he's confessing to the murder of a man in Florida among other things . . . other things concerning you, Mr. Hartford, and your personal life. I couldn't urge you strongly enough to come right on down here. We have no way of knowing how long this lucid phase will last. He could easily slip right back into coma."

But Robert was no longer listening. He was running. He charged across the room, dropping the telephone on the edge of a desk as he ran. He barged through the door, and across the reception area to the elevators, and the words of the doctor rang in his ears. Graham was confessing to a murder. In Florida. Oh, God, dear God, could Paula's story have been true all along?

It was a very nasty gym, and the smell of male bodies—their new sweat, their old sweat, and the disturbing aroma of their intermediate secretions—was unequivocal. The stench was the thing you noticed first, because everything else was half hidden in the gloomy twilight that permeated the windowless room. When you walked across the ancient carpet, it pulled at your feet, not actually sticky but clinging,

like yesterday's lover. Dotted around the dungeon were what seemed to
be instruments of torture, wicked contraptions of chipped metal, rich
with pulleys and mobile weights. Gloomy music wafted through the
fetid air, Bach, or Handel in somber mood, the funereal dirge rich
with the sense of ritual and the unmistakable message that here
sacrifice would be required.

Caroline Kirkegaard slid through the empty room. Around her
hourglass waist she wore a thick brown belt, six inches wide, strapped
together in front by three silver buckles. Above, her mighty super-
structure loomed like the bridge of an ocean liner, and below, the
sheet steel of her abdominal musculature rippled beneath the jet-black
high-cut leotard. Her da Vinci legs, anatomically perfect, were naked
all the way down to her man-size feet, and they padded across the tacky
carpet to the man who stood in the shadows by the wall.

"So!" she said.

He held his head down low as if too nervous to face the full frontal
force of her gaze, and he found something dull to do with his hands,
which were buried in the pockets of an expensive but too-well-cut
Armani suit. He coughed to clear a clearly dry throat.

"The lawyers say it's watertight. They've talked to Hartford's people
and they haven't got a case. They may bluster for a week or two, but
they won't even get a holding injunction."

"Good." It was only a word, but why should she tell him of her joy?
Why should she warble on about the glory of revenge and the
sweetness of victory? It was no part of her plan to let him know she was
grateful. It was her intention to show him.

He looked around him, blinking in the dim, religious light.

"It's not the L.A. Sports Club. It's where the *real* people work out."
She laughed as she spoke at the expense of the committers of
aerobicide in their sanitized, designer gyms, with their bonded teeth
and odorless sweat, their smooth, useless muscles.

Plutarch could see that. He could also see that Caroline and he were
the only people there, and that she was not a real person at all. She was
a fabulous prototype for some new and deeply wonderful form of
humanity, and there was no position in the world more exalted than
to be her servant.

Again he cleared a thickening throat. "Where is everyone?"

"They're not here." It meant "They won't be."

He swallowed hard when he heard both messages. She knew what
he was feeling. It was how it should be—the fear and the longing; the
deep dive in the adrenaline sea to find the mystery at the bottom; and

all the time the difficulty in breathing, the sensation of drowning in the saliva of your own anticipation.

"You want me, don't you, David Plutarch?"

She smiled at him cruelly, her mouth splitting open to show the glistening teeth. She put one hand on her hip and she thrust herself out toward him with all the haughty arrogance of the owner for the owned.

Again he could not face her, nor anymore could he speak. His head rose and fell in the hopeless gesture of assent.

"But if you want me you must work for me, musn't you?"

His furtive eyes said he didn't know. At last the billionaire knew nothing except that he would obey. Since the first day he had seen her it had been coming to this. Early on he had resisted. But her blitzkrieg assault had defeated him, and in her triumph and his debasement he had found a perverse joy. In the topsy-turvy world of sadomasochism he had discovered the dark secrets of his soul.

"Take off your coat and shirt," she commanded.

He dropped them on the filthy floor, the two-thousand-dollar suit jacket, the four-hundred-dollar Sulka silk shirt.

His stringy chest blinked beneath the neon half glow, ashamed of itself in this temple of gutter narcissism. In his mind he could see them, all the grunting, groaning pumpers, their sleek pudding biceps wet with their male juices, their round featureless steroid faces red with the heat of their pointless exertion. Would Bach or Handel play for them, or would they perform their self-love in soundless privacy?

Again he gulped back the nonexistent saliva from his throat. If they had been here, they would laugh at him and his apology for a physique. Or maybe they would be too self-obsessed for that, as they strutted by and showed him their greasy bodies and smiled smiles of satisfaction as they watched him watch them.

"Take off your shoes and socks."

Cole-Haan loafers, black silk knee-length Bijan socks, fell among the rest of the crumpled finery on the dingy floor.

"Over here," she said.

He shuffled behind her, his eyes glued to the swerving gluteal muscles, as she led him toward her objective. They passed posters of sculpted men, signed with cheerful, childish signatures, men whose jocks contained the minuscule appendages that alone they couldn't exercise. They passed notice boards full of cheap messages about cheaper apartments and worthless things for sale. They passed racks of dumbbells and gargantuan weights, and all the time they passed deeper into the conspiracy of minds that promised the alien communion of bodies.

She had reached her destination. She turned to face him. Both hands behind her, her face alight with the exhilaration of her power, she undid the buckles of her belt, letting it clatter to the floor. She filled her lungs, inflating the upturned triangle of her phenomenal torso, and she flexed her legs and rose up on tiptoe in the pose of a bodybuilder, her muscles rippling and bulging with the effort. She reached for the shoulder straps of the one-piece body suit, pulling down one and then the other, and then she swept them away in a single movement and her breasts stood there unveiled, gleaming white in the gloom, the vast circular areolae surrounding tense, spiked nipples.

His eyes bulged and his bare chest shuddered with the uneven rhythm of his breathing. His hands flicked by his side, wanting to move toward her.

"No!" she commanded quietly.

She pushed the black material down, revealing the vertical slash of her belly button, the scarcely believable evidence of her humanity. Then it was her hips, her lower stomach, the tantalizing borders of her blond pubic hairs. There she stopped, and she watched him, as he prayed for her final act.

Her voice was softly deadly. "This is what you want, isn't it? This is what you dream of."

He reached for her, unable to stop himself.

"Don't *touch* me." Her voice cut like a knife. His hovering hands fell back.

She stepped aside. Behind her the black leather platform stretched up from the floor at a forty-five-degree angle. At its top end a heavy leather strap lay unbuckled.

"Get onto the platform."

He hurried to obey. Face upward, head downward, he lay flat on the sloped bench. She moved toward its top end and, looping the strap across his ankles, she fastened the buckle around his legs, pulling it tight so that he couldn't move below the waist.

"Sit up," she commanded.

It was easy the first time. David Plutarch tensed his abdominal muscles and hauled himself up against gravity to a sitting position. But he couldn't see her anymore. She was somewhere behind his head, and he wanted so very much to see. . . . He twisted around.

"Lie down," she barked. "Then sit up. Do it till I tell you to stop."

Down he went, and up again, and down and up and up and down, until slowly but surely the muscles in his stomach began to complain. His smooth movements became more jerky, as the lactic acid built in his tissues and the merely uncomfortable merged into pain as his breathing speeded and his motion slowed.

"I have . . . to rest . . ." he grunted.

"Go ON!"

On. He had to do it. She commanded it. In the eyes of his mind he could see her, naked, magnificent, the extraordinary heart of her so near to him, so far. Red-hot pokers jabbed into his abdomen, and the impossible fullness throbbed between his legs as he prayed to be allowed to rest.

At last his strength had gone. He lay still.

"I'm sorry, I can't do any more," he murmured.

Caroline Kirkegaard stepped forward. She spun around and she backed up until her legs straddled Plutarch's resting head. Her crotch was directly above his staring eyes, maybe three feet above them, maybe more.

The vision exploded into his mind, banishing all thoughts of comfort or pain. The cruel predicament nipped him tight in the vise of its paradox. At long last she had given him the gift he had always dreamed of at the precise moment his body was all but incapable of accepting it. "If you want me you must work for me," she had said. Now he knew what she had meant.

Above him was the prize. In his body there was a new power; in his heart there was a wild joy. So he screamed to himself, and the reserves of strength uncoiled, and the muscles that had died were reborn in the reincarnation of passion.

Very slowly, like a pale ghost rising at midnight from an exposed grave, David Plutarch rose up from the black leather of the bench. His mouth was open, and his hungry tongue darted in the dryness, as his head arched toward the nirvana that lived between Caroline Kirkegaard's legs.

TWENTY-ONE

A larm bells were ringing. They blared in Paula's mind as they summoned her up from the depths of sleep. She surfaced by stages, and the anxiety faded, to be replaced by irritation. Because it was only the telephone. She tried to focus her thoughts. Some idiot had disobeyed her standing instructions and put through a call to her bedroom in the middle of the night. It was a firable offense unless the hotel itself was on fire, or worse . . . whatever that might be.

She screwed up her eyes and tried to focus on the luminous dial of the Braun travel clock. Five to midnight. Great! Brilliant! Which particular well-drilled soldier of the switchboard had chosen this particular hour of the night to go crazy? She reached for the phone. It seemed like the only way to stop it.

"Paula!"

Oh God, not him. Not now! Not all over again. *Woof,* away went the bottom of her stomach. *Wham,* went the anguish and the excitement in her brain. *Pow,* the bat punch to the small of the back and all the other crazed, disorienting feelings that went by the name of shock.

"Who is it?" As if she didn't know, but she needed precious time. Was he about to scream at her all over again? Accuse her of stealing his staff? What did he want, in the middle of the godforsaken night when only bad things happened and bad vibrations vibrated? There was a shortage of air in her lungs as she practiced her counterwrath, and the insects banged up against each other in her floorless guts. You fucking bastard, was all she could think, why were you so beautiful to love?

"It's me, Robert."

It didn't sound angry, the silken pseudovoice that belonged in the junkyard where they crushed the secondhand hearts. It sounded friendly, this voice of the man who had no friends—only enemies and lovers.

"What is it, Robert?" In her voice there was the wariness of the abused child, and her tone was soft, too soft to be wise, in the face of cruel experience.

"I'm at Cedars-Sinai. I've just talked to Graham."

"Graham? You can't. He's in a coma." It came out like an excited question.

"He just talked to me. He talked to me, and he died."

Robert on the telephone. Graham dead. At five to midnight and out of the blue in the blackness.

"Wait! Wait, Robert, what are you saying?" Graham had died. He had talked to Robert. Robert was calling her. What had Graham *said*?

"Paula . . . I don't know what to do. . . . I mean, I didn't believe you. I'm so terribly sorry."

Oh, what?! Thank you, God, for so little so late. Too late, when love had gone, when it didn't matter anymore. Thank you, Robert, for calling me a crippled hooker and throwing me out of your life when I worshiped you and wanted to live with you forever.

Thank you, Graham, for your belated decency. Damn you for dying, and leaving me alone like all the others.

Her tears came fast; a bubble of grief had burst in her.

"Oh, Robert. Oh, Robert."

She curled up around the phone like a baby in the womb as she hovered on the brink of a new life.

"Paula. Paula. Don't cry. I'm sorry. I'm so terribly sorry. He told me everything. That what you said was true. That he loved you. He heard you once, talking to the doctor, but you didn't know he could hear. He wanted to die without telling me because he wanted me to hate you, and you to hate me. But he heard you, that day. It made the difference." His voice hurried on, eager not to be cut off.

At Paula's end of the telephone there were just the sobs—just the wild hope—just the frantic anger.

"Paula. Listen to me. Don't cry. Please don't cry."

Can you forgive me? He would ask that now. In the movies he would ask that as the housewives wept and the teeny-boppers drooled and everyone wanted to forgive the man who had been given everything, but who had been born with a shriveled heart.

"Can you forgive me, Paula? Could you ever . . ."

"Oh, Robert, shut up. Shut UP!"

A helpless rage burst from her. Why? Because she loathed him. Because now she was an L.A. woman with the instincts of Attila, and God help the stragglers on the long march through the enemy territory of life. Oh yes? Oh really? Was she ever? Why did she want him to shut up? Because he was inside her again. Because he had never left. Because she could see at last that she no longer belonged to herself. She belonged to him.

He knew that. Somehow he knew.

"I must see you. I must say I'm sorry. I must . . ."

All those things he must do, and what must *she* do? Forgive him? Love him again? Marry him?

"Robert, I don't know . . ."

"Can I come over now?"

"No! I'm asleep. I mean, I'm in bed. . . ."

"Then tomorrow morning. Can I come to the Madrid? Can I come at nine? I must see you, Paula. I can't live with this. . . ."

Her whole body was in flames, but her voice was cold as charity. "Robert," she said, "you threw me out of your life once before. Now get the hell out of mine."

And she put the telephone down on the man she loathed, as the tears tumbled down her cheeks for the man she loved.

Robert prowled the lobby of the Château Madrid as if it were the dangerous no-man's-land between the trenches of the future and the blood-soaked emotional dugouts of his past. All around him was the success that spelled the failure of the Sunset—the beautiful people, the low-pitched hum of excitement, the rare combination of opulence and superb taste—but he hardly noticed it. He was thinking of Paula. She had refused to see him. He was here to change her mind. But why should she? Why should she change her mind about a harebrained Othello; a little boy lost inside the movie armor full of the sound and fury that signified nothing but the wounds of a tortured childhood, and the devastation of a world without parental love? What momentous event had occurred to make Paula forgive him? He had merely taken the spectacles of jealousy from the famous bedroom eyes. That was all. Nothing else. And with that she was supposed to roll over like an innocent puppy and pretend that the horrible words had never been spoken, that the dreadful behavior had never been behaved. He swallowed nervously as he thought of her pride, of her strength, of her screw-you arrogance when she was treated unfairly or underestimated. They were the things he loved about her. They were the part of her he knew best. They were the bits that threatened to wreck the delicate machinery of his feelings all over again.

He looked at his watch. It was five to nine. Five, possibly, to Paula. Five to a future he hardly dared to hope for. Five to a rejection that he hadn't the strength to face a second time.

He stalked over to the Château Madrid newsstand and picked up a magazine, staring at it intently without the faintest idea what he was seeing. Almost immediately he slammed it down, and his hunted eyes darted around the lobby. The reception desk, discreetly hidden from general view behind a dense bank of simple white daisies, was directly across from him. He took a deep breath and he walked toward it.

The charcoal-gray-suited assistant manager looked up as he approached. "Good morning, Mr. Hartford, sir." He had recognized him instantly.

"Morning. I'd very much like to see Ms. Hope," said Robert. His voice was as casual as he could make it. He'd never realized that acting could be so useful.

"Is she expecting you, sir?"

Robert's heart sank as he ran into the brick wall of a superbly trained male employee.

"Not exactly," said Robert.

"If you don't mind I'll just check with Ms. Hope, sir." He picked up the telephone.

Robert leaned nonchalantly against the desk. He eyed the elevator bank, and he wondered where the stairs were. Should he make a dash for it, like a groupie at a pop concert darting past the cordon to get where he wanted? He peered at the ceiling. Closely he observed the floor.

"Ms. Hope? Jenkins. Front desk. I have Mr. Robert Hartford here to see you. He doesn't have an appointment."

Jenkins smiled a reassuring smile at Robert as he spoke. He was simply playing it by the book. It had not occurred to him for a single second that his boss wouldn't see Robert Hartford, appointment or no appointment. This was, after all, Hollywood.

A puzzled expression replaced the smile. Ms. Hope had answered, but she wasn't answering. "Miss Hope?" he said.

Robert looked away. He couldn't bear this. He fought back the desire to snatch the phone and lay down the law about the seeing of Robert Hartford when he wanted to be seen.

The smile-turned-puzzled, now became puzzled-turned-anxious. "You'd like him to wait?" he repeated in the tone of voice that suggested that he had either misheard or misunderstood. "Here in the lobby?" He flicked an uncertain glance at the back of Robert Hartford's head. In this town Robert Hartfords did not wait, and if, as the result of some monumental screw-up, waiting was required, it did not, repeat not, take place in public. The movie star would now walk straight out of the Château Madrid. It would be unlikely that he would ever set foot in it again.

But Robert Hartford did not walk. He turned around to confront the astonished employee, and he smiled one of his laziest smiles.

"I'll wait," he said. "Did Ms. Hope say how long?"

"I'm certain not long, sir. Are you sure you'll be all right there on the sofa? Can I get you anything to read, sir? Is your transport being taken care of . . ."

Even in his state of internal confusion Robert took time out to admire the performance of the Madrid front desk man. The solicitous attention, the polite efficiency, the determination not to give offense. The word *transport* was itself a work of art, covering everything from a self-driven Lamborghini, via a chauffeur-driven limo, to a bicycle. This was the way staff should behave, and Robert knew the blood, toil, sweat, and tears it must have cost Paula to achieve it. Paula, who was making him wait; who, right this minute, was trying to make up her mind whether or not to see him; who held his future in the palm of her hand, as he had once held hers.

He wandered over to the sofa, and he sat down as the horrified eyes of the assistant manager followed him. He took a deep breath and the old saying flashed into his mind, Everything comes to he who waits. It had *not* been his experience of life.

Paula sat behind the vast desk that usually made her feel very big, and she felt very, very small. She was a child once more after all the tragedies that had turned her into a bona-fide grownup. She rearranged the pencils, fiddled with the blotter, flicked the switch of the dictating machine. On. Off. On again. She stared out of the big picture window in the search for inspiration, but Los Angeles, as always, had troubles of its own and provided no answers to the questions she was asking. What should she think? What should she feel? What in God's name should she *do*? The sleepless night hadn't

helped, and, on the two or three occasions when she had managed to
drop off, neither had the dreams. They had been a docudrama of her
life so far, and they had left a legacy of total confusion. Prosecuting
counsel and defense attorney had argued the case of Robert Hartford
before the jury of her heart and the jury of her brain. Both verdicts
were on the table. Not guilty. Guilty. It made sentencing impossible,
abstension the only possible course. But how did you pass on the
grand passion of your life?

She dipped her head into her hands and she looked at her watch. It
was twenty minutes since she had told them to tell him to wait. Would
he still be there, in the dock of the court? Would he be fuming
deliciously in his unaccustomed dilemma, smoking like a trout as
some poor penance for the agony he had caused her? She brightened
at the thought. The bastard! The stuck-up, insensitive bastard, with his
slimy sexuality and his box of cheap sensual tricks! He had elevated
self-love to a fine art form. He was obsessed with himself, lost in the
ultimate affair, as he compacted lovers like used cars and sold them off
for scrap. Was he still there? The string pulled at her heart, and again
the trapdoor opened in her belly. Had he left already? She had to
know. The telephone would tell her.

"Is he still there, Jenkins?" she whispered as if afraid Robert might
overhear.

"Yes, but I think he's getting a little impatient, madam."

Robert Hartford was no longer impatient. Ten minutes ago he had
been that. Now he was angry, and it was getting worse. He crossed and
uncrossed his legs, and he stared around the lobby, murdering with his
eyes anyone who dared to catch them. He arched his long neck and he
clenched his fists as he fidgeted against the rich upholstery of the
Tower-designed sofa. This was deliberate. He was being punished, and
although on paper maybe he deserved it, the reality was totally
unacceptable. He was a grown-up man. Paula was a grown-up
woman. Misunderstandings should be settled in an adult fashion. This
was puerile. When he saw her he would say so to her face before he
made his formal apology—if, indeed, one was technically needed.
Once again he looked at his watch. Half an hour. He had actually
been sitting there, on public display, doing nothing, for half a whole
hour! If she was going to see him, why make him wait? If. The word
ran around like a rabbit in his mind. If. What if she *wouldn't* see him?
What then?

He jumped up. He sat down. Damn her! He was furious. She had misunderstood him. This was not the way to treat Robert Hartford. If she thought that then she didn't begin to know him.

Jenkins called out across the twenty-foot space.

"Ms. Hope will see you now, sir. You press P in the elevator, sir. I'm sorry you've been kept waiting."

The bell of the elevator sounded like a siren in Paula's mind. She stood up. She could feel him near. Not since the Coriarchis' party had she seen him in the flesh, but she had seen him in her dreams. He had played every role, from sadistic lover to gentle child-man. He had been tender and soft and his hands had played her until her body had cried out and she had awakened in soaked sheets to hear her own voice repeating his name as wakefulness banished the blissful illusion. He had been hard and vicious, foul-mouthed as he insulted her, and she had wept in her sleep as she had learned to loathe the one she had loved, and on waking, her fists tight with anger, she had vowed vengeance in the darkness on the man who had so capriciously given, and then taken away, her happiness. She had been sorry for him, feared him, laughed with him, made love to him, but she had never been indifferent to him. And there had never been anyone else—that, too—neither before nor after her life's one and only love.

She smoothed down the material of the Yves Saint Laurent navy-blue pencil skirt, and she took a deep breath as she tried to prepare for him. In seconds the doorbell would ring, and she would say, "Who is it?" and he would say, "It's me, Robert." That was all she knew.

When the doorbell rang, she said nothing. She simply walked across the room and she opened the door.

He charged into the room, pushing past her, not looking at her.

"I've been waiting in that lobby for the best part of an hour," he said.

"Maybe you'd like to go down and wait a little longer until you get yourself into a better mood," she replied.

The anger flashed in her eyes as she turned to face him. The irritation pulsed in his as he turned to confront her.

"I don't wait in lobbies."

He threw back his head in defiance and he stared straight at her, and it was there that she could see the change in him, in his dear, wonderful eyes. The light had gone from them. They were wounded eyes, defeated eyes. They had always been the gateways to his soul. Before they had danced to the music of desire, and they had been straight, no-nonsense eyes that flashed danger and demanded respect as they had gazed into the heart of her. Once they had beamed power and mastery, but she had taught them how to transmit love and tenderness, and how to be vulnerable. Now they were the sorrowing eyes of a man who had sinned against her but mostly against himself. And they were the eyes of a man who didn't know how to say sorry.

"I do apologize for keeping you waiting, Robert Hartford. I hadn't been expecting you."

Her words were heavy with sarcasm, but there was the beginning of a smile on her face. She was winning. She was in control. Of herself. Of him. Somehow that mattered more than anything.

His head flicked down, unable to hold her gaze. Then he looked up again, and he ran his hand through his hair in the gesture that signaled his acute unease. "I came to say sorry," he said. "I had to see you to say it. To say it to you directly . . . I mean."

"Oh . . . it was nothing, really." Paula flung out a dismissive hand and the laughter was almost there in the words, as her smile broadened.

He was thinner than he had been. God . . . she wanted to touch him. That *was* what she wanted.

He looked puzzled by her reaction. Where was the stream of abuse, the tears, the recrimination? Where were all the tricks of the feminine armory, the ones he knew how to neutralize so effortlessly? She seemed to be treating him as if he were a joke.

"Maybe I shouldn't have come. Maybe . . ." But her face had filled up his mind and siphoned the breath from his lungs. The curves of her body swept through his brain, and the scent of her, jasmine fresh, wafted into his soul. In his ears he could hear the howls of her desire and his arms could feel all the shuddering surrenders as their bodies had bathed in the liquid union of flesh. There was nothing else but those memories, nothing else but the desperate necessity for the past to become the future, to become the present.

"Robert!" It was her invitation.

"Paula," his voice was husky in its acceptance.

"Come here," she said.

She lay across him, hot and wet, in the blissful interlude before the glory began all over again. Her blond hair lay across her sweat-soaked forehead, and she rested her cheek on his. He closed his eyes and he breathed in deeply, taking the wild scent of her deep within him, feeding from it, drinking it, loving it in the lungs that were so close to his heart. Robert's fingers traced the moisture on her cheek.

"I love you, little girl," he murmured, his voice the gentlest caress, softer, lighter than the pressure of his flesh against her face.

In answer she crushed her leg closer to his and she breathed out, fanning him with her warm breath. She reached down beneath the back of his neck and drew his wonderful face toward her, watching it closely like a connoisseur the finest of fine paintings.

He opened his eyes, unable any longer not to see her.

"Oh, Robert!" The love light in her eyes gave his name all the eloquence in the world, and the long, shuddering sigh of satisfaction rolled from her.

" 'Oh, Robert', what?"

"I love you."

He smiled his own satisfaction. How little minds knew. How much bodies did.

"A year just disappeared." He rolled over onto one elbow, leaving his legs entangled in hers, and the fingers that had drawn on the wetness of her face traced the graceful line of her naked breast.

"One year, and three months, and two days," she said with a rueful smile.

"I knew that, too." He laughed as he became the competitor in the love game. He *had* known that.

"But it didn't disappear for Winty. It didn't disappear for Kristina." She looked away from him as if to break the spell of his body. They had made love. Soon they would have to talk.

The frown flew across his face. "You heard about Kristina."

"I think everybody did. What did Caroline Kirkegaard *do* to her?"

"God, I don't know. Kristina was always easily influenced, but I think Caroline had been working on her for ages. She took me to a Destiny meeting in the Sunset once and I was so appalled I got Livingstone to ban them. Kirkegaard was always evil. I just hadn't realized how powerful she was."

"I love Kristina. Isn't there anything we can do? Anything I can do?"

"I don't think so. She won't speak to me. I've written. I've called. I've even tried to get to her at the Sunset. There's no way. The place is like Fort Knox, and apparently Kristina has round-the-clock bodyguards. If I could just see her, maybe I could make a difference. . . ." His voice trailed off uncertainly. "Maybe not."

"God, how awful for you. How awful for her."

"*She* doesn't think so. She's got that Destiny stuff up to her eyeballs. She's just not my daughter anymore. She was the only person I had. . . ."

Paula clung close. But not anymore. Now you have me again. Now I have you.

"We might not be able to get to Kristina, but we can get to Caroline

Kirkegaard. *I* can get to her. It would be the easiest thing in the world."

"To do what?"

"I don't know. Just to check her out. To find out about Kristina. Anything. Something. God knows what she might say."

"She's hardly likely to talk freely to the girl I'm going to marry."

Paula smiled fondly down at him. That was the second time he'd said it with his lips. The thousandth time in the lifetime of this morning's lovemaking that he'd said it with his body.

"But she doesn't know about this morning, does she?" said Paula. "I've hardly had time to know about it myself."

Caroline Kirkegaard stood up, towering above the pink-clothed table, and everyone in the Star Room at the Sunset Hotel turned to look at its new owner. They had been sneaking glances at her from the moment she arrived, but she had been half hidden by the flowers, and the folded copy of the *Wall Street Journal* that for some extraordinary reason she appeared to be reading. Now that she was upright, it was all there to see, the bits of the channeler that the Chanel didn't cover, the powerful scent of power floating out into the room to merge with that of the bagels and bacon, the hash-browns and the steaming coffee.

She put out her hand and flashed a warm smile of greeting. "Welcome back to the Sunset Hotel," she said. "I hope that the memories aren't too painful."

Paula took her hand. "Times pass, times change," she said. And then with a half smile. "People come. People go."

Caroline laughed, as the waiters hovered and the maître d' pulled out the table to allow Paula to sit down.

"We never really got to know each other, did we, Paula Hope? I hope we can change that now." Her tongue snaked out to moisten already moist lips, and she placed both her hands on the table in a gesture that said they contained no hidden cards.

"Coffee, madam?"

She nodded briskly.

"I apologize for the present sorry state of the hotel. Not up to the Château's high standards, I'm afraid, but we will put that right. Poor Robert had let things go. And dear Kristina lacked experience."

Caroline floated the bait over the water. Two names. What would be the reaction? It was common knowledge that Robert Hartford had thrown Paula out and broken her heart, and the popular wisdom was that she had never forgiven him for it.

Whatever her feelings she had certainly wreaked a poetic revenge. She had built the Château into the best hotel in Los Angeles and she had humiliated Robert Hartford and his beloved Sunset in the process, stealing his staff, hijacking his guests, and raping his reputation. It was difficult to believe that she had any feelings for him now but contempt, but in this life you could never be sure. Then there was Kristina. Paula and she had been friends, but the friendship had faded after the breakdown of Paula's engagement to her father. Later, running two competing establishments, they had been rivals but, according to Kristina, never enemies. What did Paula feel about Kristina now, and Kristina's close relationship with Caroline and Destiny? During the course of breakfast she would find out.

She looked carefully into Paula's eyes. It was important not to misread them.

"Never underestimate the egos of movie stars. Never overestimate their intelligence," said Paula.

There was a glint in the younger girl's eyes as she spoke. Caroline saw it. The words had a sharp edge, and Paula's tongue curled around them as her lips enjoyed the mouthing of them.

"Yes, he's made a terrible mess of the Sunset. There are horror stories of his behavior here. The staff couldn't wait to get rid of him."

Again the Kirkegaard eyes zeroed in for the wince of pain in Paula's that would ring alarm bells, but there was just the spark of flint, hard and cold and cruel.

"It's funny, isn't it," said Paula. "I was devastated when he broke off the engagement, but, looking back on it, it was the best thing that ever happened to me. I mean, the Château and Winty leaving me all his money, and Tower Design . . ." She looked out across the room, the smile on her face Cheshire-cat wide, as she savored her good fortune.

Caroline watched her, almost convinced. Once again she floated the bait. "Do you remember that time I was having dinner with him and you caught him in the middle of one of his ridiculous passes. You were furious, but so was I. I was *dying* to experience his technique. You know, it would have been a bit like playing tennis with Steffi Graff!"

Caroline laughed as she joked, but there was a wistful look in her eye.

Paula laughed too. "You didn't miss much. Mostly it was done with mirrors."

"And Robert peering into them, I imagine." Caroline giggled.

All around the room the necks craned and the ears flapped to discover what two hundred million dollars' worth of feminine beauty had found so funny.

"God, if Robert could hear this conversation, he'd die. He'd just die." Paula laughed through tear-filled eyes.

"We'd better send him a tape." Caroline giggled again.

Gradually the laughter subsided.

"Goodness," said Caroline. "I haven't laughed so much since that movie he did—do you remember—the one when he was an angel, and somebody had told him to put on a British accent because they wouldn't speak English with an American accent in heaven?"

"You'd better believe I remember. I had to sit through all his old movies. That wasn't an accent, that was an accident!"

"Oh dear, you are funny, Paula."

"Well, *you* certainly had your revenge on Robert," said Paula. "How on earth did you persuade Kristina to give you the shares?"

Caroline paused, with the successful person's suspicion of a question that required an answer. She seemed to debate whether to deflect it. "You don't really understand about Destiny, do you?" she said at last.

"Not really." Paula sounded only marginally interested.

Caroline leaned forward, the convivial lunch partner no more. Her eyes sparkled with a wild enthusiasm, and she was suddenly charged with energy. "It's my dream. It's all our dreams. It should be yours, Paula. It can be, if you let it. Destiny is all there is, and some day the world will know it. It's why I wanted this hotel, to act as its headquarters, to use its reputation to spread the message to those who do not yet know the truth. Kristina opened her eyes to her Destiny. It was easy. I showed her how."

Her hand snaked across the table and caught Paula's arm. "I can show you," she breathed.

Paula could feel Caroline's strength throbbing against her skin.

She said nothing, anxious not to provide ammunition for the charms of the sorceress. She felt stripped of her resolve in the disturbing currents of power that had been so dramatically unleashed. There was no need to question anymore what had happened to Kristina. This had. She fought to concentrate, and she muttered to herself a mantra to protect herself from the swirling might of the wickedness that was alive in the room. Don't listen to this crap. Don't think about it. Don't even try to understand it.

"Women can do anything," whispered Caroline Kirkegaard. "We are so strong. We can join in the sisterhood of Destiny and the world will worship at our feet. Kristina understands that. You could, beautiful Paula."

"In a way, that was what I wanted to talk to you about." Paula forced out the words, knowing that she was not supposed to speak. The sound of her voice cut into the wave of hypnotic vibrations that threatened to engulf her. The shock registered in the Kirkegaard eyes. Paula could actually see the confusion as she lost the mesmeric concentration and the spell she was casting began visibly to fall apart.

But Caroline recovered quickly. She sat back in her seat, and her hand moved away from Paula's arm as the fires that had burned in her eyes began to dim.

"You had a reason for seeing me?" asked Caroline.

Paula tried to keep her voice matter-of-fact. Slowly, the other-worldly atmosphere of mystical coercion began to fade.

"Oh, it was nothing specific, but I just thought we ought to meet, and open up the lines of communication. I know the Sunset's been having problems, and I have to admit that I caused some of them, but I want you to know that's over now. Robert's Sunset isn't the same as your Sunset, Caroline. Okay, we're still rivals, but there's more than enough business for both of us. I just wanted to signal to you that from now on I'm happy to play softball rather than hardball. I mean, no poaching. No dirty tricks. Just straightforward, honest competition."

"I hoped you'd say that. I thought you would, but I wasn't certain. Kristina maintains you were never aiming at her." Caroline's tone was conversational. Her disturbing flexing of psychic muscles was apparently forgotten.

"I always liked Kristina. I have nothing against her. Or you," said Paula. "We should all be friends. If you want any help with design or running things, I wouldn't say no. You just have to ask, although I sense that you'll have it all back together in no time. That's what I wanted to say. We can help each other. For instance, the guy that heads up your computerized accounts department, Ferris, I think his name is, is talking to the Four Seasons. If he goes to them he'll probably take your programs, and he'll almost certainly raid your client list. I'd ax him, and get your attorneys to frighten him in the process."

"How did you know that?" Caroline's voice was sharp.

"You hear things. In this business everyone knows everything. Pretty soon you'll know things like that. Hang around the bar. Talk to the waiters. Listen to the gossip. That way you get to do things to people rather than have them do things to you."

Caroline simmered quietly inside. Ferris. She didn't even know the asshole's name but already she hated him. But there was another cause for irritation. She, Caroline Kirkegaard, whose enemies always perished in eternal flame, had taken a dent in her reputation. Paula had appeared tougher and more efficient than she.

"People who cross me live to regret it," she said ominously. "Francisco Livingstone would have told you that."

Paula didn't react, but she seemed to be listening . . . just. Caroline felt the humiliation rise within her. The younger girl would be thinking "talk is cheap"—something like that. Already she had showed considerable strength in resisting the Kirkegaard influence.

"Or should I say, die to regret it," added Caroline Kirkegaard.

"Yes, poor old Livingstone really went out the way he wanted to. I wonder what the hell he was doing in the bath to make him blow a fuse. Something pretty kinky, I expect. The old fart was into that," said Paula.

Caroline's face went knowing. "Let's just say," she said, "that it was a thoroughly sticky end. You have my word on that."

Paula cocked a quizzical head to one side, as Caroline beamed the telepathic message across to her. Don't underestimate me, said the Kirkegaard eyes. I'm lethal. I can be deadly. I have been. I will be.

"The old pervert got what was coming to him," said Paula at last. "He and Robert deserved each other."

"I expect they used to compare notes on young girls," said Caroline Kirkegaard, and her eyes swept speculatively over Paula as once again the unsettling tongue snaked out to wet her glistening lips.

TWENTY-TWO

et me get this absolutely straight, Robert. You and Ms. Hope are telling me that Caroline Kirkegaard had Francisco Livingstone murdered and you want me to arrest her for it."

The Beverly Hills police chief watched the movie star carefully as he summarized the story. He hadn't been at all prepared for what he had just been told. He had met Hartford once or twice before, and when he, and Paula Hope, the young and trendy owner of the Château Madrid, had asked to see him urgently he had jumped at the opportunity for a little mutual back scratching. Robert's political clout and his legendary fundraising abilities could help the police department in all sorts of different ways.

But Caroline Kirkegaard was also a somebody. What's more, she was a close friend of David Plutarch, who was friends with senators, and judges, and whose money meant that he could be friends with anybody . . . or their enemies. This whole thing would have to be handled with the greatest care. Already it was beginning to look like a "no win" situation for him. Who to offend? This heavy hitter, or that one.

Hartford seemed to be enjoying the role of D.A. He leaned forward emphatically toward the old policeman's desk, adjusting and readjusting the horn-rimmed glasses around the bridge of his nose in a gesture that emphasized the steel-blue eyes behind them. "No, Antonio, we're not saying that. What we're saying is that there may be probable cause here. Kirkegaard had the motive. She couldn't have known about Livingstone's will, and she knew he was implacably opposed to her buying his hotel. With Livingstone dead, and myself unable to complete the contract I had signed, she and Plutarch knew that the estate would fall over itself to sell the hotel to them. Now, on top of motive, we have Caroline Kirkegaard's intimation to Ms. Hope that she was responsible for Livingstone's death. Ms. Hope will sign a deposition regarding that. What we're asking for is an autopsy. There was no postmortem done on Livingstone. He was ill. He died in the bath. Natural causes were assumed, not proven. Now I think there is new evidence that justifies digging him up."

"You want me to ask for Livingstone to be exhumed, and a forensic investigation carried out on his body."

"That's *exactly* what we want."

The police chief looked at him doubtfully. Then at Paula. Then at the hangnail that had been irritating him all morning. "Isn't it a bit much to ask anyone to believe that a person like Ms. Kirkegaard would have someone murdered just so that she could buy his hotel?"

His words carried absolutely no conviction. In L.A. a dented car was a reason for murder. The Bloods and the Crips gunned down innocents in the street because they didn't like the color of their clothes. Gang violence was altering life-styles, even in Beverly Hills.

"Chief, I wish I could explain to you the kind of person she is," Paula said. "You can feel the evil in her. You can almost touch it. And the disgusting thing is it's actually attractive. You're drawn toward the rocks by the siren music. Look at the way she's taken over Robert's daughter. Your department must have had hundreds of complaints from the families of that Destiny cult she runs. She told me she'd killed Livingstone. She as good as spelled it out."

Terrlizese nodded. It was true there had been complaints about Destiny. Nothing dramatic, but they added up to a minor irritation. "Tell me again what she said. *Precisely* what she said."

"Well, I can't remember the precise words, but she said, 'I promise you he met a sticky end.' And before that she had said 'People who cross me live to regret it,' and then she changed the 'live to regret it' to 'die to regret it.' But it was the *way* she said it, the expression on her face, the wicked glee. If you'd been there you'd have arrested her on the spot."

"You see, Ms. Hope, you can't use this evidence. She'll deny it, or she'll say she was joking and you took it the wrong way. Or she could say that it was just bravado. You know, she was trying to impress you with what a macho lady she is . . . you both being competitors in the hotel business."

He smiled carefully, not letting too much patronization out, but he was rather pleased with his speech. It had the virtue of being true, and it should go a long way to making them see that this was a long shot, hardly worth the trouble, certainly not worth the trouble he could be in if he irritated someone like Plutarch.

Robert put out a hand and rested it on Paula's knee, in a let-me-handle-this gesture. "Of course," he said, "nobody's going to *object* to a Livingstone exhumation because there's no next of kin except those distant cousins in Pasadena, and Livingstone hardly knew them. You dig him up quietly and see what the pathologists come up with. If it's nothing, forget it, sorry, I owe you one. If not, then of course it would be your duty to investigate his murder." He emphasized the word *duty*.

The chief of the Beverly Hills Police Department had seen carrots and sticks before, but few so neatly disguised. He pushed his fingers together and he looked at Robert, at Paula, and at Robert again. "No next of kin," he said.

"Precisely," said Robert Hartford.

"Dig him up, cut him up, and stick him back if everything's kosher?"

"In a nutshell, and no front-page ads in the *Herald-Examiner*."

"Nobody would know," said Terrlizese to himself.

"Except us, and we . . ."—he paused dramatically—"would be eternally grateful." Terrlizese allowed himself to dream of the Hartford/Hope gratitude. Dinners at the Château. His wife on the arm of the superstar at the odd premiere. The mayoral, the *presidential* candidate of the moment draped around Terrlizese's shoulders like a security blanket. Then there was the new police building in the grand Civic Center expansion on Santa Monica scheduled for completion in a year's time. Anything that could expedite *that* would be a help in getting him out of this inconvenient, makeshift office in City Hall. The new Charles Moore–designed police facility was going to be just about the most impressive building in Beverly Hills, as befitted a place where the liberal "haves" were more than usually interested in hanging on to what they'd got. More money would always be needed to get the Art Deco fountains to play, the mosaic tiles inlaid, the palm trees planted around the magnificent monument to law enforcement. Robert Hartford knew how the town worked. He wouldn't forget a favor. Kirkegaard and Plutarch could complain only if they were accused, and without the forensic evidence there would *be* no accusation. With it, they would be indicted murderers, and then it wouldn't matter what they felt.

"Well, Robert, it's not really 'by the book,' but from what you both say I think maybe we should have a look at poor old Livingstone. Of course the doctor who examined him at the time of death didn't smell a rat, but then he wasn't looking for one, was he?"

Robert stood up, and so did Paula. He put out his hand.

"Thank you, Antonio. I won't forget this. You've gone out on a limb for me. Let me know how I can do the same for you. Anytime. Anyplace. You'll keep me posted?"

"Yes, of course. By the way, where are you staying now? Not at the Sunset anymore."

"No, I've rented Rod Stewart's house in Bel-Air." He looked down, as several thoughts came to him at once. "Oh, and Antonio. No word of this to anyone. In particular I don't want people putting my name and Ms. Hope's together. Kirkegaard thinks we're hardly the best of friends. I want to keep it that way."

He smiled gently at Paula. Soon the world could know it all, and he would no longer live in a rented home. Together, he and Paula would march in triumph into the Sunset.

"How long does it *take?*"

Exasperation was alive in Paula's voice as she paced the Mexican-tiled floor of the bedroom in Robert's rented Spanish-mission-style mansion.

"Terrlizese said we would hear something this morning. They did the postmortem late last night."

Robert lay back on the bed and watched her. How had he ever let her go? What, in the whole of his miserable life, had he ever done to deserve the second chance he had been given?

"I want her dead," said Paula. "I want to *be* the cyanide that crawls up her nose." The awful thought occurred to her. "They would gas her, wouldn't they?"

"With Plutarch's lawyers on her side? Forget it. They'll probably give her house arrest and community service." He laughed bitterly. "But that doesn't matter. Whatever happens, a guilty verdict would finish her. She'd have to do *some* time, and then we can get Kristina helped, and some judge to nullify the deed of gift on the Sunset shares. It would be easy to prove a convicted murderess used undue influence. My troubles would be over."

"I still want her dead. I had to sit through that lunch, Robert. I had to hear the things she said. I had to agree with them. I'll feel dirty about that forever. She's evil, you know. I've never met that kind of wickedness before . . . not even Seth Baker. . . ."

Robert sat up and the pain shot across his face, as he saw it pass across hers.

"Can you ever forgive me?" said Robert, and he got up and walked toward her, taking her hand.

"I forgave you," she said. "The other morning. Last night. Maybe twenty other times. I lost count." She smiled away the sadness as she joked with him. There had been so much sorrow, so much hatred.

Now there would be love, and more love, all the love in the world.

She walked over to kiss him, to make it twenty-one, but the telephone interrupted them.

Robert reached for it, motioning to Paula to pick up the extension.

"Robert? Antonio." The policeman's voice was excited. "Goddamn it, you were right! Cause of death, suffocation. No doubt about it, even after a year and a bit in the ground. And listen to this. The forensic team found traces of cyanoacrylate in the mouth, nostrils, and eyes. That's superglue."

"Superglue?"

"Yeah, isn't it incredible? It seems someone glued up his nose and mouth so he couldn't breathe."

Paula couldn't hold it back. "That's what she meant. She said it. That was what she meant by 'sticky end.' "

"That's wonderful, Antonio. So you arrest her and charge her. Have you done it already?"

There was silence.

"It's not quite as easy as that, Robert. My legal people are all over me now. There's no evidence to tie Kirkegaard to the murder, apparently. Her remarks to Paula just aren't enough. She'd walk out of a courtroom, and they could probably do my department for wrongful arrest. I'm afraid the very best we can do is keep her under surveillance, interview her. Maybe persuade her to confess . . ."

"She's not going to *confess*, Antonio! Christ, the woman has brass balls. I'd rather try to intimidate the Ayatollah. What the hell is this, Antonio? Is this some kind of a cover-up? I'm sorry. I didn't mean that. Forget I said that. But it's just that we're so close, and we all know she did it. . . ."

"Robert, I could give you the names of a hundred murderers walking the streets of L.A. right this minute, and I don't mean the ones on furlough. It's called living in a free country. She's not guilty until she's proven guilty in a court of law, and nobody cares what you or I 'know.' Don't blame me, blame all the bleeding-heart liberals. They do their bleeding in the corridors of power, while my officers are doing the real thing out on the streets."

"There must be some proof. We've just got to find it."

"That's the worst part of all. There is."

"There is, and that's the worst part? What the hell do you mean?"

"Well, obviously the killer cleaned him up after he'd croaked. They used a solvent to wipe away the evidence of the glue, and the forensic boys have found traces of that. But more important they've found a human hair in his nostril. A red one."

"A red one? But Caroline's hair is blond."

"And they found a blond hair under Livingstone's fingernail."

"Her assistant has red hair," said Paula, her voice bubbling with excitement.

"So do maybe a hundred thousand girls in Los Angeles," said Terrlizese. "That's most of the ones that aren't blond."

"And there's no way to identify the hair as positively belonging to Caroline and the girl who works for her?" Robert's voice was full of disappointment.

"Funnily enough, there is. It's a new technique that they've been using in England since 1985. It's called DNA fingerprinting. DNA forms the building blocks of the amino acids that make up the cells' protein. Identical twins have the same DNA structure. Nobody else does. The pathologists have a technique that can compare the DNA structure on two samples of tissue. If we could get one of Caroline's hairs, we could find out if it matched the hair beneath Livingstone's nail. Same with the girlfriend."

"And that evidence would stand up in court?"

"It's a definite 'maybe.' They convicted a rapist in Florida using the test late last year, and they've used it successfully in some paternity cases."

"It wouldn't matter that the hair's been in the ground all that time?"

"No, apparently not. Livingstone's coffin was lead lined, and DNA is tough stuff. They're using it to decide a ten-year-old rape case in Illinois. And anyway hair lasts longer than most body tissue. No, that's not the problem. The problem is that the D.A. won't have Kirkegaard arrested on the evidence so far obtained. I've argued it out with him, but he's adamant. Says he's not prepared to go up against Plutarch's girl. I think he's wrong, but it's his decision and he's made it. I'm very sorry."

"You're telling me that a sample of Caroline's hair would clinch it, but you can't ask her to provide a sample."

"I can ask but I can't get, without arresting her, and I'm not allowed to arrest her without more proof. It's Catch Twenty-two."

"Fuck Catch Twenty-two," said Robert, biting his tongue to avoid saying any more.

"I know you're disappointed. *I'm* disappointed, but that's the end of the story, I'm afraid."

"Like *hell* it is," said Robert as he slammed down the phone.

He looked helplessly at Paula. "How do we get a sample of Caroline Kirkegaard's hair?"

"Easy," said Paula. "We cut it off."

*   *   *

"You touch my hair and I'll sue your faggot ass from the Redwood forests to the Gulf Stream waters, okay?"

In the mirror, the Kirkegaard eyes flashed as a backup to the message, and behind her the hairdresser wilted like a waterlogged houseplant. The makeup girl, her brush poised in midair, froze.

"You, too, Kanga," added Caroline Kirkegaard loudly. "We agreed to turn up for a disease, not amateur night at a stylists' convention. When I want my hair cut I'll get someone to do it who thinks hair is something more than a way to get a part on 'Knots Landing.' "

Giles Ramillies put down the scissors and wished he hadn't bothered. It should have been the best. Paula Hope's AIDS fashion show at the Château Madrid had been a crimper's dream. The word had spread like wildfire all over town and every makeup artist, every stylist, every color person in Los Angeles had been waiting patiently for the summons that would be the ultimate sign of acceptance among the people who really mattered. AIDS was the hot ticket to the charity circuit. Everyone would say yes, nobody would dare to say no, and that was what had happened. The usual AIDS people were out in force, the Liz Taylors, the Richard Geres, and the newer people too, whose hot box office opened charity doors as well as movie ones—dirty dancer Patrick Swayze, fatally attractive Glenn Close, cheerful Kirstie Alley. But poor Giles had had the rotten luck to draw Caroline Kirkegaard and her sidekick, Kanga. The woman was a deadly weapon, pointed right at him.

"Miss Hope asked that we tidy up everyone's hair." He nearly bit off his tongue as he heard his own implication, that the Kirkegaard hair was untidy. It wasn't even true. The stark geometry of the sculpted cut was formidably neat. But his instructions from Paula had been quite clear—"tidy it up."

Quite suddenly Caroline Kirkegaard reached out and put her hand on the makeup artist's chin, and she pushed. The girl, paintbrush in one hand, blusher in the other, wasn't expecting it. The Kirkegaard fury had seemed to be aimed at the hapless barber. In the world of "beauty," makeup artists were distinctly inferior to hairdressers and were often treated as such, so she had been rather enjoying the discomfort of her "superior." Now, however, her head traveled about a foot at the end of Caroline Kirkegaard's palm and as a result she fell back, lost her balance, and fell in a heap to the floor.

"Fuck!" she said.

"Problems?" asked Paula sweetly from the doorway.

The makeup girl, her legs in the air, lay covered by a fine dust of highlighters, blushers, and powders from her upended tray. Ramillies was white as a sheet, his sensitive face contorted with the pain of the Kirkegaard insult. Kanga, pouting, sultry, sat quietly at the dressing table next to Caroline. The leader of the pack, cheered by the distress she had so comprehensively caused, beamed into the mirror at Paula.

"No problems," she said sweetly. "I just told the gay boy to lay off my hair. And I was tired with the princess fiddling around with my face like this was a movie set. How are you, Paula? You look good enough to eat."

Paula smiled easily, as she took in the scene. "You're right, Caroline. Your hair is just great as it is. Better than great. Who does it for you?"

"Dan Galvin from London. David sends the jet for him once a week."

Paula walked toward her and stood behind her, right up close, as the makeup artist, mumbling unmentionables, picked herself up off the floor.

"I'm so glad you could come, Caroline . . . and Kanga," she added as an afterthought. "I really wanted this gala to be special, and you've made it that."

"Well, AIDS is AIDS, but you are you," said Caroline. The meaning was unmistakable, and despite herself Paula felt her face reddening.

To cover her sudden confusion she introduced the girl who was standing by her side. "Caroline. I don't think you know my assistant. This is Greta. Greta, this is Caroline Kirkegaard, and this is her assistant Kanga."

"Hi," said Greta, but nobody bothered to look at her.

"How's it going, Paula?" Caroline asked. "Are the stars shining bright? Are the glitterati oiling their checkbooks? Are they all making block bookings in your hotel?"

Paula caught the drift. Charity in Hollywood was a two-way street. Apart from tax deductions there were other kickbacks, social advances, career opportunities, business deals. But she smiled to herself. Her ulterior motive was as far from the obvious as it was possible to be. "I wish they could," Paula laughed easily, "but I'm booked solid for months."

"Don't worry. My new Sunset will relieve some of your strain."

"I'm counting on it. Running this place is too much like hard work."

"You should meditate. It's a whole new world."

"You should teach me."

"Maybe I will."

Again the electricity crackled and Caroline smiled into the mirror—the special smile, the one that melted souls.

Paula found herself caught by the eyes. They seemed to bore inside her. They were enormously compelling and the feeling that came with them was above and beyond such words as *pleasant* and *unpleasant*. It was impossible to say whether the sensation was nice or nasty, far more difficult to determine whether it was good or bad. With an effort she tore her eyes away from Caroline's reflection, glad as she did so that the full force of her eyes was diluted by the glass. Was this what had unhinged Kristina, and the girl called Kanga, who had killed for her?

"Caroline, I think your hair looks out of this world, but I wonder if Kanga would object to having hers piled up a bit for our eighteenth-century theme. She wouldn't have to have much actually cut, would she, Giles, just the smallest bit off the back."

"Okay," said Caroline easily. "I guess I can live with that." She spoke as if Kanga didn't exist.

Paula motioned toward the chastened hairdresser to get on with it. "It's going to be a wonderful show," she said. "Valentino and Armani. Johnny doing the commentary. I can't believe that everyone got it together at such short notice."

"It's your charm," said Caroline. "You could make people do anything."

"Anything?"

"Anything."

Caroline spun around in her seat and the dressing gown she wore flipped open, as the naked breast, iceberg magnificent, sailed into glorious sight.

Paula swallowed despite herself. Nobody should underestimate this woman. She had the devil within her, with all his power, and all his charm, and all his consummate wickedness. "I'll bet," Paula laughed, "you wouldn't allow me to cut just one lock of your hair."

"For your locket?" smiled Caroline. The air was suddenly sprayed with the fine mist of supersexuality.

"Maybe," breathed Paula.

"Take some," said Caroline.

In slow motion Paula moved forward and picked up the scissors from the table. She came closer, and every millimeter that she advanced she felt the aura of Caroline Kirkegaard closing in on her. She had turned once more to the front and there were two breasts now, dazzling in their awesome symmetry. Paula struggled to remember her purpose.

"Just a little bit," said Paula to cover her sudden confusion.

Caroline watched her. She didn't find the request strange. In her life the strange had changed into the commonplace. She had but to get close to people, and the magic began to work. Now it was Paula Hope, beautiful, influential, and the ruler of the Château Madrid, the deadly rival to her Sunset Hotel. The girl with the swimming-pool eyes wanted a lock of her hair. Soon she would be wanting other things.

Snip.

"There!" said Paula with a giggle of embarrassment. "Here, Greta, will you look after that for me." She handed it to her assistant like it was the Holy Grail.

"Sure," said Sergeant Greta Kandinsky of the Beverly Hills Police Department.

"You have the right to remain silent . . ."

The uniformed officer was playing it by the book, and he was not alone. This wasn't just a straightforward homicide arrest. The deputy D.A. was there, and a police department doctor, and even the guy who handled publicity for the Beverly Hills P.D. It was only with difficulty that the ones who had them had resisted the temptation to bring their agents.

Kanga sat quite still, her face stricken but together. She didn't cry and she didn't plead. She just endured it as they read her Miranda rights and charged her with murder in the first degree. Well before they had charged her, they had searched her apartment and they had gone through her drawers, and her address books, and they had put everything loose into big cardboard boxes, but first they had enclosed everything in plastic, wearing rubber gloves as they did so. She had seen it coming like a tornado across a rough sea, but still she could think only of Caroline. If they knew about Kanga and her part in the Livingstone killing, then the chances were that they knew about Caroline, too. But how, after all this time, could they possibly know what had happened?

"You have the right to an attorney. . . ."

"Can I call my lawyer?" she said.

"You are allowed one call," said the policeman. "You can make it from here, or from headquarters. Whatever. And you say you have no knowledge at all of the whereabouts of Ms. Kirkegaard?"

"None," said Kanga. It was true. She didn't know where Caroline was. Usually she would be at Plutarch's house this time of the late evening, but the police and a battery of warrant-toting lawyers from the D.A.'s office had apparently checked it out. Already the dragnet was in operation, and the all-points bulletins would be burning up the wires and the airwaves, but so far Caroline was at large in the big city, almost certainly oblivious to the tragedy that was about to engulf her. Kanga fought to think calmly as the room went spinning round. She had one call. One chance to warn the woman she worshiped of what was about to happen. If only she could sound the alarm, then Caroline would know what to do.

One call. One try. Plutarch's house with its live-in legal department?

No, that would be wasted. The cops had been there. Plutarch, too, would be trying to alert Caroline. Then she remembered it. The car phone. The unlisted number that nobody else but she possessed. Was Caroline out there in the Mercedes somewhere? At nine o'clock at night? Hardly. But wait a minute. Tonight was the night of Emilio Steinbeck's dinner party at the Bel-Air hotel. Caroline had been invited by the New York agent because he was handling the auction of the sequel to her best-selling book, *March to Destiny*. It was just possible that she was running late. Perhaps this very second she was handing the keys of her car to the Bel-Air's valet parkers.

She leaped to the phone, not caring that the policeman at her shoulder took down the numbers as she punched them out.

For an age it rang, and then, at last, there was the irritable voice. "Yes?" barked Caroline Kirkegaard.

"It's Kanga."

"Christ, Kanga, I'm late for Emilio's party. What the hell is it?"

Kanga knew she hadn't much time. The cop at her elbow had all but climbed inside the telephone. "I'm being arrested for the murder of Francisco Livingstone," she blurted out. "The police are here now, and they're looking everywhere for you." She jammed the telephone down as they rushed at her.

"Did you get the number?"

"Yeah, Sarge. It's right here." The plainclothes cop started to punch frantically at digits.

"It's a cellular phone. Get a subscriber trace. It's probably her car. She's out there somewhere in a car. Feed it into the APB. Did they get a diary from the Plutarch house? Is there one here? She may have an engagement tonight. Find it, for chrissakes, don't just stand there."

He swung around to confront Kanga.

"Okay, wise-ass, you're deep in it, believe me. There's no holes in this case against you, or against Kirkegaard. You talk, you help me find her, and there's a good word in it for you. Hear what I'm saying?"

"Go fuck yourself," said Kanga.

Caroline Kirkegaard turned off the ignition, and she rolled up the window she had just rolled down. The small parking lot at the Bel-Air was full to the bursting point as the literary high rollers of Tinsel Town disgorged from their top-end cars for the Steinbeck dinner, and inside her car the telephone was still warbling. But she knew not to answer it anymore. Kanga's words had been shot from the barrel of a gun. Anybody else on the private line would be foe not friend.

It was quiet in the eye of her storm. Her mind ground on,

steamroller smooth, in the preanger, prepanic phase where there was only information, only facts. Kanga had been arrested for Livingstone's murder. So what. Kanga wouldn't implicate her if they stretched her on a rack. But there was an arrest warrant for her, too. That meant there was evidence against her, good evidence, the kind that could convict. It was then that the drums began to beat within her. Convicted of murder. Found guilty. Sentenced to die. At the very least all her dreams would vanish in the messy trial—Destiny, the power and the glory, the Sunset Hotel. She might be freed through the contortions of the lawyers, but she would never, ever again be free to be what she had to be, to become what she had to become.

It was all unraveling. At the moment when she had climbed every mountain and achieved every objective, her carefully constructed world was about to fall apart.

She looked down at her frilly dress, Lacroix on a roll. The frothy exuberance of it, the black tulle, the ballerina tutu frame for her world-without-end legs was the cruellest paradox in the universe. It was created with only joy in mind, and now she wore it while all the frustration and fury were boiling deep within the cavity where her heart had once been. Her instinct screamed at her. Robert Hartford was behind this. There was nobody else. Somehow he had found out about Livingstone. The body had been dug up, the cause of death determined, and the link between her and the murder somehow established. Her mind raced over the last few weeks. When had she ever mentioned the long forgotten Livingstone?

Paula! "A sticky end" she had bragged to the seemingly guileless girl. The meeting had been a fishing trip, and she had risen like a greedy novice to the bait. She and Paula had laughed at Robert Hartford in the easy conspiracy of the feminine wronged. But all the time Paula had been in Robert's camp, his lover once more, and she, Caroline, had dug the ditch that threatened to become her grave. The events of the last few days flashed before her. The fashion show, arranged at such short notice at the Château Madrid. Would dear Caroline and beautiful Kanga model the clothes to save the sick, and cement the friendship between the two most exotic hoteliers in the world? Could Paula, Robert Hartford's Paula, have a lock of her hair?

Such a business had been made of it. The hair. Hers. Kanga's. Yes, that was it. That must be it. The hair had in some way tied them to the murder. The New York Times had carried a story on it a while back. Body tissue of any kind could be identified like fingerprints. Science had undone the perfect crime.

She reached out and she turned the key in the ignition and the engine roared into life. Emilio Steinbeck wouldn't be getting a book on reincarnation after all. He would get another book. A far better book. A book called *Revenge*.

As she headed out onto Sunset Boulevard a plan was forming in her mind. One phrase ran through it like a theme song. It was everything, a symbol of all she had ever wanted, a sign of the totality of what she was. It represented the desires of those she hated. It would be the weapon of her retribution. It was all she could think about, filling up her brain, expanding like a balloon full of the vapor of loathing. The Sunset Hotel. The place she had longed for. The place she would destroy.

The Mercedes screeched to a halt at the gas station, and she spoke fast to the Mexican on duty, well aware that the hundred-dollar-bill dangling from her hand was speaking faster. Two cans of gasoline. Yes, ninety-two octane, for the car of her friend, stranded, can you believe the luck, in Bel-Air.

Outside the Sunset the scene was as she imagined. It was swarming with police, the crackling of the radios merging with the flashing blue lights to create the sense of panic so dear to police forces all over the world. They were looking for her there. But they wouldn't find her.

She parked the car in the side street, and she slipped across the ice-smooth grass by the bungalows, weighed down by the twin cans of gasoline, the smell of the fuel warring with that of her Paloma Picasso scent. Nobody was watching. Nobody saw the Christian Lacroix superwoman and her bizarre cargo. She hurried along the path, then disappeared into the bushes where she would be least likely to be seen. Using her master key she unlocked the side door to the ballroom. She knew that there was no function planned for the evening. She opened the door and hurried up the steps, the heavy cans of high-octane fuel light as feathers in her powerful hands.

The ballroom stretched out before her, the heart of the Sunset Hotel. It was deserted, prostrate at the feet of the mistress of Destiny.

For fifty years the room had not changed because Livingstone had loved it as it was. The faded, polished wood of the ancient floor gleamed in the moonlight that flooded in from the high windows, its boards worn by the feet of a million dancers. Love had blossomed here and alliances had been forged, marriages ended, as happiness had lived and died. The curtains, heavy damask, ran from the floor to the high ceiling, and across the back of the wooden bandstand, rich tapestries hung proudly, a defiant statement that the new world was no less grand than the old one. The tables and the chairs were stored away, magnifying the vastness, and the memories scurried around, cavorting with the moonbeams like happy children playing in a deserted house.

But Caroline saw Robert Hartford's face, smiling at her in victory. She saw Paula, proud on the arm of the man who had won. She saw Kristina, saying the things that the shrinks wanted to hear, muttering the meaningless phrases that would result in the withdrawal of the gift of her shares. In the terrible eye of her mind she saw the door banging shut on her freedom, and she watched in fascination as the upturned pyramid that was Destiny crumbled at its shattered foundation.

She reached down and she undid the caps of the gasoline cans. She kicked one over and watched the juice of potential fire spreading out like a bloodstain over the old wood of the floor. Then she walked with the other across to the bandstand, climbed up, and splashed the tapestries and the drapes, and the dry boards of the platform with the petroleum. There was so much of it, and she poured as she walked, leaving a river of gas trailing behind her. The uneven boards channeled the liquid. This way and that it hurried, defining the low parts, leaving areas of relative high ground surrounded as it found its level. But Caroline didn't notice as the floor became a chain of scattered islands, enclosed by a sea of flammable wetness.

Whatever else happened, Robert Hartford would never own the Sunset Hotel. It would die. It would burn. It would be gone forever. The fiery furnace that she would start here could never be contained. The ballroom was the core of the hotel. Nothing would survive.

She bent down and she flicked at the lighter, and she dipped it into the gasoline.

The flame raced away from her, quicker, stronger than she had imagined. It darted to the left, and it scurried to the right, and it flew like an arrow to the bandstand. It jumped up the steps, scaled the walls, and ran crazily to the priceless tapestries. It seized greedily at the thick damask of the drapes. Already the flames were crackling as they ate at the floor. Caroline stared in fascination at the extraordinary destructive force she had unleashed. Then she turned around and looked toward the door through which she had entered. There was a corridor of dry wood between her and the escape route, covered only by tiny pools of fuel. She walked backward fast as all around the sheets of flames sprang up, not yet hot, but already high, already beginning to sizzle and fizz with the excitement of fire. She hurried toward the door, but she couldn't resist looking back, to savor the destruction she had wrought and to dream of the sadness it would bring to those she hated.

And then she slipped.

Her foot, neat in its Manolo Blahnik black satin shoe, the heel so high, the sole so smooth, stepped into the middle of a pool of gasoline. She slid a foot or two on the ice-rink floor, and her flailing arms kept her upright as they windmilled in the air. But she knew she was going to fall. She went backward and she landed on her bottom, the frilly black tulle of the frivolous Lacroix skirt floating on the puddle of gasoline like a lily on a pond.

The flames saw her. Alligators on the edge of a jungle swamp, they eased themselves toward her. A tongue of flame darted across her escape route, cutting it off with a solid wall of fire. Another curled around her in a semicircle, hungry, stalking her, creeping close.

She tried to get up but she was slippery with gasoline, sliding, swimming on the polished floor. There was a pain where she had fallen, but there was a far worse one in her mind. Because now she knew what was going to happen to her. She was going to burn. She was going to *be* the bonfire that she had started. She herself was going to be the fuel that destroyed the Sunset Hotel.

At first her scream was not loud. It was a cross between a shout and a warning, devoid of agony, but its volume increased as it poured out of her.

"Noooooooooooooo!" she howled.

Yes, said the flames. They rushed at her, wanting the dress more than they wanted her. They were crazy for the flimsy material, like avaricious billionairesses in the front row of the Paris collections. They walked all over it, licking it, loving it, making it their own. They didn't mind that they made the flesh on Caroline Kirkegaard's legs bubble like hot tar. They didn't care that they turned her skin red, and black and white and whole bits of her that had been firm hissing, liquid soft. They were fond of her hair, too, and they reached it from the back of the dress, bridging the gap of skin with no problem at all until she was nothing but a flaming torch as she sat, upright, on the burning floor of the ballroom of the Sunset Hotel.

Her tongue, still wet inside, wanted to speak through fiery lips— something about terror and a pain more horrible than pain could be, but it was warming up inside her skull, as the furnace wrapped her head in its embrace. So she forgot what it was she wanted to say as she toppled sedately over to one side and cocked a fiery leg at the ceiling. As she died there was one lingering message left inside.

"This is the last life, Caroline," said a hideous voice. "Only joking about rebirth."

EPILOGUE

The glow from the setting sun sent the finger shadows dancing across the pool. Above, the sky was blazing with all the Los Angeles colors, the orange-yellows, the purple-browns, and the deep red-magentas, and all around the wind from the desert, warm, sensual, scurried through the canyon like a lover in the twilight.

Robert Hartford breathed in deeply, his head buried in his hands. Paula stood beside him in the fading light, tall and statuesque. She put out a hand to touch his shoulder, and, absentmindedly, he covered it with his. "Can you believe that Plutarch killed himself?" she asked, staring off into the distance. Billions couldn't protect you from obsession. Nothing could.

"Kanga would have done it, too, if they didn't have her locked up," said Robert, his voice full of awe as he contemplated the extraordinary power that Caroline Kirkegaard had wielded.

The silence closed in. The wind was gathering pace, rustling the pine trees, shaking their needles into the immaculate pool.

She sat down beside him and leaned against his shoulder. He leaned back at her, his body hard against hers, for support, in affection.

"Will Kristina get over her?" said Paula.

Robert sighed. Had his daughter and Caroline been lovers? He hadn't dared to ask the psychiatrist, and the doctor hadn't volunteered the information. Perhaps he'd never know. Perhaps that was the best way. "The doctors say yes. Apparently it has to do with time. The Kirkegaard influence didn't last long enough to be permanent. They

374

have techniques to counter the effects of brainwashing. She'll remember it as a sort of bad dream."

"Poor, *poor* Kristina," said Paula.

"It's funny, even now I can't really forgive her for what she did. I know it wasn't her fault, that it was like an addiction. I know that intellectually, but I can't *feel* it. I *feel* she betrayed me."

"That's nonsense, Robert. If the courts say she wasn't in her right mind when she deeded the Sunset shares to Caroline, then that's the truth. It wasn't something she could help."

He rocked his head backward and forward. "I know. I know. I'm just telling you what's inside. I'm always going to do that from now on. You'd better get used to it."

He smiled and she felt his mood lighten, and hers with it. "Well, anyway, she burned on earth and she's burning in hellfire right this very minute."

"Only talk good of the dead," said Robert in mock solemnity.

"Good. She's dead," said Paula, laughing.

"I never thought I'd thank God for a sprinkler system," said Robert.

"It was the three-minute delay before it was activated that I'm thankful for. I wouldn't have wanted anything to put her out. She'd have never given up, you know. Whatever happened to her—jail, anything—she'd have been there somehow to harm us."

She stood up, and she reached for Robert's hand, pulling him up beside her. Over the sea, the orange sun was sitting on the pencil line of the horizon, and Paula linked her arm through his as she led him across the lawn to the edge of the pool terrace.

"Will they charge Kanga with Livingstone's murder?"

"She'll get off on an insanity defense, I guess, then get psychiatric help."

"An exorcism would be more effective," said Paula.

She shuddered as the memory of the Evil scudded across her mind like the clouds hurrying across the burning sky. Above her head the evening wind rustled the fronds of the palm trees. The Santa Ana was picking up—the wind from the desert that longed for the sea. "So the Sunset is safe," she said, and she cuddled in close to him to ward off the chill of the wickedness that had so very nearly destroyed the happiness they now shared.

"Yes, the deed of gift will definitely be nullified. It's safe. But not from me, and not from competition from that pushy old hotel run by that genius from the Florida Everglades." He turned toward her, and he laughed as he spoke.

She smiled back at him. "You mean the one that's about to change its name from the Château Madrid to the Sunset Hotel, run by that girl who's about to change her name from Hope to Hartford?"

"There's no answer to that. Winty would have had one, wouldn't he? He always did."

They laughed at the bittersweet memory as she melted into his arms, and the warm wind washed over them as if they were a single person, joined together at last for the wonderful future they would share.